HEADHUNTER

HEADHUNTER

MICHAEL SLADE

Cemetery Dance Publications
Baltimore, Maryland
2017

Cemetery Dance Publications Trade Paperback Edition 2017

Cemetery Dance Publications
132-B Industry Lane, Unit #7
Forest Hill, MD 21050
www.cemeterydance.com

The characters and events in this book are fictitious.
Any similarity to real persons, living or dead,
is coincidental and not intended by the author.

Trade Paperback Edition

ISBN-13: 978-1-58767-628-4

Cover Artwork and Design © 2017 by Elder Lemon Design
Interior Design © 2017 by Desert Isle Design, LLC

The mind of man is capable of anything—because everything is in it,
all the past as well as all the future.
—Joseph Conrad, *Heart of Darkness*

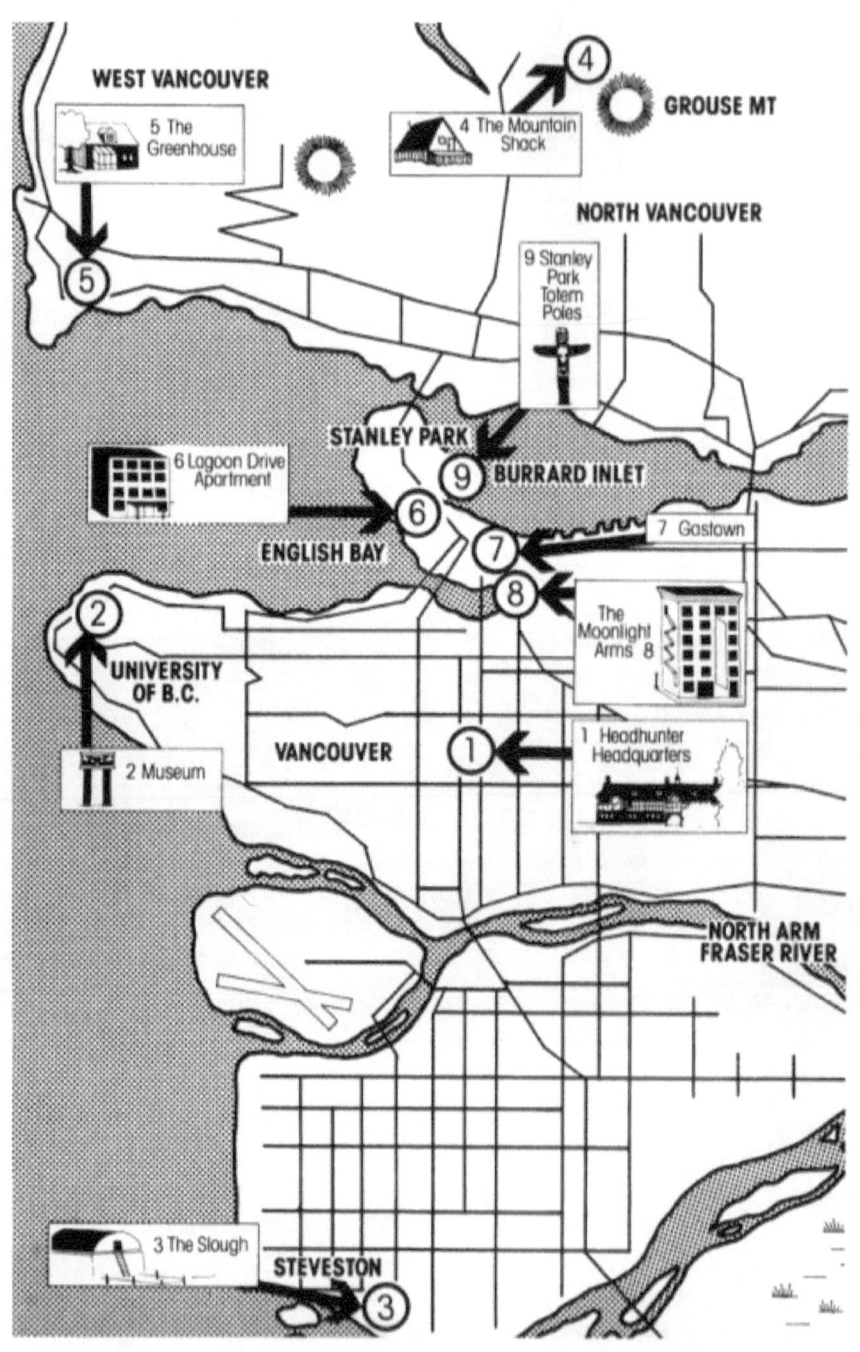

Part One

HORSEMAN

Old is the tree, and the fruit good
Very old and thick the wood.
Woodsman, is your courage stout?
Beware! The root is wrapped about
Your mother's heart, your father's bones;
And like the mandrake comes with groans.
—Robert Louis Stevenson, *Fables*

THE NIGHTMARE

Medicine Lake, Alberta, 1897

The body hangs upside down from the ceiling by nails driven through both feet. The head is missing, the neck severed to expose artery and vein, muscle and bone in a circle of raw flesh. What's left of the corpse is dressed in the bright scarlet tunic of the North-West Mounted Police. The arms in sleeves with gold braid dangle down toward the plank floor. Blood as red as the uniform pools under the headless Mountie. Blood drips from the fingertips, but the sound of the drops hitting the floor is masked by the rhythmic thud of a drum beating overhead. The drumbeat booms down from atop a trapdoor in the ceiling.

Thump...thump...thump...thump...

He awoke with a start.

His muscles tense.

His mind alert.

His nerves as taut as a bowstring at full draw.

Under the blanket he used as a pillow, Blake closed his right hand on the Enfield's grip and eased back the hammer with his thumb. The telltale click as the sidearm cocked was smothered by the multiple folds of the coarse blanket. Slowly, the manhunter eased the revolver out from under his head and into the bitter cold. Then he lay stock-still in his buffalo robe. Silent. Listening. Waiting.

Thump...thump...thump...

The night was cold and moonless. To the north, the aurora borealis trembled across the frozen landscape with that weird flicker the Indians call the Dance of the Dead Spirits. Above the Mountie, countless stars pierced the ink-black sky, while east of the Rockies, beyond the endless flatlands of the Canadian plains, a meteor shower stabbed the ruddy smudge of dawn.

It was 6 a.m.

During Blake's hours of fitful sleep, a storm from the Arctic had shrouded these mountains with a sheet of thick, fresh snow. Now the midnight blizzard had passed and frost crept down from the hoary peaks to encrust his camp with ice. Around him, the whole world seemed to sleep in savage desolation.

Thump...thump...thum-thump...thump...

The Mountie was camped in a thicket of pines on the rim of a frozen lake. Though he strained his ears to the silence, not a sound cracked the brittle air of this snowbound valley. But in his gut—his primal core—Blake *knew* something was out there.

Enfield in hand, breath held, the Horseman rose to his feet.

Wilfred Blake was a tall man with firm, unflinching eyes. As protection from winter, he was bundled up in a beaverskin hat and a thick buffalo coat. For nineteen years, the Scotsman had served in the British colonial army. That was followed by decades more in the Mounted Police. Although he was now almost sixty years of age, that lifetime of fighting and exposure to the world's harshest climates had failed to sap his strength. Muscles still roped his broad shoulders and barrel chest to a backbone as straight as a ramrod down a rifle barrel.

In 1857, Blake had been with the Highlanders posted on the Ganges River. During the Sepoy Mutiny, he was garrisoned at Cawnpore. There, he slept through the screams of captured comrades being skinned alive and nailed to makeshift crosses by the mutineers, and he saw the well near the Bibighar filled with the heads, limbs, and bodies of dismembered British women and children. That bloodbath fueled the revenge the Highlanders later wreaked at Lucknow, where Blake—kilted and shouting "Remember Cawnpore!" as his battle cry—spiked and slashed with his bayonet, taking no prisoners and showing no mercy as the bagpipes drove him on. Finally, returning to Cawnpore, he forced the Indian rebels to lick every drop of British blood off the Bibighar's floor.

After clashing in China in the Second Opium War and suppressing the Red River Rebellion in western Canada, Blake had served with the Black Watch on the Gold Coast of Africa. Half a century earlier, in 1823, the British governor, Sir Charles MacCarthy, had foolishly invaded the inland Ashanti empire with woefully insufficient troops. The Africans cut off his head, and the Ashanti king had from that point forward used MacCarthy's skull as a drinking cup and paraded the trophy annually through the streets of Kumasi.

In 1874, Sir Garnet Wolseley had recruited Blake for a new Ashanti campaign. On January 31, the Ashanti attacked with a force five times larger than that of the British colonial army. Against wave upon wave at the Battle of Amoafo, Blake exhorted his men to "Fire low, fire slow!" as African bodies piled up in front of the Black Watch rifles. On entering Kumasi, the Highlander faced the grisly remains of human sacrifice, and while torching the king's palace, he recovered MacCarthy's gold-rimmed skull.

In London, the queen herself had pinned the Victoria Cross to his chest.

Through forty years of advancing the flag in far-flung corners of the British Empire, Wilfred Blake had embraced the soldier's crowning lesson: cunning honed on instinct is the key to survival.

Honed on instinct then.

And honed on instinct now.

So as dawn began to redden the jagged peaks, the manhunter crouched on his heels and shivered in the keen hoarfrost, listening intently for any sound that might give his quarry away. The frostbitten fingers that gripped the Enfield were going numb.

Thum-thump...

The ice encrusting Medicine Lake creaked from the weight of the overnight snowfall.

Thum-thump...

A white-on-white snowy owl hooted from atop one of the pines.

Thum-thump...

An alpine breeze made the trees whisper like conspirators.

Thum-thump...

Nature sounds. Nothing human.

The only man-made noise was the blood throbbing in his ears.

Thum-thump...

Wilfred Blake had jerked awake from the clutch of a haunting nightmare, the genesis of which went back almost thirty years. The black delirium had seized him in the darkness before dawn. It too had commenced with a pounding in his ears. Now, as he crouched listening to the hammering pulse from his heart, he wondered if the night tremor alone had wrenched him from sleep...

Thump...thump...thump...drip...

No! Blake thought as the unbidden nightmare plagued him again...

It's not the thumping that rattles him. Nor is it the dark. It's the ghastly collection of still-bleeding scalps nailed to the fortress walls. This room without windows has lurked in his mind for close to three decades. The plank door braced with ironwork is bolted firmly shut. The hand-hewn logs are stacked one on another. Mud is packed between the logs to keep out the cold.

Again, it's a winter month in 1870.

Again, this room is where the fort does its Indian trade.

Beside him are sacks of feed and crates of ammunition. A candle on a table casts the only light. Along the nearest wall lean eight oblong crates, the lid of one pried off and lying on the floor. The candlelight illuminates a barrel within. At twenty rifles to a crate, that's a hundred and—

The attack came without warning.

As happens in the Rockies, the breeze reversed direction. Barely strong enough to bend smoke or twist a feather, a frigid zephyr puffed in from the edge of the woods. Instantly, two dogs awoke and turned in that direction. The huskies were sleeping near the dogsled.

Dogs? Blake wondered. *They're nae in this dream.*

Then reality bit and shook him loose from fantasy. In the cold light of dawn, the Horseman understood that his cross-country manhunt was done.

Aye, laddie, Blake thought. *It's a good day to die.*

The Plains Cree churning toward him was hardly out of his teens. He wore the winter dress of his tribe, but it offered little protection against this harsh environment. He'd stuffed his ice-caked leather leggings and moccasins with dead moss to insulate his limbs. His naked chest was cloaked by a snow-covered buffalo robe. On his head, Iron-child wore a horned bison cap adorned with broken feathers and tattered weasel skins. While one hand paddled the deep drifts to propel him across the valley to where the Mountie was camped in the pines, his other gripped the barrel of a rusty Winchester rifle and wielded it as a war club.

A jolt of adrenaline hit the white man's blood. Addicted to life-or-death combat, Blake thrived on the thrill of a kill. For forty years, he'd lugged his battered regimental trunk around the British Empire, adding trophies to the macabre collection concealed in its false bottom. Here was another memento mori to join those glories on his return to NWMP headquarters in Regina, Saskatchewan.

Come and get it, laddie!

The Scotsman aimed his frosted handgun. Beyond the sights of the Enfield, Blake watched the Cree warrior shed the buffalo robe that was encumbering his attack. As war paint, the fugitive had streaked his face and chest with charcoal, likely scraped from a tree struck by summer lightning.

"Dinnae fire till ye can see the whites of their e'en," Sir Andrew Agnew of Lochnaw had told his Royal Scots Fusiliers before they cut down French infantry at the Battle of Dettingen in 1743. This morning Blake adopted that tactic, not to ensure that his bullet would drill the forehead of its oncoming target, but to savor the glory in smiting another heathen for his God.

When Iron-child was close enough to glimpse the hate in his eyes, the Horseman pulled the trigger…and the Enfield refused to fire! Either his finger was frozen or the mechanism was jammed.

The Cree's war whoop shattered the solitude, rousing nature from its hibernation. With flapping wings, the snowy owl took flight from atop the pines, soaring up the surrounding mountain peaks. As powdered snow sifted down from the wobbly branches, Blake jammed his left mitt into his mouth, bit hard, and wrenched the stiff glove from his fingers. Gripping the cold revolver with both bare hands, he tugged the trigger as hard as he could to free the mechanism and fire the reluctant weapon.

Ten feet away, Iron-child clawed through the knee-deep snow, his breath billowing out in wispy white clouds. His arm rose to slam the rifle down on the Horseman's head, but then—as if his protecting spirit had warned the brave of certain death—he ducked from the Enfield's muzzle.

A flash of yellow blazed at the heart of the shocking explosion. The revolver lurched in Blake's grip as the blast roared out at the towering peaks, echoing back like a multi-shot barrage unleashed by a British colonial army firing line.

The bullet missed its target and zipped over Iron-child's head, smashing against the breech of the Winchester. A fragment ricocheted off the metal, striking the Cree just above the temple, slashing down his cheek, and lodging in his shoulder. The velocity stunned him, and the force of the slug hitting the rifle hurled him back into the snow.

With a crack, Iron-child's leg snapped below the knee.

Gasping, he passed out.

Thump…thump…thump…drip…

JUNKIE

Vancouver, British Columbia, 1982
Monday, October 18, 5:02 a.m.

In this city, it often rains. Geography demands it. Beyond the western islands roll endless miles of ocean, while northeast at the city's back jut jagged mountain peaks. With the slate-gray skies of autumn come the cyclone westerlies, raging winds and roiling clouds that storm in from the sea. In waves, these bloated bellies tear open on the peaks, and rain rattles down from each gut.

To live in this city, you learn to stomach rain.

The woman stumbling through the early morning downpour was soaked to her skin. Staggering up Chinatown's Pender Street with one arm clutching her abdomen, she flailed her other arm wide for support from the derelict buildings along the sidewalk. She was tall and slender, this jitterbugged junkie splashing through puddles stained with garish neon, this long-legged, black-haired hooker in her early twenties. Despite the October chill, her drenched coat flapped open to expose a scoop-neck T-shirt that flaunted her breasts and clung to her puckered nipples. Shivering, tired, hungry, and sick, she was badly in need of a fix.

Chinatown at 5 a.m. had lost a century. At this hour of the morning, the inscrutable mystery of the East was tangible. In rundown facades as ornate as Chinese theater masks, the windows above the street watched her like dead men's eyes. In some of these buildings, sinister tongs had met in secrecy as thick as the smoke fuming from their opium factories. In one, Dr. Sun Yat-sen had lived out his exile.

None of this the hooker knew, for she was new to this city. The addict had squirmed in Vancouver's clutches for only four days.

"Johnny. Help me, Johnny," she mumbled as she wobbled.

Twenty minutes had passed since the bulls let her go. They had stopped her at nine last night out front of the Moonrise Hotel. She was leaning against the corner of that sleazy dive, with her back to the stinking side-alley where working girls scrawled messages on "the Wall" to warn their sisters about sadistic creeps on the prowl. Her raincoat hung open to offer the erotic wares of her dangerous trade, and with each curb-crawling car that slowed down to check out her tits and ass, the streetwalker bent forward to deepen her cleavage and blow the cruising john a kiss.

The bulls had used a bait car to take her by surprise. The mud-spattered vehicle advertised 24-HOUR PLUMBING and had a phone number on the doors. The windows were shut against the rain when it pulled in to the curb, so she sashayed out from under the eaves in her tight top, miniskirt, and high-heeled boots to tap on the glass and ask, "Wanna party, boys?"

"Sure," said the bull riding shotgun as he flashed his badge. "Suck on this."

"Hey, that's entrapment. I know my rights."

"You hear that?" Shotgun asked the bull behind the wheel. "Southern accent as thick as hers, she's got to be Scarlett O'Hara."

"Rights?" scoffed the Wheelman. "This ain't the US of A."

"What gives?" the hooker asked.

"Routine check." Shotgun opened the door and climbed out of the passenger seat. "Nothing personal. We roust all you working girls."

"I said 'party.' There's nothing sexual in that."

"You speak Latin?"

"Huh?"

"*Res gestae*. Mean anything to you?"

"No."

"It's a legal term for words that form part of a physical act."

Shotgun poked one of her breasts.

"The physical act is you bouncing your eye-popping rack. And the words are displayed on your T-shirt."

The T-shirt read DEEP THROAT.

"Your tits speak volumes. So get in the car."

The cop shop was just a few blocks away. It too was in the skids. Because Shotgun rode in the back with her, she couldn't ditch her stash. Normally, the junkie would have carried the cap in a plastic balloon in her mouth, ready to swallow the H before any narcs could clamp her with a chokehold. Work, however, trumped that. You can't chat up johns if your yap is stuffed with a balloon.

She hoped these cops were vice bulls working the pussy patrol.

But of course, they were narcs.

They parked the car in the alley behind 312 Main, beside the door to the elevator that rose to the jail. Rain drummed on the trash cans out back of the neighboring greasy spoon, thrashing tin like a wannabe heavy metal rocker in a garage band. Waterfalls gushed from the gutters gurgling overhead, then foamed out to the storm sewers draining Cordova Street.

"Let's play a game," Shotgun said. He was the younger of the two, a beefy bully with mean eyes and a sneer like Elvis Presley's.

"What kinda game?"

"From down south. Called Mississippi Gambler."

"Gimme a break."

"I'm doing that, hon. A fifty-fifty chance."

"What's the bet?"

"I say your stash is hidden in one of your boots. No question you're a druggie. It's written all over you. Want to pass me your footwear or suffer a cavity search?"

The Wheelman turned in the driver's seat and slipped her a wink. His embalmed features were blotched with drinker's veins. "Take the bet," he said. "It's less invasive."

Shotgun nodded. "Good advice. If you bet the cavity search, I'll *know* your stash is tucked away in one of those come-fuck-me heels."

The junkie knew they had her, so she relinquished her boots. Turning the footwear upside down, Shotgun smirked when the balloon with her cap of H fell into his palm. Worse for her, the junk was for tonight's fix. Just one more trick hooked off the stroll out front of the Moonrise Hotel and she'd have cooked the smack up in a spoon and spiked it into her arm.

The lift took them up to the city jail attached to the police station. By the time they'd booked her in, rolled her prints, and snapped a photo, the mug in the shot was beaded with sweat. Then they locked her in a cell on the fourth floor and let withdrawal have her.

Before long, her eyes, her nose, and the pores of her skin were running. She stewed in her rain-dampened clothes and her own body juices. She jerked from fever to shivers. Too weak to stand, she flopped on the bunk and curled up into a ball. Her legs twitched as her vision blackened around the edges. A phantom hand squeezed her heart until she thought she would die. Finally, the bulls hauled her out and dragged her to the interview room. With the monkey weighing heavy on her back, she had to clutch her guts with both arms to keep them in.

"You look like shit," Shotgun said as he dropped her on a chair.

The room was claustrophobic, with tight walls, a scarred table, and two wooden seats. Shotgun sat down opposite her, and the Wheelman stood by the door. Grabbing her wrist to extend her bare arm, the narc exposed the crook of her elbow, where the vein had retreated back to the bone to hide from probing needles.

"Keep jabbing that spot," he said, "and it's gonna get infected."

The Wheelman dumped the contents of her purse onto the table. Cosmetics, condoms, combs, and tissues tumbled out with her wallet. Rifling through the billfold, Shotgun extracted her birth certificate.

"New Orleans, Louisiana. I pegged you right, Scarlett."

"That was Atlanta."

Her voice was no more than a whisper.

"Close enough," said the bull. "The South's the South to me." He held up the cap of H he'd recovered from her boot. "The penalty for possession is up to seven years. The shape you're in, seven minutes will seem longer than that. Appears you swapped the Big Easy for the Big Hard."

He dropped the cap on the table amid the scatterings from her purse.

"Mississippi Gambler. Let's play again."

Shotgun flicked the cap with his finger so it rolled toward her.

"You want to go back to your cell? Or you want to pick up the contents of your purse and vamoose out the door?"

"*All* the contents of your purse," the Wheelman emphasized. "*Everything* on the table."

"We're reasonable men," Shotgun said. "Poor sick girl like you."

"Name your pusher."

"Name your pimp."

"Or give us something better."

"The choice is yours."

"The jackpot awaits."

"You can be a winner. But give us nothing, and what can we do?" Shotgun shrugged his shoulders with his palms up, like Frenchmen do.

So she told them to fuck off and the narcs made good on their threat, caging her in with the monkey until she thought she'd go insane.

Then—about twenty minutes ago—they'd issued her an appearance notice and chucked her out in the rain.

The first thing Helen Grabowski did on getting sprung from the can was totter down Cordova Street to the grotty room she shared with Johnny, her pimp, in a rat-infested hotel. HOT AND COLD WATER IN EVERY ROOM—REASONABLE RATES, read the dingy sign outside. A drunk had passed out in the doorway with a bottle of Aqua Velva aftershave in his hand. Rodent-like—so fitting for this dump—the sot had a pointed, stubbled face and yellow buckteeth. As Helen stepped over him, he came to life and took a sloppy swig that dribbled down his chin and pooled with the puddle of piss in the alcove.

"Gotta find Johnny," the junkie muttered as she zigzagged up the stairs.

But the room was empty.

Johnny was gone, and so was their stuff.

Strung out and dreading the torture in not getting fixed, Helen lurched down the stairs with bile in her throat and tried to squeeze by the wino at the door.

"Gimme a kiss," the bum slurred as the jumpy junkie flattened herself against the walls, and that's when the feel of the bricks on her palms reminded her of the messages on "the Wall" at the Moonrise Hotel.

Johnny, you rotten bastard! You better have left me a note!

Struggling two blocks along Carrall Street to Chinatown, she turned left up Pender Street to double back to her skid row stroll. From the pioneer days of Vancouver—when pigtailed coolies got shipped in from China to punch a railroad through the Rocky Mountains, and whores serviced the men of the nearby logging camps—hookers and Asians have shared this vice-plagued street in the poxiest part of town.

So now she stumbled up Pender Street in the early morning rain, gasping as severe withdrawal cramps cinched her insides. A cold burn seared her goose-bumped skin as ants crawled through her muscles. At the corner of Main and Pender, she tripped and her feet skidded out from under her. Her hip struck the ground with a bone-jarring wrench as the traffic light at the empty intersection turned red, suffusing the rain with a hue so intense that it seemed as if blood poured down on the city.

With her head bent and her black hair plastered across her anguished face, she sat in a crimson puddle and cried until sobs racked her body. When the light changed to green, she heaved herself back up on her feet and locked her blurred eyes on the neon Moonrise Hotel sign sputtering at the next corner. The giant letters climbed down the front of the six-story building to the marquee of its ground-floor pub, the Moonlight Arms. Sloshing her way toward the beacon and unaware that she was being stalked by a car, Helen veered to her right just before the pub to enter the message board alley.

The Wall was painted with red-and-white stripes like a flat barber's pole. Hookers—and occasionally pimps trying to contact their girls—scrawled notes between the red lines. *Light blue Pontiac: This one's a beater*, or *Look out (shank!)* with a BC license plate.

Hunched over to protect her shaking hands from the rain, Helen struck match after match in the darkness to search for any word from Johnny.

"God, no!" she gasped with rising panic. "He hasn't left a message!"

Engine noise from the mouth of the alley drew her attention back to the street. A car had pulled in to the curb and sat idling with the passenger's window down. The dim silhouette of the driver stared out at her.

Helen Grabowski's life had shrunk down to this: earning the price of a cap. A quick blow job would score enough scratch for her to go hunting for H.

On faltering legs, she approached the car and bent over to flash her cleavage.

"Wanna date?" she croaked.

The driver lurked back in the shadows.

It wasn't a light blue Pontiac, but hers was a perilous profession. Yesterday, she'd heard of a local working girl snuffed by a bad date. The creep had used the girl's own nylon stocking to strangle her to death. At this hour of the morning, Pender Street was a wasteland. So Helen, desperate though she was for money to go score junk, probed the gloom inside the car for a benign face.

"Forget it," she said on glimpsing the eyes, and turned away from the window.

"Wait a minute, lady."

"Fuck off," she replied over her shoulder.

"You don't look well. You look strung out. You look like you need a fix. I want you for a friend of mine. He'll throw in a cap of junk."

"No!" said the hooker. But then the iron crab of withdrawal cramps clamped its vicious claws on her guts again, worse this time.

Moments later, Helen climbed into the car.

The driver hit the gas and they drove off into the dregs of night.

FLOATER

Monday, October 25, 11:45 a.m.

It's common knowledge among those who have traveled the world that for physical setting, there are six stunning cities: Hong Kong, Sydney, Cape Town, Rio de Janeiro, San Francisco, and Vancouver. The torrential rains of last week had given way to sunshine, and this morning showed why Vancouver—if not for its iconic rain, rain, rain—would be home to a billion people by now.

Seen from the whitecaps of English Bay, this greenhouse, attached to a seaside bungalow at the foot of the North Shore Mountains, threw off sunbeams in a burst of blinding glare. The maple trees above it were turning a riot of autumn colors: red, orange, and yellow. Viewed from inside the dazzling panes, a breathtaking panorama swept the south shore of the bay. Stanley Park and the Lions Gate Bridge hid the inner harbor and downtown core to the east. Ahead, the sandy beaches and cliffs of Point Grey were topped by the evergreen forest surrounding the university. And to the west, beyond the dragon-like silhouette of Vancouver Island, the pounding breakers of the blue-green Pacific stretched all the way to China.

They thrived in here, the roses.

Pen and paper in his lap, the man in the white wicker fanback chair was besieged by a profusion of vibrant blooms growing in tropical wells and artificial gardens. Lately, he had taken to hybridizing his own yet-to-be-christened variety of rose, a deep maroon plant flowering by the door to the bungalow. In the years since Robert DeClercq had retired early from the Mounted Police, this hothouse had become a psychological refuge against the dark demons of his past. In here, he had written his first book, *Men Who Wore the Tunic*, a frontier history of the hard-hitting, straight-shooting Horsemen—the Riders of the Plains—who made Canada the only nation known chiefly for its police force.

Horsemen like the manhunter who, almost single-handedly, had forged the legendary saying "The Mounties always get their man": Inspector Wilfred Blake.

This morning, DeClercq was trying to work on his follow-up book, a chronicle of serial killing from an investigator's point of view. "Write what you know" is the motto for all who put pen to paper, and before the Job had tragically cost him his first wife, Kate, and his young daughter, Jane, the superintendent was pegged as the rising homicide hotshot in the federal RCMP.

Judging from the pile of crumpled paper on the floor, the writing was not going well.

DeClercq was hemmed in on all sides by every major work on Jack the Ripper. The history of serial killing always starts with Jack—hence the books littering the ex-Mountie's desk and the tiles around his feet. Not only did that Victorian psycho have all the tropes in spades—from the name that will never be rivaled by those who skulk in his footsteps, to the degenerate, gaslit hunting ground of East End London, to the madcap taunting of the beleaguered bobbies at Scotland Yard, to the butchered skid row tarts with their missing body parts—but the hunt for the Ripper was such a botch-up in so many ways that it's the classic lesson in how *not* to investigate.

Given DeClercq's background, writing this book should have been a piece of cake.

But instead, he was going stir crazy.

Like the fictional character Nero Wolfe, growing orchids in his brownstone greenhouse in New York, DeClercq was in a cell of his own making. Shattered by the heartrending aftermath of Quebec's October Crisis, the Mountie had fled from Montreal to West Vancouver, purchasing this waterfront hideaway before property prices blew through the roof. Here, he'd settled into the life of a lonely recluse, until horrific nightmares of Jane's death had forced him to seek help.

Sometimes the wheel of fortune spins you a second chance. Having made you suffer hell on earth, fate will randomly hand you a windfall. And so it was with the psychologist who took on bedeviled DeClercq. It helped that she too was a transplant from Quebec, a francophone steeped in anglophone culture. The fact that she was so damned good-looking also didn't hurt: twenty years younger than he was, with wild auburn hair and green eyes sparking with intelligence, she had high cheekbones and full, sinful lips, and the knockout figure of a femme fatale. She turned male heads from ages nine to ninety. But most of all, she exorcised the horrors from his sleep. And having patched up his cracked psyche, she married him within a year.

Genevieve was his salvation.

DeClercq, however, was still caged in his glass fortress. On working days, his wife would leave for the university, often returning late if she had night classes. Here, he'd sit scribbling at his antique desk, faced by three photos of those he'd loved in the past and present: Kate onstage in Manhattan, the night he'd fallen in love at first sight while watching her perform Ibsen's *Rosmersholm*; Jane sitting in a pile of autumn leaves, her head thrown back in laughter, with sunlight caressing her curls; Genevieve on their honeymoon, beachcombing the South Seas, wearing a white bikini and holding a conch shell to her ear. If he became restless—like he was now—DeClercq would exit to a knoll on the shore and watch the world pass him by.

His cabin fever dated from the Clifford Olson case.

Serial killing—the big time—had sunk its fangs into Canada with those vicious murders. Over a nine-month spree, from November 1980 to July 1981, Olson had sexually assaulted and killed eleven local kids. He'd pick them up with offers of a job with good pay, then render each helpless with a Mickey Finn spiked with chloral hydrate. The girls were raped and stabbed; the boys were raped and bludgeoned. Olson used a sixteen-ounce stainless-steel hammer to crush their skulls. He was Maxwell Silverhammer in his sexual fantasy, and like the crazy head-cracker in the Beatles song, he would—*Bang! Bang!*—bring his silver hammer down upon his victims' heads until he was—*Clang! Clang!*—sure that they were dead. In one instance, he used the hammer to pound nails into the brain of a boy who was still alive.

DeClercq had watched from the sidelines as a bizarre deal was struck to solidify the case. In what the media would later call a "cash for corpses" scam, the authorities paid Olson $10,000 a body for information about the murders and directions to his dump sites. Ten months ago, on January 11, 1982, that psycho pleaded guilty to eleven counts of first-degree murder, and the judge sentenced him to eleven life terms, with a recommendation that he never be paroled.

The fallout from that notorious case tarnished the Mounties. For a number of reasons—overlapping jurisdictions, turf wars, staff transfers, personality clashes, lack of coordination, fouled lines of communication—a monster had been able to prey unchecked on the kids of Vancouver. When the Horsemen finally got it together and began to hunt for links, it took less than two weeks for them to get their man.

Guilt.

That's what DeClercq had felt.

Gnawing guilt.

He hadn't been there for his daughter, and he hadn't been there for those eleven kids.

All his life he'd trained himself to hunt rabid killers, to put real-life teeth to the mythology of the Mounties. But when a full-blown psycho had run amok, he'd sat here in self-imposed exile writing a *history* of serial killing.

Maintiens le Droit. Uphold the Law. That was a Mountie's sworn duty. And when the call to duty had come, where was he?

This book was going nowhere. He was spinning the wheels of his mind. Unable to sit still any longer, DeClercq set his pen and clipboard of paper down on his book-cluttered desk, uncrossed his antsy legs, got up, and picked his way through the minefield of Jack the Ripper texts to stand at the hothouse windows and take in English Bay.

Move 'em in and move 'em out, he thought.

Freighters and container ships waiting to offload foreign cargoes and onload Canadian resources rocked at anchor on the choppy waves, queuing for a berth in the port sheltered by Stanley Park. Those sailing to parts unknown plowed through a flotilla of windjammers launched to catch the billowing breeze of this glorious day before foul weather returned. A lonely tugboat ran the gauntlet across the harbor's mouth, chugging fast to avoid getting rammed broadside.

DeClercq's robust reflection belied the cracks within. Tall and slim, with a fencer's build that was quick to parry attacks and riposte with a lunge to his adversary's heart, the ex-cop worked out three times a week with an old Hungarian master. His hair was dark and wavy, with gray at the temples. His aquiline nose and narrow jaw could have belonged to Julius Caesar. Only his guilt-ridden, brooding eyes betrayed the demons in the dungeon of his mind.

When the door to the bungalow opened, he turned his attention to his wife. Having had the morning off, she wore a gray tailored pantsuit over a maroon silk blouse for her afternoon class. The Greenhouse was bright with sunlight, and dangling prisms threw rainbows across the rows of roses. Yet it seemed to DeClercq—as it always did—that Genny added uplifting zest to his workspace.

Lucky me!

"Eh bien, Robert," she said in French, for in this bilingual house they switched languages day by day. "*Est-ce qu'on prendra un lunch aujourd'hui?*"

"*Oui,*" he replied, weaving among the plants to close the gap between them. "*J'aimerais bien. Combien de temps as-tu?*"

"*Juste une heure. J'ai une classe de seminaire en fin de la journée.*"

Fetching a pair of gardening shears, DeClercq snipped a rosebud off the plant he had hybridized and held it in front of her heart for a perfect maroon-on-maroon match.

"*As-tu pensé à un nom pour ta rose?*" she asked.

The name of the nameless rose faced him.

"Genevieve," he said.

———

One of the boats DeClercq had watched—the lonely vessel cruising fast to avoid getting cleaved by a freighter churning out to sea—was a BC government tug returning from a salvage check up the bite of Howe Sound, northwest of the outer harbor. The young man leaning on the port rail, his blond hair whipped forward by the incoming wind, enjoyed the same view that Jonah had the moment before he was gulped down the gullet of that biblical whale. For that's how Dan Heller had imagined this inlet—one of a million indentations that make up the ten thousand linear miles of the rugged West Coast—ever since he was a boy, when his tug captain dad would take him on nautical adventures. The Hollyburn, Grouse, and Seymour Mountains, the teeth along the North Shore, were the lower jaw of the whale. Stanley Park was the uvula at the throat of First Narrows, which fed the stomach of the inner harbor beyond. Point Grey was the flat tongue of the whale's mouth, sticking out as if to lick Dan off the sea.

Gulp, he thought, grinning.

Down where the mountains met the waves, sunlight flashing from a greenhouse just this side of the Point Atkinson Lighthouse blurred the seaman's vision. For a moment, his mind's eye imagined this inlet as seen by British crewmen on Captain George Vancouver's ship *Discovery* in 1792, when it engaged Spanish explorers on two galleons beneath the towering sandstone cliffs of Point Grey. Back then, all this was an evergreen forest as far as the eye could see, with Native longhouses built where the salmon fishing was best, and where lookouts could spot Kwakiutl war canoes crossing the strait from the Land of the Headhunters.

"Dan!" yelled a voice from the wheelhouse. "Coffee break?"

Wiping his bleary eyes and sucking in lungfuls of salty air, Heller rounded the bow, scaled the bridge ladder, and ducked into the wheelman's cabin. After pouring himself black coffee from a thermos on the chart table, he joined the pilot at the controls.

"Hair o' the dog?" Glen Simpson asked, wagging a hip flask of brandy.

"Don't mind if I do." Heller held out his cup.

The spiked coffee burned his throat on its way down.

Seen from up here, tide lines snaked across the harbor—dark green on one side, light green on the other. Logging debris tossed on the waves like corks in boiling water. High above them loomed the crumbling cliffs of the peninsula, topped by the soaring glass windows of the Museum of Anthropology, a storehouse for totems spirited away from the Land of the Headhunters. As the tug rounded Point Grey, Dan took in Tower Beach's blockhouse gun emplacements, designed to blow Japanese ships and subs out of the harbor during the Second World War. Wreck Beach, at the tip of the tongue, would be teeming with nudists come summer.

"To scopophilia." Dan raised his cup.

"Scopo-what?" the pilot asked. Under his quilted vest, he wore a T-shirt emblazoned with spinach-eating Popeye.

"The fun in sneaking a peek at naked female flesh."

"I'll drink to that."

"Remind me to buy a stronger pair of binoculars this June."

Having rounded the tip of Point Grey, the tug labored inland up the North Arm of the Fraser River. Across the muddy water came the roar of jets taking off and landing at the international airport on Sea Island in the delta. Lifting off from one of the log booms lining the banks of the river, a blue heron soared up to join the planes. Boats zipped around the delta channels like fish slipping through a net. As the tug neared the government wharf of the Ministry of Lands and Forests, Heller scrambled down the bridge ladder for hawser ropes to moor it to the dock...and that's when something in the water bumped along the hull. Assuming a wayward log was to blame, he reached for a gaff to hook it. Seconds later, he whistled up to catch Simpson's attention, then sliced his hand across his throat as a cue to cut the engines.

"What gives?" the pilot yelled down.

"We got a floater."

"A body?"

"Yeah. A naked woman thumped against the hull."

Whupping rotors drowned them out as a chopper landed on the wharf's helipad. Simpson scurried down from the bridge to join Heller at the rail. Leaning out over the tire fenders on the side of the hull, he followed the gaff down to the dirty brown current.

"Scopo-whatsit, my ass," Simpson bellowed over the chopper's noise. "It's no fun sneaking a peek at *that* naked female flesh."

The seamen stared transfixed at the bloated, half-submerged, fish-nibbled horror.

"See what I see?"

"Yep. The floater's got no head."

—

Commercial Crime Section (Special "I": Electronic Surveillance)
Target: Steve Rackstraw (aka "The Fox").
Tape installed: October 25. 0900 hours. (Tipple.)
Tape removed: October 25. 1130 hours. (Tipple.)
U/M known only as "The Weasel."

Outgoing local call: 1122 hours

Weasel: Hey.

Fox: Hey. Hey.

Weasel: Sorry. Forgot to call ya. Forgot all about it.

Fox: Ya did, huh?

Weasel: Sorry.

Fox: Well, better grab yo' ride and get yo' black ass over here.

Weasel: Can't. Not now. Maybe later.

Fox: That Ms. Billie Holiday I hear behind you, man?

Weasel: Yeah, pussy purrs for her. She da cat's meow. I need time, man. To corral this filly in m' stable.

Fox: Uh-huh.

Weasel: Y'know? Get this filly broken so I don't need no rope to keep the bitch from splittin'.

Fox: Don't use yo' dick. Use Sister H.

Weasel: Can't hear ya. Hold a mo'. (Shouting: Turn that music down.)

(U/F: Come on, baby. Make me fe-e-el good.)

(Weasel: In a bit. Get yo' selfishness ready.)

Weasel: Ya still there, man?

Fox: Sounds like ya got yo' hands full. Take heed, cousin. Voodoo juju's comin'. Ya better be ready.

Weasel: I be ready.

Fox: When the Wolf calls, have yo' shit together.

Weasel: (Inaudible)…zombie walks.

Fox: By the by, where's H.G.? Bitch been split a week.

Weasel: I know. Cold. Real cold.

Fox: Better find her, man, 'fore the Wolf finds out. You'll be cold—stone dead cold—if there's a leak.

Weasel: Hear ya.

Fox: Be cool. Waitin' on y'all.

Weasel: Bye.

Fox: Huh. Huh.

(End of call.)

THE MOONLIGHT ARMS

Tuesday, October 26, 8:15 a.m.

No man was ever born to his job quite like Sharma Satalkar. He could trace his decision to become a forensic pathologist all the way back to the abolition of slavery on Trinidad's sugar plantations in 1834. Five years later, the British had imported "coolies"—indentured laborers—from India to cut sugarcane. But Hindus had a religious problem in crossing the Kala Pani, the "black water" of the sea. Their customs said that crossing the sea not only cut a voyager off from the regenerating waters of the Ganges River (essential for reincarnation), but also caused him to lose caste, thereby knocking him down to a lesser level. The British quelled those fears with a two-pronged response. First, they stocked their ships with cauldrons of water from the Ganges to ensure the reincarnation cycle extended beyond the Kala Pani. And second, they hired a Brahmin priest—Sharma Satalkar's direct ancestor—to conduct the purification rituals necessary to *reinstall* lost caste in the West Indies.

What the Brahmin ritualist was not prepared for was the rampant opium use among Trinidad's Asian immigrants. To curb the lucrative traffic in that work-sapping narcotic, colonial rulers decreed that only medical practitioners could dispense the drug. No slouch at thriving in the British Caribbean, the Brahmin priest got himself qualified as a drug dispenser, thereby establishing the tradition that all Satalkar offspring are destined from birth to become medical men.

Reincarnation.

So that's why, earlier this morning, Dr. Sharma Satalkar had parked his car at Richmond General Hospital and set about his gruesome daily task of turning dead bodies into dugout canoes. Three corpses awaited his attention in the morgue: a pair of road-racing teens barbecued late last night in a fiery collision on Highway 99 (likely caused by the bottle of tequila the responding officers found smashed in the charred driver's lap), and yesterday's headless floater fished from the Fraser River.

As a lifelong fan of hard-boiled crime thrillers, Dr. Sharma Satalkar, Medical Detective, was well suited to his grisly job. A thickset man with a bowling-ball head shaved to the scalp, he resembled—in his own eyes too—Lex Luthor, the arch-villain of Superman. Nothing engaged his whatdunit mind more than a cadaver with a questionable cause of death, so instead of turning to the foolish crispy critters killed in the fast-and-furious drag race, he began his day by focusing his forensic skills on the floater.

Question: Was she dead or alive when she went into the water?

Question: Did a passing boat propeller behead her?

After changing into hospital greens and a plastic apron of the same color, Dr. Satalkar entered the autopsy theater with its off-white tiles and stone terrazzo floor. The morgue had several dissecting stations, each one fixed to the floor with its own sink, garburator, scales, and water supply. There was an isolation chamber for decomposing remains, and that's where the morgue attendant had wheeled the gurney with the floater, locking it in toe-tagged foot to sink.

Music played softly so as *not* to wake the dead.

The pathologist stood in the crook of the L-shaped dissecting station and scanned the waterlogged corpse from neck to toes with a powerful light. Unnaturally white in color and its abdomen bloated with gas, the body was partly decomposed from at least a week in the water. Where fish had nibbled at the naked flesh—for the floater was found with no clothes—fibrous strands of muscle clung to exposed bone.

Dr. Satalkar would have to open her up to determine if she was alive or dead when she went in the water, but he could establish the cause of the beheading with an external examination. Armed with a strong magnifying glass fit for Sherlock Holmes, the morgue sleuth peeled back the soggy tissue that had closed in around the neck bone and homed in on striations scratched into the top vertebra.

A minute later, Dr. Satalkar peeled off his gloves and strode purposefully to the phone on the wall to dial the homicide cops at Richmond RCMP.

———

Corporal James Rodale had never been one for blood and gore. Not even horror movies. When he became a Mountie, he knew that attending postmortems was part of the job. Sure, he'd felt queasy at his first autopsy—what human wouldn't at such a stark intimation of mortality?—but he was certain that would soon pass.

Nope.

Rodale had been elated when he and his best friend through Mountie recruit training at Depot Division in Regina, Saskatchewan, were posted to the same RCMP detachment here on the West Coast. But then one tragic night, his buddy was ambushed in a routine traffic stop, and Rodale arrived to find him shot through the heart. After a ramming car chase at a hundred miles an hour that's now legend in the Mounted Police, two avowed cop haters were arrested at gunpoint.

Determining which of the two was the shooter required a detailed autopsy to track the course of the bullet, and rookie Rodale—as exhibit man—had been forced to watch the pathologist peel away his buddy's skin, muscles, lungs, and heart, all the while thinking that this could also be his fate if he road-stopped the wrong car.

The stench of the autopsy theater—with its vats of formaldehyde for fixing specimens, and the nauseating smells wafting up from various body organs—was burned into the coils of Rodale's brain and still brought bile to his throat with every postmortem he attended. So the last thing he needed on starting shift just after breakfast this sunny morning was a call from Dr. Sharma Satalkar summoning him to the dissection of a headless corpse that was floating in the river for a week before it was fished out.

Luckily, winter had arrived early within the four walls of the morgue. To retard decomposition, the air was cool and light condensation glistened on the stainless steel. Rodale could almost see the breath billowing from his bilious throat, and on spotting the gruesome mess on the autopsy gurney, he might very well have thrown up had the room been hot and muggy.

"What's up, Doc?" he asked.

The corporal wore the brown serge working uniform of the Force. Self-conscious about his receding hairline, he didn't remove his peaked hat. The Horsemen's regimental badge—a bison head circled by maple leaves— sat in the center of his forehead. Whereas everything about Satalkar was exotic and piratical—it was easy to imagine him with rings through his ears and a cutlass in his hand—Rodale was ordinary and bland but for one feature: he had eyes of different colors. One iris was reddish brown, the other green. Back when he was bullied as a featherweight in junior high (a prod to don the red serge for its authority), thugs had dubbed him Stoplight.

"Floaters," said the doc, "are run of the mill for me. Some bob down the river, and others come in with the tide. The missing head isn't unusual, with all those estuary boats put-putting around. The floater bumps against a hull and the prop whacks off its head."

"Clean as a guillotine, eh?"

"But not here, Corporal. Take a look."

The queasy cop's stomach lurched as the sawbones passed him the magnifying glass.

"See the zigzag striations across the top vertebra?"

"Yeah," said Rodale, bending his head and feigning a look through closed eyelids.

"You don't get marks like that from the clean cut of a whirling propeller. You get them from sawing with a nicked blade."

"She didn't drown?"

"I doubt it. I'll know more when I open her up. The lungs of drowning victims are typically full of water. People suck it in in their struggle to breathe as their blood oxygen level falls. Coughing makes it worse by triggering an inhalation reflex. Water-filled lungs—pulmonary edema— aren't conclusive, though. The lungs of any corpse submerged for several days after death will passively fill with water. I'll do the usual tests for drowning. Did her beating heart pump diatoms through her bloodstream to collect in her bone marrow? And I'll do the Gettler chloride test to see if we're looking at a saltwater or freshwater drowning."

"But your bet's against that?"

"Yes."

"You're thinking murder by beheading?"

"That would be stretching it from just the decapitation. No matter how she died, the saw marks could be from getting rid of the body."

"After death? While cutting it down to stuff in a trunk or something?"

"Uh-huh. But not the stab to her throat."

As Satalkar pointed to several vertical punctures on both sides of the neck, the Horseman squinted his eyes to blur the ghastly stump of artery and vein, muscle and bone in its circle of waterlogged flesh.

"Someone stabbed her sideways through the throat," said the pathologist, "using a knife or a pointed weapon with a thick blade."

"Like a Bowie knife?"

"That would do it."

"Sex attack?" asked the Mountie.

"There's bruising around her genitals, but that could be from prostitution. Note the needle marks on the interior aspect of both arms. Addiction to drugs often leads to the sex trade. But the slash across both breasts, bisecting the nipples, suggests a sexual element to the attack. It cuts deep to the sternum."

"Semen?"

"Too long in the water for a swab to be productive."

"Okay, Doc, from what you see, how's this for a theory? Junkie hooker runs afoul of a vicious john. While they're going at it, he stabs her through the neck for sadistic kicks. To make a statement, he also slashes her breasts. Then, to impede the ID, he cuts off her head and dumps her body in the river."

"Maybe," the sawbones slowly replied. "But if he decapitated her to hinder identification, why not snip off her fingertips as well?"

Satalkar leaned over to take scrapings from under each fingernail. Then he injected glycerin into the wrinkled tips to smooth them out. After Rodale had fetched a fingerprint sheet from his briefcase, the doc pressed the arches, loops, and whorls into an inkpad, then he rolled each finger across the form. On retrieving the exhibit, Rodale labeled it and filled in a box with time, date, place, and his regimental number.

If the vic was a junkie hooker, odds were a drugs bust had left her prints on file.

Who were you? the Mountie wondered.

1:15 p.m.

To: Richmond Detachment, RCM Police

6900 Minoru Blvd., Richmond, BC

Attn.: Cpl. James G. Rodale

From: Vancouver Police Dept.

312 Main Street

Vancouver, BC

Repl.: Det. Bernie Zebroff, Drug Squad

Re: Fingerprint Enquiry/Floater (Fraser River)

ID confirmed.

Helen Ann Grabowski, aka Patricia Ann Palitti.

Outstanding charges: NIP heroin (October 18, 1982), Vancouver (Moonrise Hotel, Moonlight Arms).

DOB: June 12, 1961, New Orleans, Louisiana.

Check with FBI.

Mug shot to follow.

Description from booking sheet: white female; height, 175 cm; weight, 50 kg; slim build; large breasts, unusually firm (believe me, that's what it says here); black hair to collar; brown eyes; needle tracks both arms; long scar down center of spine (skin search by nurse).

B. Zebroff (Det.)

3:45 p.m.

To: "E" Division, RCM Police

Richmond Detachment

Attn.: J. G. Rodale (Cpl.)

From: "N" Division, RCM Police

Ottawa, Ontario

Re: 4722067

FBI confirmation print record: Helen Ann Grabowski, aka Patricia Ann Palitti.

New Orleans Police Department.

Soliciting (April 12, 1980). Suspended sentence.

Known prostitute. Pimp: John Lincoln Hardy, aka "The Weasel."
No record.
Pictures to follow.

5:33 p.m.

It hit you as soon as you came through the door. Nothing definite, nothing concrete—just a gray, amorphous atmosphere that hung in the air like the opium smoke from Chinatown's sinister past. You sensed at once without being told that this was Junk City. Junk time ruled here, with real time suspended. The fifty patrons in the Moonlight Arms made no more noise than twenty. Most were content to lurk in the gloom of this cockroach haven, nursing a beer until it was time to shoot up again and watching each other furtively through tombstone eyes. The only drunk was a fat, slovenly Native woman who banged on the top of the jukebox offbeat to a Loverboy tune. In the rooms upstairs, there were probably a dozen hypes lolling on crumpled, stained sheets in various states of un-dress, nodding in and out of life with needles clinging to their arms like glass leeches.

Odds were, on sensing this, you backed out the door.

The Amazon who was slumped against the wall on the far side of the bar would have been striking had she taken care of herself. Six feet tall, with a muscular, statuesque figure, she resembled Ursula Andress in the Bond film *Dr. No.* Same high cheekbones. Same honey-colored hair. Same almond eyes. But in her demeanor, the likeness slipped away. Her clothes were loose and grubby. Her nails were painted with chipped red polish. Her sloppy makeup failed to mask the dark smudges beneath her sleepless eyes. And at least a week had passed since her rat's nest of greasy hair had last felt a comb.

The woman was jittery and jumpy…

Her eyes jerked here and there…

Beseeching all who were pushing…

I need junk!

The Indian who strode into the bar had headhunting in his blood. That history was proudly emblazoned on the T-shirt just visible in the gap of his frayed jean jacket:

The photo harked back to a time when his ancestors were feared warriors on the West Coast, before white men arrived to pollute their land with plastic and malls. Now, his people were ground down to drinking on shabby reserves and trolling through downtown dives like this to eke out a living. His tattooed arms were bare from the shoulder down, the sleeves of his jacket and T-shirt torn off to boast his thick biceps. The short, stout man wore soiled jeans cinched with a Harley-Davidson belt. Strung round his neck was a whale's tooth dangling from a leather thong. From under the brim of his dirty Stetson leered a pockmarked face punctuated by eyes cold with the meanness of the streets.

"Are you lookin'?" the Indian murmured as he weaved among the tables.

"Are you lookin'?"

"Are you lookin'?"

The pusher's version of the hooker's "Want a date?"

When he spied the twitchy blonde across the bar, his mouth cracked into a grin of yellow, rotting teeth. Like a wolf on the prowl, he zeroed in on his prey.

"Are you lookin', baby?"

"You got?" the Amazon asked.

"Uh-huh."

"How much?"

"Sixty for one."

"Where?"

The Indian—whose street name was Bax (for Baxbaxwalanuksiwe)—rolled his bloodshot eyes toward the pub's rear door.

"Meet me out back in five."

Turning on the heels of his cowboy boots, he quickly walked away.

IS SOMEONE HUNTING HEADS?

Wednesday, October 27, 9:34 a.m.

"Gumby!"

"Nose-honker!"

"Poo stain!"

"Bitch!"

The tiff between the five-year-old twins was heating up.

"Bitch" was the word their dad had spat repeatedly at their mom in the volatile days leading up to their parents' recent split. "Bitch" was also the word their mom used to refer to their dad's new girlfriend, Roz. Mom never said the name Roz—she just hissed "That bitch!" whenever she mentioned the pretty young woman who'd moved into their old house to live with their dad after the separation. Whatever "bitch" meant, it was obviously a big step up from "Gumby," "nose-honker," and "poo stain"—the usual taunts in their girlhood lexicon. So as tempers flared in the current argument—about whether to break Mom's strict "Don't go near the creek!" rule in order to explore a tattered tent spotted at the foot of the hillside—first one twin and then the other had pulled out the loaded word and hurled it at her sister.

"You're a *double* bitch, Cindy!" retorted Diane, standing nose to nose with her rosy-cheeked twin in a matching yellow slicker, her arms akimbo like Mom's when she snarled, "That bitch!"

"Scaredy-cat! Stay here. I'm going down," Cindy said, poking a red curl back under her yellow hood before stomping off to the clifftop fence that separated the backyard of their new home from the leaf-strewn hillside that plunged to the whitewater creek.

"Hey, wait up!" Diane yelled. "I'm no scaredy-cat!"

All their lives, the siblings had been battling to determine who was the alpha and who was the beta, and Diane was not about to let Cindy claim the Queen of Adventure crown and lord it over her.

Their mom had sent them out to play while she screamed at their dad on the phone about alimony or something, and no sooner had they peered over the fence to see what was down there than Cindy spied the tattered tent in the undergrowth on this bank of the stream.

"No, Cindy! Mom says."

"Poo on that."

So Diane had grabbed her rebellious sister by one arm and pulled her toward the recently rented house, igniting the tiff that escalated into "Bitch!" versus "Bitch!" Having broken free and tromped back to the rickety corral, Cindy scaled the fence and slung one leg over the top rail, then jumped down on the far side. But no sooner did her rubber boots hit the ground cover of soggy leaves than her feet slipped out from under her, skidding the girl over the edge of the muddy cliff. Bump, bump, bump bounced her bum in a wild plunge down the incline, until she was tossed in the air by a hillock at the bottom and crashed back down to earth in front of the tattered tent.

Cindy screamed.

For when her fall-breaking hand sank into a shallow grave near the slashed canvas, a clutch of rib bones burst out of the muck and clamped onto her arm.

11:55 a.m.

Corporal James Rodale didn't relish this drive across town through gridlocked midday traffic. Greater Vancouver was chunked up by too many west-to-east waterways, so his south-to-north route required him to cross too many bottleneck bridges. Every municipality had once had a choice to make: Did it want to contract with the national Mounties to set up a local RCMP detachment, or did it want to recruit its own police force? Consequently, Greater Vancouver was a patchwork of conflicting police turfs, and that was one of the reasons—no, the *main* reason—why Clifford Olson had found it easy to abduct, rape, and kill eleven kids.

Divide and conquer: the feudal politician's fiefdom fantasy.

Richmond Detachment—Rodale's home turf—policed the largest island in the Fraser River delta. To reach the city of Vancouver, which had its own police force (including the drug cops who'd busted Helen Grabowski out front of the Moonlight Arms a week ago), Rodale had to cross a bridge over the Fraser, just east of where her body was fished from the river. His drive across the city took him past RCMP "E" Division Headquarters, in the center of the Vancouver Police Department's jurisdiction. To the west, at the tip of Point Grey, sat University Detachment, where the Mounties patrolled the campus. East of Vancouver, the Burnaby Detachment policed the suburbs, and beyond that, the New Westminster Police Department served upriver. False Creek—actually an inlet of the sea—divided Vancouver, so a second maddening bridge funneled Rodale downtown. There, the causeway through Stanley Park—a forest lost in the jungle of high-rises—conveyed him to the worst logjam: Lions Gate Bridge. Arching over the waterway between the outer and inner harbor to give access to the foot of the North Shore Mountains, the bridge divided West Vancouver, which had its own police force, from North Vancouver, which was guarded by the Mounties.

Divide and conquer.

The perfect hunting ground for a serial killer.

At the far end of Lions Gate Bridge, the corporal took the right fork into North Vancouver and followed Marine Drive east along the inner harbor. By then, road rage fostered by poor city planning had him fantasizing—cop though he was—about rat-a-tat-tatting the choked midday traffic with machine-gun fire. But before he snapped, Rodale came upon a knot of RCMP cars parked at the mouth of the creekside path that led to the crime scene.

They drove *me to it*, he thought.

That would have been his defense in court had he opened fire.

The Mountie stepped out of his vehicle under an ominous overcast sky. The Indian summer of the past week was giving way to an Arctic front. Not only did this chilly weather force Rodale to bundle up, but the cold air was conjuring fog out of the moist earth. After flashing his badge at the uniformed constable blocking the path, the corporal snaked his way up a gully overhung with shedding maples, while the stream beside him gushed over smooth rocks, and phantom harbor ships bellowed mournful horns.

"Corporal."

"Sergeant."

"Thanks for coming. Sorry to drag you across town—"

"Olson."

"Right. Olson. Can't be too careful."

"So what've you got?"

"Like I said on the phone, a slashed tent, a shallow grave. And a headless corpse."

"Let's hope it's a coincidence."

"Not anymore."

"Huh?"

"While you were on the road, I phoned Dr. Satalkar."

Sergeant Jack MacDougall of North Vancouver Detachment had the straight spine and shoulders-back bearing of a military man. With piercing blue eyes that would drill a guilt-ridden suspect to his rotten heart and a pencil mustache befitting Errol Flynn, MacDougall looked like the poster boy for RCMP recruitment...circa 1940s. His voice had an edge of authority. His lips held a determined line. And though the others working the leafy scene were wilting from the dampness seeping out of the ground, MacDougall—despite his trenchcoat straight out of a film noir—seemed ready for a *GQ* shoot. Even a fedora wouldn't have looked out of place.

"Did you hear the news coming over?"

"No," said Rodale.

"The house on the bluff has been vacant for a year. A woman who split from her husband just moved in with two kids. One of the girls climbed over the fence and tumbled down here. Her landing bared rib bones, and her screams brought the mom running. Mom unearthed the headless corpse and phoned her husband to rip a strip off him for driving her out to rent a graveyard like this. Hubby called us."

"So you called me."

"Better safe than sorry. I saw the piece on your headless floater in this morning's paper."

"Why call Satalkar?"

"You'll see when you take a look."

Those who make murder their business were hard at work. Ident techs had cleared a trail through the undergrowth to the tattered tent, where they crouched in the mud amid fingers of fog that seemed to threaten to drag them down into the putrid grave. A tech was taking photos. A tech was measuring distances and sketching a map. Other techs combed through the leaves around the maggoty remains. Meanwhile, moving out from the grave, a dog handler "read" his German shepherd as it sniffed along the slope, the path, and the creek. Downstream, a tech with a metal detector called out hotspots for others to sift for clues.

Bile rose to Rodale's throat as he forced himself to squat on his heels beside the rotting body. At least there was no decomposing head with worm-eaten brains leaking out. Small mercy.

"The hole in the rib cage was punched by the tumbling girl," said MacDougall.

Averting his eyes from the squirmy torso, Rodale ran them down the skeletal legs to focus on the jeans looped around the ankles.

"Looks like rape," he said.

"Which fits the bruised genitals of your floater. The reason I phoned Satalkar was to quiz him about these zigzag marks on the neck bone."

The corporal took a look.

"Christ! They match ours," he said.

"The doc says such scratches are from a nicked blade, probably a knife. My gut tells me the same blade was used to rip the tent."

"And the breastbone?"

"That fits too. See the gouge across the sternum, near the hole punched by the kid?"

"So we've got another Olson."

"Yeah, and the news is out. The hubby of the mom on the hill works at a radio station. He didn't call us because he's a helpful citizen. He put two and two together—your floater and this vic found by his kid—and asked us to comment on the catchline they're broadcasting: 'Is someone hunting heads?'"

"That's on the air?"

"Remember when I asked if you'd heard the news?"

"Damn!" said Rodale.

"When this headhunter thing goes large, the shit…will hit…the fan."

2:34 p.m.

They don't make newspapermen like Skip O'Rourke anymore.

The Skipper's nickname dated from his youth in the merchant marine, before his first landlubber job as *The Vancouver Sun's* waterfront reporter. A dinosaur from the good ol' days, O'Rourke had an appearance that reflected his roots: iron gray, flattop brush cut; skeptical, rheumy eyes; nose blotched from too much drinking; beer belly from the same; hula girl tattoo on his arm that irked *The Sun's* feminists.

Back in the good ol' days of yellow copy paper and hand-set hot metal type, when the paper was printed in the old Sun Tower at the gateway to Chinatown, the newsroom ran on booze. Newshounds would drink in the darkroom of the photo department, tossing their empties behind the huge built-in filing cabinet. When *The Sun* later switched premises and the cabinet was removed, out poured an avalanche of bottles.

In those days—thanks to antiquated liquor laws—Vancouver was rife with bootlegging joints and bring-your-own-bottle clubs. One morning, Skip was drinking his eye-opener in a longshoremen's watering hole when a thug walked in and shot one of the patrons. O'Rourke got the hell out of there and ran back to the paper. As he came in the door, the editor yelled, "Where have you been? Someone just shot up the longshoremen's club. Go cover the story." So Skip returned to the dive from which he'd just escaped, wrote up a piece that read as if he'd actually seen the action, and was promptly promoted to crime reporter. The crime reporter got to go on raids with the cops, so for years Skip swaggered to work with a .38 stuck in his waistband.

By the sunset of the good ol' days, Skip had climbed the totem pole to news editor. The newsroom back then was a madhouse come deadline. Harried reporters pounded their typewriters. Copyboys zigzagged around desks to transfer yellow paper. Rewriters dreamed up catchy headlines at the U-shaped "rim" circling the "slot," the pneumatic tube that sucked copy up to the typesetting floor.

The grunt job of the year was covering the *Sun's* Salmon Derby. Pity the poor reporter sent to capture the flotilla of fishing boats bobbing in the harbor around the mouths of the creeks that fed the Pacific.

Too many years of salmon derbies had used up most of the angles, so one year the reporter wrote from the point of view of the winning catch, a chinook weighing almost thirty pounds. The copy sucked up the tube to the linotype room read:

A sleepy chinook, fat, sassy, and happy with life, yawned and hastily gulped his Sunday breakfast.

Too hastily.

With one munch, there in the cold, clear predawn waters off Seal Rock, that fat fish, all 28 pounds and 12 ounces of him, had become exhibit A in The Sun's 25th annual Salmon Derby...

For half an hour after deadline, Skip could "chase" the paper. Typos in the front-page proofs could be caught before *The Sun* went to press. But that was a hot summer day on the Tower's cafeteria deck, so the chasing window had passed when Skip—puffing on his first cigar of the workday—wandered in and ran his eyes down the derby story:

A sleepy chink, fat, sassy, and happy with life, yawned and hastily gulped his Sunday breakfast...

Some typos you can live with—and some typos you can't. The cigar dropped from O'Rourke's mouth, scattering sparks that set the offending page proofs on fire, and that's how the Skipper got to bellow the words sacred to every editor but rarely heard in the newsroom...

"Stop the presses!"

Those Wild West days of *The Vancouver Sun* were now the stuff of legend. Typewriters, yellow copy, and hot metal type had given way to VDTs, computer paste-ups, and cold web offset printing. The hell-raisers of yesteryear had evolved into the choirboys of today, leaching the fly-by-the-seat-of-your-pants fun out of this job. If only a time machine would take

Skip back to the good ol' days for a last hurrah, he'd gladly be pensioned off to the Old Reporters' Home.

At least the page proofs still came in for him to review, so for half an hour after the two o'clock deadline for *The Sun's* five-star edition—the final print run of the day—he'd chased the clock to catch any typos before the presses took over.

Now, 2:30 had passed.

Time for a cigar.

The Skipper lounged back in his swivel chair and propped his Hush Puppies up on his desk. His thumbnail scratched a wooden match into flame, and he passed it back and forth across the end of his stogie. Soon, his office filled with thick blue smoke as he wondered if tomorrow would put flesh on the bones of today's skeletal story. This morning's edition, the three-star, had run a brief piece on yesterday's headless floater. Before noon, a local radio station was broadcasting that a *second* headless body had turned up in North Vancouver, but with no police confirmation, that news had missed the four-star's twelve o'clock deadline. The newshound in Skip had already dreamed up the perfect moniker for such a serial killer, and in an ideal world, the edition just put to bed would have screamed this front-page headline in ninety-six-point type: HEAD-HUNTER STRIKES AGAIN!

But alas, no.

Still no confirmation sufficient to kick out all the stops.

Ah well, perhaps tomorrow.

The woman who entered Skip's office fanned her hand in front of her face both to see where she was going and to keep from getting cancer.

"Someone left this at the front desk," she said, dropping a manila envelope marked PERSONAL: EYES OF EDITOR ONLY on the desk before beating a retreat.

Skip slit open the package and dumped out its contents: a magazine cutting paper-clipped on top of two photographs. The cutting was a subscription form for a bottom-feeding men's magazine called *Buns and Boobs Bonanza*. It depicted a woman naked to the waist with the biggest pair of breasts Skip had ever seen. The caption under the image read, "Looking for these?"

Shaking his head at whatever wanker had delivered this, O'Rourke plucked off the paper clip to expose the Polaroid pictures.

Out in the newsroom, free from the stress of the five-star deadline, the choirboys and choirgirls of today's newspaper business sat caged in their cubicles, soberly typing features for tomorrow's edition, when out of Skip's office bellowed a cry they thought they'd never hear:

"Stop the presses!"

Again, the cigar butt had tumbled from the Skipper's mouth, for staring up at the startled editor from the photos in his hand were the black-haired, dead-eyed, slack-lipped heads of two women, hacked off at the neck and stuck on upright wooden poles.

THE MAD MOUNTIE

Medicine Lake, Alberta, 1897

Iron-child emerged from the black void caused by the wounds to his head and leg to find himself staring down the barrel of a .476 Enfield revolver.

"Aye," said Blake in English. "I see yer alive."

The Mountie pushed the beaverskin hat back from his weathered forehead to expose a patch of scabby skin, then rubbed and picked at the rawness until it bled.

"Are y'in pain, laddie?"

The white man stood between the Cree and the blazing ball of the sun. From where Iron-child lay sprawled in the blood-spattered snow at the edge of the lakeside thicket of pines, the manhunter was a black silhouette haloed by the glare off the jagged Rockies. Blake cast a long, dark shadow over his shivering foe. As the Cree's squinting eyes adjusted to the morning light, he took in clues that exposed his adversary: the square-cut forehead seeping blood down one side of his face; the bushy eyebrows hoary with ice; the pale gray, hate-filled eyes that met his gaze. The British imperialist glowered down from on high as if he *knew* that up there was his rightful place in the world. His cheeks were ruddy, not just from the harshness of winter but also from too much firewater (known to his kind as Scotch whisky). The Cree could smell it in the breath that billowed from the sneer beneath his drooping white mustache. A lanyard was tied to the butt of the gun in his bare hand so that if he dropped it in the heat of battle, it would hang at arm's length for him to grab again. The lanyard snaked out through the unbuttoned throat of the Horseman's frost-encrusted, black buffalo coat, in the V of which the Cree could see the scarlet uniform of the North-West Mounted Police.

"Dinnae fight 'cause there's hope o' winning," said Blake. "T'is much finer to fight when it's nae use. That's Cyrano de Bergerac. Be that yer philosophy, lad?"

The white man's whistle brought a pack of wolf-like huskies bounding out of the thicket. The sled dogs circled the half-naked Indian, sniffing his blood in the air. The alpha dog, Cerf-vola, closed in on the prey and licked his rough tongue up Iron-child's cheek, trailing a smudge through the charcoal designs of his warpaint and the blood that was trickling down from his head wound.

"Dinnae think we're blood brothers," the Mountie said, distracted by his own red hand. "Truth be, I loathe ye heathens. Yer an affront to God. But part o' ye will yield a bonnie memento mori to join the other glories in the trophy collection hidden in m' trunk."

With a sweep of his arm, the Scotsman yanked the buffalo-horn cap from Iron-child's head. Having smeared the Cree's blood across the heel of his palm, he glared at it, as if transfixed, then mimicked the dog by lapping it up with the tip of his tongue.

"Nae much of a trophy, is it, Cree? Nae like my scalp would have been. Aye, that gives ye young bucks pride. Taking a gray-haired scalp."

Blake licked a drop of his own blood from the bristles of his mustache.

Not many moons before Iron-child was born, his father, White Owl, had fought alongside Sitting Bull at Custer's Last Stand at the Little Bighorn River, known to Natives as the Greasy Grass. To escape the wrath of the Long Knives—those of Custer's men who'd survived—Sitting Bull and his followers had fled north, crossing the medicine line to the safety of the North-West Territories. Soon after, Blake had galloped into Sitting Bull's camp with his fellow redcoats to lay down the law. When he discovered that White Owl had stolen some horses from a local rancher, Blake put Iron-child's father in handcuffs and leg irons, earning himself the nickname One-Who-Ties.

That was the last time White Owl was seen alive.

"D'ye grasp English, laddie? It dinnae matter to me. Let's have a wee talk while we got the time. I'll do the talking as ye do the dying."

Iron-child didn't understand a word Blake said. Listening to the gibberish roll off the Scotsman's tongue, the Cree was hypnotized by the trilled r's of the Highlander's burr. So severe was his shivering that the bones of his broken leg rattled against each other. If only death by freezing would set his spirit free, he could perish as a warrior and cross the Bridge of the World.

"I know ye Crees on Chief One Arrow's reserve dinnae like being boxed into sixteen square miles when ye once had a thousand miles o' prairie to roam. And I know ye dinnae like starving because there are nae buffalo. But, lad, that's the price ye Crees must pay for backing Riel in his failed rebellion against the government. Ye cannae stop the settlers from coming.

"I'm nae saying that Sergeant Colebrook was the best o' officers. Aye, he had a checkered record and had been up for breaches o' discipline. But when he caught up with Almighty Voice that morning as he was breaking camp, Colebrook dinnae draw his pistol. This is nae Tombstone or Dodge City, and the Mounted Police are nae Yankee barbarians. So tell me, laddie, why did yer redskinned blood brother have to shoot Colebrook through the neck with a double-barreled shotgun?

"Aye, that put pressure on us. Settlers cowering in their homes, afraid the Mounted Police cannae hold the thin red line. But the *real* pressure came from *within* the Force. 'Cause no one, lad—redskin or white—gets away with killing one of our *own*.

"This Almighty Voice. He was a piss-poor—"

Blake stopped talking.

The Mountie's eyes lost focus.

His attention wandered from the sights of his gun to the blood spatters reddening the snow.

Drip...

Drip...

Phantom sounds echoed in his brain.

Rub...

Rub...

He clawed his temple as if it caused him pain.

He shook his head...

His eyes cleared...

His focus returned to the Cree sighted down the barrel of his Enfield.

"Ye think I'm rambling, lad? Well, I'll tell ye. Malaria got me in the tropics. The Ashanti War, it was. Still plagues me, though it's been twenty-five years.

"This Almighty Voice. He was a piss-poor leader to follow in yer foolish escapade. What'd ye three young Crees think? He'd bring back auld lang syne and drive us demon white men from yer land? Nae, it's *our* land now. A lesson for yer learning."

Thum-thump...

"Ye renegades made a mistake. Aye, ye made a bad one. It was nae killing Colebrook. And it was nae killing the others. It was prodding Herchmer to put *me* on yer tail."

Thum-thump...

"Herchmer says I'm excessive. But ye'll nae find a black mark on m' record."

Thum-thump...

"'Cause, Cree, the Mounted Police need me more than I need them. When there's a job o' tracking, who d'ye think they call on?"

Thum-thump...

"A legend is born, laddie, when a man beats the probabilities o' life."

Thum-thump...

"I'm the one who gets the ones who ought to get away."

Thum-thump...

Drip...

"Hear me, Cree. Hear me well. The legacy o' the Mounties will be the legacy o' *me!*"

Blake lashed out with the Enfield and pistol-whipped Iron-child across his mouth. With a sickening crack, the Indian's teeth exploded into a spray of shattered enamel. Screams of shock and pain roared up and down the Rocky Mountains, the echo of each colliding with the shriek of the one following. Tossing aside the brave's buffalo-horn cap, the mad Mountie grabbed him by the braids of his hair and yanked his head off the ground as he choked on fragments of teeth.

"Dead or alive?" Blake spat in the face of his prey.

Releasing the braids, the Horseman threw the Cree back into the snow.

"It's either/or to the Mounted."

He cocked the hammer as sunlight danced along the Enfield's barrel.
"But I tell ye, laddie..."

Iron-child stared down the dark muzzle.

"It's nae either/or to *me*!"

With a flash of yellow and a blast of thunder that bounced around the towering peaks like the cannonade from the artillery pieces that had blown apart Almighty Voice and two of his renegades at Duck Lake, Saskatchewan, seven months ago, launching Blake on the manhunt that led him here, the Highlander pulled the trigger and shot the Cree between the eyes.

Thum-thump...

Drip...

As Blake scraped the flesh of his temple down to bare bone, he raised the revolver to his nostrils and sniffed gunsmoke into his lungs.

———

The Enfield had blown out an exit wound the size of Blake's fist, splashing gobs of blood and brains across the dazzling snow. Grabbing the corpse by its braids, the Mountie hauled the Cree to his overnight camp in the lakeside pines and dropped the body near his unhitched dogsled. Rummaging among his food supplies for breakfast, he whistled for the huskies to join him in the trees. While the dogs fed on dry moose meat, the Horseman ate biscuits and pemmican washed down with slugs of whisky.

Thum-thump...

Thump...thump...

Drip...

In the early years of the nightmare, he'd thought it was an after-effect of malaria, a feverish dream that followed him here to the Great Lone Land, where it drew its dark contents from his pioneer exploration of the wilderness. But now he knew it was more than that. Not just a nightmare that vexed his troubled sleep, but also a black daydream that seized him as a conscious echo. Never when he was in barracks, though, surrounded by British civilization. Only when he was alone on the hunt in Indian territory.

Was he haunted by the heathens he'd killed to stock his trophy collection?

Or was he going mad?

This time the nightmare's echo had almost cost him his life. It had distracted him at the moment when he most required his wits: when he was primed to meet the threat of Iron-child's attack. Fortunately, he was able to pull himself out of the bloody hallucination, but because the echo had not played out in front of his eyes, the throbbing pressure within his head got worse with each heartbeat.

Thum-thump…

Thump…thump…

Drip…

The Scotsman busied himself with breaking camp and packing the sled. One by one, he attached the huskies to the train with traces, back bands, and collar straps. As usual, Cerf-vola and Spanker fought over the lead, and also as usual, Cerf-vola won. Finally, Blake heaved Iron-child's body on top of the heap, then lashed it to the sled, spread-eagled and facedown with its shattered head forward. Climbing onto the rear of the skates, he flicked a whip at the dogs, urging the huskies to tug the load out of the trees.

Once in the open, the Mountie paused to gather up his trophies. He tucked the old Winchester the Cree had wielded as a club into the lashings and strapped the buffalo-horn cap in front of the gory head wound like a ship's figurehead. He contemplated tracking Iron-child's footprints around Medicine Lake to their origin farther west at Windigo Mountain. But then—

Thump…thump…

Drip…

—the pain in his head got worse. Red streaks flashed before his eyes like arrows sinking into his brain and the blood trickling down from his forehead froze to his face, so he climbed back onto the runners and cracked the whip at the dogs.

For hours the huskies panted as they hauled the heavy sled, dipping their snouts to lap up refreshing mouthfuls of snow. They zigzagged into cloud that clung to the eastern peaks, and eventually they reached it: the Indians' Bridge of the World—that hinge where the Rocky Mountains face a thousand miles of plain stretching across the North-West Territories to the Great Lakes.

Reining in the dog train, Blake brought the sled to a halt. A false step here would plunge them into a mountain gorge. Wiser to wait for the noonday sun to burn off the haze and unveil the pass through the frontline spurs of the Rockies. To kill time, the madman set about adorning his trophy, the buffalo-horn cap, with Iron-child's braids. Stepping off the runners and drawing a knife from his boot—the *sgian-dubh* used by Highlanders for skinning and cutting meat—the Horseman trudged to the front of the sled to harvest the Cree's hair, but when he gazed down at the hellhole drilled through the Indian's brain—

Thump...thump...

Drip...

—the nightmare's echo sucked him in.

It's not the thumping that rattles him. Nor is it the dark. It's the ghastly collection of still-bleeding scalps nailed to the fortress walls. This room without windows has lurked in his mind for close to three decades. The plank door braced with ironwork is bolted firmly shut. The hand-hewn logs are stacked one on another. Mud is packed between the logs to keep out the cold.

Again, it's a winter month in 1870.

Again, this room is where the fort does its Indian trade.

Beside him are sacks of feed and crates of ammunition. A candle on a table casts the only light. Along the nearest wall lean eight oblong crates, the lid of one pried off and lying on the floor. The candlelight illuminates a barrel within. At twenty rifles to the crate, that's a hundred and sixty guns to trade with the Cree. Joining them as barter for pelts are blankets, beads, colored cloths, handkerchiefs, and ribbons. On the other side of the table looms the wealth of the fur trade: piles of buffalo, bear, mink, beaver, fox, and marten stacked to the ceiling, where there hangs the carcass of a deer, its head bent back from the weight of its antlers, the rack points crooked at him like accusing fingers.

The candle illuminates just half of the room. Where it fades into darkness, he can barely make out another shape hanging from the ceiling, but primal fear raises the hackles on his neck and instinct tells him not to explore whatever lurks in the shadows.

Drip...

Drip...

Is that from the scalps?

Or does it come out of the darkness?

Now the walls are closing in like the sides of a grave. The candle sputters as it drowns in a pool of its own melted wax. As claustrophobia strangles him, he stumbles to the door, draws the bolt, and throws it wide to escape outside. But there is no escape. There's only hell on earth.

The Hudson's Bay Company fort overlooks the Saskatchewan River. A five-sided stockade of twenty-foot-high logs and corner bastions, the fort is open to the Indian wigwams camped along both banks. As fat white snowflakes tumble from the sky to shroud the smothered, frozen landscape, a horde of ghostly Plains Cree stagger into the trading post. Red spots pustulate the skin of the pale apparitions, all of whom are whiter than the terrified frontiersmen cowering behind every window inside the fort. Moaning, wailing, and bleeding from the blisters rotting their flesh, the specters lurch around the yard, spitting on door handles and smearing pus from their putrid faces across the windowpanes.

He knows why the dying, disfigured Indians are here.

The Cree are bringing smallpox back to its source, in the desperate hope that this will somehow release them from the white men's curse.

Now a medicine man appears at the gate to this red-and-white chaos. His headdress is of ermine skins, and his deerskin robe is embroidered with porcupine quills. Tears of blood trickle down his wrinkled cheeks as he spreads his arms wide to encompass the Native zombies shambling around the yard. Like Christ curing the lepers, the shaman shucks the scarlet carrion from the bones of his suffering people, melting it like the wax dripping from the candle on the table. As each distorted face dribbles off the ivory skull beneath, as each shedding body becomes a walking skeleton, the medicine man swings his left hand forward and points it directly at the Mountie standing in the doorway.

Blake slams the barrier shut and rams the bolt into place.

Soon the first tomahawk strikes the wood. Blow upon blow vibrates the door as the skeletons assault it, then the blade of a hatchet splinters through one plank. As the breach widens, skulls peer in, until finally the wood disintegrates into kindling.

Thum-thump…

Thum-thump…

Thum-thump…

Blake's heart pounds in his ears. As he backs toward the darkness to seek refuge in the shadows, the candle on the table sputters and dies. By the light streaming in the door, the skeletons smash through kegs, bottles, and furniture to retrieve the scalps from the walls. Can it be these too are pelts in the fur trade, skinned off the skulls of Cree warriors and not the skulls of whites?

Drip…

Wet hits his head and runs down his cheek.

Drip…

Blake hears bony feet shuffling toward him.

Groping in his pockets, he finds a match and strikes it against a tinderbox. Sulfur flares yellow as the next drop hits him. While smoke from the snuffed wick mingles with pungent whiffs of rum and whisky, he cranes his neck to squint up at the cause of the dripping.

The body hangs upside down from the ceiling by nails driven through both feet. The head is missing, the neck severed to expose artery and vein, muscle and bone in a circle of raw flesh. What's left of the corpse is dressed in the bright scarlet tunic of the North-West Mounted Police. The arms in sleeves with gold braid dangle down toward the plank floor. Blood as red as the uniform pools under the headless Mountie. Blood drips from the fingertips, but the sound of the drops hitting the floor is masked by the rhythmic thud of a drum beating overhead. The drumbeat booms down from atop a trapdoor in the ceiling.

Thump…thump…

Drip…

Thump…thump…

Drip…

Blake identifies the scarlet tunic as his own.

Bony fingers claw him as the Horseman starts to climb. A ladder used to hoist the body leads to the trapdoor. On his way up, Blake slows to grab the Enfield from the dead man's holster. The holster's empty. The gun is gone. As vengeful bones clasp his ankle, he kicks back viciously, splintering the skeleton into pieces. But no sooner do those fragments clatter to the floor than they reintegrate into a snarling, skeletal windigo monster gnashing its razor-sharp teeth as it climbs the rungs after him.

Shoving the trapdoor open, Blake scrambles onto the roof. Up here, the drumbeat deafens him as he whams the hinged door down on the monster, pulverizing it.

Bone dust chokes him amid the feathery white flakes, and he perceives an overwhelming horror closing in on his last stand. Like Custer, Blake is surrounded by heathen warriors. A yellow peril of Chinamen swarms in from the Far East: pigtails and dragons and fireworks wrapped in a haze of opium smoke. Those stomped by the jackboot of Britain in the Opium Wars are coming for him with gleaming knives in their fists, intent on flaying him alive with the death of a thousand cuts. Black men surge in from Africa on his other flank: an impi of darkies in leopard skins grinding white teeth that have been filed to points, their arms holding cannibal pots above their kinky heads. Those enslaved to cut cane in the British West Indies and those who fell to British guns in the Ashanti War are coming to stew his flesh to devour at juju feasts.

Thump…thump…

Thump…thump…

Thump…thump…

The drumbeat summons the hordes.

Sitting cross-legged on the snow-covered roof is a naked Ashanti witch doctor adorned with snake skulls, juju fetishes, and a leopard tail around his waist. Blake recognizes the conjuror as one he killed in Africa and the voodoo fetishes as trophies now secreted in his regimental trunk. Wielding a massive buffalo bone, the necromancer pounds rhythmically on a drum made from the severed head of an inspector in the North-West Mounted Police. The Horseman's face is bashed to a bloody pulp, but Blake registers the man's white pith helmet as his own.

With a jerk, his head snaps back when someone yanks his hair. The cold steel of a knife blade slits across his throat. A gush of warm blood cascades down the front of his chest, spraying from his arteries to curtain the nightmare behind red mist.

As he gurgles, chokes, and gasps for air, the unseen attacker whispers behind his ear:

"Shu-kwe-wee-tam."

Thumpthumpthumpthumpthump…

———

Blake came out of his madman's trance to find the snow around him spattered with blood. With his right hand—bloody and gripping the sgian-dubh from his boot—he was pounding against his temple like the witch doctor bashing the severed head.

Thump...

Thump...

Thump...

The Mountie was jarred to find his other hand clutching Iron-child's scalp. Blake had no recollection of having skinned the Cree's skull. So not only had the first echo distracted him at the moment when he most required his wits—repelling the Indian's attack—but now, Blake had lost control of his body in the grip of his madness.

Was this a hex for culling so many shamans, soothsayers, witch doctors, medicine men, sorcerers, obi-men, voodooists, spirit-raisers, necromancers, conjurors, magicians, idolaters, spellbinders, warlocks, and finger-flingers for God, Queen, Country, and the White Man's Burden?

Was he jinxed by juju creeping from his trophy collection?

By now, the noonday sun had cleared the peaks of mist. From here, where the Rocky Mountains stood sentinel over the plains, he gazed across an expanse so vast that every hill, lake, and woodland in Alberta, Saskatchewan, and Manitoba appeared flat to the eye.

Aye, this was a grand territory to add to the British Empire, the rulers of which had gathered in London this past June of 1897 for Queen Victoria's Diamond Jubilee. Thanks to Blake and imperialists like him, it truly could be stated, "The sun never sets on the British Empire."

But now it was evident that Blake had done his bit. In stalking Iron-child across the plains to the Rocky Mountains, he had silenced the last war cry of all the Indian nations: the rampage of murder by the Mountie killer Almighty Voice, known as Shu-kwe-wee-tam to his people.

Blake was almost sixty. Time for him to retire. To sit by the fire, his pipe in one hand and a dram of Scotch in the other, while Jennie, her blue eyes sparkling under a lace-bordered cap, waited on him hand and foot like a young housekeeper should.

Aye, she's a bonnie lass. The prettiest poke in Regina. The wee bairn'll be about one year old by now. Siring a son's a serious matter in any man's life. And having a father like me...

Yes, with all his conquests in the British colonial army and the North-West Mounted Police, Inspector Wilfred Blake had a legacy to pass on.

DOGFISH MORTUARY POLE

Vancouver, British Columbia, 1982
Thursday, October 28, 5:16 a.m.

Joanna Portman, the maternity ward nurse, wondered if she or the birth mother was more exhausted from delivering this baby.

At just after seven yesterday morning, Harry Walker had rushed his pregnant wife, Elizabeth, into St. Paul's Hospital on Burrard Street in downtown Vancouver. The mother-to-be's water had broken forty minutes earlier, and Harry was anxious, this being their first child.

"No drugs. No forceps. No trauma," the jittery man demanded, fumbling in his pocket for a cigarette and matches. "We want the birth natural. Who's your obstetrician? I don't want some doc fresh out of med school fooling around with my wife and kid."

The nurse told him not to smoke in the admitting hall.

"I don't trust hospitals. I want that clear from the start. Isn't this where they left a sponge in some poor bastard? Where they cut off a left leg instead of a right?"

Snapping the cigarette in two, he tossed it into a trash can. Then, absentmindedly, he shook another from the pack as he watched his wife waddle off to be admitted.

The complications had begun late that afternoon, not long after Joanna clocked in for the evening shift. Taking over as the nurse in charge of Mrs. Walker, she'd seen her through a pit drip to induce labor, an epi needle to her spine to cope with the pain of the baby's skull pinching her pelvis, Mr. Walker's meltdown on overhearing a nurse say this was the obstetrician's first delivery (but missing the part about how lucky the hospital was to have him after a stellar twenty years on the job in Britain), the episiotomy cut to enlarge her vagina, the forceps required to twist the baby in the birth canal as Mrs. Walker cursed her fucking husband for doing this to her, and—the cherry on the cake—Mr. Walker's freak-out when a plug pulled loose during the delivery and flatlined the monitor tracking the baby's heartbeat, causing him to sob and shriek, "You *killed* my kid, you butchers!"

Phew!

What a day!

Normally, Joanna's shift would have ended at midnight. But she became a neonatal nurse to help birthing mothers, and that meant refusing to abandon a woman in medical distress simply because the clock struck quitting time.

With the baby finally born, Joanna served Mrs. Walker a cup of tea. Her last sight of Mr. Walker, as she stood waiting for the elevator, was of him gazing into a glowing nursery window in a dark corridor, wiggling his pinkies at a squiggling incubator.

Now, almost as exhausted as if *she'd* given birth to the baby, Joanna stepped out of the hospital into the darkness that precedes dawn and flipped the collar of her coat up against the chill wind blowing down the high-rise canyon of Burrard Street. Founded by the Sisters of Providence in 1894, St. Paul's Hospital was a rambling red-brick building at the heart of the city. As always, Joanna turned and winked for luck at the statue of St. Paul in his heavenly nook under the Christian cross atop the roof.

"See you tomorrow," she said.

The 22 Macdonald bus stopped right in front of St. Paul's, so the nurse sat in the bus stop shelter, waiting for it to pull up. Joanna was a petite woman, twenty-three years of age. On shift, she wore her long black hair in a bun, but now she pulled the pins and let it tumble free. Wild strands whipped in the wind like those of the heroine in a classic romance novel, and she felt like shouting "Heathcliff!" into the surrounding night, to summon him off the Yorkshire moors.

But then the Macdonald bus arrived, so she climbed on board instead.

The route took her over the Burrard Street Bridge and along Kitsilano Beach on Point Grey Road. Peering out the window across the onyx bay, she tracked the lights of the North Shore halfway up the mountainside, where human inhabitants relinquished the upper reaches to undeveloped nature. Ten minutes later, she got off the bus where the beach road met Macdonald Street at Tatlow Park.

Dry leaves rasped along the deserted pavement while Joanna Portman stood alone at the corner. Those blown off the whispering trees flitted like bats. Chimney smoke from last night's embers dying on nearby hearths added bite to the autumn air. The shortest path to her upstairs suite in a renovated house three blocks west was through Tatlow Park, an urban oasis of small footbridges across a meandering stream. In summer, she would skirt one side of the tennis courts, then traverse the grass to Bayswater Street, where it was a quick walk up to Third. There, a flight of stairs would see her home.

Tonight, however, she knew that would be insane, what with the media screaming about a headhunter on the loose, so bone-tired Joanna took the long way round.

She was two blocks from her door when she heard the purr of an engine sneak up behind her. With it came apprehension, for not a single light burned in the old houses on the chestnut-lined street. The curb-crawling car stalked her along the dim sidewalk.

Easy, girl, she told herself. *Go on, take a look.*

Prepared to run like hell if need be, Joanna glanced back over her shoulder.

Then she sighed, relaxing, as the car pulled up beside her.

Friday, October 29, 1:53 a.m.

The chill of the day before was plunging to bitter cold. If Chris was going to strip the clothes off the sorority girl he'd met at last week's frat party, he'd have to keep the engine running and the heater going full blast. The windshield was already fogged from their passionate necking, and slushy snowflakes swirled around the pricey car in its secluded spot not far from the reconstructed totem village out front of UBC's Museum of Anthropology, high atop the sandstone cliffs tipping the tongue of Point Grey.

"It's two o'clock," Sue said, consulting her watch. "Time to call it a night."

That was about as far as you could get from what the horny frat boy had in mind, for tonight was the night he hoped to tap this sexy chick's ass.

"Toke?" he asked, sticking a fat joint between his lips. Striking a match, he filled the car with the sweet smell of Mary Jane, then offered the pot to Sue.

"Jeez, Chris! Come on! I've got an early class."

"Hey, I do too."

"And you also have a rich family. My mom tends bar in Quesnel so I can study at UBC. It'll break her heart if I flunk out from party hardy with you."

"It's *gooood* shit, Sue. Don't know what you're missing." He groaned from straining to speak while holding the smoke in his lungs.

"Yes, I do. You want me to wake up naked and find you wearing my underpants, my belly a canvas of Lascaux cave paintings done in lipstick."

"Now you're talking!" Chris enthused, and—*Cherchez la femme, old boy!*—he ran his hand up her silky thigh beneath the short skirt and flicked his middle finger—

Whap!

She actually slapped him.

Fuuuuck, didn't that go out with 1940s movies?

"Screw you!" Sue snapped. "I'll find my own way back to the dorm."

With that, she opened the passenger door and stepped out into the night, stomping off into the snowfall that was whitening the bluff.

"Women," Chris muttered, and sucked in another toke.

With the high of the potent bud came a headful of visions. Sue, blinded by the snow, tumbling off the cliff. Did she fall or was she pushed? Him in the hot seat and having to tell the Mounties, "I went for her pussy, so she dashed off and fell to her death." Or what if the Headhunter got her? The psycho all over the news? That would make him the doofus who set her up as prey for the killer. Would his frat brothers blackball him as a coward? And if Sue made it to the dorm, would she tell every sorority girl that he was a piggy date rapist? Think of all the tail that would cost him in the future!

Shoving open the door, Chris wobbled out. He flicked the joint from his fingers, spewing orange sparks from its red tip. Slipping and sliding on the slush, he jogged toward the totem village in front of the museum, the shortest route to UBC's Totem Park dorms, where Sue was a resident in Kwakiutl House. Ordinarily, he'd have been able to see the sixty-foot-high glass walls of the university's world-renowned showcase for West Coast Indian art, but tonight it was lost in the whiteout.

Chris almost pissed himself when Sue let out a bloodcurdling scream. His mind's eye envisioned her plummeting to the rocks of Wreck Beach below.

But then—

"Uh!"

—he ran into Sue and sent them both flying across the snow-covered gravel to crash down just this side of the Dogfish Mortuary Pole.

Backed by two squat cedar longhouses and five stand-alone totem poles, all of which were mostly obscured in the maelstrom of snowflakes, the mortuary pole consisted of two posts supporting a horizontal cross-piece. In shape, it reminded Chris of a giant croquet hoop. In West Coast Indian culture before the white man arrived, a burial box filled with the mortal remains of a chief or an honored elder would be slotted in behind the crosspiece, which was known as the frontal board. The board was carved and painted with a lineal totem crest—in this case a dogfish figurehead from Native myth. Dogfish are small bottom-feeding sharks, fierce, solitary, wandering creatures in Haida art. The dogfish carved on this mortuary pole had huge bug-eyes with elliptical pupils, parallel lines symbolizing gills in its cheeks, flaring red nostrils above a downturned mouth full of square teeth, and a big red tongue protruding from fat red lips that reminded Chris of the Rolling Stones' logo.

None of which had made Sue scream.

What *had* wrenched the scream from Sue was the butchered body of a headless woman who had been crucified to the frontal board of the mortuary pole by nails driven through both palms. She was posed in such a way that the dogfish crest was a mocking substitute for her missing face. Her torso was draped in a white nurse's uniform, its front ripped down to expose her flesh from the neck to the hair of her crotch. Chris gawked at the blood streaming down from her severed neck and the brutal slash across her bare breasts to drip from her legs, where it collected in a pool of gore creeping across the slush toward him.

NIGHT SHIFT

2:09 a.m.

The call came into the VPD in the wee hours of the morning. Had the dispatcher not been nursing a bad hangover from too many rums in the Police Athletic Club—a euphemism for the city cops' private bar—he might have caught the error. But he was, so he didn't.

"Police. State your emergency."

"A dead body, man!"

"Where?"

"Hanging from a totem pole. It's got no head!"

"The totems in the park?"

"That's what I said. There's blood all over the place. It's weird, man. *Weird!*"

"What's your name?"

"Chris."

"Stay on the phone, Chris, while I send help."

With headphones clamped to his ears and a headset mike in front of his lips, the hungover dispatcher flipped a toggle switch to send his voice out to the night-shift patrols prowling the city in radio cars.

"Code 4. A possible 212 in Stanley Park."

"Copy that," a patrol replied. "Where in the park?"

"The Brockton Point totem poles."

A moment before the dispatcher patched himself through to Homicide, he heard the wailing siren of the patrol car kick in, and he envisioned the red-and-blue lights on top streaking toward the urban forest that choked the throat of the harbor like a chunk of meat requiring the Heimlich maneuver.

"Major Crime. Detective Flood."

"It's Jenkins in Dispatch. Call just in of a DB at the totems in Stanley Park. Response is on the way. The caller says the body's headless and hanging from a totem pole."

Working at his cluttered desk in Homicide, Flood glanced at yesterday's headline on *The Vancouver Sun*: HEADHUNTER STRIKES AGAIN! The newspaper and the two Polaroid photos left for its editor lay on top of the Helen Grabowski file, which had been handed off to Major Crime by Detective Bernie Zebroff in the drug squad.

"Prob'ly a hoax," the dispatcher said. "It's almost Halloween."

"Yeah, the witching hour, when cranks and ghouls come out. See if the caller's still on the line. A crank'll have hung up by now."

"Right," said Jenkins.

"And let me know ASAP what the street guys find."

Meanwhile, with wipers slicking slush from the windshield and red-blue-red-blue wigwags flashing in the dark, the squealing police car circled around the park. With the forest on their left and the harbor on their right, the cops fishtailed past the rowing and yacht clubs, the monuments to Queen Victoria and the poet Robbie Burns. Just shy of the Nine O'Clock Gun, a naval cannon fired daily as a timekeeper since 1898, the car veered off the waterfront drive and slid to a halt in the parking lot between the rugby lawns and the totems at Brockton Point.

The blue riding shotgun was the first cop out of the car. His hand on his .38 in case the Headhunter burst out of the snow to whack him with a machete, he ran toward the Stanley Park totem poles, which, as BC's most visited attraction, have drawn tourists by the millions since the 1920s. With spread-winged thunderbirds on top and mythic crests stacked down their spines, the first poles were brought from the Kwakiutl village at Alert Bay, where they were featured in the 1914 silent film *In the Land of the Headhunters*.

The cops searched every totem.

They failed to find any trace of a headless body.

Detective Al Flood was no fan of Halloween. Sure, it had been his favorite holiday when he was a kid. What boy didn't want to be a vampire, werewolf, mummy, zombie, or Frankenstein's monster? As a baby boomer, he was around for the birth of rock 'n' roll and heavy metal, and he grew up on shock rock by Alice Cooper and Black Sabbath. But then he became a homicide cop, and Halloween turned deadly.

Flood was a broad-shouldered cop with an unruly thatch of strawberry-blond hair, a clean-shaven face against the VPD trend toward mustaches, and blue-gray eyes that didn't miss a thing. Last year, he'd been left alone in the Major Crime bullpen when the other detectives went out to answer Halloween crimes, the worst of which was a robbery committed by a street gang in trick-or-treat costumes. As the last man standing, Flood took the one call that mattered that night.

"Major Crime. Detective Flood."

"My son's dead!" a father in hysterics choked out at the end of the line. "Someone in the neighborhood handed out poisoned candy."

It turned out the poisoner was the dad himself. Deep in debt, he hatched a plan to cash in on his kid's life insurance, falling back on every parent's fear of tampered Halloween treats. Having laced some bubble gum with cyanide, he slipped a wad into his son's bag of goodies and watched him convulse to death before calling the cops.

Two years before that, Flood had caught another Halloween squeal. A homeowner had opened his door to what he thought were kids in costume. Instead, a grown-up disguised as the Joker shot him through the head with a handgun concealed in a paper bag. Flood nabbed the shooter, who was a lesbian with a crush on the vic's wife. The plan was to get rid of hubby but keep his estate, allowing the lovers to travel the world in style for the rest of their lives, without the inconvenient baggage of having to work.

All of which is to say that at this stage in his police career, Flood saw Halloween as the Devil's Night, not a lark of harmless pranks like egging houses and TP-ing trees.

He was, however, still a fan of Alice and Sabbath.

Ring-ring.

"Major Crime. Detective Flood."

"Jenkins again. The totem's a hoax. Street patrol found nothing in Stanley Park."

"Did the caller hang up?"

"No. He's still on the line. I told him to wait until responders secured the scene."

"What's his name?"

"Chris."

"Okay, put me through."

Flood sat surrounded by unmanned desks and silenced typewriters, drumming his fingers on the Grabowski file and watching the clock throw seconds into the room. One of the fluorescent tubes was on the fritz, casting a wonky flicker over the graveyard shift.

"Chris?"

"Yeah."

"Detective Flood. What's with the hoax?"

"Huh?"

"We didn't find a body."

"That's impossible! It's hanging headless from a totem pole for all to see. While we're yakking, the killer's getting away. You don't believe me? Talk to Sue."

"Hello?" A quaking female voice came on the line.

"Sue?"

"Yes."

"Detective Flood. Did you see a crucified body?"

"Yes."

"Where?"

"In front of the museum."

"What museum?"

"The one at UBC. The Museum of Anthropology, near the Totem Park dorms."

Uh-oh, Flood thought. *Jenkins fucked up.*

The *same* mistake that let Clifford Olson kill again and again and again. The body was actually hanging in the Horsemen's realm. But for some reason, the dispatcher had erroneously code 4'd a VPD prowl car to the totem poles at Stanley Park's Brockton Point, instead of out to the campus totems at the tip of Point Grey.

"Sue?"

"Yes."

"Hang on while I call the Mounties."

2:31 a.m.

Constable Rick Scarlett had joined the Mounted Police for action, action, action, and to kick some serious butt. Though Scarlett saw himself as an alpha male, he was, in fact, an insecure bully. Back when he was the leading track star in his high school, the accolades that came with athletic trophies weren't enough, so he bolstered his craving to be top dog by picking on those he perceived as weaker than him. Becoming a Mountie was the next step in his quest for power—for not only did the bison-head badge give him the means to advance his bullying, but the red tunic also scored him a lot of ass off chicks who fall for knights in scarlet armor.

Rick Scarlett.

What better name for a Mountie?

Because his social life revolved around a co-ed gym, Rick was in even better shape than he had been in high school. His dark hair got cut by a *stylist*—no barbershop for him—and his suave mustache made him look like one of those flyboys in Spitfires who'd won the Battle of Britain. Now in his mid-twenties and just over six feet tall, the Mountie worked out five times a week on the gym machines, focusing more on the hard-bodied babes in tight-fitting skimpies around him than on his own body image. But later, after bouncing back and forth between the steam room and the pool, Scarlett would pose in front of a mirror for personal inspection, and if there was any hint of a blemish on his buff physique, he'd work out a regimen to weight-lift it away.

Too bad his bloated self-esteem was blighted by this posting, for in the coast-to-coast-to-coast realm of the RCMP, there was no dinkier a detachment than this one at UBC. For a cop who yearned for action with his fists and his gun, there was no pleasure to be had in busting petty thieves at the university bookstore. The bully in him, however, had found satisfaction in cruising past rowdy parties on Frat Row. Scarlett, boasting only a high school diploma, resented the cocky fraternity studs and their holier-than-thou swagger. At this moment, one of the animal houses was hosting a toga party, and the bully in Rick was itching to pull over some piss-tanks and watch 'em squirm in their seats as he demanded their IDs. To that end, he was almost out the door of UBC Detachment when the phone rang.

"Constable Scarlett."

"My name's Flood. Detective. VPD Homicide. You've got a code 4—a headless body—at the totem poles out front of the MOA."

Scarlett was out the door in a sprint befitting his track-star days. It took him no more than a few minutes to speed along Wesbrook Mall to Chancellor Boulevard and skid to a halt at the campus-side doors to the museum. Sweeping his torch over the slush ahead to make sure he didn't tread on any footprints the killer may have left, the constable skirted one side of the building to reach the totems bordering the cliff. Snow swirled around him as he stared up in awe at the surreal corpse hanging from the Dogfish Mortuary Pole. No matter how many more years he served in the Mounted Police, Scarlett knew he'd never have a case as big as this.

Play his cards right and this murder could be his ticket up the ranks.

Who should he call?

2:48 a.m.

Sergeant Jack MacDougall felt like an underworld criminal. It had been fifteen years since Pierre Elliott Trudeau, in appealing to parliamentarians to decriminalize homosexuality, famously declared, "There's no place for the state in the bedrooms of the nation." While it was true that being gay was no longer a criminal offence, Mounties could still be fired for it. Should the day come that MacDougall was outed as a homosexual cop, the Horsemen would tear the red serge tunic off his back before tossing him into the dung heap.

The closeted sergeant had even chosen a home with a private back entrance so his lover could sneak in and out unseen. Jack and Peter had spent this evening taste-testing the chef's new cookbook, the last chance to tweak its recipes before publication. Now, as Peter snored softly on the pillow beside him, the Mountie was wrenched from his sleep by the phone on his bedside table.

"MacDougall," he answered gruffly.

"Sarge, it's Constable Rick Scarlett. UBC Detachment."

"You'd better have a much stronger reason than *that* for waking me up."

"I'm standing in front of a totem pole at UBC. A headless woman is nailed to it. The tongue of the totem is sticking out at me. Her clothes are torn and there's a slash across her breasts. The killer staged the scene for dramatic effect. I found a jug with traces of blood at the foot of the pole. Looks like the blood was poured over the corpse."

Ottawa, Ontario
6:30 a.m.

Commissioner François Chartrand had no neck. That's partly why the ranks called him the Bullet. The top cop's head was round at the crown and flat at the bottom, and it sat squarely on his shoulders like a slug in its casing. Back when they were new to driving, Chartrand and three teenage buddies had taken a spin in one brother's convertible. The car was struck from behind by a drunk driver, whiplashing the joyriders so hard that three required neck braces. But because Chartrand had no neck, he suffered no injury. On the second day of his first posting as a Mountie in rural Nova Scotia, Chartrand responded to a domestic dispute. Before the cop was out of his car, the husband—drunk, berserk, and waving a gun—burst from the farmhouse and opened fire. The ensuing shootout saw the Horseman go down with lead in his leg, while his return shot drilled the Wild East gunslinger through the heart. The Bullet took a bullet and the legend was set.

Chartrand was filtering his morning coffee when the call from the West Coast interrupted him. The ramifications of finding a *third* headless body were so great that news of the killing rapidly made its way through the chain of command and across three time zones to the commissioner's home near RCMP HQ in the nation's capital. There, the Bullet listened intently to what the deputy commissioner of "E" Division in Vancouver had to say, then he carried a cup of coffee and his cigarette case to his sealed balcony to mull over the Headhunter's latest taunt.

The commissioner's apartment overlooked the Supreme Court of Canada, the Parliament Buildings, and the Ottawa River. Plucking a Gauloises cigarette from the engraved case, Chartrand lit the smoke and puffed it as he sipped his black java. Through the double-glazing that shielded him from Ottawa's harsh climate, he watched the pale light of dawn overtake the city as a flock of Canada geese in V-formation crossed the hunter's moon.

"François," the West Coast CO had warned, "we're going to have a media feeding frenzy on our hands. A jurisdiction cock-up bought the Headhunter time to escape. If we don't take control and muster a high-profile manhunt, the public will revolt."

"Leave it with me. I'll get back to you."

"Soon, I hope. Or they'll do *more* than burn us in effigy."

Stubbing his cigarette in a windowsill ashtray, the commissioner opened the silver case to fetch another one, and as he tamped its tip on the metal to pack the loose tobacco, the engraving on the box transported him back to the tense days of the October Crisis.

Commissioner François Chartrand was a meat-and-potatoes cop. Tourtière, pea soup, and poutine were his style, and hockey and Gauloises his passions. So when he was teamed up with Robert DeClercq, the RCMP homicide hotshot, to manhunt the Front de libération du Québec terrorists who had kidnapped the British trade commissioner, James Cross, and killed Pierre Laporte, Quebec's minister of immigration and labour, they were mismatched partners. To Chartrand, Robert DeClercq was an exotic beast. Not only did the homicide honcho shuck Canada's national game for crossbow shooting and fencing duels, but like frontier Mounties in the Wild Northwest, he fused military tactics with police and forensic techniques to take down modern monsters.

Squeezing his underworld snitches—the Horsemen's scouts and turncoats of old—DeClercq located the Chenier and Libération cells, freeing the ambassador from his abductors and nabbing the minister's killers. But two weeks later, for revenge, a gang of thugs invaded the Mountie's home, ripped his wife apart with a machine pistol, and fled with his young daughter, Jane.

The powers that be sidelined DeClercq from that manhunt, so he launched a rogue one-man dragnet. Using the same informers who'd smoked out the FLQ, he pinpointed where the punks were holding Jane, and moved in with his crossbow and gun to get her back.

The action was over by the time François Chartrand arrived at the scene. The Laurentian backwoods cabin sat in a sea of fallen maple leaves, the ground around it a fiery hell of reds, oranges, and yellows. DeClercq had picked off one of the thugs with a crossbow bolt to the eye as he exited the cabin for firewood. The second went down from a bolt to the throat when he came out to look for the first man. Having dispatched those two in a stealthful manner, the Mountie kicked in the door with his revolver blazing, shooting the third in the hideout before strangling the last kidnapper with his bare hands.

But he had burst in too late.

Shortly before DeClercq arrived, the punks had argued over what to do with their captive. Two wanted to let her go—drop her off in the woods and see if she could find her own way back to civilization—but the more reckless of the four wanted to eliminate the witness. The hotheads won out...and broke the girl's neck. When Chartrand arrived, he found DeClercq slumped on the floor, weeping with his broken daughter cradled in his arms.

"*Mon ami*," soothed the Bullet, easing the limp girl out of his partner's sorrow. "Let me help carry your burden."

There was an internal investigation into DeClercq's rampage. By tradition, he couldn't have a lawyer speak for him, just another Mountie. Chartrand maneuvered to make sure *he* marshaled the defense, and since those sitting in judgment had never taken a slug for the job, they listened intently to what the Bullet put forth. DeClercq had been sidelined. He hadn't been ordered. By law, he had a right to protect his family. Self-preservation kicked in when he saw the odds were four to one. The police had found a machine gun—the same one used to kill DeClercq's wife—in the cabin. And the Mountie had public sympathy on his side.

"Let's be *rational*," Chartrand said, before he sat back down.

DeClercq wasn't punished, and he never stood trial in a courtroom. But that didn't matter. He was wracked with guilt and decided to retire. "Westering" is what it's called when the broken-hearted head west until the Pacific Ocean brings them to a halt. After DeClercq abandoned Quebec for the West Coast, he and the Bullet lost contact. But when it was later announced that Chartrand would be the next commissioner of the Mounted Police, Robert had sent him the cigarette case he now held in his hand—a case so slim that it carried no more than five smokes. François grasped the hidden meaning in DeClercq's note: *Congratulations. Gauloises are an addiction. Don't let the stress of the job push you up to several packs a day. Make it five cigarettes from dawn till dusk.*

Some days he failed, but most days he made it.

This morning, as he tamped a second smoke on the metal too close to dawn, the Bullet's eyes took in the words etched into the silver: *Maintiens le Droit.* Translation: "Uphold the Law." The duty every Mountie swears on donning the scarlet tunic.

In a moment of epiphany, Chartrand knew what to do. Out on the West Coast preyed a serial psycho with the potential to become the Mounted's undoing. When you command an organization with a larger-than-life myth to live up to, you use your best manhunter.

Even if you no longer have him.

Vancouver, British Columbia
8:17 a.m.

Genevieve was dying.

The night shift for the RCMP and VPD was over by the time Robert DeClercq returned home from his early morning fencing session with the old Hungarian master. In the car, he'd caught the news about the headless woman nailed to a totem pole, and he'd listened to the commentators speculate that divided police jurisdictions had cocked things up yet again.

While his wife was in their bedroom getting dressed for work, he poured himself a cup of coffee from the pot on the stove and carried it to the Greenhouse. As he made his way to the glass walls to gaze across the sea to the Museum of Anthropology on the cliffs of Point Grey, he glanced at the hybridized rosebush just inside the hothouse door and was jarred to find it wilting from blight or disease.

Examining one of the rosebuds, he found two minuscule white dots where it joined the stalk.

That's the problem with exotic plants, he thought.

Exotic diseases.

The phone inside the house was ringing. It stopped when Genny answered the bedroom extension. After a moment, she called, *"Robert, on tu demande au téléphone."*

Exiting the Greenhouse, he crossed the pegged wood floor past the cold hearth to the entrance hall, where he picked up the main phone.

"DeClercq," he said.

"Hello, Robert. It's François Chartrand."

"François! I'll be damned. What can I do for you?"

"Maintiens le droit," said the commissioner of the Mounted Police.

HONKY TONK

"Honky Tonk Women" by the Rolling Stones rocked from the jukebox in the Moonlight Arms. The honky tonk women in this pub were of the skid row kind: reduced by life and drugs to selling their bodies for the price of a cap of junk, or drinking away another day on their welfare checks. Today, like every day over the past week, the bedraggled Amazon sat slumped against the wall on the far side of the bar. Her greasy hair, sloppy makeup, and unkempt clothes didn't deter the barflies from hitting on her, but the glare they got back snarled, "Buzz off!" Through furtive, strung-out eyes, she watched the slinking down-and-outs come and go. One she dubbed "Miss Havisham," after the jilted spinster from the Dickens novel. Like that character, the befuddled woman with the daze of a simpleton still wore her wedding dress—now soiled grubby gray—and slowly twirled around the bar as if dancing with her beau. She was just one of many walking wounded left to wander skid row when the government emptied Riverside to decrease the cost of keeping mental patients. The most pathetic of these honky tonk women was a crippled Native hooker known as the Skirt Lifter. Her come-on was to hike her dress up to her rolls of belly flab and flash her bare pussy at every john cruising the stroll outside. When she was unable to shuck the monkey from her back on the street, she weaved among the tables in here and flashed for every barfly.

Showtime! thought the Amazon when a shiver rippled through the fix-hungry crowd and all eyes locked expectantly on the street door.

Bax is back with smack.

Unbeknown to the blonde and the hypes around her, Bax was holding *heavy*. This afternoon, the man had fronted him two bundles of H. "Sell it fast," the pusher said. "Harness bulls get a whiff o' this, they'll kick in the door ablastin'. Shit this good'll have buyers on their knees beggin'."

"Why the front? That ain't the usual you."

"I trust you, man," the pusher said. "Stiff me and you die. Where'd this motherfucker be without a little trust? But sell it fast. I need the green."

The way the Indian figured it, he'd push forty-five caps to hypes in the Downtown Eastside bars. That would leave him five caps to crank a borderline fix. Mix it with bouncing powder, and the speedball would skyrocket him to the heights that separate life from death.

His radar was fixed on Blondie as he bebopped across the bar to Status Quo's "Bye Bye Johnny." She was a *big* girl, with a rack to die for. A cap wouldn't hold her long, so odds were she'd want to stash up with heroin this good. And with a bod like hers, money'd be no problem. She could earn a bundle in minutes turning tricks out back in the alley.

"My man," she whispered as Bax sidled up. He sat down facing the door in case the Horsemen rode in on a drug sweep.

"Bad news, Blondie. Got nothin' for you."

Behind caked makeup and sleepless eyes, her face twitched like dead matter coming to life.

"Oops! My mistake. Got some after all."

It was the old pusher's joke. Cooking up the market. Feeding off the interplay of hope and fear on strung-out faces. The power to give or withhold. He opened his mouth so she could peek through his rotten teeth and see the balloon near the back of his throat, to swallow in the event of a bust.

"Price?" she asked.

"Depends," he said. "How many caps you want? It's *d-e-e-luxe* goods this time, Blondie. Seventy-five a hit. Discount if you buy in bulk."

The blonde was about to negotiate when the Indian held up his hand to stop her. His eyes were fixed on the huge black man entering the bar. The giant wore a blue denim shirt strained by his muscular chest and shoulders. Bright red suspenders held up his loose-hanging jeans. His glowering face was crisscrossed with livid scars from a knife fight. A red toque hid his hairline. Gold chains glinted in the V beneath his jaw, and a gold stud pierced one ear. Flaunting jewelry was asking for it in this crime-ridden part of town, but only the brain-dead would try mugging this Hulk.

"Chill a mo, Blondie. Back in a jiff."

Bax nodded toward the rear of the pub and the heavyweight retreated out the front door. Skulking away, the Indian vanished amid the toilets out back, tailed by the Amazon. As he slipped out the door to the alley, she veered into the women's can. The filthy latrine was a toxic dump of human waste; puddles of piss and puke and a dirty Kotex littered the floor.

The window above one of the stalls was cracked to let out the stink. The seat was missing from the toilet, so the Amazon had to balance on the rounded rim of the bowl. Through the opening, she peered down into the trash-filled alley and saw Bax exchange something with the black man.

Before returning to the pub to haggle with the pusher, Constable Katherine Spann entered the U/M's description in her undercover notebook.

5:40 p.m.

The railway hut used by the RCMP for this ongoing drug operation sat on the waterfront side of the tracks, beside the western terminal of the coast-to-coast Canadian Pacific Railway. The freak snowstorm of the night before had all but melted away, so Spann sidestepped the slippery patches and stuck to the shadows to avoid blowing her cover. To the squeal of wheels on rails and the smash of boxcars being shunted, she ducked into the hut to meet her control.

"I'm on to something," Spann said, locking the door. "A rung up the ladder."

"Yeah?" replied her boss with venom in his voice. The corporal had little piggy eyes and a beer belly so porky it drooped over his belt.

"Before I scored two caps off him, fifty-six hooked up with an unknown male out back of the Moonlight Arms. A *big* black guy. They swapped something."

"His source?" asked Piggy.

"That's my bet."

The animosity coming off her boss was palpable. For a hundred and one years, from 1873 to 1974, the Mounted Police had been a fraternal domain, a hard-riding cavalry regiment born from the British colonial army.

Only eight years had passed since women first breached the ranks, and their presence wasn't welcome in the old boys' club. Spann realized from the get-go that she was adrift in a sea of frat boys plotting panty raids. Fresh out of training at Depot Division in Regina, she was posted to a small Saskatchewan detachment. As usual, her regimental trunk was sent ahead. On reaching the boonies to take up her post, Spann found her trunk sitting in the middle of the squad room with a pair of plastic breasts strapped to the lid. The lock had been broken so the men could drape the breasts with her bra, and the puckered nipples were inked in red with her regimental number.

Every woman she knew in the ranks was exposed to sexual harassment. Without a union and subject to a strict command structure, the Mounties were a law unto themselves. Women who wanted in had to cut the mustard. No mollycoddling for those in red serge. To adapt the words of President Truman, "If you can't stand the heat, *stay* in the kitchen." Second-wave feminism was rapidly taking hold out there in the real world, but within the Mounted Police, time virtually stood still.

Even now.

1982!

For years, Katherine Spann had put up with cops like Piggy. Every time she entered the railway hut to hand in buys and report on her progress, his eyes homed in on her tits before they did her face. Had he heard the yuk-yuk about her trunk? It certainly seemed as if he was trying to read her regimental number off her breasts. Spann could feel him stripping her as she went about her work: dropping the gelatin capsules of H into an evidence pouch; sealing the pouch with her reg number, the date, and "56 C"; and transferring the contents of her undercover notes to her large black court book.

Back in the drug squad office at RCMP HQ, Bax had become number fifty-six on the target board the first time Spann bought off him. The "C" on the current evidence pouch meant this was her third score off him. Once Bax had become a target of the drug sweep operation, his photo got snapped with a telephoto lens, and now his mug was also stuck up on the board. When the time came for the Horsemen to bust their targets for jail, Bax's photo would be on the arrest sheets issued to the bulls.

"Write the U/M up in detail," Piggy ordered Spann.

"He won't be hard to spot. The unknown male's a black giant with knife scars on his face. With luck, I'll have him up on the target board soon."

"No such luck," Piggy replied contemptuously. "You've been pulled."

"Pulled?" The undercover frowned. "What gives?"

"The Headhunter, Spann. Chartrand's put together a special squad. Word is, Robert DeClercq's coming back to head it. And guess who's his golden girl?"

So that's it, thought Spann. *The source of Piggy's venom. Bad enough that women had breached the barricades, but now they were climbing the ranks at his expense. He thinks Chartrand and DeClercq are kowtowing to PR wonks and leapfrogging me over him because I've got a vagina.*

"Report to HQ. The Heather Stables. Ten a.m. tomorrow."

Spann took in the loathful look Piggy shot her.

If looks could kill, she thought.

MARDI GRAS

New Orleans, Louisiana, 1957

Jazz echoed up on the hot night air from the muggy streets below. A musical mix of ragtime, bop, boogie-woogie, and swing, it soared above the drunken French Quarter revelers, a mishmash of rich and poor, black and white, priest and libertine crowding the curbs eight deep to watch the krewe floats and masquers parade by. The smell of the Mississippi River and the salty Gulf of Mexico mingled with strains of "When the saints..." and scaled the facades of the houses, where women flashed their breasts and called out, "Throw me something, mister!" Krewes on the passing floats tossed doubloons, strings of beads, and Zulu coconuts painted with blackface to hands outstretched for "throws." Coins from the pockets of unsteady gawkers guzzling potent pink cocktails from hurricane glasses were tossed as thanks to flambeau carriers whose wild gyrations and flourishes led the carnival procession down the timeworn streets. The brassy jazz rose up from the flamboyant throng of bizarre masks and disguises—"He-Shebas" vamping as butterflies and snails, King Kong and the Queen of Hearts and fig-leafed Adam and Eve, the Big Shot of Africa and a cowboy garbed in white leather except for his bare behind—up from the purple, green, and gold banners and streamers, until the music slid softly through the wrought-iron balcony where the black girl stood watching.

"Want a snort?" a husky voice asked from within a set of open French doors.

"Yes," said Crystal, turning.

"Here. Ice your brain."

The black girl padded naked into the top-floor room of the eighteenth-century mansion to join the white woman, who was chopping coke with a razor blade on a glass-topped table. In here, the jazz of Mardi Gras gave way to the strains of Elvis begging Crystal not to be cruel. The fireworks in the black sky outside seemed to explode in the stoned girl's head, for the aftershocks of too much cocaine and too many female-on-female orgasms still had her tingling.

Suzannah gave the seduced girl a rolled-up hundred-dollar bill. "Sniff as much as you want," she said. "There's lots more where this came from."

The girl bent over the table and used the nose tube to suck up the blow. She moaned when the dominatrix cupped her breast and slipped a finger inside her. As sweat trickled down Crystal's back from the heat of the night, Suzannah lapped it up with her hungry tongue.

"Ebony and ivory—that's you and me, honey."

Suzannah was a femme fatale who dripped sex appeal. She'd shaved her head to accommodate the many wigs needed to fulfill the sexual fantasies of the men who paid top dollar to gain entry to this horrific, blood-soaked house of discipline. Her breasts had the ripeness of forbidden fruit, and when she leaned over the table to fill her head with snow, Crystal's eyes swept down her spine to the six gold rings piercing her labia and glittering in the black hair of her crotch.

Snort.

She sucked the dust up one nostril.

Snort.

Another line took the parallel route.

Wetting a finger, the cokehead wiped the residue from the glass table and rubbed it around her gums.

Then, as if a sixth sense told Suzannah that Crystal was ogling her snatch, she craned her neck to slip her young, caught-out prey a lascivious wink.

"Pussy's addicting, hon."

The rush of the coke had Crystal's heart flapping in her chest like a caged bird trying to break free. Masked by the color of her skin, her flushed cheeks felt frozen and she had no sensation in her teeth. She had the jitters so bad that she *had* to circle the room, and as she moved around the carved rosewood furniture by the cabinetmaker Prudent Mallard, paranoia creeped her out into thinking the myriad empty eyes on the walls were stalking her.

A Bobo-Wule tribal mask. A Senufo firespitter. An Ashanti fertility head. An Egyptian mummy's mask. A Roman mask of Pan. A Japanese *gigaku* mask. A Chinese *t'ao t'ieh* face. An Incan death mask. A Salish spirit mask. An Iroquois False Face. A Hopi Kachina doll. A hussar *Totenkopf* busby. A *Oedipus* mask from Stratford. A New York Yankees catcher's guard. A First World War gas mask. A hood of the Ku Klux Klan...

In Crystal's manic, dizzy mind, the threatening eyes lusted after her naked body with the same incestuous intent as her father had every night in the chemical-smelling room above his dry-cleaning shop. There, the motherless girl was forced to her knees in front of his smelly cock, or bent over the table while he humped and grunted like a randy hog from the bayou. But yesterday, a stylish woman had come in to pick up her cleaning, and while Crystal's dad was looking through the plastic bags on the runner, Suzannah had whispered in her ear, "I had a father like him. Meet me out back in ten minutes and I'll save you from this shit."

Now here she was, in a Lafon house furnished with expensive antiques, being fed fine food and cocaine by a sexy savior teaching her the uselessness of men.

"*Hot* love, honey," Suzannah had purred last night while peeling off her scarlet corset for the coked-up girl. "Strip for me and I'll make you come until you melt."

Which she had done, and was doing.

Circling the room brought Crystal back to the open French doors. A black silhouette in a candelabra-lit doorframe, she peered out into the darkness. At the far end of the cul-de-sac, where it met Royal Street, Comus trundled past on a glitzy float depicting a giant green frog spewing Mississippi water from its yawning mouth. To chords of "Jambalaya" from distant Bourbon Street, Suzannah slinked up behind her Mardi Gras plaything and reached around to palm her melon breasts, weighing them as if for juiciness to sell in a sultry night market.

"Do we have to miss the party?" Crystal pouted.

"Of course not, precious. It'll go on all night. But first we must earn money at a party of our own so I can afford to fly you to Paris tomorrow."

"What sort of party?"

"A *secret* masquerade ball."

"Can I wear a costume with a mask like the ones on the walls?"

"That's why I took you shopping for the white undies that look so *yummy* against your chocolate skin. To fashion a *new you* from that lingerie all the way out to your Mardi Gras mask."

"What's my costume?"

"Have you read *The Prisoner of Zenda*?"

"No."

"The Man in the Iron Mask?"

"No."

"How'd you like to be Zenda, a beautiful woman who escapes from a cell in the Bastille prison to become the most famous courtesan in eighteenth-century France?"

"Yes, please!" said Crystal.

"Then, sweetheart, that's who you'll be."

"Why are you so kind to me?"

"Because we're *sisters*, baby. Chocolate and vanilla made to suffer by evil men. No one came to help me, but I can help you. And that gives me revenge against my abusers."

"Against your father?"

"Yes, and my husband. Mine was a double whammy of sexual assault."

"In New Orleans?"

Suzannah shook her head. "In Canada."

"That's a long way from here."

"Closer than you think, hon. Were you not taught in history class how the British army conquered the French colony of Acadia in the 1700s? During the French and Indian War, the bloody British deported the Acadians south from Atlantic Canada to the French colony of Louisiana, where they settled here in New Orleans. That's how the Cajuns of today came to be."

"'Cajuns' means 'Acadians'?"

"Aren't you smart?" Suzannah cooed, hefting Crystal's breasts and flicking her nipples with both thumbs.

"Are you Cajun?"

"No. My ancestors stayed in Canada to spy for France. But I inherited this house from the Cajun branch of my Acadian family."

"Did your Cajun relatives keep slaves?"

"Heavens no, cream puff! No doubt you've heard of Marie Laveau, the notorious Voodoo Queen of New Orleans? Some of my Cajun ancestors performed rituals in this very house with leading voodoo queens from the black community. Could be *your* ancestors conjured here."

"Where'd your dad assault you?"

"In Montreal."

"And your husband?"

"Far to the north, in Arctic Canada. He was a Mounted Policeman posted to a snowbound one-man detachment in what's called the Northwest Territories. Igloos and Inuit—that's Eskimos to you. He used to whip a dogsled across the snow on Arctic patrols."

"Like *Sergeant Preston of the Yukon* on TV?"

"Exactly," said Suzannah, chuckling throatily as she recalled dumping his emasculated corpse through a hole in the ice on a frozen tundra lake. That was the last time he ever used the dog whip on her, then chased her naked through the snow to fuck her with the whip handle when he caught her.

"Why'd you marry him?"

"To make up for my crap dad. My husband was old enough to be my father, and he looked so dashing in his red serge uniform. I was young and stupid. Simple as that."

"Why'd he abuse you?"

"Because he was a weak man with a limp dick. His dad was the most famous Mountie in the Wild West. You know how they say, 'The Mounties always get their man'?" The girl nodded. "That's based on him. Inspector Wilfred Blake. He vanished on a manhunt in the Rocky Mountains late last century, leaving behind a bastard son he'd spawned with his housekeeper. With a towering father like that, my sniveling Mountie husband couldn't live up to the legend, so he took his inadequacies out on me. He beat me to get his cock hard, then forced me to perform demeaning sexual acts. When I asked why he was treating me so bad, he spat on me and said, 'Because I'm up here and you're down there.'"

"So you divorced him?"

"I divorced him all right. But not in the usual way."

From the wall behind them, a Gustav Becker clock chimed half past eleven.

"The witching hour approaches. Time to get dressed, Crystal. A special guest is coming to our masquerade tonight, and the festivities *must* start at twelve fifteen precisely."

"Why?"

"History, baby. *History*."

———

The Fat Man was singing "Mardi Gras in New Orleans" as they crossed the candlelit Mask Room and entered Suzannah's bedroom. It too was awash in candlelight, for Mardi Gras—Fat Tuesday—was a time to relive the past. The bedroom was a riot of red and black: walls of red satin, curtains of red velvet, red sheets on a bed rumpled by Crystal's orgasmic trashing, soft red cords used to bind her wrists to the headboard posts while Suzannah played her come zones like a piano—all set against a dresser, wardrobe, and mirrored makeup table of ebony and red onyx. The naked black girl fit in with the dual color scheme, but the ghostly woman was vampiric white.

She was the shade of a bloodsucker.

Like a wraith, Suzannah slinked to the table and rummaged in a shopping bag for the white bra and white panties they'd bought that afternoon.

"Here," she said, passing the scant wisps of lace to Crystal. "It's a crime to cover up luscious beauty like yours, but let's see how you look."

The accent was on "small" in the small clothes the girl put on. Her firm, flawless breasts bulged erotically from the flimsy push-up cups, and her pubic thatch peeped through the filigreed holes in the white V hugging her vulva. *Va-va-voom, Lolita!*

The Fats Domino double play began "Ain't That a Shame" as Suzannah crossed to the closet and pulled open its double doors. From the top shelf, she took down the largest hatbox Crystal had ever seen, then set it on the carpet. Balanced on the lid was a thick pack of crisp hundred-dollar bills. With a fluid underarm throw, she tossed the wad to Crystal.

"That's for you. Mad money. To spend lavishly in Europe."

The young eyes almost popped.

"Let's do London with Paris. Would you like that?" Suzannah asked. "Tour the Tower of London and check out the Crown Jewels. See Madame Tussauds Wax Museum—"

"And the Chamber of Horrors?"

"If you want."

"Yes, please!" enthused the girl. "We can pretend we've got our crap dads jailed down there so they can suffer like we did."

"Speaking of jails…"

Lifting the lid off the hatbox, Suzannah reached in and eased out a resplendent Zulu Krewe mask with rainbow feathers crowning an iron face grille.

"I give you Zenda, the mysterious Woman in the Iron Mask, recently freed from imprisonment in the Bastille during the French Revolution!"

"For *me*?"

"Who else? But before you try it on, help me with my costume. Rouge my nipples, honey, while I paint my Mardi Gras face."

Suzannah set the Zulu mask down on the lid of the box. She pulled the chair back from the table so Crystal could kneel between her and the mirror. While the girl reddened the tips of her tits with rouge from a small jar, the dominatrix used grease paint to blacken the lids of her eyes. After cleaning her hands with cold cream, she chalked the surrounding skin to a deathly pallor.

"Bloody my lips."

The novice stage dresser reddened the puckered Cupid's bow mouth with a shade of lipstick that matched the diva's crimson claws.

From a drawer in the makeup table, Suzannah withdrew a vial of cocaine and a tiny spoon, along with a pair of fishnet stockings and a scarlet garter belt. Turning the chair sideways, she hooked the belt around her narrow waist and raised a long, shapely leg to pull on one of the nylons and tether its top with snaps. Lifting her other leg, she sheathed it too. When she stood up, the garters ran down her thighs like blood.

"How do I look?" she asked the girl.

"Peachy," Crystal replied.

Little Richard tore into "Rip It Up" as Suzannah sashayed across the carpet, swinging her bottom. Retrieving a black leather corset from the wardrobe, she wriggled it over the top of the garter belt. The low-cut top flaunted her lush cleavage. Black leather straps ran up from her armpits to a silver-studded collar. Red lacing stitched the sides of the garment. Two circles cut in the bodice exposed her rouged nipples. The black shoulder-length gloves she fastened to the collar had cut-off fingertips that bared her red nails. Stepping into spike-heeled, knee-high, red-laced boots, Suzannah zipped them up her calves. Finally, she attached the rolled-up dog whip her husband had used to abuse her and then reached back in the closet for the weirdest wig in New Orleans.

The dominatrix reeked of fetishism.

The leather creaked and the stockings rasped as the woman returned to the table and sat down to put on the wig. The girl could see Suzannah's pulse throbbing as she gazed at the network of veins under the shaved scalp before it disappeared into a nest of serpents.

"Are those snakes *real*?" Crystal asked.

"They were before they were stuffed. A taxidermist made me this Medusa wig out of rattlers, cottonmouths, copperheads, and coral snakes. All the mouths are open to bare their fangs."

"Who does the costume make you?"

"Guess," Suzannah replied.

"Marie Laveau, the Voodoo Queen of New Orleans?"

"Aren't you the smarty-pants? That deserves a hit." Opening the vial and dipping the spoon into the white powder, she stuck it under Crystal's nose and let her suck it up. After scooping a second spoonful for the girl's other nostril, the seductress then froze her own brain.

Catlike on the balls of her stiletto-heeled feet, Suzannah retrieved the Zulu mask from the hatbox lid and eased it down around her groomed prey's skull so the open collar rested on her shoulders. Peering in at the face through the iron grille, she told the prisoner of Zenda to hold still while she secured the Mardi Gras mask in place. By closing the collar and slipping a padlock through two eyebolts, she had Crystal shackled like a slave.

"Feast your eyes, baby. Here comes the finishing touch."

Swiveling the chair so it faced the table, the Voodoo Queen plucked a leather thong from the drawer and angled the mirror at her sex. While the El Dorados doo-wopped into "At My Front Door," Suzannah spread her thighs wide and laced together the six gold rings piercing her labia as if she were doing up a shoe. Tying the black thong into a knot, she left the ends dangling from her crotch.

The clock in the Mask Room began striking midnight.

Bong...bong...bong...

THE STRATEGY WALL

Vancouver, British Columbia, 1982
Saturday, October 30, 5:30 a.m.

Surprisingly, DeClercq could still get into the uniform. Years of fencing at the break of day had kept his body firm. This morning, he donned the semi-formal garb of a Mountie superintendent: blue serge tunic with chest and hip pockets, a white shirt, a blue tie, blue "banana pants" with a yellow side stripe, and congress boots with spurs. The crowns and pips on his epaulets, the gleaming collar dogs, and the buttons on his chest stamped with the insignia of the Force—all shone gold. As Genevieve entered the bedroom, he positioned his forage cap—blue with a yellow band above a bar of perma-gold on the peak and the badge of the RCMP in the center. With a wink, his wife passed him a cup of coffee.

"How do I look?" he asked.

"You know what they say about women falling for a man in uniform?"

DeClercq puffed out his chest. "No, what do they say?"

Genevieve put an academic finger to her cheek and furrowed her brow as if in deep thought. "It's the knight-in-shining-armor syndrome," she said at last. "The fairy-tale mindset of the female psyche. A man in uniform exudes chivalry. He's a father figure, the embodiment of heroism, protection, and power. A whiff of menace, risk, excitement, and adventure wafts off a uniform. It makes the common man look dominant and authoritative. A strong gravitational pull."

"Never wed a psychologist," DeClercq groaned, rolling his eyes. "Is that the attraction for you? It turns me into a father figure?"

"No, it's baser than that. The outfit comes with *handcuffs*."

"You're an evil woman."

"Guilty," she replied with a sly smile.

He wasn't an insecure man, just a realist. With each passing year, the gap between them widened. When he reached eighty, she'd be sixty. Because he knew advancing life would one day end this nirvana, he'd resolved to relish every moment of her precious company. And though he loved all her dawn-to-dusk transmutations, the feral Genny of early morning was his favorite. Her wild auburn hair was rumpled from sleep. Last night's bedroom eyes were not yet tamed from greeting the sun. And her nightwear—even these flannel pajamas patterned with teddy bears— clung to her entrancing shape in a cuddle-me-all-you-want way.

"Excited?"

"That I am, my siren."

"I'm talking about your job. What's the Mountie term? Back in harness?"

"That's the lingo."

She turned to go. "And about women falling for a man in uniform"— Genny pointed to the scarlet tunic still hanging in the closet—"when do I get to see you in *that* one?"

"When I catch this monster."

———

Daylight saving time had almost spent itself broke (the clocks would fall back an hour on Halloween), so the cosmos above was black. With his back to the foggy harbor, DeClercq left his seaside home by the mountain- side door and trudged up the steep driveway to his car on Marine Drive, where he'd parked it to protect against sliding and crashing after yesterday's freak snowstorm. The nip of autumn harbingered the winter months to come, and before he could shake it off, the smell of smoke and the scratch- ing of dry leaves clawing the ground reminded him of that Laurentians cab- in where he'd failed to stop the vengeful hoods from snapping Jane's neck.

"*Out, damned spot!*" he thought, like guilt-ridden Lady Macbeth.

Traffic was light as hibernation closed in. DeClercq's 1966 Citroën DS 21 Pallas in Olympic gold—further proof that he marched to the beat of a different drummer—slipped through the spectral haze like a shark's fin. Crossing Lions Gate Bridge to Stanley Park, he parted the trees and the high-rise canyons beyond to glide over False Creek on the Cambie Street Bridge and reach the RCMP's Heather Stables atop Little Mountain, with its panoramic view of Vancouver. After parking his car at the corner of 33rd and Heather, he strode up the leaf-strewn lawn, past the tall flag-pole with its billowing Maple Leaf, and into the newly commandeered Headhunter Headquarters.

Code name: HH HQ.

Formally known as the Fairmont Barracks but dubbed the Heather Stables in Mountie-speak, this heritage structure in the Tudor-revival style gave the impression that Shakespeare might have lived here. From 1921 to 1937, the barracks housed two hundred Horsemen; four stables sheltered more than a hundred steeds. Later, the officers' mess and drill hall became an RCMP training center. Now, ongoing renovations had screeched to a halt to accommodate the Headhunter squad.

For a minute, DeClercq stood in the doorway and surveyed the high-vaulted entrance hall. A wide staircase ran up the left-hand wall to the second-floor mezzanine, which led to the superintendent's new office in the front right-hand corner of the building. On the ground level under the mezzanine, a huge lecture hall was being hastily reconfigured as the squad room. There, he would meet the Headhunter task force later that morning. Between the stairs and the bullpen, a flight of steps descended to storage.

What made DeClercq a legendary cop was a sixth sense he called the Zone. When he lost his parents in a traffic accident, the orphaned child was raised by an unmarried aunt who took him to historic sites around the globe. The hours he spent recreating in his imagination the events that took place at those now static sites gave him the ability to "see" what had most likely occurred. It was like a yo-yo superimposing the past onto the present so he could view a film of Back Then being projected onto the Here and Now.

Hindsight in the literal, not the figurative, sense.

The entrance hall before him was a stripped-down shell, but Robert slipped into the Zone and time-traveled back to the Fairmont Barracks of old. He could smell the horses in the stables outside. In the squad room, where work crews had spent the night wiring in phones and setting up desks and filing cabinets, he saw long-dead Mounties in shirtsleeves, jodhpurs with suspenders, and riding boots with spurs, guzzling whisky and smoking cigarettes in the hazy officers' mess as they played billiards or tossed darts. Mounted on the balcony above the stairs, a phantom stuffed bison head gazed down at him. As DeClercq climbed the staircase, a line of paintings and photos depicting the colorful history of the Force ushered him up what was in reality nothing more than a bare, pictureless wall.

At the top of the stairs, he angled right and followed the balcony railing to his office. Before opening the door, he yo-yoed back out of the Zone.

A good magician never reveals his secrets, and Robert would *never* confess to using pseudohallucination to solve murder cases.

Cops don't understand visionaries who "see" things.

That's hallucinating.

And that brands you as nuts.

———

"Good morning, sir," Sergeant Jack MacDougall said as DeClercq entered his office. He and Corporal James Rodale stood at the Strategy Wall.

"Coffee?" asked the corporal, holding up a thermos and an empty mug.

"Thanks. Black," said DeClercq.

Rodale poured.

"Here's the duty roster of those we pulled in for the squad." MacDougall passed DeClercq several sheets of paper. "As requested, Flood's on loan from the VPD."

"Good, that deals with the turf war exposed by Olson's rampage."

Like the rest of the building, the superintendent's office was under construction. Three Victorian library tables, arranged in the shape of a horseshoe to the right of the door, served as DeClercq's desk. The high-backed barley sugar chair, an antique from the early days of the Force, was found gathering dust in storage beneath the officers' mess. The desk and chair were turned so he could look out at Queen Elizabeth Park. Overnight, at his request, carpenters had sheathed that side of the room with corkboard to construct the Strategy Wall. Like a general deploying toy soldiers on a campaign map, he would use the wall to arrange evidence of the Headhunter's crimes, then—secretly—analyze it in the Zone.

Now, as DeClercq sipped his coffee and studied the duty roster, he was surprised to see a name that dated back to before Jane's death and the October Crisis.

You? he thought, smiling.

After yesterday morning's call-up from Commissioner François Chartrand, DeClercq had summoned MacDougall and Rodale to brief him on the murders and help him map out the Headhunter Squad. From noon on, the three Horsemen had worked in an office at North Vancouver Detachment, reading, discussing, culling, and organizing the mounting piles of photos and reports generated by the beheadings. Both investigators—and particularly MacDougall—demonstrated that they were clear-thinking detail men, so DeClercq confirmed them as his deputies. He assigned them to assemble the squad, with two provisos: for the sake of Force morale, they were to find a role for Constable Rick Scarlett, so that he and other Mounties in the lower ranks wouldn't think first responders got shut out of big cases; and they were to recruit Detective Al Flood, the point man on the VPD's half of the Grabowski floater case, so that separate police jurisdictions wouldn't result in a loophole that benefitted the psycho.

Late in the day, word came in that DeClercq's request to commandeer the Heather Stables for his headquarters had been approved, so the three had driven over to map out the floor plan. Before going home with copies of the crime scene photos to process in the Zone, the super had suggested they meet here early this morning to plot the Headhunter dragnet on his Strategy Wall.

"Okay," said DeClercq, draining his coffee, "let's start with the first killing."

Mountie detectives wear plainclothes. MacDougall was impeccably dressed in a white shirt and a red tie with a tailored blue blazer and sharply creased gray slacks. His shoes were Italian. Seemingly bland Rodale wore a nondescript brown suit. But just as the men turned their attention to the corkboard wall, DeClercq's sixth sense superimposed a full-face mask over the corporal's head so his reddish-brown iris stared out through one eyehole and his green iris out the other.

Heterochromia iridis, thought the superintendent. *Never pull a bank robbery, James, or the Zone will use that telltale clue to take you down.*

Lines divided the Strategy Wall into three parts. The left-hand section depicted the first Headhunter murder: MacDougall's victim in the shallow grave. Pinned in the center was the Polaroid that had been delivered to editor Skip O'Rourke at *The Vancouver Sun.* There was no need for DeClercq to call on his sixth sense. The photo fleshed out the crime: the head of a young woman in her late teens was hoisted on a pole and set against a white background, probably a sheet. The photo ended two feet down the shaft, so the ground was out of frame. The teen's eyes had rolled back in her skull, and only slivers of pupil peeked out from beneath her lids like crescent moons. Matted with blood, her jet-black hair was tangled about her face. Strands slithered down like hellbound snakes to shreds of skin where her neck had been severed. Her mouth hung open slackly in a silent scream.

"Has the teen been ID'd?"

"No," said MacDougall. "The tattered tent"—he indicated the crime scene photos circling the Polaroid—"was made in Switzerland and sold exclusively in Europe. Except for the jeans around her ankles, the clothes left in the tent and the fabric fragments recovered from the grave are European too. My guess is she was a tourist, backpacking here."

"Interpol's missing persons?"

"Nothing yet."

"Immigration?"

"Ditto."

"Local missing persons?"

"Negative."

"So Jane Doe was here on her own."

"Odds are she came to Vancouver and crossed the harbor to camp in one of the North Shore's ravines. The Headhunter came along the path and surprised her at her tent. Or he followed her from somewhere back to her campsite. He took the time to bury everything but the head, which means he didn't want the body to be found. Everything points to the tent being the crime scene. If he'd killed the camper elsewhere, why bury her here? The Headhunter would have had a slew of more remote dump sites to choose from."

"Forensics?"

"Time of death's about three months ago," said Rodale. "The entomology report says she's full of insects that move in then."

"So the end of July."

"Summer camping season. When school's out in Europe."

"Anything near the grave?"

"No," said MacDougall. "Sifting soil and searching the creek failed to uncover the weapon. It's large, like a Bowie knife, and the killer took it with him. A chopper sweep with infrared recorded no hotspots. She's the only body buried in the ravine. Nature's had months to erase forensic traces."

"Witnesses?"

The sergeant shook his head. "Summer foliage hid the tent from the creekside path. And the only house at the top of the bluff was vacant till recently."

"Polaroid?" DeClercq tapped the copy on the wall.

"Except for those belonging to the editor who opened the envelope, the lab found no fingerprints on the original photo or the *Buns and Boobs* subscription form. Except for *Sun* employees, prints on the envelope are unidentified. No one saw who dropped it off and we can't find the sender. There are no other forensic traces. No saliva on the flap means the lab guys can't tell us the blood type. The envelope was likely sealed with water. The lab did identify the typeface of the address. It's from a portable Commodore made in Toronto. Find the typewriter the sender used and the techs'll be able to match it. The letter *C* is off-kilter and holds up the carriage."

"So those knife marks on the buried bones are our best lead?"

MacDougall nodded.

The autopsy photos were pinned lower on the wall. One displayed scratch marks on the top vertebra, where the psycho had sawed off the camper's head. Another showed gouges across the rib cage consistent with someone having slashed horizontally through her breasts.

"The lab confirms that the marks on all three bodies were made with the same knife," said Rodale. "The nick in its blade left identical striations.

Snags in the canvas of the tent indicate the Headhunter used the same weapon to slash the shelter to shreds."

DeClercq stepped back from the Strategy Wall and slipped into the Zone.

"Here's how I see it," he said. "The tent was hidden from the path, so we know this psycho didn't chance across a random victim in the ravine. The Headhunter selected her for a specific reason. She fit his victim type. Most likely, she was a stand-in for someone in his past, someone he wanted to hurt or take revenge on. Either he stalked her to the tent and took her by surprise, or they met elsewhere and traveled there together. Perhaps he offered her a break from the outdoors at his home. They went to the campsite to get her stuff and that's when he attacked her. The jeans around her ankles indicate rape. The slash across her breasts has sexual undertones. Gripped by frenzy, he ripped the tent to tatters. Then he used the nicked blade to saw off her head. After burying the headless body in a shallow grave, the Headhunter carried the trophy back to his lair. There, he stuck the head on a stake in front of a white sheet and snapped the Polaroid."

"Question?" asked MacDougall. "What did he do with the head? After he took the picture, I mean. Unless he froze it, the flesh'll have rotted by now. Did he keep the skull as a trophy?"

"Psychologically that would fit. Fetish fed his fantasy between murders. He probably used the trophy as a masturbation aid until the compulsion to act out his sexual fantasy in the real world drove him to stalk, rape, and kill another victim."

"If the Headhunter hid the camper's body and kept the photo of her head for three months, why change MO with Grabowski?"

"Anonymity no longer gives him sufficient kicks. In ramping up to the next level, he's boasting. He's saying, 'Look at me. I'm your worst nightmare.'"

"Helen Ann Grabowski, also known as Patricia Ann Palitti," said Rodale, taking over from MacDougall when the cops turned to the middle section of the Strategy Wall. "Date of birth June 12, 1961, in New Orleans, Louisiana. Arrested out front of the Moonlight Arms pub on Pender Street in Chinatown at about nine o'clock on Sunday, October 17. She was hooking, but the bust was for drugs: a cap of heroin was found hidden in one of her boots by Detective Bernie Zebroff of the VPD's drug squad. The bulls charged her with narcotics possession, then set her free at four thirty in the morning on Monday, October 18. That was four days after she arrived here from New Orleans—and the last anyone saw of her until seamen on a government tug fished her out of the Fraser River delta a week later."

Once again, the overview of the crime centered on the Polaroid shot of a woman's severed head stuck on a stake. Again, the trophy was set against a white background and the picture was cropped well above the ground. The head had belonged to a junkie in her early twenties, once attractive but now ravaged by drugs. Her collar-length black hair was plastered to her skin. Her eyes had rolled so far back in her skull that only bloodshot whites showed. Her mouth hung open, spilling her tongue. Blood trickled down both cheeks from her eye sockets, and down her chin from the corners of her lips.

She looked like a zombie in a cheap horror film.

Pinned above the Polaroid was a copy of the *Buns and Boobs* subscription form sent to the editor of *The Vancouver Sun*. Its caption read "Looking for these?" and beneath that a naked woman lifted up the largest breasts the cops had ever seen.

"As before, no prints or forensics on the originals. The clipping's from the skin mag's July 1982 issue."

The Polaroid of the taunting head was flanked by two mug shots. One had been snapped at the VPD jail after the bust at the Moonlight Arms. The other, dated April 12, 1980, had come north from the files of the New Orleans police.

"At first, we thought the floater had drowned and lost her head to a boat propeller. But the autopsy nixed that. The lack of water in her lungs proved she didn't drown. The saw marks on her vertebra, the stab wound through her neck, and the slash through her breasts meant we had a killer. Her genitals were bruised, probably from rape. She'd been in the water for a week. Because she was fished from the estuary where the Fraser meets the sea, we don't know if the floater came from upstream or was washed in with the tide."

Rodale knuckled the VPD mug shot.

"Fingerprints led us to Grabowski's drug arrest. A week in the water means time of death was shortly after she got out of jail. The prints also linked her to a soliciting bust in New Orleans."

His knuckle jumped to the NOPD mug shot.

"I phoned New Orleans and spoke to a cop named Jefferson. He told me that Helen Grabowski was a known French Quarter prostitute with a pimp named John Lincoln Hardy, aka the Weasel. Hardy has no record, but he's mixed up in an ongoing NOPD investigation into drug trafficking, a mobile prostitution ring, and—are you ready for this?—an active *voodoo* cult. Jefferson wired this mug shot of Grabowski. And this photo taken surreptitiously of the Weasel."

Rodale tapped a grainy wire photo.

"No shots of Mr. Toad, Mole, Ratty, and Badger?" asked DeClercq.

Rodale frowned. He didn't get it.

"*The Wind in the Willows?*" the superintendent prompted. When Rodale still looked puzzled, he said, "You need a trip to Disneyland."

Back before the October Crisis turned his world upside down, he'd read that children's book to Jane, but he'd never got to take her on Mr. Toad's Wild Ride.

DeClercq studied the wire photo beside the headshots. It captured a muscular black man as big as a heavyweight boxer, with a receding hairline above a sadistic face crisscrossed with livid scars that likely came from a knife fight. His ear was pierced with a stud.

"Do we know why Grabowski and Hardy came to Vancouver?"

"No," said Rodale.

"Is Hardy still kicking around?"

"As near as we can tell. Four days before she got busted, he and Grabowski took a room in a flophouse on skid row. On the night she disappeared, Hardy left that dump. We don't know where he went. We've turned up no sightings of Grabowski after she got out of jail. But hookers and drunks at the Moonlight Arms ID'd the Weasel and said he was hanging around in the week after she vanished."

"Pushing drugs?"

"Could be."

"Does he pimp other women?"

"None have surfaced. We've followed the obvious lines of inquiry when a junkie hooker is snuffed." He held out his hand and started counting off on his fingers. "One, was she killed by a vicious john? Two, did she run afoul of her pimp? And three, did she rip off the pusher supplying her drugs? That was my thinking until the first victim turned up."

Stepping forward, DeClercq examined both Polaroids closely.

"Here," he said, pointing to the neck of the unidentified camper. "See this slit perpendicular to the cut that sawed off her head?"

He returned to the Grabowski Polaroid.

"See the slit in the *same* place here? It's the top half of the stab wound through her throat that the pathologist spotted."

DeClercq retreated from the Strategy Wall and viewed the Grabowski section through the psychological overlay of the Zone.

"Here's how I see it," he said. "Like the camper, Helen Grabowski was chosen because she's the Headhunter's victim type. She was another stand-in for someone in his past. What both victims have in common is black hair. So does the third victim. Is the psycho a hair fetishist? Slashing the women's breasts has sexual undertones, but it also equates to mother mutilation. The cutting from the *Boobs* magazine fits that psychology.

"The facts suggest the Headhunter waylaid Grabowski the morning she got out of jail, then drove her somewhere secluded to rape and kill her. My gut tells me that stabbing her through the throat during forced intercourse gave the rapist sexual kicks from her death throes. From the lack of decomposition and the freshness of the blood, we can assume the Polaroid was snapped a short time after the woman was knifed and beheaded. Having collected his trophies, the killer lost interest in the body. He dumped it in the water, where it might have washed out to sea. But then in rapid succession, you found *both* bodies. That's when the Headhunter's MO changed and he sent the Polaroids to *The Sun* for maximum exposure."

"Like Jack the Ripper?" said MacDougall.

"So it seems."

"Is the Weasel a dead end?"

"No," said DeClercq. "Skulls are used in voodoo, and we don't know what the Headhunter does with the severed heads once they rot away. What if the camper ran out of money and crossed the harbor to hook on a downtown stroll? What if she worked out front of the Moonlight Arms? We know Grabowski was starved for junk when she got out of jail. Did she go hooking there too? Is that what they have in common? A sexual predator trolling Vancouver's hooker strolls to find his victim type? Or did they both run afoul of a pimp—John Lincoln Hardy—who's involved in some sort of voodoo cult?"

"To answer that, we need to know if Hardy was here at the end of July, when the entomology tests inform us the camper died," said Rodale.

"Check with Immigration."

A map of Vancouver and its suburbs down to Washington State was affixed to the top of the corkboard and marked with the Headhunter's crime sites.

"The floater was fished from the river at the foot of UBC's cliffs," said DeClercq. "The nurse was nailed to a totem pole on the campus above. Both crime scenes are in the jurisdiction of University Detachment. I assume Richmond Detachment took over because it's bigger?"

"Yes," said Rodale.

"That means Constable Scarlett had *two* murders wrenched from his hands?"

"As you requested, he's on the duty roster."

"Good. Have him investigate the John Lincoln Hardy lead. That'll give him a task linked to one of the bodies found on his turf."

"That should make for a good team," said MacDougall. "He's in one of your flying patrols, and his partner's been undercover for months buying drugs in the Moonlight Arms."

"Name?"

"Constable Katherine Spann."

THE AXEMAN OF NEW ORLEANS

New Orleans, Louisiana, 1957

The man with the briefcase chained to his wrist had a date with Death. As he skulked through the hard-partying streets of the French Quarter, wending his way toward Suzannah's House of Discipline, he checked the watch on his other wrist and throbbed with sadomasochistic anticipation as the minute hand crept inexorably toward the Axeman of New Orleans's killing hour: 12:15.

Like the Mardi Gras masquers around him, he was dressed to kill. They were dressed to kill figuratively—these costumed nobodies made bold by anonymity—while he was literally dressed to kill. The axe head looped in a sling under his sweaty armpit was cold against his heart.

His earliest boyhood memory was of lying in a musty canopy bed on a scorching afternoon in the crumbling Louisiana mansion built by his eighteenth-century ancestors when the Mississippi River delta was green with sugarcane plantations worked by African slaves. The land was later auctioned off to pay gambling debts, but not his forbears' haunted antebellum manor, a Southern Gothic hothouse of incest and insanity that was home to his maddened mom and her young son.

How he loved to smell the perfume she dabbed between her pillowy breasts and into the other secret nooks of her body. He loved to be near her on those beastly hot days, when she hugged him so tightly against her naked flesh that it hurt, while through the French windows came the fragrance of the massive southern magnolia, its huge white blossoms nestled in glossy leaves. Later, while "The Mysterious Axeman's Jazz (Don't

Scare Me, Papa)" played on the gramophone, his mom would clean out her "naughty boy" with a soapy enema and scrub his skin raw with a stiff brush as they bathed in her clawfoot bathtub.

"Who do you love?" she would ask as she scrubbed his genitals.

"You, Mama," he'd reply, biting his tongue to endure the delicious pain.

On one of those oozy afternoons, as they lay entwined in the damp hooded bed, his mom told him how his grandpa had helped form the Ku Klux Klan in shadows cast by the Civil War, recruiting the ghosts of fallen Confederate soldiers to mount up and gallop with him. Dressed in white pointed hoods with dark eyeholes and white ankle-length robes, they thundered through bayou country, chasing down freed niggers to lynch from mossy trees and burning their churches and schools to the ground as a warning to others still alive.

"Do you hate niggers?" she would ask.

"Yes, Ma," he'd reply.

Then she told him how her pa and his Klansmen rode up and down the street out front of the theater showing D.W. Griffith's *Birth of a Nation*—what stronger recruiting hook was there than the cross burnings in that film?—and that's when the old nigger voodoo woman stepped off the curb in front of his horse and cursed him with her black magic.

"How?" he asked, wide-eyed.

"She stuck a pin through the head of a Klansman doll."

"Then what happened?"

"Pa became the Axeman of New Orleans."

His mother was scrubbing his cock and balls when she told him about the Axeman. Before they'd climbed into the tub, she had played "Axeman's Jazz" again. Her father's headaches began the day after he was hexed by the voodoo curse. Month after month, the pain grew worse as the hole in his brain got bigger. Eventually, her dad became a zombie with no brain at all, and that's when the voice of the old voodoo woman echoed into the hole, ordering him to sneak out at night and hack up white people.

"Did he?"

"Sure did. Pa was *possessed* by her."

The Axeman's reign of terror began in May 1918. Come dark, her pa would slip out and prowl about the French Quarter and beyond. Selecting an unlucky home, he would chisel a panel out of the back door and feel his way to the dusky bedroom. There, he'd close in on that night's slumbering prey. Raising an axe high above the snoring heads, he'd smash it down to cleave the skulls apart. Then he'd escape into the night, leaving the gory axe behind as his calling card.

"How many sleepers did he kill?"

"The toll's not clear. Six, seven, eight…And he hacked up a lot more."

She told him how the Axeman sent a taunt to *The Times-Picayune*. By then, the choppings had New Orleans in a panic. Its citizens were afraid of every sound, wary of every shadow, and loath to go to sleep in case they awoke to glimpse the Axeman about to split their heads. In the morning, they'd open the newspaper with trembling hands to see if another ill-fated Orleanian had been whacked overnight.

The taunt in *The Times-Picayune* read:

Hell, March 13, 1919

Esteemed mortal,

They have never caught me and they never will. They have never seen me, for I am invisible, even as the ether that surrounds your earth. I am not a human being, but a spirit and a demon from the hottest hell. I am what you Orleanians and your foolish police call the Axeman.

When I see fit, I shall come and claim other victims. I shall leave no clue except my axe besmeared with the blood and brains of those I have sent below to keep me company.

To be exact, at 12:15 (earthly time) on next Tuesday night, I am going to pass over New Orleans. In my infinite mercy, I am going to make a little proposition to you people. Here it is:

I am very fond of jazz music, and I swear by all the devils in the nether regions that I shall spare every person in whose home a jazz band is in full swing at the time I have just mentioned. If everyone has a jazz band going, so much the better for you people. One thing is certain: some of your people who do not jazz it on Tuesday night (if there be any) will get the axe.

The Axeman

There'd never been, his mom told him, a more raucous evening in New Orleans than St. Joseph's Night on March 19. Every dance hall was stuffed to capacity, and bands jazzed it up at hundreds of house parties all over town. True to his word, the Axeman didn't strike.

"Why jazz?" the boy asked.

"Niggers like boogie music, so the voodoo hag turned Pa into a boogieman."

"Did the Axeman kill again?"

"Several times. His last chop was in October 1919. Then, like Jack the Ripper did last century, the Axeman stopped as abruptly as he'd started."

"Why, Ma?"

"Pa begged me to save him from the voodoo curse. So I drove a silver needle through his brain the same way you free a vampire with a stake through the heart. Pa's bones are moldering in an unmarked grave by the roots of the magnolia tree outside our bedroom window."

For Mardi Gras the year after she told him the tale of his grandfather's rampage, Ma dressed him up as a pint-sized Axeman of New Orleans. As they strolled along Bourbon Street hand in hand, marveling at the masks and floats swirling through the French Quarter, a pickaninny with a rag doll let go of her granny's hand and ran toward them with Raggedy Ann outstretched.

"Voodoo!" shrieked his mom. "Don't curse my son!"

From her bonnet, she yanked an eight-inch hatpin and fell upon the black girl in a stabbing frenzy. Before police could pull her off and slap her in handcuffs, his mom had stuck the pickaninny full of bleeding holes.

The judge said his mom suffered from paranoid delusions and shipped her off to the loony bin. There, they zapped her with electric shocks that fried her brain, put her in a straitjacket to stop her from going berserk, and dug in her head with a scalpel to lobotomize her. He was taken into care and sent to a foster home. The family mansion was sold to cover his mom's debts. Later that year, they told him she had died from a stroke. None of this would have occurred if not for that nigger and her doll.

Well, now it was Mardi Gras, decades later. He'd made a lot of money from the nuclear technology that had incinerated all those Japs in Hiroshima and Nagasaki, and now kept America safe from the Russkies. His guilt demanded punishment for what had been done to Ma, and his groin ached for the erotic pain that she had bestowed on him. Ergo, the briefcase chained to his wrist was full of cash to pay Suzannah to scratch his S&M itches, and nestled in the money was a clutch of his dead mom's hatpins.

Voodoo pins, he thought.

Around him, the streets of the French Quarter buzzed with Mardi Gras masquers. He felt as if he were lost in a canvas by Hieronymus Bosch or Salvador Dali, with heads of birds and beasts on human bodies; human heads on birds and beasts; Comedy and Tragedy concealing the front and back of a head; a woman with a bone through her nose wearing a leopard skin draped with skulls; mermaids, satyrs, man-bats, monks, and demi-fishes; a sea of exhibitionists letting it all hang out as they laughed, sang, shouted, drummed, and tossed trinkets about. And in their midst snaked this *new* Axeman of New Orleans, his body cloaked in a black robe once worn by a nighthawk of the Ku Klux Klan, his face hidden behind a Masque of the Red Death from Poe's story.

All the clocks in the city lurched toward 12:15 as the Axeman angled off Royal Street into the dim cul-de-sac ending at the door to Suzannah's Pit of Pain.

LAND OF THE HEADHUNTERS

Vancouver, British Columbia, 1982
Saturday, October 30, 7:36 a.m.

Dawn was breaking by the time DeClercq, MacDougall, and Rodale moved on to the section of the Strategy Wall reserved for the killing, beheading, and crucifying of Joanna Portman. Once again, the collage revolved around a woman's headshot—in this case, her graduation photo from her nursing training at a Catholic hospital in Winnipeg, Manitoba. Dressed in nurse's whites and cradling a bouquet of pink roses, the graduate smiles at the cops from the corkboard, her jet-black hair crowning a beaming face ready to step out and make a mark on the world.

She reminded DeClercq of his first wife, Kate.

"Joanna Portman," MacDougall said, taking the reins back from Rodale for the third briefing. "Twenty-three years old. Born in Winnipeg. Catholic girls' school, Catholic church, and Catholic hospital there, before she came west to nurse at St. Paul's Hospital. Night before last, she worked late with a difficult birth and got off at five in the morning. Portman caught the Macdonald bus out front of the hospital, rode it along Kits Beach to Tatlow Park, and stepped off alone at the stop three blocks from her apartment in a house on Third. Somewhere between the park and her door, the Headhunter got her."

"Witnesses?" asked DeClercq.

"Nothing helpful. The bus driver says the street was deserted when he last saw Portman walking down Macdonald, staying clear of the park. That hour of the morning, the neighbors on Third were asleep. Portman had the next day off, so no one missed her at work. The following morning at two, a pair of students at UBC chanced across her butchered remains nailed to a totem pole."

"Her killer's either lucky or very street-smart."

"Lucky, for sure," said MacDougall. "Everything worked to his advantage. First, the freak snowstorm masked the daring crucifixion. The paved loading area beside the museum meant no tire tracks. The path from there to the totem pole is loose gravel, so no footprints. All we found are pits in the stones left when he dragged Portman's body and the ladder used to hoist her up. Imagine the effort it took to nail her to the mortuary pole. Haul her up the ladder in the snowfall. Drive a spike through one palm, then raise her so the severed neck tucks up under the dogfish carving on the crosspiece. Then hammer a spike through her other palm. End result"—MacDougall swept his hand around the crime scene photos orbiting Portman's headshot—"a crucified woman with a substitute head sticking its tongue out at us."

"Forensics?"

"Nothing. Even the snowfall played into the Headhunter's hands. Instead of preserving footprints and tracks, it covered up any traces. All Ident found at the scene was a jug smeared with Portman's blood at the foot of the totem."

"The blood's weird," said DeClercq.

"Talk about making a statement. The Headhunter abducts the nurse on Thursday morning. He carts her off to wherever he rapes and kills her. Cutting off her head sheds a lot of blood. The psycho collects it in a plastic jug, then after he crucifies her on the mortuary pole with her white nurse's uniform ripped open to her crotch, he pours the blood over the corpse to make it ultra macabre."

"For dramatic effect."

MacDougall nodded. "A horror show."

"And the postmortem report?"

"The stab wound in her throat was the likely cause of death. Same knife scratches on the top vertebra from sawing off her head. Breasts slashed like the other two victims. This time there's no question about rape. Portman had severe bruising and trauma to her genitals. A vaginal swab tested positive for semen. Motility is lost about six hours after intercourse, and this sperm was immotile. Most tails had broken off. As a rule, spermatozoa aren't found thirty-six hours after rape. But according to the lab guys, it depends on the manner of death and body cooling, quantity of ejaculate, sterility in the male, and acidic/alkaline balance in the vagina. The timeline here fits rape."

"Did Portman have a boyfriend?"

"None that we've uncovered. The doctors, nurses, and admin staff at St. Paul's paint a picture of her as a dedicated, well-liked, kindhearted maternity nurse, strong on religious beliefs and faith in the basic goodness of human beings."

"So of course she's the one who falls prey to this monster."

"Only the good die young," said Rodale.

"Portman proves these are definitely sex crimes," DeClercq stated. "Question: Is this serial predator a sexual psychopath killing for personal gratification? Or are we after a sexual psychotic whose sick mind has broken with reality?"

"My bet's the latter," said Rodale. "This psycho's lost in a fantasy world of hallucinations and delusions."

"Or *not* lost," countered DeClercq. "Could be the Headhunter lives in a borderline state, slipping in and out of psychosis like Jekyll and Hyde."

"Is he linked to UBC?" asked MacDougall. "The floater under the cliffs and the nurse on the bluff. What if the European camper was a student checking out UBC for postgrad studies?"

"Did she go to a dance or frat party?" wondered Rodale.

"Is the killer a student?"

"Or a professor?"

"Serial killing could be a blind," said DeClercq, "used to mask the fact the Headhunter is tied to *one* of the women. To guard against tunnel vision, we must investigate that too. But my gut says that's not the case here. There may be a strong personal link to one of the women, but the other two aren't a smokescreen. All three play an important part in the sexual fantasy he's acting out."

Once more, DeClercq stepped back and slipped into the Zone.

"Here's how I see it," he said. "Three months ago—assuming the camper was his first victim—the Headhunter met and selected the black-haired European for rape, murder, and beheading to act out revenge on another black-haired woman who abused him as a boy—his mother, his stepmother, or a female guardian. So he wouldn't be caught, the crime was to be kept secret. A European backpacker far from home and camping alone in the woods was an ideal stand-in. He went to her camp and indulged his warped fantasy, then buried the body and carried his trophies off to masturbate over later.

"Reality, however, never lives up to fantasy. So three months later, his compulsion forced him out to rape and kill again. He chose another black-haired stand-in unlikely to be missed—a junkie hooker wandering skid row in the darkness before dawn. Taking her somewhere safe, he raped her, knifed her, hacked off her head, and dumped her body in the water, never to be found. But already his MO was changing, whether he knew it or not, because discarding her in the river or sea undercut secrecy.

"Once more, reality fell short of his fantasy. The thrill of the kill was weaker than he'd imagined, as it is for all serial killers. That's why they kill repeatedly—to *perfect* the fantasy the next time they act out. The Headhunter failed twice in his desperate need to get even, then fate dealt him a trump card. The media frenzy whipped up when we found the first two bodies in rapid succession gave him a taste of public notoriety. Overnight, the Headhunter became the terror of the town. Now, all black-haired women were in fear for their lives. The Polaroid taunts sent to *The Sun* fueled the hysteria, and instead of trolling skid row, he headhunted Joanna Portman in upscale Point Grey. After ritualizing her death in his lair, he crucified her under the dogfish head on the campus totem pole. The chutzpah that took! It's the crime of a madman morphing into a Nietzschean superman."

"When will he strike again?" Rodale asked.

"Soon," said DeClercq. "Feeding off that volatile mix of fear and notoriety, the Headhunter undoubtedly plans to outdo Portman's murder."

The Horsemen were interrupted by a knock on the door.

"Enter," called DeClercq.

The giant who stepped into the room stood six foot four and weighed 285 pounds. In girth, he was as massive as an old-fashioned beer barrel. He wore a Russian fur hat with the earflaps tied at the crown, and he had to duck to cross under the lintel. Standing normally, his posture was stooped to shrink him to the size of most people. He had obviously come from the airport, judging by the suitcase in one hand and the Murder Bag in the other. When he doffed his hat, his slicked-back white pompadour added inches to his height. His gray eyes encircled by wire-rim glasses made him look like Arthur Ellis, Canada's most famous hangman. It was a fitting comparison, for had hanging not been abolished in 1976, the many killers caught by this scientist's forensic expertise would have plunged from the gallows.

"Hello, Robert. Are you busy?"

"Not too busy for you. When'd you get in?"

"Early this morning."

"Sounds like a grueling flight."

"When you're my size, flying cattle class is like being locked in Little Ease."

DeClercq grinned. He knew the reference. Little Ease was a four-foot-square dungeon in the Tower of London, so confining that no one held there could stand, sit, or lie down, except in a fetal position with his knees drawn up to his chin. That's where Guy Fawkes was crammed for his part in the Gunpowder Plot, the plan to blow up London's Houses of Parliament in 1605.

"Doctor Joseph Avacomovitch," said DeClercq, "meet Sergeant Jack MacDougall and Corporal James Rodale, the backbone of the Headhunter Squad. Jack and Jim, meet Joe."

The men shook hands.

"Joe has me to thank for his discomfort," said the super. "When the commissioner asked me to head up this task force, my one condition was that Joe be flown here from Ottawa's crime lab to provide forensic assistance for the duration of our manhunt."

"Welcome aboard," said MacDougall. "We'll leave you two to catch up. There's a lot to do before the press briefing at nine. And even more to do before the squad meets at ten."

As soon as the Mounties departed, the Russian shucked his overcoat and hung it up with his hat on the antique coat rack by the door. Then—as these two friends had done many times in the past—he joined DeClercq to play "forensic chess" with the pieces on the Strategy Wall.

"Fill me in," he said.

The son of Ukrainian farmers slaughtered by Hitler's Einsatzgruppen during the Nazis' blitzkrieg on Stalingrad, the academically gifted Joseph was selected for a first-class Soviet education in the postwar years. By his thirties, he had four university degrees and was a top-notch forensic sleuth in the Russian Academy of Sciences. In the shadow of President Kennedy's *"Ich bin ein Berliner"* speech, police were baffled by a series of homosexual slayings tied to the Red Army. Five Germans were found in bombed-out buildings, bound, sodomized, and slowly strangled with garrotes looped around their necks. The act of repeatedly tightening and loosening the cords clenched their anal sphincters for the psycho's sexual pleasure. When news leaked that local detectives had discovered, clutched in the hand of the fifth victim, a button torn off a Russian occupier's uniform, anti-Soviet sentiment ignited a riot so incendiary that army troops were mobilized to suppress it.

Consequently, Moscow dispatched Joe to East Berlin.

An hour before the Russian forensic scientist arrived, the so-called Red Strangler struck again. Thriving on the notoriety of his crimes, the killer upped his game. The sixth victim had been buggered and throttled to death, like the others, but this time the body had a hangman's rope noosed around the neck and was tossed naked off the roof of a bombed-out ruin to hang above the street for all to see.

So concerned were the responding cops with the social—but not forensic—ramifications that they cut the corpse down at once and threw the rope aside. Arriving at the scene to work his magic, Joe found the Red Strangler's hemp discarded on the ground and immediately picked up on its puzzling configuration. Loop, loop, then an elongated circle out to one side, like Halley's Comet orbiting the sun, then loop, loop, and a second ellipse, and finally loop, loop again.

In the twists of the rope, Joe noticed flecks of paint.

Using the latest chromatographic equipment, he identified vehicle make and year: a Nazi Volkswagen, circa 1943. After the Soviet bombardment in the closing days of the war, few Nazi cars in Berlin remained roadworthy. Those that did were soon surrounded by East Germany, and were now constantly monitored by Stasi agents in a never-ending battle to curb Western spies.

"The car you're looking for," Joe explained to his bosses, "is a 1943 VW Type 82 'Kübelwagen' in wartime camouflage paint with a rusting rear bumper. To keep the bumper from breaking away and hitting the ground, the Strangler looped it twice with hemp rope, then pulled the rope up over a metal bar in the ragtop's frame, before repeating the same configuration and tying the whole thing off around the bumper. When he got the idea to hang his sixth victim above the street for terrifying effect, he used the bumper rope, which not only had picked up chips of paint from the car, but also had taken on the loop, loop, ellipse pattern after months of rain and sun stretched and shrank its fibers into that unique shape."

Moscow was elated when the so-called Red Strangler turned out to be a West German sexual predator recruited by the CIA and fed into East Berlin through Checkpoint Charlie. When America dismissed that charge as Russian propaganda, the Kremlin announced that Dr. Avacomovitch, who'd just been awarded the Order of Lenin for his forensic work, was going to West Berlin to prove the allegation.

Sadly, Joe never got to accept that lofty decoration, for no sooner had he touched down on the *free* side of the Berlin Wall than he defected to the West.

Goodbye, Mother Russia.

After his debriefing, he chose to settle in Canada because the harsh winters reminded him of his happy childhood before the Einsatzgruppen machine-gunned his parents and left them to rot in a field on the family's conquered farm.

With a reputation for always getting their man, the Horsemen had promptly offered the Russian defector a job in their crime lab. The first investigator to use Joe's forensic expertise to help him solve a puzzling murder case was Robert DeClercq, the rising homicide hotshot. The two men had instantly hit it off and forged a friendship. Each recognized in the other the willpower that only kids orphaned young understand.

You and me, buddy.

I've got your back if you've got mine.

In chess game after chess game, they'd checkmated killers. Robert lived in Montreal and Joe in Ottawa, a driving time of two hours and fifteen minutes apart. Many a night as Old Man Winter prowled around the house, Joe had joined Kate and Robert for dinner. Then the two men would retire for cognacs by the hearth, discussing murder while baby Jane slept in the Mountie's lap. How he had treasured that time with his surrogate family. And how he lamented the day that he and Robert had opened the door for another session of manhunting by the fire...and came upon Kate ripped apart by a machine pistol.

Now here they stood all these years later, once more out to defeat a rabid monster on the chessboard of Robert's Strategy Wall.

"So what do you think?" the Mountie asked after briefing the scientist.

Avacomovitch closed in on the crime scene photographs pinned around Portman's headshot: some from a helicopter hovering over the totem village high on the cliffs of Point Grey; others of the headless body nailed to the Dogfish Mortuary Pole, its crest a mocking substitute for her face, with its bugged eyes and elliptical pupils, its flaring red nostrils and downturned mouth full of square teeth, and its big red tongue sticking out from between its fat red lips.

"The totem pole is significant," said the Russian. "Too much effort and danger went into creating this taunt for it to be nothing more than attention-getting. Somehow the Headhunter's psychology is linked to Native history, culture, or myth. Weren't you going to write a book about Wilfred Blake?"

"Yes."

"What happened?"

"I got distracted writing another book that recently bogged down."

"Will you return to Blake?"

"Perhaps."

"I see a motive for revenge in his legacy that you and I as orphans grasp better than most."

"Residential schools?"

Joe winked. "We still see eye to eye."

The lost patrol of Wilfred Blake is the most baffling mystery in the history of the Mounted Police. After the British colonial army suppressed the

Red River Rebellion in 1870, the Scotsman was dispatched by dogsled that winter to cross the Cree and Blackfoot territory to the Rocky Mountains, then report back with recommendations on how to settle the Northwest. His report led to the formation of the Mounted Police in 1873, the Great March West that painted the Prairies imperial red, and the Indians losing their land. Generations of Native kids were torn from their families and placed in church-run residential schools, where they were brainwashed into forgetting their culture and preyed on by sexual predators. And Blake? In 1897, he vanished into thin air after tracking Iron-child—who was wanted for killing cops alongside Almighty Voice—up into the Rocky Mountains. The search party sent to find him after the spring thaw uncovered nothing but his Enfield revolver on rocks at the foot of Windigo Mountain.

"If you were an Indian boy," said Joe, "subjected to cultural genocide and years of rape in one of those government schools—and later a hate-filled man caught up in the extremist backlash of Red Power and the pan-Indian resistance—how would you make white folks and the Mounties understand that you reap what you sow?"

"Racial attacks on white women *always* get to white men. First, I'd take 'scalps' as trophies for *personal* revenge, then I'd expand my atrocities into a full-blown reign of terror to taunt the Mounted Police."

"Like the Zebra Killings."

There was no need for Joe to explain that case to Robert. Less than a decade ago, over a six-month period in 1973 and 1974, a splinter group of the Nation of Islam called the Death Angels had attacked and killed at least fifteen whites and wounded many others, plunging the city of San Francisco into panic. These Black Muslim racial extremists believed that white people were an inferior race created six thousand years ago by a black scientist named Yakub. By killing the "blue-eyed devils" or "grafted snakes," the Death Angels earned points that would get them into heaven. At one point, they kidnapped a homeless man from Ghirardelli Square and tied him naked to a post in the loft of their hideout, Black Self-Help Moving and Storage. Each man chose a weapon—a meat cleaver, knife, or machete—and they took turns hacking their captive to pieces. They disposed of the body by dumping its parts into San Francisco Bay. They were called the Zebra Killings not because they were black against white, but because the cops were assigned a special Z radio band to use during the manhunt.

Joe flicked one of the photos of Portman hanging headless from the totem pole. "The missing heads remind me of Swift Runner."

Robert recalled that case as well.

The Windigo is a man-eating spirit from Native Canadian myth, strongly associated with winter, snow, famine, and the North. Gaunt to the edge of starvation, the monster has ash-gray skin pulled tight over flesh-less bones and eyes sunk deep into the sockets of its skeletal face. Its lips are tattered and bloody, and it reeks of decay. The creature looks like it has crawled out of a frozen grave. It howls with the cry of a cannibal lusting after human meat, and it grows in size with each man it consumes.

Swift Runner was a Plains Cree used as a guide by the Mounties in the earliest days of the Force. Rumor ran rife among Natives in the harsh winter of 1878 that he had been possessed by the Windigo demon, and had murdered his wife and six children to cook their flesh and eat it. Wilfred Blake was dispatched to Swift Runner's camp north of Fort Saskatchewan to investigate. There, he found human skulls and piles of bones cracked open for their marrow. In December 1879, the cannibal became the first person hanged by the Mounted Police.

"Today, we recognize Swift Runner as the classic example of Windigo psychosis: a culture-bound syndrome found only among Native North Americans, in which madmen believe they've been transformed into a Windigo monster and lack the ability to control their cannibalistic impulses."

"Far-fetched?" Joe asked.

"Not to me." Robert shook his head. "We're thinking along the same lines."

"What's your theory?"

"The Lekwiltok and their Hamatsa cult."

The superintendent realized how much he had missed this: bouncing a murder puzzle around with a mind as versed in *all* aspects of criminality as he was.

"Of all the Native peoples in North America," Robert explained, "none is more fascinating to me than the Lekwiltok, the Southern Kwakiutl of

Vancouver Island. When whites arrived on the West Coast in the wake of Captain Cook, the Lekwiltok were highly aggressive headhunters who preyed on other tribes all the way down to Puget Sound, where Seattle is now. They would cross the Georgia Strait to the mouth of the Fraser River in their war canoes, passing under the bluff where we found Portman and heading up the river by the bank where Grabowski floated ashore. When they came upon an enemy tribe, they would strike quickly, hacking off heads to take home as gory trophies. Then they'd paddle back to their own villages, where the heads would be used as part of a Hamatsa ceremony. During the ritual, a young man of the tribe would be possessed by the spirit of Baxbaxwalanuksiwe, the cannibal god."

"That name's a mouthful," Joe said. "No pun intended. Know what it means?"

"I've seen it translated as Man-Eater at the North End of the World. And also as He Who Is First to Eat Man at the Mouth of the River."

"Description?"

"The Kwakiutl depict Bax as a hungry monster whose body is covered with mouths full of gnashing fangs. He lives in a spirit house high on the slopes of the Coast Mountains. Day and night, blood-red smoke billows from his chimney. One of his sidekicks is Hok Hok, a supernatural crane with a long beak used to crack open the skulls of men and suck out their brains. Hok Hok's the crest you see on Kwakiutl totem poles. His beak is so prominent it sometimes requires support at the tip. The Hamatsa cult's cannibal dance—which included real-life man-eating—was the main ritual of the winter ceremony. Ethnologist Edward S. Curtis captured the dance when he filmed *In the Land of the Headhunters* here in 1914."

"Why headhunting?"

"The Kwakiutl believed the soul resided at the crown of the head. To reincarnate, the soul had to travel down the gullet to the stomach. Severing a warrior's head cut his soul off from his stomach, ensuring that he couldn't come back to life and take revenge against the beheader. They also believed that releasing an enemy's soul by decapitation would pass the headless man's supernatural powers to his killer. The more trophies a Kwakiutl carried back to his village, the more powerful a man he was perceived to be. So headhunting became their signature act of war."

"Cannibals from myth come to life?"

"You could say that. There are stories about Kwakiutl headhunters in the colonial records. For instance, two men named Hunt and Moffat reported seeing Kwakiutl warriors chase down, kill, and butcher a runaway slave on a beach by Fort Rupert. While the men squatted around the corpse chanting, 'Hap! Hap! Hap!'—'Eat! Eat! Eat!'—dancers in bearskins growled and fed them the meat in order of seniority. The Kwakiutl carved a rock at the spot in the likeness of Baxbaxwalanuksiwe."

"What suppressed their headhunting?"

"In the 1860s, European material goods became the symbol of power in potlatch ceremonies. Headhunting no longer had the prestige it once did."

"Is the Dogfish Mortuary Pole Kwakiutl?"

"No, Haida."

"So how do you see it?" asked Joe.

"Pan-Indianism and Red Power blend Native cultures. For example, the sun dance of the Plains tribes is now performed here on the West Coast. If the Headhunter is a psycho who split from reality thanks to sexual abuse in a residential school, what will count to him is getting even—on both a personal and a communal level, for *all* suffering Natives. The Dogfish Mortuary Pole is the *best* head substitute. Cults and psychos latch on to unconventional motives. The Son of Sam listened to his neighbor's talking dog. The Manson Family killed because of a Beatles song. The Zodiac Killer gazed up at the stars. The Lekwiltok claimed spiritual possession."

"Like Windigo psychosis?"

Robert nodded. "Or maybe it's Hok Hok at work."

"Does the Headhunter crack open his victims' skulls to eat their brains?"

"Could be. We don't know what Jack the Ripper did with the organs he harvested."

"Hmm." Deep in thought, Joe took in the three beheadings on the Strategy Wall. "So where do I start?"

"I doubt there's much to glean from the buried camper or the floater remains. Too degraded by decomposition. Portman, however, is fresh and the crime screams ritual. Search the corpse and the murder scene, and assess the reports. Something fetishistic's going on here. This fellow"—he flicked the photo of the Weasel, next to the Polaroid of Grabowski's head—"is mixed up in New Orleans voodoo. As yet, a Native suspect hasn't surfaced in our manhunt. But what if a Kwakiutl mug shot ends up here?"

As he tapped the blank space left next to Portman's grad photo, the Mountie winced from shock. All his life, Robert had controlled when he slipped into and out of the Zone. But *this* was like the jolt Dr. Jekyll got the first time he switched to Mr. Hyde without drinking the potion.

He hadn't tossed the yo-yo, but the Horseman was in the Zone.

And staring at him from that blank space on the Strategy Wall, he "saw" a Polaroid of Portman's head stuck on a pole.

THE MEAT HOOK

New Orleans, Louisiana, 1957

Bong...bong...bong...

As the clock in the Mask Room struck midnight, Suzannah pulled open a secret panel in one of her boudoir's red satin walls and revealed a circular staircase that funneled down into the eighteenth-century bowels of the Lafon mansion. Fetching some matches, she lit a torch bracketed to the mouth of the stairwell, then removed it to light her descent.

"Come see Madame Suzannah's Chamber of Horrors, Crystal," the dominatrix coaxed, sweeping the flambeau around the dark shaft.

Shivering, the stoned girl hesitated as she struggled to swallow the bitter taste of the coke dust dripping from her caked nostrils into her dry throat.

"Don't be silly, precious. It's only theater. Men who've sinned in the past sometimes *need* punishment. So I get paid gobs of money to straighten them out. The carnival masks hide their faces and help them shed their inhibitions. What we earn tonight will let us live like queens in Europe for a year. Would you rather go back to fucking your pig of a dad?"

The muddle-headed girl reluctantly tailed Suzannah down the cork-screw steps as the torchlight warped their shadows up the brick-lined walls and the fetid air got clammier the deeper they sank into New Orleans's sordid past.

"There used to be a smuggler's vault under the house," said Suzannah. "Used by pirates and privateers like Jean Lafitte and his brother. 'Yo-ho-ho, and a bottle of rum.' A tunnel led from the Mississippi River to the secret crypt, but my Cajun kin sealed the passage."

The stairwell bottomed out at a flagstone floor and a heavy plank door set into a curved wall. The hinges squealed as Suzannah pushed the protesting door and stepped into stygian darkness to light a second torch near the jamb.

"Duck," she cautioned the girl, "so you don't snap your mask feathers."

As the dominatrix circled the drain in the center of the stone floor, the medieval torture chamber exposed its horrors. To the left of the door was a tableau with an Egyptian motif. Painted like the sarcophagus from King Tut's tomb, an iron maiden stood open to show a naked wax figure bleeding from holes pierced by spikes leveled at the mannequin's groin. On the floor in front was a potter's wheel with a foot pedal to spin it. Rolls of bandages and two buckets sat on a workbench nearby. One pail was half full of plaster of Paris and the other brimmed with water.

"What's that for?" Crystal asked, her voice quivering.

"We're going to make a mummy. A Freudian mommy, in fact."

"I don't get it."

"You will, baby. Tonight's guest has special needs that pay *very* well."

"I'm scared, Suzannah."

"Good. That's the intended effect. Remember what you said upstairs about Madame Tussauds and the Chamber of Horrors? As I recall, you suggested we pretend we've got our crap dads jailed down there so they could suffer like we did."

"I said *pretend*."

"This is pretend. When we're in Paris, I'll take you to the Théâtre du Grand-Guignol and you'll see similar horrors."

Suzannah circled clockwise to the next tableau. Here, a wax figure hung in chains from a gibbet, like a real-life version of Hangman. Another mannequin had been skewered on a stake, like all those Turks executed by Vlad the Impaler, the model for Dracula. In front of them stretched a bloodstained rack with wheels and limb cuffs at its ends. In its middle was a hump designed to raise up the buttocks of whoever was clamped in. Fanged grins leered from a rack of skulls, the empty eye sockets overlooking a table spread with flogging implements and razor-sharp surgical tools. Beside that stood a propane-fueled brazier with several branding irons dangling from its rim. One brand bore the letter *S*.

"Men are swine, lover. You and I know that. They believe it's a man's world out there. But I know sex is the clock key that winds them up, and they are *not* superior to their own psychology. Men cling to a foolish delusion of what it means to be male. But the truth is that they were conditioned—like Pavlov's dog—by their mothers. And that's what I drive home down here."

"Who's Pavlov?"

"You'll see before tonight's through."

Suzannah plucked a cat-o'-nine-tails from the whips on the table.

"Rum, sodomy, and the lash. This beauty—off a British ship from the last century—taught shirtless seamen in checked pants why they must never wear stripes and checks together."

Suzannah flicked the cat's nine knotted thongs over her shoulder and let the "claws" lovingly caress her back. Then she switched the whip for another on the table.

"This one's a seventy-year-old Scottish tawse. See how the leather strap is split at one end? The hardened tips bite bare bums like an adder."

She swapped the tawse for another relic of corporal punishment.

"This, my sweet, is an English birch. The closest there is to poetry in the discipline of flogging. Have you ever been to a circus?"

"Yes," said Crystal, shaking.

"So you've seen how the ringmaster"—Suzannah swept her arm around the circular crypt—"uses a whip and a chair to tame the lions?"

The girl nodded.

"Stand back, honey, and I'll show you how I tame men the same way."

Winding up like a baseball pitcher on the mound, Suzannah whirled in a tight pirouette on the ball of one stiletto-heeled boot and lashed out with pinpoint accuracy at the hump on the rack. Her relentless *fwip-fwip-fwip* filled the glow from the flickering torch with dust and made Crystal aghast with coke-addled alarm. Each thwack of the rack drew Suzannah's cruel lips back from her teeth in a sadistic snarl, flared her nostrils like those of a bull goring a matador, and nubbed the nipples poking through the holes in her black leather bodice to knots as hard as those tied in the cat's nine tails.

Circling the drain...circling the drain...

As Crystal's wonked-out brain spun into a swoon, her whirling head angled up to the dome above the hole in the floor and caught sight of a meat hook waiting for a carcass. Blood from the meat—

Circling the drain...

—would flush away down the hole.

From the rack, Suzannah's Chamber of Horrors circled around to a guillotine, where a waxwork executioner held up a severed head. The large iron grille to the right was where the smuggler's tunnel came in from the Mississippi River. As Crystal's legs buckled and tipped her back against the grate, a hungry Doberman pinscher, its slavering jaws confined in an iron muzzle, ran up the passageway that had once fed contraband into the cave and clanged against the metal bars keeping it from the overwrought girl.

Clang...clang...clang...

The vicious dog tried to sink its teeth into her.

Whapping the whip back onto the table, Suzannah pounced across the vault like a panther going for the kill. She grabbed the Mardi Gras mask encasing Crystal's skull and reached into the shadow cast by the open door for a chain attached to the wall. Slipping a lock at the end of the chain through the loop at the back of the black girl's collar, she tethered her like a Southern slave.

"Don't mind him," Suzannah said, nodding at the ravenous beast. She might have added, "He's the cleanup crew for tonight's festivities."

"Take me home!" Crystal blubbered through her feathered face guard.

"Sweets, you're worth too much moola for us to say goodbye now. Play your part right, and tomorrow you can choose between Paris and your crap dad. Tonight, however, I'm casting you in a Grand Guignol play. These props'll help you get into character."

From a hook on the wall, Suzannah took down shackles used on a sugarcane plantation before the Civil War and clamped them around the terrified girl's wrists and ankles. The chain between the cuffs ran through the body of a grotesque voodoo doll mimicking a devilish Raggedy Ann.

Beneath her skimpy bra, Crystal's heart was pounding in her rib cage.

The hairs on her skin bristled.

Mewling with dread, the desperate girl made a mad dash for the door, skirting around a four-foot metal box between her and the open frame, until the leash tautened and yanked her off her feet, crashing her to the floor in front of the solid cage. The only breach in its face was a peephole through the steel at the same height as the gold rings piercing the sadist's labia.

Crystal shrieked when an eyeball behind the peephole blinked.

"I told you I was married. *That's* what he forced me to spawn." The dominatrix sneered with feminist hatred as cold as Canada's Arctic. "If you don't have the one you hate, you punish the one you've got. In there is my *special* project."

Through the tiny peephole, a sobbing child beseeched, "Mommy! Mommy! Forgive me, Mommy! I'm sorry, Mommy! *Please!*"

———

At 12:15 precisely, the doorbell rang.

The Axeman of New Orleans was here to wallow in Mardi Gras.

FLYING PATROLS

Vancouver, British Columbia, 1982
Saturday, October 30, 9:35 a.m.

After months of living as an undercover junkie, Katherine Spann had cleaned herself up as best she could. Yesterday's reassignment had come too late for her to have a salon cope with her rat's nest of greasy blonde hair, so she'd simply washed it, combed out the tangles, and trimmed it herself with scissors in the bathroom mirror. Her sloppy, slutty makeup and baggy, rumpled clothes had been replaced by a freshly scrubbed face and a black leather jacket over a gray top, with trim-fit black jeans and a silver buckle.

Ready to rock 'n' roll…and don't mess with me!

The sun was shining as she stepped out of a taxi at 33rd and Heather. She paid the fare and tipped the cabbie, then paused for a moment to take in the scene before commencing the long stroll up the walk to the Tudor facade of HH HQ. To the left of the door, a man in blue serge was holding a press conference, fending off a phalanx of mikes while a horde of reporters peppered him with questions.

So that's DeClercq, thought Spann.

As soon as she'd pushed through the front doors, she understood why he was holding the scrum outside in the autumn sunshine. HQ was a shambles of renovation chaos. The squad room ahead was bustling with mostly male cops, and many of them ogled her like a slab of beef in a meatpacking plant. It was all so tiring, but what can you do? No police force has a longer-standing macho culture, and too many Mounties view "respect" as a personality disorder.

The constable spied a woman sitting by herself in the briefing area and wormed her way through the crush of men, a few of them copping a feel on the sly, to join her sister-in-arms.

"They sure like you," the woman said.

"Pigs at the trough."

"Haven't seen you before."

"Got smuggled in from back east for an undercover op. I've been slumming it for the past few months. Today's my first on the surface."

"I'm Monica Macdonald."

"Katherine Spann."

The women shook hands.

"Assignment?"

"Flying patrol. Whatever that is," said Spann.

"Me too."

"Know the score?"

"I hear they're partner units."

"You and me?"

"I wish. Flying patrols pair male and female."

"Great," Spann groaned. "We get to play Russian roulette. Spin the cylinder to see if we get the chamber loaded with the sexist jerk."

"You're way too generous."

"Huh?"

"You mean the *three* chambers loaded with sexist jerks."

The women laughed.

Macdonald was at least five inches shorter than the six-foot Spann. Her body was *zaftig*, for want of a better word, which made her the target of sexual harassment as well. Her brown hair was pulled back in a chignon, and her brown eyes were suspicious. She wore a loose cream sweater over blue jeans, but it couldn't hide her voluptuous breasts. Clusters of men around the room locked eyes on her chest, then nudged each other and sniggered in conspiracy as they shared jokes.

"The ones who really irk me are the *sly* ones," said Macdonald.

"You mean the guys who pretend they like women in the Force? The ones who are too weak to say anything to your face, then fuck you in your service file?"

"Yeah. At my first post after Depot, I came down sick. So I called in ODS. My boss could have put down 'off duty sick—flu.' But no, he's gotta trace a circle around a dime and fill it in red to mean I've got my period. Every guy since who's seen that file laughs at me."

"The first corporal I worked for," said Spann, "was henpecked at home. So of course he took it out on me. He couldn't comprehend the idea of women in harness. He scored my first assignment as poor, but did say mine was 'a very well-written report.' Thankful for any crumb, I told him I'd tried to present the information in a factual, concise manner. 'No,' he said. 'I mean you have neat, easy-to-read handwriting.'"

"Jesus Christ!" said Monica. "Where do they find these dorks?"

"At the old boys' club."

"Y'ever try to file a complaint? We're the only police force in Canada without a union. There's no one to report to except the guy harassing you or his buddies."

"The first thing we've got to do is scrap our uniform," said Spann. "I didn't join the Mounted to look like I'm in the ladies' auxiliary. I joined to wear the Stetson, pants, boots, and spurs. We're caught in a culture of discrimination. What's with the silly hat, skirt, and pumps we're forced to wear?"

"I hear you, Boudica."

"You with me?"

"We'll storm the barricades," Monica agreed. "But in the meantime, how 'bout a bet? Five dollars says my flying patrol partner is a bigger jerk than yours."

"Make it ten. And a six-pack of beer."

———

At ten on the dot—*A message?* thought Spann. *When I say ten, I mean ten exactly*—DeClercq entered the squad room and took the podium.

"Good morning. I'm Superintendent Robert DeClercq. The commissioner has asked me to lead this investigation. Each of you has been handpicked for the Headhunter Squad. You know the pitfalls we faced during the Olson manhunt. This team's been organized to prevent that happening again. My second-in-command is Inspector Jack MacDougall."

DeClercq turned to the well-dressed Mountie on his right.

"That frown on the inspector's face is because he was unaware that he's just been promoted. Expect a similar reaction from Sergeant James Rodale, my third-in-command."

He turned to the Mountie on his left.

"He too has been recently promoted."

Clever, thought Spann, sitting front and center with Macdonald. *He chose blue serge to convey the perfect image of command. No plainclothes, so folks watching the press conference don't see a janitor at the helm. No red serge, so no one—including us—sees a preening peacock running things. And no brown serge, so he doesn't look like a pile of horseshit.*

The brown serge working uniform was loathed by the brass. Brown jacket, tan shirt, blue tie, brown pants, blue socks, brown shoes—ugly, ugly, ugly. Rumor had it the god-awful outfit was designed by a color-blind fashionista trying to hide her poor eyesight.

Nor were the promotions lost on Spann.

Another message? Do good work, she thought, *and you too will climb the ranks.*

Seventy cops in plainclothes were crammed into the room. Some sat on chairs, some on desks, while others leaned against the walls. As he addressed the squad, the superintendent's gaze moved from face to face, making contact with each cop's eyes. For a moment, DeClercq and Spann forged a personal bond, then the superintendent moved on to do the same with Macdonald.

"Apart from our own disquieting experience with Clifford Olson, there's a lesson to be learned from the recent hunt for the Yorkshire Ripper. Between 1975 and January of last year, Peter Sutcliffe smashed the skulls and mutilated the bodies of more than a dozen women. In 1978, the police received an audiotape and the first of three letters signed with the name 'Jack the Ripper'; the tape and the letters confessed to the murder of Joan Harrison in 1975. Swabs from her vagina and anus had tested positive for semen from a secretor with the rare blood group B. The same blood group was in the saliva that sealed the flaps of the envelopes. Experts analyzed the voice on the tape and concluded that the speaker had a Geordie accent and came from the Sunderland area, which is also where the envelopes were postmarked. Consequently, the officers hunting the Yorkshire Ripper issued a special notice to all police forces to eliminate suspects who didn't have type-B blood or a northeastern Geordie accent. One of those interviewed and discounted because he had a local West Yorkshire accent was Peter Sutcliffe, who went on to kill three more victims while police wasted eighteen months on that red herring. After his arrest last year, the Ripper went down for thirteen murders, *but not that of Joan Harrison.* The letters and the audiotape turned out to be a cruel hoax.

"So," said DeClercq, "let's smoke out our enemies."

He held up a finger.

"One: red herrings. Tips that misdirect can sidetrack our investigation. Once latched on to, red herrings become hard to shake."

He held up a second finger.

"Two: tunnel vision. No human being is an objective surveyor of the world. All cops filter sensory input through their own experiences to create beliefs. Quick to form, beliefs are resistant to change. The danger is that more weight gets placed on evidence that supports our theories and less on evidence that undermines them. Tunnel vision develops when cops become so focused on an individual or an idea—like the Ripper's supposed Geordie accent—that no other person or idea registers in their minds."

He held up a third finger.

"Three: groupthink. Human beings are governed by the herd instinct, a reluctance to think critically and challenge the dominant theory. Instead, we go with the flow. No one wants to tell the emperor—that's me—that he has no clothes."

Laughter filled the room.

"So how do we guard against red herrings, tunnel vision, and groupthink? Well, I'm a historian, so I say we reach back into our past. In 1886, Commissioner Lawrence Herchmer took command of the Force. He transformed a bunch of military men into civilian police by introducing the patrol system. First, Mounties were distributed in small detachments throughout the North-West Territories. Next, each detachment sent Horsemen out on patrol so they could keep an eye on every settler and Native resident. While riding his beat, each cop had to fill in a patrol report noting the movement of any suspicious characters. Each settler was asked if he had any complaints, and then he had to sign the form to show he'd been visited. A copy of each report and a map were sent to headquarters, where they were assembled into a comprehensive picture of crime on the plains. It didn't take long, however, for smart crooks to learn how to evade detection. So in 1890, Herchmer added flying patrols."

Macdonald elbowed Spann in the ribs.

"Here it comes," she whispered. "Want to raise our bet on who-gets-the-jerk to twenty?"

"You're on, sister."

"Most of you," said DeClercq, "have been assigned to the Central Corps—the patrol system—of the Headhunter Squad. Computers are a new policing tool. The cops hunting the Yorkshire Ripper didn't have any. We do. Computer Command is under Inspector Eric Chan, the man bringing the Mounties into the modern age. That's him standing over there. Use his expertise."

Spann took in the egghead leaning against the wall.

"Members of the Central Corps will receive a daily printout from Inspector Chan listing suspects and avenues of inquiry. Feel free to pose questions to Computer Command; you'll get software-enhanced answers back ASAP.

"Vancouver is a patchwork of police jurisdictions, but I won't tolerate divide and conquer. Enough said? The man standing by the door…"

Attention swiveled.

"…is Detective Almore Flood of VPD Major Crime. Uh-oh, he's wincing."

"It's *Al* Flood, *please*. I hate my given name."

Chuckles all around.

"Detective *Al* Flood," DeClercq emphasized, "is our VPD liaison. Detectives from other municipal forces will join him. Teamwork reigns. No personal agendas. Also, to guard against copycats, we can't have leaks. Nothing goes to reporters except through Inspector MacDougall or me. Loose lips sink ships, as they said in the war."

Everyone nodded in agreement.

"By 1890, Herchmer's patrol system had revealed its weakness. Though the Mounties were covering one and a half million miles a year, crooks knew when *not* to commit their crimes—they'd go to ground and hide out till the Horsemen passed through. So Herchmer added flying patrols that didn't follow regular routes and timetables. Instead, they functioned as a backup squad of irregular, independent commandos.

"Ten of you—paired up in five flying patrols—will have the same duty. No one knows the hunter like the hunted, so each team will have a female partner. Because your only interaction with the Central Corps will be through Sergeant Rodale, you'll be the squad's defense against red herrings, tunnel vision, and groupthink. Like the flying patrols of Herchmer's day, your job is to follow your instincts to the Headhunter's lair."

Macdonald nudged Spann. "Time to see who wins that six-pack."

"Superintendent," an urgent voice called from the back of the room, "you'll want to see this before you dismiss the squad."

All heads turned to an Ident tech wearing latex gloves and carrying a brown manila envelope forward to the podium. He didn't hand the package to DeClercq, but reached in gingerly to withdraw some papers and hold them out for him to read.

"What's going on?" Macdonald whispered.

"Something big," said Spann.

The pause stretched out for a minute before the super finally said, "We have a new development. I'm staring at a Polaroid of Joanna Portman's head on a stake. It's just like the Polaroids of the first two victims. The other document's a note constructed from clipped newspaper headlines. The note reads: *Welcome aboard, Robert. Do you think you're up to this?*"

MACHO/MACHA

11:05 a.m.

"Scarlett, you poor bastard," laughed Mad Dog Rabidowski on reading the list of flying patrol partners taped to the wall of the downstairs locker room. "They got you pussy-whipped by some broad named Katherine Spann. You'll never see me let a skirt have my back when there's a chance some punk'll start a firefight, though I might let her blow me to pass the time on a boring stakeout."

"Hey, Rusty," called Scarlett to a male cop hanging his jacket in one of the metal lockers. "Any idea who this Spann dame is?"

"That would be *me*," someone behind him said coldly.

The men turned to face two women at the foot of the stairs.

"Lordy!" said Mad Dog. "It's *Attack of the 50-Foot Amazon*. No, wait. She can't be an Amazon. She's still got both tits."

The bare-chested man flashed Spann a leer with lots of teeth, then spun his hand as if to say, "I haven't got all day."

"I get it," Spann replied.

The Amazons were mythic female warriors who supposedly cut off their right breasts so they could steady their bows and draw their arrows straight across their chests.

"Ignore him," Scarlett said, slipping her a wink after his eyes gave her the once-over. "Your tits look *great* to me."

"So you're my partner?"

"Lucky you."

"I fear this will cost me dearly," she said.

"What d'ya mean?"

"Twenty bucks. And a six-pack of beer."

"I don't get it."

"Hi, Monica," said Rusty Lewis, closing the door of his locker and joining the group at the posted list. True to his name, he was a redhead, with a freckled nose and the sleepy eyes of the actor Robert Mitchum. "I see the roster has us partnered up."

"Thank you, Jesus," Macdonald muttered, crossing herself and pressing her hands together in prayer before she held out an upturned palm to Spann.

Spann greased the palm with a twenty.

"Don't tell me you girls bet on who'd get the least handsome partner?" said Scarlett.

"Not exactly," said Spann.

For decades, this room under the Heather Stables had been used for storage. A dusty, musty basement hiding the antique furniture now in DeClercq's office, it was cleaned out yesterday and equipped with several lockers to serve as a dressing room for the flying patrols and SWAT cops, known in Mountie-speak as the ERT—the Emergency Response Team. Thanks to Rabidowski, it already smelled like a locker room. Before the briefing, he had pumped iron at the gym, adding muscles to the muscles that ripped his powerful frame. With no time for a shower, he'd high-tailed it to HQ, exuding this musky odor of maleness that he was currently civilizing by slapping deodorant into his hairy pits. If ever there was a throwback to the hard-knuckled, sharp-shooting Horsemen who'd policed the wild frontier, it was Constable Ed "Mad Dog" (from "Rabid") Rabidowski. As the son of a Yukon trapper, he was a man's man who could shoot the eye out of a squirrel at one hundred feet before he was six. When he went hunting on his days off, it was for elk on Pink Mountain or grizzly bears at Kakwa River. On days at work in the city, he hunted for bigger game: punks in shootouts or standoffs with the ERT. In sizing him up while looking down (she was taller than he was), Spann took in the jet-black hair and Neanderthal brow, the drooping macho mustache around his sardonic grin, and the "Maintain the Right" tattoo—an alternative translation of the Mounties' official motto—in big black letters on his inside right forearm.

Ugh, she thought.

Obviously pissed off at having to look up at her—*You should see me in high heels,* Spann thought—Mad Dog wrenched a pack of cigarettes from his jeans, shook out a smoke, and plucked it from the foil with his lips. Then he scratched a wooden match with his thumbnail for flame.

"Definitely an *m-a-t-c-h-o* man," quipped Spann.

Laughing, Monica broke into a chorus of "Macho Man" by the Village People, its lyrics extolling the virtues of working out and staying fit.

"Don't sell Mad Dog short," said Scarlett. "Y'oughta see his trophies. For my money, Rabid's the best marksman we got in the Force."

"Word is DeClercq's better," said Spann.

The macho man guffawed. "You call that a marksman's weapon? Crossbows went out with the Middle Ages."

"A kill is a kill. And it's silent."

"See?" said Rabidowski, turning to Scarlett. "Broads lack what it takes to be tough cops. This is why bitches will *never* serve on assault teams. With her watching your back, you'll get your ass shot to pieces. Then I gotta step over the mess to save her sweet butt."

"I can take care of myself," she said. "*And* look out for my partner."

"Bull-fuckin'-shit."

"Want to put your money where your mouth is, Mad Dog?"

The ERT cop reached down and gave his packet a heft, jingling the coins in his pocket. "Want to put your mouth where my money is, Kath?"

"I mean it."

"Are you *challenging* me? You wanna have a duel with Barbie dolls at dawn? When it comes to hardware, lady, I got you licked."

He flicked his tongue between his teeth in a meaningful way.

"Don't tell me you're *chicken*?" Spann taunted, crouching down a few inches to look him straight in the eye.

That did it.

Waving a red flag in front of a bull.

"You wanna play with the big boys? Try this on for size, Barbie. You got a four-man Emergency Response Team, and you gotta arm it to cover all the angles. We're talkin' firepower. We're talkin' shots per second. We're aimin' for accuracy. You wanna take the bet?"

"How much?"

"Say fifty bucks?"

"Sounds good to me." Spann withdrew fifty dollars from the pocket that lost twenty to Macdonald. "Who holds the pot? Who decides the winner?"

"Scarlett."

"No way. He's your lapdog. How 'bout Monica?"

"I'm a big fan of girl-on-girl action, but not when it comes to cold cash."

"So that leaves him." Spann crooked her thumb at Lewis.

"Fine by me."

"Monica?"

"He'll be fair," replied Macdonald. "Won't you, Rusty?"

"Yes, ma'am."

"Give me your history," said Spann.

"I was born on a ranch in Alberta," said Lewis, "and raised in the saddle. I just got through a stint in the Musical Ride. Currently, I'm training to help Chan computerize the Force. He's putting together a 'skinner file' of all known sex offenders. This flying patrol, I suspect, is a test."

"Sold," said Spann. "He judges."

"Ladies first?" Mad Dog offered gallantly, his voice dripping sarcasm.

"Shouldn't a team leader *lead*?"

"Okay," said Rabidowski, taking up the gauntlet. "Long barrels first. I'd arm two guys with pump-action Remington Model 870 12-gauge shotguns. Why's obvious. Scatterforce! Number three gets a sniper's rifle, the Remington Model V for Varmint, heavy barrel, caliber .22–250. The small bullet with high velocity means pinpoint accuracy combined with a flat trajectory, so no compensation required. The last guy gets a Heckler & Koch Model HK 93 assault rifle, caliber .223, with telescoping stock and roller-locking mechanism. That's German manufacturing—the current state of the art—so I'd choose semi-automatic over fully automatic. Better target control. Finally, I'd sidearm each guy with a whizbang of a short barrel: the semi-auto Beretta Model 92S pistol, caliber 9-millimeter Parabellum, with a mag capacity of fifteen rounds plus one in the spout. The Beretta's double action. The whole shebang means *Kapow!* You'll never top that, lady. So, Lewis, hand me the cash."

"James Bond uses a Beretta," Scarlett added.

"Used," corrected Spann. "M made him switch to the Walther PPK in *Dr. No.*"

Scarlett's eyes narrowed as a smile curled Macdonald's lips.

"Come on, Spann. Admit defeat," Rabidowski pressed. "Better brains than you and me put that team together. Go down gracefully."

"Better minds than yours and mine are rethinking it, Rabid. For the sake of argument, I'll keep the long barrels the same. But let's chuck those Berettas and replace them with four Ruger Security-Six .38 Special revolvers spitting either .38 Special +P ammunition or .357 Magnum. I'd take the four-inch barrel over the two and three-quarters. The Ruger's also double-action and easily field-stripped."

"Don't be a fool. Your Ruger's got only six shots compared to sixteen in my Beretta. The buzzwords in this exercise are 'greater firepower.' That means semi-auto. Not revolver."

"What about accuracy and reliability? If you don't hit the target with your first few shots, what does it matter? All four women on the team'll be dead—"

"Women! That'll be the day. We're talkin' action, not pushin' paper."

"Fact is, your firepower is in those long barrels. You're going to use the sidearm only if you're right against it. If a semi-auto misfires and jams, you're fucked. If a Ruger misfires, you pull the trigger again. Stopping to clear a Beretta wastes precious time. The Ruger's reliable."

"No go, smart broad. What about transportation? A semi-auto's thinner, and more easily concealed and holstered than a bulky cylinder. To reload, you got speed. Eject one mag and pop in another."

"Irrelevant," said Spann. "A speedloader quickly rearms a revolver. Also, the Beretta 92S is fussy in what it feeds. No good with Glaser Safety Slugs, hollow points, flat noses, wadcutters, or armor-piercing cartridges. With the Ruger, if it goes in the chamber, it fires. No choice of ammo makes the Beretta a bad pick."

All heads turned to Rabidowski, who'd run out of arguments.

Smelling blood, Spann closed in for the kill.

"You do realize that you've put the team at risk, right? Semi-autos spew hot casings out with every shot. What if one hits the guy running beside you? A second means survival, and you just dumped a red-hot cartridge down his shirt. And what about the floor? You want the team roller-skating on spent Beretta casings? The Ruger avoids that danger. In fact, why does the squad need sidearms at all? For tactical response, it's long barrels that count. But if you crave a handgun, my Ruger's the one."

"Amen," said Macdonald, turning to Lewis. "Well, judge?"

"Kathy wins."

"Mad Dog, you bum!" Scarlett groaned. "She waxed you!"

Wagging her finger at Rabid, the macha Amazon said, "That'll teach you. Times are changing, macho man. You're not the only Mountie with marksmanship crowns on the sleeve of your red serge."

The flying patrols laughed.

But Rabidowski did not.

———

The roster taped to the wall told the flying patrol cops to report to Sergeant Rodale, so they left Rabidowski below to stink up the locker room and climbed the stairs to the front hall, where Rodale stood waiting.

"You heard the super," the sergeant said, "so you know the drill. Flying patrols work apart from the main investigation. Rusty, you program computers. Monica, you work sex crimes. Inspector Chan wants you to turn his skinner file into a *practical* manhunting tool. He's up the street at Computer Command, where every sex offender case is being fed into what will eventually grow into our linkage analysis system."

"Heady stuff," said Macdonald.

"So off you go."

While Monica and Rusty made for the door, Rodale turned to the other flying patrol. "Rick, Katherine, come with me. You're also teamed up for a specific reason."

They climbed the stairs to the mezzanine and followed the railing to DeClercq's vacant office. Ushering the constables in, the sergeant led them around the horseshoe desk to the corkboard wall. "This is the super's Strategy Wall. It's where he posts all the relevant evidence for a case. Seeing it all laid in front of you like this can help you focus in on what matters and get you asking the right questions. For instance, what if the Headhunter isn't a random killer? What if his motive is tied to *one* of these three victims, while the other two are random or some kind of a smokescreen? Rick, Helen Grabowski washed ashore on your patch. Katherine, she hooked the stroll out front of the Moonlight Arms, where you've been working undercover for the past few months. Your flying patrol is to focus on this crime alone"—he tapped the center section of the Strategy Wall—"and figure out who would have wanted her dead. And one more thing: this killing is somehow linked to voodoo."

"Voodoo!" said Scarlett.

"I'll leave you two alone. Unlike the rest of the squad, you *can* have tunnel vision."

———

"So where do we start?" asked Scarlett.

"I know where we start," said Spann. "Problem is, I don't want to share it with you."

"Huh? Why?"

"You'll no doubt fuck it up."

"Wait a second, lady."

"Don't 'lady' me, *boy*. I weighed your balls in the locker room and the scales found 'em ounces short. That's what cost me the twenty."

"What *are* you talking about?"

"My bet with Monica. We put twenty on who'd get saddled with the biggest jerk. Now I've got this bag of fat hanging from my belt. Is your brain big enough to grasp just how fed up I am with sexist lightweights like you? I joined the Mounted to become a cop and work with *men*. But from the moment I first heard your voice at the bottom of the stairs, nothing's come out of your mouth but gender-based drivel aimed at my ability to do the job. 'Suck it up, baby. It's a man's world.' 'If you can't stand the heat, get out of the Force.' 'Challenge me and you'll end up in the penalty box, getting all the meaningless jobs and frozen smiles. The guys above me think the same and will back me to the hilt. And the black marks on your record will follow you through time.'"

"I'm not stupid."

"You're friends with Rabid. And I judge a *boy* by the company he keeps."

"We're not friends. We went through Depot together."

"Whatever."

"Look, let's hit the reset button, Spann. This is the biggest case you and I will ever have. I want to shine and climb the ranks, and so do you. I take back my comment about your tits. They're no great shakes."

Katherine looked stone-faced.

"Come on, smile. It's a joke. And I forgive you for that snarky comment about my humongous balls, which, by the way, are truly awesome to behold…Hey! What's that? A hint of a grin?" He smiled. "Want to bury the hatchet? Get on with the job? What say we shake hands?"

Spann eyed his paw with suspicion.

"Kathy, I was first man up on the Grabowski and Portman cases. I have a right to investigate this. With or without you."

"Truce? You mean it?"

"Hell, the way you waxed Mad Dog at his own game, it's *you* I want watching my back."

They shook hands.

"Good," he said. "So where do we start?"

"With this guy," said Spann, approaching the wall and tapping the NOPD photo of John Lincoln Hardy. "I saw him push drugs to a Native Indian named Bax in the alley out back of the Moonlight Arms."

———

Commercial Crime Section (Special "I": Electronic Surveillance)
Target: Steve Rackstraw (aka "The Fox").
Tape installed: October 30. 0900 hours. (Tipple.)
Tape removed: October 30. 1630 hours. (Tipple.)
U/M "The Weasel," now known as John Lincoln Hardy.
U/M known only as "The Wolf."

Outgoing local call: 1444 hours

Weasel: Hey.
Fox: Hey. Hey.
Weasel: What's happenin', nigga?
Fox: Waitin' on a call.
Weasel: I'm ready.
Fox: 'Bout that house youse knows?
Weasel: All moved in.
Fox: An' the filly?
Weasel: Hooked on Sister H. Now she hooks for me.
Fox: Biz good?
Weasel: Uh-uh. Stroll's too crowded. So many ladies out last night, they shoot at you, no need t' shoot at them. Pussy failed to drive them white boys wild.
Fox: H.G.?
Weasel: Nothin'. No worry, bro. Done an' dusted.
Fox: Play this right an' you'll move up.
Weasel: I ready.
Fox: Good. Be gettin' yo' juju soon.
(End of call.)

Incoming long distance call: 1557 hours

Fox: Hey. Hey.
Operator: I have a collect call from Mr. Wolf. Will you accept the charge?
Fox: I will.
(Pause.)
Wolf: It's cooking on the second. Pot boils over at midnight.
Fox: The cous'll be down to see ya.
Wolf: Better not fuck up.
Fox: He won't.
Wolf: *Au revoir.*
(End of call.)

Outgoing local call: 1601 hours

Weasel: Hey.
Fox: It's on. Time a nigga caught his ride an' was gone.
Weasel: Will do.
Fox: Enjoy the gumbo. Tell Momma hello from me.
(End of call.)

JACK-O'-LANTERN

5:40 p.m.

Tonight, the moon was almost full. And after midnight, it would become Halloween.

Double trouble.

Cops, firemen, shrinks, and bartenders don't need almanacs to tell them that the nights before a full moon experience more violence, unbridled emotion, and just plain weirdness than other times of the month. It has long been known that psych ward patients engage in their most bizarre behavior in the twenty-four to forty-eight hours preceding a full moon. The word "lunatic" says it all.

At 5:40 p.m., the hunter's moon—the blood moon—poked its pocked face up over the dark horizon and shone its eerie glow down on the jagged North Shore Mountains. Later tonight, it would stalk the Headhunter's soon-to-be Halloween victim through shadows cast by skeletal trees on the Indian reserve.

8:21 p.m.

"Sparky."

"Shut up! Go away! Leave me alone!"

"Sparky, really! Is that how you talk to your mother?"

"You're dead and buried! You're not here!"

"Oh, but I am, child. I'm down here waiting. Come downstairs and stroke my hair."

"No!"

"*Soft, soft, so soft. Come see how black it is. Black, black, black, child. As black as your evil heart.*"

"I'm not evil! You are! You make me do horrible things!"

"*Discipline, Sparky. Heed Mama's advice. There is no pleasure without pain.*"

"What you did to the Axeman! What you did to Crystal!"

"*Tsk-tsk, Sparky. What you did to the hippie. To that poor girl in Ecuador.*"

"That wasn't me! That was you!"

"*I wasn't even there.*"

"Yes, you were!"

"*Not really. Only in your head.*"

"Well, you can fuck off! I won't do what you say."

"*Yes, you will. You'll do anything I command.*"

"No, I won't!"

"*Yes, you will.*"

"No!"

"*Yes.*"

"No! AUUGGHHHH!"

"*See what I mean?*"

"Please, Mommy. No more. My head will explode!"

"*Dry those tears, Sparky. Do what Mama says. Let me hear your footsteps on the stairs. Come, child. I'm waiting. Come and stroke my hair.*"

"Please, Mommy. I'm scared! Why'd you make me look?"

11:19 p.m.

For as long as she could remember, Sister Angelica had feared All Hallows' Eve. Born in a state-funded, church-run Irish home for unwed mothers—her own had died in the ordeal of giving birth to Angelica—the devout nun had spent her entire life within Catholic confines. As a girl in a Catholic orphanage, she had shuddered to one sister's tales of terror about how Samhain, the pagan festival of the dead, had become All Hallows' Eve, when the veil between our world and the otherworld is the thinnest, allowing all kinds of ghosts and monsters to skulk among the living. The pagans would gather in covens to sacrifice beasts and humans to their unholy gods, lighting huge bonfires to keep the undead at bay. The only shield against such demons was the Catholic Church, so Angelica had taken vows to enter its protective embrace, and now as she sat alone on a pew in St. Paul's Indian Church, she nervously turned the wedding ring on her left hand that signified her as a Bride of Christ.

Sister Angelica was a virgin, like the Virgin Mary.

Hers was the purest of biblical loves.

If she could only find peace somewhere in this wicked world, and not live in fear of the unholy lust of both bestial men and priests.

Back home, in Ireland, Satan himself had infiltrated the church. Rumors were rife of priests and monks sodomizing altar boys, and of an unmarked grave at the home where she was born, filled with the bodies of hundreds of babies. There—like tonight—she'd sit alone in the parish church and stare blissfully at the nearly naked Christ on the huge crucifix towering behind the sacred altar. But as those blasphemies darkened her mind, paranoia seeped in, and with it came visions of horned priests and bewitched nuns peering in at her through the stained glass windows. Possessed by Satan, they burst in and tore the habit from her cowering body, forced her down on her hands and knees, and used her bare back as a shaking altar for their obscene Black Mass orgy.

Then the horned priests…

Then the horned priests…

Defiling the Bride of Christ in front of her husband's eyes…

And Sister Angelica *knew* she had to escape from that hellish place.

In searching the world for a Catholic community reflecting true Christian values, she discovered the Mission Reserve on the north shore of Vancouver's harbor. There, in 1863, the Oblate Fathers had established the Sacred Heart Mission among the Squamish Indians. For hours, the nun had gazed longingly at photographs of St. Paul's Indian Church, with its two Gothic Revival towers spired with blazing crosses that could be seen for miles, and its grounds ringed by humble Native houses.

As fate would have it, God was dying in this secular world. Convents no longer attracted the faithful in number to their cloisters, as they had in the pioneer days of 1898, when Bishop Paul Durieu wrote to the Sisters of the Child Jesus in Lepuy, France, asking the nuns to come to the Mission Reserve to establish a residential school for Squamish children.

And because the faithful no longer came, Sister Angelica's emigration from Ireland was a godsend to the struggling Mission Convent.

Peace at last.

Or was it?

For there were ghosts here too.

Sister Angelica tore her eyes from the body of crucified Christ to check her watch. She needed to keep track of the witching hour, which would drop the black veil to the otherworld and herald All Hallows' Eve. Time to go, for she had an uphill trudge to the convent.

Locking the church, she stepped into the ominous night. From across the stygian waters of the polluted harbor, she saw electric eyes by the hundreds of thousands leering at her from the phallic commercial towers that over time had dwarfed the steeples in their midst. But over here, on the Indian reserve, with its rundown, ramshackle dwellings and its junk-filled yards, dim porch lights were the only beacons guiding her through the dark. Whatever peace she'd hoped to find on this side of the world had dissolved in the welter of rumors about St. Paul's Indian Residential School. There, it was said, Satan had possessed the faithful too. So now, as Sister Angelica skirted the unholy site where that school had once stood, she could hear the ghostly whimpers of the Squamish children who'd been mentally, physically, and sexually abused in a state-funded, church-run hellhole designed to brainwash the Indian out of them.

Suddenly, the nun began to cry.

"Mother Mary," she prayed, "release me from this torment."

As she crossed the road and shuffled up the quiet side street to the gateposts of the walled convent, the moon beamed down upon her. The wimple about her head, neck, and shoulders was as white as her face. The cowl over the wimple was as black as the blackest hair. Black too was the habit draping down to her feet. The only bit of ostentation came from the silver crucifix glittering on her breast and the silver rosary strung down her right flank, each one gleaming as her black cloak flapped with each stride. The hand clenching the cloak round her throat flashed a silver ring.

The jack-o'-lantern unnerved her.

It stopped her in her tracks.

The carved pumpkin hadn't been glaring down from the gatepost earlier tonight, when Sister Angelica left the convent to go pray at the church.

And it hadn't been set out by the nuns to ward off Halloween demons.

No, this jack-o'-lantern was malevolent in the extreme. Its baleful eyes wavered from the candle burning within. Its nose flared as if it had whiffed the acrid sulfur of hell. Its fiendish grin was a maw of fangs and carnivorous appetite.

Sister Angelica crossed herself in the face of evil.

Creaking open the gate, the spooked nun sought sanctuary in the garden of Christ within. No sooner did she step into the shadows of the ivied wall, however, than a gloved hand clamped over her mouth and shoved her down on the ground. A punch to the forehead quelled resistance and left her dazed and confused. Vaguely, she heard material ripping and felt the chill of night cut a swath down her bare belly. She realized this was rape a moment before the hardness stabbed between her splayed legs. In stark terror, she gazed up at the demon humping her, while leather fingers muffled her cry. The Headhunter was sheathed in Gore-Tex against the spray of blood, but through holes in a black mask stretched as taut as a stocking, the nun glimpsed eyes more hateful than she thought possible in a human being. In that instant, she understood that her lifelong dread of piercing the veil to the otherworld on All Hallows' Eve was deathly *real*...

Then the knife in the killer's free hand stabbed sideways through her neck.

Sunday, October 31, 1:22 a.m.

Whatever peace and tranquility the Catholic convent had known in the past, it was gone forever. The quiet side street forgotten by time was now ablaze with flashing red-and-blue wigwags on the roofs of multiple police cars, and the night squawked with walkie-talkies as Mounties locked down the crime scene. German shepherds sniffed and barked outside the yellow tape as RCMP dog handlers tried to pick up the trail left by the fleeing killer. So tight was space that DeClercq parked a block away and hoofed back to where Jack MacDougall and Joe Avacomovitch were waiting.

"Any doubt it's the Headhunter?" he asked.

"None," replied MacDougall.

"How bad?"

"He's upped the ante from the totem pole victim."

DeClercq braced himself.

"This way," said Avacomovitch. "Let's approach from the rear. Because the back gate was locked, we know the Headhunter didn't come and go that way. Ident has yet to comb the path of contamination, so we don't want any shoes tromping in and out the front gate."

The two Mounties followed the scientist around the convent's wall to an entrance off the alley, now guarded by a cop. Once through the back gate, they moved along a walkway skirting one side of the three-story Victorian convent. Glancing into a bow window as he passed, the superintendent saw bewildered nuns huddled together in prayer. As a failed Catholic, he wondered how many of them would abandon their faith after this horrid Halloween.

Switching on a flashlight, Avacomovitch veered off the cobbled walkway at the inside edge of the garden and led both cops toward the front gate by treading across empty flowerbeds unmarked by footprints. He wanted to ensure that no forensic clues were compromised by their approach. The ground was mottled with light and shadow where the moon cast beams through overhanging trees still laden with leaves fighting a last stand against autumn. The nun lay spread-eagled near the high brick wall, a few feet to the right of the front gate.

"Christ!" muttered DeClercq.

The superintendent had seen too much of death to be shocked by atrocities. But this murder was so far beyond the pale that it defied stoicism. The headless nun lay exposed in the pool of light thrown forward by Joe's torch. With her arms stretched left and right and her bloody thighs spread wide, the nun looked as if she'd been crucified. The slash across her breasts resembled the cuts on the previous victims. But this time, the substitute for her head—which had been carried away with its cowl as a sacrilegious trophy—was a jack-o'-lantern alight with a guttering candle. Judging from the amount of blood, the Headhunter had held the nun's severed head above the pumpkin to drizzle it with enough gore to taunt DeClercq with what was surely Satan's diabolic grin.

Welcome aboard, Robert. Do you think you're up to this?

"Who's the victim?"

"Sister Angelica," said MacDougall. "She left the convent early tonight to pray at St. Paul's Indian Church on the Squamish reserve. While she was gone, someone mounted this jack-o'-lantern on one of the gateposts. A neighbor walking his dog noticed it there at about eleven. Later, when Sister Angelica hadn't returned to the convent, a nun looked out from an upstairs window and spied the jack-o'-lantern flickering in the garden. She went to investigate…and screamed bloody murder."

"Another crucifixion, like the totem victim. Is this the killer's signature?"

"Think it's a religious nut?"

"Could be," said DeClercq. "Perhaps the first two victims were posed like crucifixions too, before the bodies were buried or dumped in the water. We know both the nun and the nurse were Catholic. What about the hooker? And did the camper run into her killer at church?"

"Black Mass? Satanic cult?" suggested MacDougall.

DeClercq shrugged. "Halloween fits."

"So does voodoo," said Avacomovitch.

"Which brings us back to John Lincoln Hardy," said the superintendent.

"Scarlett and Spann are hunting for him," said MacDougall. "They put out an APB on the Weasel after yesterday's briefing."

"New Orleans was founded by the French," said DeClercq. "That ties in not only the Catholic Church but voodoo rites as well."

"Voodoo gods!" MacDougall shook his head. "Sounds more like horror fiction than real life."

"Psychosis *is* horror fiction in real life."

"Do we know the color of Sister Angelica's hair?" asked the Russian.

"No," replied MacDougall.

"I doubt that matters," said DeClercq. "Black hair is symbolic to the killer. My gut says the black cowl was enough. We'll know when we get the Polaroid."

"Too bad the pumpkin's smeared with blood," said MacDougall. "There go any fingerprints."

"Not necessarily," said the scientist. "I'll try Krazy Glue."

"Krazy Glue?"

"You'll see. It's a nifty new technique."

"Hamatsa? Lekwiltok? Pan-Indianism?" said DeClercq. "Sister Angelica went to pray at St. Paul's Indian Church. There was a lot of abuse of Squamish children at St. Paul's Indian Residential School. The nun may have been followed back to the convent and attacked at the gate by someone psychologically traumatized in that school during his youth. In those dark days, every Native kid was wrenched out of his or her home and subjected to brainwashing—and worse—from as early as age four."

"The ravine where the camper was buried is near the reserve," said MacDougall. "A lot of Native women end up on the stroll in front of the Moonlight Arms. And then there's the totem pole."

DeClercq scratched his chin. "We need a house-to-house on the reserve."

"That won't go down well," said the inspector. "They'll see it as racial profiling. To say the Natives are wary of all whites is putting it mildly. There is, however, a Plains Cree I've had my eye on for a while. He's currently using his tracking skills in the forensic lab, but he's going to climb the ranks. His anglicized name is Bob George. But he prefers to go by Ghost Keeper."

"The Human Vacuum Cleaner?" said Avacomovitch.

"That's the guy."

"Then you and I will come to blows. I've got my eye on him too. For the Ottawa lab."

"Have Ghost Keeper question the people on the reserve," DeClercq told MacDougall.

Turning back to the corpse, Avacomovitch shone the flashlight on the nun's bloody thighs, then up toward the jack-o'-lantern leering down at the naked torso.

"Virginity aside, this rape was brutal," he said. "She's torn apart. Sexual savagery of this magnitude is what I'd expect from a psycho spawned by abuse in a church-run residential school. But then why weren't the other victims Catholic nuns as well?"

"How do you see what happened?" MacDougall asked his boss.

DeClercq slipped into the Zone.

"The Headhunter carved the pumpkin and brought it with him. His target was any one of the black-cowled nuns residing in the convent. He staked out the gate and followed Sister Angelica down to the church, then came back and mounted the jack-o'-lantern on the post as an apparent prank. Hiding just inside the wall, he surprised her when she came through the gate, then raped, killed, and beheaded her in the shadowed garden. Finally, he reached up and took the jack-o'-lantern down from the gatepost. Planting the pumpkin above the nun's severed neck, he drizzled it with her blood as a grisly taunt and carried his cowled trophy off into the night."

DeClercq pulled the yo-yo back.

Then...

Was he overtired?

He had—ever since the call from Chartrand—been running on minimal sleep.

Or was it something more insidious?

Were the cracks in his psyche beginning to split?

For a second time, DeClercq slipped back into the Zone against his will. Aghast, he watched as the blood from the nun's neck was sucked back into her body, then gushed out from between her legs to pool around his feet.

The psycho-hunter's blessing was now a curse.

RIOT

Dawn

To live in British Columbia is to know the conflagration that can come with a lightning strike. Long before the white man set foot upon this shore, West Coast Natives depended on trees. Trees for longhouses, trees for canoes, trees for totem poles, trees carved into masks and costumes for sacred rituals. Then the white man came and the forest industry boomed, and the British colony earned its keep on trees, trees, trees...so much so that logging is *still* BC's economic foundation. Come the summer months, the forests are tinder dry. And all it takes is a lightning strike for the province to go up in smoke.

Until Clifford Olson, this lotusland was free from serial killers. That rampage, however, had withered its sense of security, and now, just a year later, Vancouver's women were falling prey to a psycho as sadistic as their worst nightmares.

Three women found raped, slashed, and beheaded in a few short weeks—all of them snatched off streets patrolled by the Mounties and local police.

All it would take was a lightning strike to ignite a conflagration. And this morning, Vancouverites awoke to a lightning strike in ninety-six-point type: HEADHUNTER STRIKES AGAIN, blared the banner headline from every copy of *The Province* newspaper.

NUN AS FOURTH VICTIM, screamed the subhead.

The same way a fire jumps from tree to tree to engulf a forest, fear was spreading from mouth to mouth to whip up panic.

The city of Vancouver was about to go up in smoke.

Artie Fripp made a decent living as a bottom-feeder. Well, not a "decent" living, given that his primary stock-in-trade was anything titillating to do with sex. "Titillating" was in fact Artie's kind of word. Anything having to do with "tit" was okay by him. Artie Fripp was president of Get-A-Whiff Productions, one of the city's low-rent purveyors of porn mags, books, videocassettes, sex toys, and marital aids. The shelves of his warehouse and storefront in a seedy part of town were stocked with titles like *Hump Happy* and *The Hungry Husband*. He peddled penis-shaped cigarette lighters called Flick My Dic; cartons of Prolong Cream, Lustfinger, and Hap-penis; boxes of the Anal Intruder, complete with batteries and a free butt plugger; and—a big seller with guys too shy to make it with girls—Brandy: Your Wild Teen Nympho, a life-size doll with gargantuan tits, spreadable legs, and three self-lubricating holes for your private personal pleasure.

Ka-ching! Money, money, money! Artie's business was good.

Well, that depends on your definition of "good."

Artie Fripp saw himself as a product of the sexual revolution. For him, 1967's Summer of Love was the big bang. All those drugged-out hippies and liberated women turning their libidos loose: "If it feels good, do it!" Women were on the pill, so there went the risk of preggers, and if you picked up a dose of Hong Kong dong from some GI back from Vietnam... well, diseases caught from sex could be cured by popping pills. Then came the disco years and all those swingers out to get fucked every night of the week, the dudes in their bell-bottoms and the chicks in their slinky dresses, dry-humping around the dance floor to "Da Ya Think I'm Sexy?" and other hits. Sex without add-ons got dull awfully quick. And what about all those poor schlubs without the looks to make it among the beautiful people?

Well, Uncle Artie was here.

So now it was 1982 and sex was big business, a recreational sport freed from the fears of the past, and the cash registers at Get-A-Whiff overflowed with green. Artie's sideline in Halloween costumes, candy, and fireworks had topped up the till enough to send him on a beach-hopping holiday to several topless hotspots, and that's why the porn king had wheeled his Corvette into the parking spot out front for one more day of selling junk to the great unwashed before he packed his thong and flew off into the sun.

Artie, however, was unaware that his name topped the Dirty Dozen: a hit list compiled by the Wimmin's Strike Force, a radical feminist brigade that was as mad as hell and not going to take it anymore—even before they'd heard the news about the butchered nun.

This morning, to show they meant it, the guerrillas were out for action.

Striding from his Stingray to Get-A-Whiff's entrance, Artie stuck his key in the lock and swung the door open. Before going in, he stopped to admire his window display—a harem of Brandy: Your Wild Teen Nympho dolls in sexy T&A-revealing lingerie, fawning over a Big Bill: Your Bucking Stud doll, with its foot-long plastic penis for your private personal pleasure. The orange-and-black banner arced above read, SHOW HER A TRICK AND GIVE HER A TREAT FOR HALLOWEEN.

Lost in the reflection of chest hairs and gold chains, Artie was shocked when a brick smashed through the plate glass window, spraying him with shards that cut his cheek. Whirling, he saw a gang of women rushing toward him, their faces hidden by green witch masks. Some carried bricks, others wielded baseball bats, and Artie wasn't going to stick around and confront them. Retreating into his store, he slammed the door and locked it, then dashed for the counter phone to call the cops.

In a way, Artie got his just desserts. Last night was Get-A-Whiff's annual Halloween party, when Artie laid on the largesse for his staff. The booze was flowing freely when one of the girls—all women under forty were "girls" to him, and after that, they became "old broads"—flipped open a box containing a powerful new electric dildo marketed as Hum a Different Tune and switched it on. The vibrator jumped out of her hands and hit the floor, spinning around wildly as the drunken girl giggled, "More fun than spin the bottle!"

The reverie had petered out with the dildo still on the floor. Now, as Artie dashed across the store to the phone, he hit the vibrator like a slapstick comedian slipping on a banana peel. His feet flew out from under him in a clown's pratfall, and he crashed down hard on the floor, twisting his ankle, breaking his elbow, and wrenching his spine.

Writhing in pain, Artie saw Get-A-Whiff's window display hurled out into the street. Then the front door was kicked in, splintering the lock.

A pair of steel-toed workman's boots stomped toward him.

"Pig!" snarled the woman wearing the boots.

Then, as hard as she could, the guerrilla kicked the porn king in the teeth.

———

It isn't fair, thought Kurt Schmidt, throwing his pencil down in disgust on the ledger sheet. *How can a change in technology gut a business almost overnight? Damn videocassettes!*

For two decades, Schmidt had owned the Kit Kat Klub and Theater on Hastings Street, an underground emporium of peep shows and skin flicks. For their personal pleasure, members of the not-so-exclusive Klub could rent voyeurs' cubicles by the half hour and gawk through keyhole-shaped mini-windows at down-and-out women masturbating. The cinema next door was what's called a grindhouse, a venue for raunchy sexploitation films like the current fare: *Hot Dames on Cold Slabs.*

In a long-running heroic (depending on your definition of "hero") fight against the forces of repression, Kurt Schmidt had battled Canada Customs over its refusal to allow fuck films across the border, the provincial censor over in-and-out footage, and the VPD vice squad's attempts to shut him down. Charged with obscenity, he'd gone to jail twice, and twice he'd fought himself free in the courts. It looked like he'd go on forever peddling his cheesy filth and pocketing his ill-gotten gains…but then some fucking asshole invented videocassettes.

Now most Kit Kat wankers and jack-off voyeurs preferred to stay home and watch hardcore porn queens steam up their TVs, bleeding Kurt's business dry.

He was bankrupt!

Ergo, there could not have been a worse time for the phone to ring.

"Yeah?" he barked into the handset.

"Trouble, Mr. Schmidt." It was the box office clerk. "A bunch of feminists stormed in without buying tickets. And now they're tossing paint."

Slamming down the phone, Schmidt pushed away from his desk and waddled his girth through the door to the Kit Kat's lobby. The theater looked like a scene from *The Texas Chainsaw Massacre*, there was that much gruesome red splotched on the walls. From the shouts and curses booming out of the auditorium, it was obvious where the intruders were at this moment. Yanking open the door, Schmidt was outraged to find several black silhouettes spattering *Hot Dames on Cold Slabs* with balloons of paint.

"That screen cost a thousand bucks, you dykes!" he bellowed.

In the shaft of light cast in from the lobby, a witch mask turned toward him.

"You skank snatch!" fumed the porn peddler.

Though his fuck flicks didn't have the gravitas of films by the Master of Suspense, the multi-chinned Kurt Schmidt looked rather like Alfred Hitchcock. Lumbering like a hippopotamus toward the witchy woman, an urban guerrilla in combat pants and workman's boots, one toe of which was caked with fresh blood, the livid lecher clenched his hand into a fist and pulled it back to punch.

"Pig!" snarled the woman as she took a swipe at him with a cutthroat razor like the gleaming blade his grandfather had used to shave.

Luckily for Schmidt, he was also built like Alfred Hitchcock. The razor slit through his shirt and slashed across his belly. If not for the flab insulating his gut with inches of jiggly blubber, the cut would have dumped his intestines onto the floor.

———

While the Wimmin's Strike Force worked down through the Dirty Dozen, several less radical feminists were setting up for a noontime Take Back the Night rally in Robson Square, between the old courthouse and the new law courts. Because today was Sunday and because the fear factor in Vancouver was already sky-high, the rally was certain to draw a sizable crowd. But when news of the nun's murder spread like wildfire after the city awoke, not only did that motivate thousands more to get out and protest the plight of preyed-upon women, but the anger also kicked in the snowball effect—a chain of random events increasing in momentum until it's impossible to stop.

By eleven thirty, the square was full and so were the surrounding streets. Handheld signs waving in the air read, WOMEN UNITE AGAINST VIOLENCE AGAINST WOMEN, EVERY MAN IS A POTENTIAL RAPIST, and (no mincing words) YOU CAN'T RAPE A .38. Near noon, several women standing on ladders draped a banner between the courthouse columns. It depicted a bare-chested, muscle-bound man like those on romance novel covers, but this one was lacking his handsome head. In the lower left corner was the animated Queen of Hearts from Disney's version of *Alice in Wonderland*. OFF WITH HIS HEAD! screamed the scarlet letters in the dialogue bubble billowing from the Queen's mouth.

"Off with his head…"

"Off with his head…" the crowd began to chant.

Meanwhile, across town, the bleachers of an old wooden stadium were filled to capacity with boozed-up louts and yobs waiting for the annual Old Jocks' Chariot Race, a blue-collar sports tradition dating back to the 1930s, in which men as drunk as the fans pulled carts full of manure *Ben Hur*–style around the track while charioteers pelted each other with dung.

It was all in a good cause. The five-dollar admission fee went to charity.

The snowball effect, however, kicked in when an organizer standing near the announcer's mike tuned his portable radio to the news station to hear if the race was being promoted. Instead, he picked up the goings-on in Robson Square, broadcasting what came over the airwaves through the stadium's loudspeaker to the shit-faced yobs.

"Off with his head…"

"Off with his head…"

The rally's anti-male chant riled the Neanderthal jocks.

"Headhunter four! Women zero!" a drunk yelled from the bleachers.

"Headhunter four! Women zero!" the jocks picked up the gibe.

Before long, that too made the news and got back to Robson Square, where it was channeled through speakers to a mob already as mad as hell and not going to take it anymore.

"Off with his head…" morphed into "Kill the pigs…"

Unfortunately, that expression had more than one meaning. "Kill the *sexist* pigs," yes. That was understandable, given the situation. But the words also called to mind counterculture protests of the 1960s, when "Kill the pigs" meant "Kill the police!" And the riot squad was near enough to hear.

There are no longer mounted Mounties in the city of Vancouver. The only mounted cops are with the VPD. Since 1909, the Mounted Squad has patrolled the over one thousand acres and more than a hundred miles of roads and trails in Stanley Park. In times of unrest, like the labor strikes in the 1920s and 1930s and the Gastown Riot by pot-smoking hippies in 1971, the urban cavalry is used for crowd control and dispersal. With so many protesters crowding the square, the Take Back the Night rally had the potential to get out of hand, so that's why the squad was secretly moved from its stables in the service yard near Stanley Park's Rose Gardens to a staging point in a parking lot near the space between the courthouses.

In riot gear, the mounted cops clutched long batons.

Still, the snowball effect might have been avoided had Fernand Zirpoli not decided to work the crowd.

With his straggly Einstein hair and snaggle teeth, Zirpoli didn't look like your classic Latin lover. He did, however, hail from Rome, the Eternal City, the fabled land of gigolos and bottom-pinchers, as any well-traveled female will attest. He found Canadian women less resigned to groping, and as a result, he had racked up four convictions for indecent assault. In psychological terms, Zirpoli's paraphilia was frotteurism: intense sexual arousal achieved by rubbing against unwilling women in crowded public places. His MO was to buttocks bump toward the front of a gathering of females—as he was doing now—while his arms brushed breasts beside him for an added thrill. "'Scuse me. 'Scuse me," he apologized as he advanced.

The frotteur was hard as hell in his pants as he neared the front of the rally. A rub or two more and it would be "Thar she blows!" for Moby Dick. That's when a feminist with electric-blue hair and knee-high boots came down from the stage to gather roving mike comments from the protesters. Tipsy from a liquid brunch, the two women standing between her and Zirpoli tottered on their high heels. As the feminist extended the mike to one of the wobblers, the Latin lover gave her a pump for his not-so-private pleasure, and that provoked her to yell, "Help! This pig's trying to rape me!" in amplified decibels.

"Kill the pig!" the mob retorted in sisterly support, and that was all the encouragement the other wobbler needed to whip off one of her high heels and take a swing at Zirpoli. The spike struck him in the eye and he squealed like a stuck pig, his scream so strident that it grated on the crowd's nerves like fingernails scratching a blackboard, and that ramped up clashing fight-or-flight responses.

The fighters surged to grab the rapist and tear him apart for all the fear they'd suffered from men in their lives, while the recoilers realized they could get trampled and shoved back in a desperate attempt to break out of the claustrophobic crush. Steamed by the shouts of "Kill the pigs!" and reacting to the blood-chilling shriek from Zirpoli, the commander of the Mounted Squad gave the order for the cavalry to muscle into Robson Square and clear it.

Pandemonium!

Chaos!

Panic!

At street level, it seemed like the Four Horsemen of the Apocalypse were thundering in. The clatter of horses' hooves echoed off the surrounding office towers as vapor clouds snorted from the steeds' flaring nostrils and armored knights swinging clubs rode into battle. Cries, curses, and the crack of wood on bone followed, then the screams of those trampled underfoot. One of the horses stumbled on a fallen protester, throwing its rider from the saddle into the midst of the enraged mob. "No more violence!" a feminist yelled as she pulled the baton from his hand and turned it back on him, pummeling the cop to a pulp. Soon the heart of the city wailed with sirens as patrol cars skidded to a halt and reinforcements jumped out to flush out rioters cowering in doorways and club them black and blue.

———

Handguns are hard to obtain up here because there's no constitutional right to bear arms. But down there, in Washington State, "equalizers" are readily sold to those with hard cash. This afternoon, two women returning from a shopping spree in Seattle got flagged for a random Canada Customs check. In searching under the backseat of their car, the diligent guard found fifty-two lightweight, aluminum-framed, double-action, short-barreled Colt Cobra revolvers, along with lots of .38 Special ammunition, purchased from a no-questions-asked arms dealer known to the biker brother of one of the smugglers.

Like the rally sign said: *You can't rape a .38.*

SKINNER FILE

Joseph Avacomovitch had worked through the night. Once the Ident techs were finished with the jack-o'-lantern left by the Headhunter at the nun's murder scene, he boxed up the bloody pumpkin and took it to the RCMP forensic lab in the mushroom-shaped building beside HH HQ. There, he subjected the head substitute to the cyanoacrylate-fuming method to expose any fingerprints.

Fingerprints get left behind because the ridges on our fingertips ooze sweat containing amino acids, fatty acids, and proteins. Visible prints on smooth surfaces like glass are easily photographed by dusting them with white powder, but latent prints on uneven, hard-to-dust surfaces like knife and gun handles, bloody pumpkins, and even dead bodies require the intervention of Krazy Glue.

To create as gruesome a jack-o'-lantern as imaginable, the Headhunter had drizzled blood from the nun's severed head over the pumpkin, creating gory red and orange stripes. Any fingerprints under the blood would be irretrievable, but if the forensic gods were smiling, prints hidden on the pumpkin's bare surface could be recovered.

To that end, Joe placed the jack-o'-lantern into an airtight fish tank, along with a small heater—a coffee cup warmer—and a dish of water. After squeezing a few drops of Krazy Glue into an open aluminum container, he set it down on the heater and sealed the tank. When the glue reached its boiling point, it turned into cyanoacrylate gas, the fumes of which reacted with the organic compounds in the sweat of two fingerprints on the pumpkin shell, forming a sticky white substance along the ridges.

When he opened the tank, the lab filled with a noxious odor of toxic fumes. Light-headed from the chemicals, Joe crossed to the window and watched dawn break in a red smudge behind Little Mountain. Once the fumes had dissipated, he returned to work. Reaching into the tank, he lifted up the pumpkin and carried it across to the camera bench, where he photographed the results. Now—if his luck held—the loops, whorls, and arches would match those in one of the twenty-four thousand sets of prints on file from BC in the RCMP Report Center in Ottawa.

Yawning and stretching, Joe rubbed his eyes with the backs of his huge hands. He was bone-tired but still had much to do. Leaving the lab, he paused in the morning sunshine to breathe in fresh air and listen to the song of a bird that hadn't gone south, then he walked next door to the Tudor building to have the communication center wire the pumpkin prints back east.

"Joe," Sergeant Rodale hailed him in the entrance hall.

"Good morning, Jim."

"You look beat. You should be saying good night."

"That bad?"

"Time to crash. You can't work round the clock."

"Where's Robert?"

"Upstairs. He worked all night too."

"Anything new?"

"Just got this from Interpol." The Mountie waved a bunch of printouts. "Looks like we've ID'd the North Van camper. The bones found by the creek. Liese Greiner, a German national, left Switzerland this summer to camp in the Rockies. She hasn't been heard from for months. Six years ago, she broke her leg in a car accident. Interpol wired several X-rays of her fractures."

Joe held up an evidence pouch. "Want to swap forensics? I recovered these fingerprints from the jack-o'-lantern left in the convent garden. If you'll check for a match with Ottawa, I'll compare the X-rays of the fractures with the campsite skeleton."

The manhunters exchanged packages, then Avacomovitch climbed the stairs to inform DeClercq of his fingerprint find before going to the morgue.

"Oh no!" exclaimed Monica Macdonald as she entered the cubbyhole assigned to her flying patrol in the operations building two doors up the street from the Headhunter Squad. "Don't tell me I've got a Mad Dog macho man on my hands? Are you going to crow that while I was snoozing the wee hours away, you were burning the midnight oil, slaving over that computer and crunching files till dawn?"

"No, I got in early," said Rusty. "I'm a lark, not an owl."

"Then make my day, Mr. Lark. Tell me the early bird got the worm."

"I'm still pecking."

Monica set down a paper bag on a table piled high with sex crime files, then shucked her parka and hung it on a hook. So confining was the room that it barely held the work surface and two chairs. The blank, windowless walls reminded her of a solitary confinement cell.

"I come bearing gifts," she said, opening the bag. "Coffee? Danish?"

"What kinda pastry?"

"Custard. Cherry. Got you both. I'm not cheap."

"Plunk down beside me and I'll show you what I'm doing."

Yesterday after the briefing, they'd gone up Heather Street to Computer Command, where Inspector Chan had set them up with a terminal and access to the files collected in the main room. Monica's first comment on closing the door had been, "Okay, Encyclopedia Brown, show me how all this computer stuff works."

"Computers are the future of psycho-hunting," Rusty explained. "The Geordie tape mentioned by DeClercq wasn't the only screwup in the Yorkshire Ripper manhunt. The British cops worked without a computer, storing hundreds of thousands of bits of information on handwritten index cards. The floor of their incident room had to be reinforced to keep it from collapsing under the weight of so much paper. Sutcliffe was interviewed nine times, and the Brits opened three separate files on him, each with his name spelled differently. Drowning in information and lost in a blizzard of paperwork—"

"Not to mix metaphors," Monica teased.

"—the psycho-hunters couldn't see the forest for the trees."

"Bad to worse," she groaned.

"The cops assumed those three Sutcliffes were three different men, and the backlog of unprocessed paper meant they failed to connect vital pieces of related information. Cards got misfiled, mislaid, and overlooked. And the Ripper kept butchering women."

"Sounds like Olson."

"Uh-huh. When a manhunt's plagued by turf wars, staff transfers, personality clashes, and fouled lines of communication, it all comes down to *links*."

"*Computer* links?"

"Bingo. So meet this brainy baby."

Lewis gave the hardware on the table a paternal pat.

"No doubt it's a she?"

"Huh?"

"Ships and hurricanes, until recently. Why do guys name objects and disasters after us?"

He held up both hands in mock surrender. "I'm no Mad Dog. *You* pick a name."

"Sherlock?" she suggested.

"Sherlock it is."

"Sherlock the Computer. So how does he track down crooks?"

"Imagine a future when all the forensic details of all major predators and crimes from coast to coast to coast and along the U.S. border are stored in our Ottawa database. Any cop with a computer and security clearance can type in keywords that link to similar words in those files. Let's say a psycho with gap teeth bites his victim. Typing in 'gap teeth' will pull up every criminal described as having gap teeth. The Yorkshire Ripper killed with a hammer and a knife. At the time of his arrest, Peter Sutcliffe tried to hide a hammer and a knife behind some shrubbery. Today, if we typed in 'hammer knife,' Sherlock would nab him."

"Is there a term for that?"

"Scoring a hit."

"You score a hit by linking a crime to a crook or his past MO?"

"You got it."

"How many are files in the system?"

"Hundreds."

"Doesn't sound like many."

"This is our tomorrow. It's in the early stages. That's why I want in *now*. To spearhead where it's going."

"Are most of the files murder cases?"

"Mainly. But the database is expanding to include sexual assaults."

"That skinner file that Rodale mentioned? Is that 'skinner' in the sense of prison slang for a sex offender?"

"You got it," said Rusty. "The thinking is that a sex killing is basically nothing more than a fatal sex assault. Serial psychos are driven to kill again and again. Trauma from the past gets scripted into a fantasy of revenge that the killer feels compelled to act out. Often he'll rehearse with non-fatal sex assaults before the curtain goes up. But because reality never lives up to fantasy, his killings become more grisly as he tries to get them right. That's why Jack the Ripper's last victim was literally torn to shreds. What those early, non-fatal assaults provide are links to *living* witnesses."

"Too bad the system is currently so hit-and-miss."

He shrugged. "Better than nothing."

"Okay, Captain Tomorrow. Let's give it a shot."

"Keywords?"

"Let's go with the obvious: 'severed head.'"

The wannabe cyber sleuth tapped the keyboard to set the game afoot, then sat back as Sherlock filled the screen with case file numbers. They were linked to several domestic disputes involving decapitated corpses, but the interesting lead was to a bizarre murder in a skid row flophouse full of junkies and drunks. Two men were apparently vying for the attention of the same woman. One night, she answered a knock on her door. There stood one of her suitors with a romantic gift. "I love you," he professed, offering her a plate bearing the head of the other man. In Mark 6:14–29, Salome asks for the head of John the Baptist on a plate. So the local cops—connoisseurs of gallows humor—dubbed this case the John the Baptist Murder. But when Rusty called the Riverside Unit for the criminally insane, he was told the psycho was securely locked away.

Despite the computer, links were slow to come. The database was essentially just a keyword index to thick paper files, so the two Mounties still had to shuttle to the main room for crime scene photos, police reports, and documents detailing each murder.

"Sure would be simpler," Monica said, "if the files were stored in Sherlock."

"One step at a time."

As yesterday afternoon wore on, they'd tried other keywords—"trophy hunting," "crucifixion," "totem pole"—but when those trails went cold too, they called it a day.

Today, as Rusty sat sipping his coffee and munching the cherry Danish, Monica moved her chair into position and studied the screen.

"Can I have a go?"

"Type away." Rusty held up the sticky pastry with gooey fingers. "If I gum up the keyboard, that'll be the end of my chance to join Chan's squad."

"Why are men so obsessed with women's breasts?" she asked rhetorically. "Why do guys go gaga over a pair of modified sweat glands? How many times a day do I mutter, 'Hey, my eyes are up here'? It's gotta go back to Mom, dontcha think?"

"I'm hurt."

"Not you, Rusty. You don't ogle my tits."

"It takes willpower." He slipped her a wink.

"Ah, so you're normal?"

"*Abnormal*, don't you mean?"

"No, what's abnormal is the Headhunter slashing his victims' breasts. I figure his fantasy must be about getting even with Mom. And if sex assaults were his training ground, then the keywords most likely linked to his MO are—"

She typed in "breast mutilation" and hit the enter key.

Sherlock came back with a list of skinners and their case file numbers.

In whittling that down, Rusty headed for the main room and fetched a folder labeled MATTHEW PAUL PITT.

———

"Get a load of this."

Monica passed Rusty a crumpled piece of paper covered with child-like scribbling. It came from the file amassed when Matthew Paul Pitt was arrested for—but not charged with—stabbing a stripper last year.

My drems are very weerd. I hope I can remember my drem to night cause I want a gril with tits. Maybe why I can't remember my drems is because someone is maken me forget them, so I can't write them down, or its something to do with me. I got to get out of hear. It is almost like I am be in Brain Washed every time I wake-up. I just keep on sayin to myself, I am going to meet a gril with tits in my Drem or Drems tonight. I will tell you about the drem to-morrow when I wake-up. thats if I Remember it. never know I mite meet you.

Good night, Sleep tite, and don't
Let the Bed Bugs bite.
Good night.
Tits! titstitstitstitstitstitstitstits! tits! tits! TITS!

"I'll see your bet," Rusty said, "and raise you this."

He gave Monica a notebook also from the file. The book began with a diatribe in the same childlike scrawl: *Women are like screen doors. once they get Banged a few times they loosen up.* After that, the pages were filled with hundreds of black line drawings of erect penises dotted with sores in red ink.

Monica winced. "What a weirdo. Pitt gives me the creeps."

Photos of the suspect were spread across the table between them. The mug shot depicted a scruffy, wild-eyed young man with long, tangled hair uncombed for months and a crusted, unkempt scraggle of beard circling a mouth of cold sores. His gaunt, bony features made him look like a ghoul. His filthy, open-throated shirt revealed ladders of scars climbing his scrawny neck. His shirttail hung out of muddy jeans held up by logger's suspenders, and overall, Pitt looked decades older than he was. Other photos caught hundreds of self-abuse scars on his arms and legs.

"Crazy eyes," said Monica. "Where have I seen them before?"

"Manson, minus the swastika," her partner replied, alluding to the Helter Skelter killers of the acid-tripping sixties.

The police report outlined the sexual assault. Late last year, on a foggy night, a stripper had left her workplace by the alley door. Someone was lurking in a dark doorway in the lane, and this person had grabbed her from behind, punched her to the ground, and stabbed her in each breast with a short-bladed penknife. The cops searched nearby harborside woods and found Matthew Paul Pitt—who'd recently been released after twenty years in psychiatric institutions—sleeping rough in a tent. When asked about the blood on his clothing (which turned out to have come from a slash on his own arm), he told police: "I like seeing blood on TV, but I like my own blood better. Is it true that women have the reddest blood of all?"

Detectives tossed his tent and seized a plastic bag full of matchbooks advertising local strip clubs. The breasts of the naked women printed on the covers were jabbed with pins, and that was enough for the cops to conclude that they had their man. That was also what had linked the keywords "breast mutilation" to Pitt's skinner file.

"You read the psych report, Mon?"

"The part about the heads?"

"And about his mom?"

To determine Pitt's fitness to appear in court, a Crown psychiatrist had reviewed his decades in mental institutions. His single mother had killed herself when he was four, leading to his placement in a foster home. His pathological hatred of his mother "for abandoning him" had compelled the delinquent to tear the heads off the dolls collected by his foster parents' biological daughter. His violent tantrums resulted in a misdiagnosis of "retarded but without psychosis," and for years, the boy was confined to a warehouse for subnormal children. In fact, Pitt had an IQ of 128, which was above average to superior.

What he really had was a learning disorder that undercut his ability to read, write, and count. Surrounded by inmates with whom he couldn't communicate, the volatile youth had turned in on himself and taken up residence in a fantasy world of revenge. With the passing of years, he had developed BPD—borderline personality disorder—but when the province began emptying mental asylums in hard economic times, Matthew Paul Pitt was freed to roam the mean streets of Vancouver.

"How'd he beat the stripper rap?" Monica asked.

"Insufficient evidence, according to the Crown. She couldn't ID him. The cops had no forensics. And voodoo doll matchbooks weren't enough."

"So Pitt walked."

"Yep."

"And camped in the trees."

"Same as the woman buried by the North Van creek."

"I wonder what she looked like…"

"The skeletal vic?"

"What if she ran short of cash and got a job stripping?"

"Flaunting her 'gril tits' at Pitt?"

"Maybe his revenge fantasy started with strippers and hookers, then turned to nurses and nuns."

"Pitt ticks a lot of boxes," Rusty agreed. "Loathes Mom. Beheads dolls. Sinks into BPD. Flies from the cuckoo's nest. And maims breasts."

"What if Pitt haunts strip dives to rev up his hate, watching babes bare their boobs before skulking off to kill substitutes for Mom?"

"I see where you're going." He flashed her a lecherous grin.

"What say we crawl the bars in Pitt's matchbook collection to see if he's ogling ecdysiasts wrapped around stripper poles?"

"*Ecdysiasts*?" Rusty said.

Monica held up an academic finger.

"From *ecdysis*, meaning 'to molt,'" she said.

"Who thought that up?"

"A wordsmith named H.L. Mencken. When a stripper named Gypsy Rose Lee asked him for a more dignified way to refer to her profession."

Damn!

Mad Dog Rabidowski had to concede that the Ruger Security-Six revolver in blue carbon steel finish was a good-looking handgun. Following yesterday's verbal shootout with Spann down here in the locker room, the ERT cop had placed an order for her winning suggestion with his local gunsmith at How the West Was Won. And because he was a kick-ass with the right permits, the rod was delivered fast.

Fill your fist, asshole.

Rabidowski favored the black turtleneck–sports jacket combo of Steve McQueen in *Bullitt*. With the jacket off, he strapped on a shoulder holster that hung above the Beretta secured on his hip, then he opened a box stamped with Ruger's eagle logo. Withdrawing the heavy-duty revolver, he flipped open the cylinder to chamber it with six .357 Magnum rounds. He then holstered the revolver with its butt to the front, making it possible to draw the Beretta with one hand and cross-draw the Ruger with the other for a two-gun *bangbangbang!* When it came to firefights, it helped to be ambidextrous.

Lawmen like Wild Bill Hickok had carried two guns.

Now so did he.

Standing in front of the locker room mirror, Mad Dog admired himself. The taut black turtleneck clung to his gym-pumped pecs and six-pack abs. Whoever said black and brown don't go together hadn't seen this outfit, for the straps of the brown shoulder holster running down his black chest made him look primed for action. No wonder American bulls took to the armpit look.

Cross-hand, Quick Draw Rabidowski whipped out the Ruger.

"You talkin' to me?"

Taxi Driver.

Holstering the gun, he waited…waited…then whipped it out again.

"You've gotta ask yourself one question: 'Do I feel lucky?' Well, do ya, punk?"

Dirty Harry.

Holstering the gun, he waited…waited…then whipped it out again.

"I've heard that you're a low-down Yankee liar."

"Prove it."

Shane.

"What *are* you doing?" a voice behind the gunslinger asked.

Faster than he could draw the Ruger, Mad Dog whipped around to face Sergeant Rodale at the foot of the stairs.

"Uh…practicing, Sarge."

"Is that a Ruger Security-Six I see in your hand?" The smile on his lips told Mad Dog that the sergeant knew who came out on top in yesterday's macho/macha gunfight.

"You heard?"

"The entire squad heard. These walls have ears. Glad you're taking it so well and trying out Spann's piece. Rumor had you as a sexist."

"Not me," Mad Dog lied.

"Grab your coat, saddle up, and let's take a ride." Rodale waved a sheet torn off a teleprinter. "The fingerprints lifted from the jack-o'-lantern match a local named Fritz Sapperstein. He's got a record for assault, and he lives on a farm in the delta."

"Want me to scramble the team and hit him gangbusters?"

"No. A delta farm is flat as far as the eye can see. Going in with an army means we have no element of surprise. Let's sneak up on Mr. Sapperstein and see what he has to say."

A sunny drive south from the Heather Stables took them over the north arm of the Fraser onto Lulu Island, a sprawling chunk of rich brown farmland choking the mouth of the river. They parked their ghost car this side of an open drainage ditch, then crossed the moat on a footbridge to an open-air market offering a cornucopia of fruit and vegetables harvested from the bountiful fields beyond. The proprietor was a man in a grocer's apron stocking barrels of apples. They approached him from behind.

"Mr. Sapperstein?" Rodale asked.

"Yes," the man replied, no doubt expecting a customer. Then he turned around and saw the badge in the sergeant's hand.

"Fritz Sapperstein?"

"Yes?"

"I'm Sergeant Rodale of the Mounted Police."

The farmer scowled.

Wary.

Mad Dog cracked his jacket to allow Sapperstein a peek at the butt of the Ruger.

"Yes?"

Twitchy.

"Last night, a woman was murdered. The killer left a jack-o'-lantern in place of her head. Fingerprints on the pumpkin match yours from your assault arrest."

"What? That was a barroom brawl."

"Explain your prints."

Sapperstein shook his head. "You guys are a pain in the ass. See that barren field?" He pointed to one of his harvested acres. "Weeks ago, it was orange with *thousands* of pumpkins. Not only do I sell 'em here, but I also stock Vancouver supermarkets for Halloween. See these callused hands?" He held them up. "They got like that 'cause I work this farm myself to keep in shape. Can I toss you an apple without your sidekick plugging me?" Selecting a rosy red McIntosh from the bin, Sapperstein polished it on the bib of his overalls and passed it to the Mountie. "A buck says my prints are on that apple too."

Smirking, he reached into his pocket and withdrew a dollar bill.

"I don't gamble, Mr. Sapperstein."

Dead end, said the triumphant glower in the farmer's eyes.

"If I killed someone, you wouldn't find my prints. One thing a farmer learns from mucking in manure is the wisdom of wearing gloves."

A short cab ride north on Cambie Street from 33rd Avenue to 12th and a jog west back to Heather Street brought Joseph Avacomovitch to the door of the VGH morgue. By the time he'd entered the autopsy room, the Russian quite literally felt like a ghoul thanks to jetlag, the sleep-depriving red-eye flight, and the late night amid toxic fumes in the forensic lab. Psychologically, Joe was merely *haunting* the autopsy room instead of rolling up his sleeves and concentrating on the task at hand.

I'll check the bones, he thought, *then go sleep and come back later.*

Jurisdictionally, the bodies of the four Headhunter victims should have been scattered around morgues in the city of Vancouver and its suburbs: the floater at Richmond General, the camper and the nun at Lions Gate Hospital, and the crucified nurse at VGH. The Headhunter Squad, however, was set up to prevent the turf wars among rival police departments that had let Olson go undetected, so it only made sense to bring the victims to one place. Where was the logic in having a clue missed because the four bodies weren't gathered in one morgue? Its central location made Vancouver General Hospital the best choice, and that's why Joe was here.

Armed with the Interpol X-rays and his Murder Bag.

The relatively fresh corpses of Joanna Portman and Sister Angelica were side by side on gurneys in the main dissecting room. The rotting remains of the camper and Helen Grabowski were side by side on gurneys in the adjoining isolation chamber. Evolution has hardwired humans to find the stench of putrefaction revolting and repulsive. Objectively, Joe the scientist found that intriguing. But subjectively, Joe the human fought his own revulsion when he entered this charnel cell ripe with putrid flesh.

Retreating to the dressing room, he put on a chlorophyll mask.

That was better.

Now down to work.

Back when he was a student in the Soviet Union, Joe had read every history of forensic science on the shelves of the library. His hero was the patron saint of CSIs: Sir Bernard Spilsbury, the British pathologist who shot to fame in the early 1900s through his groundbreaking work in the Crippen case, the Brides in the Bath murders, the Brighton trunk murders, the Blazing Car murder, and other puzzles. In 1924, Spilsbury entered a Sussex bungalow known as the Crumbles to help Scotland Yard piece together a dismembered woman. Patrick Mahon had butchered his lover, Emily Kaye, to keep her pregnancy from ruining his life. A trail of blood ran from the sitting room, where he'd chopped her with an axe, across a hall and through a bedroom to the scullery. There, using a knife and a saw, he'd cut his mistress apart for disposal.

Inside the Crumbles, Spilsbury caught a detective using his bare hands to scoop up mounds of bloody flesh and dump it into buckets.

"Are there no rubber gloves?" the pathologist asked.

"I never wear gloves," said the frowning cop. "No one I know has worn gloves in the seventeen years of the Murder Squad. This is how we do it."

The Crumbles case saw the introduction of the Murder Bag, a standard kit that Spilsbury put together for Yard detectives called in to investigate a homicide. The bag contained rubber gloves; brushes to dust for fingerprints; a ruler to measure distance; a compass to chart direction; a magnet, tweezers, and other means to lift clues; swabs, bags, and containers to store evidence; and (although it wasn't on Spilsbury's official list of supplies) a bottle of Scotch to fortify detectives at the grisliest of crimes.

In Moscow, Joe had put together his own Murder Bag. He stocked it with the same items as Spilsbury's, but switched the Scotch to vodka.

Now, here at VGH morgue, the Russian rummaged in his bag for the bottle of booze and a large magnifying glass worthy of Sherlock Holmes.

Removing the cap, he took a swig and mumbled a toast to himself: "*Za vashe zdorov'ye!* To your mental health!"

With the Interpol X-rays in one hand and the magnifying glass in the other, Joe bent over the camper's remains and compared Liese Greiner's fractures with the fractures of the lower tibia and fibula and the upper femur of the corpse's right leg. Their match proved that the Headhunter's Jane Doe was indeed the German tourist.

As he was straightening up, Joe's magnifier caught something else: a more recent hairline crack in the pubic bone at the lower front of Liese Greiner's pelvis. And wedged in the crack, as if the killer had kicked the corpse in the groin, was a tiny black splinter.

A bit of bark? Joe wondered. *Wedged by the sole of a shoe?*

There was no match for the hairline crack or the black splinter in the Interpol X-rays.

Puzzled, Joe fetched a small glass plate, a cover slip, and a pair of tweezers from his Murder Bag and mounted the splinter on a slide for analysis back at the lab.

JIMMY JAZZ

The Headhunter Squad was buzzing with chatter about the reports now flooding in concerning the attacks on Artie Fripp of Get-A-Whiff Productions and Kurt Schmidt of the Kit Kat Klub and Theater—not to mention the ongoing Take Back the Night riot—when Inspector MacDougall appeared at the door and called for quiet. When that didn't work, he stuck two fingers in his mouth and let out a shrill whistle.

"Listen up!" he ordered as the din died down. "Who here's got a good grounding in rock music?"

At first, there were no takers. Then Al Flood raised his hand.

"I'm a rocker," the VPD bull confessed.

"How versed, Detective?"

"Enough to have been in the audience when AC/DC performed 'I'm a Rocker' live at the Golders Green Hippodrome in October 1977. Angus Young sat on my date's lap."

The Mountie had no idea what Flood meant.

"You'll do," he said.

They left the ground-floor squad room and climbed the stairs to the mezzanine, then crossed the balcony to DeClercq's office.

"Come in," the super replied to their knock.

The first thing Flood noticed on entering was that a fourth Polaroid photo of a woman's severed head had been pinned to the Strategy Wall. Like the others, it had been snapped against a white background. Sister Angelica's head was still draped with a black cowl, and both eyes stared blankly at Flood from the top of a pole. Her face was etched with terror, and blood trickled from her nose.

Mesmerized, Flood froze in his tracks.

"Detective?"

"Huh?"

"Something wrong?"

"Uh...no." Al snapped out of his trance. "How'd the photo arrive?"

"It was left in an overnight drop box at Christ Church Cathedral. The priest found it this morning."

"Surveillance?"

"None. The Headhunter skulks like a ghost."

"Fingerprints? Hairs? Fibers?"

"Just the priest's. There's nothing but a plain brown envelope with the Polaroid and a tape."

"Tape?"

"An audiotape. That's why we need you. My taste is classical music. Jack listens to country and western. We're out of our depths here."

DeClercq was sitting at his horseshoe-shaped desk. Motioning Al and Jack to the chairs in front, he angled a tape player in their direction.

"Ready to play *Name That Tune*?"

"Ready," said Al.

The Horseman punched Play.

The tune was rock bordering on bluesy jazz. It bled in with the sort of guitar noodling you'd hear in a smoky, sleazy, low-life after-hours dive at three in the morning.

Whistling...

Jabbering...

Clinking glasses...

Then these lyrics...

> *The police walked in for Jimmy Jazz*
> *I said, he ain't here, but he sure went past*
> *Oh, you're looking for Jimmy Jazz*

> *Sattamassagana for Jimmy Dread*
> *Cut off his ears and chop off his head*
> *Police come looking for Jimmy Jazz*

So if you're gonna take a message 'cross this town
*   Maybe put it down somewhere over the other side*
*   See it gets to Jimmy Jazz*

Don't you bother me, not anymore
*   I can't take this tale, oh, no more*
*   It's all around, Jimmy Jazz*

J-a-zee zee J-a-zed zed
*   J-a-zed zed Jimmy Jazz*
*   And then it sucks, he said, suck that!*
*   So go look all around, you can try your luck, brother*
*   And see what you found*
*   But I guarantee you that it ain't your day*
*   Chop! Chop!*

As a baby boomer born in the postwar forties, Al Flood was the perfect age for the Big Bang. In the beginning, there was nothing—then suddenly, there was! Sure, purists from the American South and East Coast sophisticates will argue that the roots of rock 'n' roll can be found in this or that tune, but if you were a kid in the northern sticks or on the West Coast, the Big Bang moment was Elvis Presley's first hip gyration on *The Ed Sullivan Show* in 1956. Al vividly recalled sitting on the floor at his parents' feet, feeling as if an electric current was running through his veins, while above him, his dad choked to his mom, "Good Lord, Jean! I fought a war for *this*?!"

The timeline was perfect from then on—all that rockabilly music to keep him bopping up to puberty; in his horny teens, the British Invasion of the Swinging Sixties; heavy metal ear bleeding after the sex, drugs, and rock 'n' roll Summer of Love; all the glittery, overblown concerts of the seventies; and then the circle closed with the raw power of punk rock.

If you weren't there for the Big Bang…

Well, bad vibes, kid…

You were born out of time in the aftermath.

That's how Al saw it.

"Well?" pressed DeClercq.

"It's 'Jimmy Jazz' by the Clash, off the album *London Calling*."

"What does it mean?" asked MacDougall.

"Your guess is as good as mine. It's impressionistic. Oblique, verging on cryptic. It's gossip, rumor, Chinese whispers, and drunken mumbles. It's not so much what it says—it's the *way* it's said. Are Jimmy Jazz and Jimmy Dread two killers in cahoots or warring enemies? Are they the same person? Is there a contract out on Jimmy Dread? Or is he already dead? Is the message for Jimmy Jazz a warning? If so, who's warning him? Is it the police? Or is the narrator warning Jimmy Jazz that the police are looking for him? Myself, I've always wondered if 'suck that!' was a reference to *Taxi Driver*. You know, when gun nut Travis Bickle says, 'Suck on this!'?"

"I wonder what the Headhunter's trying to tell us?" said DeClercq.

"Or tell himself," said Flood.

———

As a lifelong fan of science fiction, Corporal William Tipple of Commercial Crime could see the future. A year and two months from now would be 1984, when George Orwell's dystopian social science fiction novel predicted a future of omnipresent Big Brother surveillance against "thoughtcrimes." In his decade of going after economic crooks, Tipple had witnessed an explosion of electronic eavesdropping. So much so that in the listening rooms behind his office—the businesslike decor of which made Scarlett and Spann think they were sitting in a bank—countless master-and-slave tape recorders caught the bugged conversations of white-collar flimflam men, corrupt politicians, stock market manipulators, corporate slicks who'd kill for money, and organized gangs from offshore triads down to local outlaw bikers. Though civil liberty lawyers vowed it would never happen, Tipple could see a future when—given the right shock-to-the-system catalyst—Big Brother would be monitoring every telecommunication, and there'd be CCTV cameras above every door and watching every corner.

Hey, call him paranoid.

But Tipple knew what he'd seen, and he knew what was to come.

Give cops a new high-tech tool, and sure as shit they'd push it to the outer limits.

Such was Tipple's job.

"What's with all this 'nigger' stuff?" Rick Scarlett scoffed, flicking the wiretap transcripts in his hand. "Every second word is 'nigger this' or 'nigger that.'"

"That's how they talk."

"I don't get it. Everywhere you turn, the word 'nigger' is getting written out of history. Agatha Christie's bestselling book was *Ten Little Niggers*. Now it's *And Then There Were None*."

"Not in Britain," said Spann.

"Huh?"

"In Britain it's still *Ten Little Niggers*."

"Yeah? That'll change. My uncle was an airman in the Second World War, one of the Dambusters who dropped 'bouncing bombs' on rivers in the Ruhr valley. The guy who led the squadron was Wing Commander Guy Gibson. When they filmed *The Dam Busters* in the 1950s, Gibson and his dog, Nigger, featured prominently. Now censors want to replace Nigger with Digger, Trigger, or something else."

"Times change." Tipple shrugged.

"Soon they'll be trying to pull *Huckleberry Finn* from reading lists. With so much bending over backwards to erase the word 'nigger' from history, I don't get why these blacks you've bugged use that supposedly hated slur so obsessively."

"They're into a new kind of music."

"Really? What's it called?" asked Scarlett, tossing the wiretaps onto Tipple's desk. "The dudes in your photos look like gangsters to me."

When it came to ethnic minorities, Vancouver had always been an Asian city, way back to its earliest days, when Chinese "coolies" were brought over to punch the national railroad through the Rocky Mountains. That done, they'd settled in Chinatown, where Helen Grabowski had reached the end of her line. Back east had been the mecca for those of African descent during the American Revolution and the Civil War, and for Caribbean immigrants during the 1960s, when immigration restrictions were lifted. But there were still so few black Canadians on the West Coast that when a woman was murdered on the highway to Whistler this year by "a black man in a red car," that was enough info for a Mountie corporal to snap his fingers and exclaim, "I know who *that* is!"

And sure enough, it turned out that guy *was* the killer.

So yesterday, after Corporal Rodale said their flying patrol was to focus on the Grabowski murder, and after Spann ID'd Helen's pimp as the black pusher in the drug deal she'd witnessed out back of the Moonlight Arms, the pair had issued an APB to all local cops concerning the whereabouts of John Lincoln Hardy. Then they'd split up to hunt for him in the haunts of skid row.

It should have been easy to spot his black face among all the whites, Asians, and Natives. Though dressed in undercover clothes, Spann stayed clear of the pubs, flophouses, and dives, so as not to jeopardize the on-going drug operation. Instead, she snuck into the rail yard hut to ask her old boss, Piggy, if there'd been sightings of Hardy after she fingered him to her control. Piggy's reply was no. Then Spann cruised the ugly streets in a battered ghost car, probing the shadows for Hardy as night took hold.

Meanwhile, Scarlett assumed the role of inside man. Never having done a stint undercover, and with Halloween coming at midnight, Rick embraced turning Jekyll into Hyde. Dressed in grubby jeans, a red lumber-jack shirt, and a green sleeveless outdoorsman's vest, he donned a hippie wig he'd once worn to a masquerade and put on the black shades of a blind bluesman. Then, tapping a white cane like the killers in *Dr. No*, he pub-crawled his way around Hastings and Main, hunting for the pimp.

As he trolled the seedy strolls and bars of the East End—including the Moonlight Arms—the eyes took in more scores of junk, grass, speed, acid, coke, and angel dust than the courts process in a year, and his ears overheard more deals for blow jobs, around-the-worlds, and straight lays than were negotiated at an accountants' convention.

Yet still no glimpse of Hardy.

This morning the partners had met for breakfast to compare notes on last night's separate patrols. While they prowled together by daylight through the squalid slum, a radio call informed them that yesterday's APB had pinned the tail on Hardy. Now here they were, in the same building where Rusty and Monica worked in Computer Command, sitting across a desk piled with paper from Corporal William "Call me Bill" Tipple.

"You think I'm a buttoned-down dork?" asked the electronic bugger.

"Not me," fibbed Rick.

"I know my stuff. You want to talk about sanitizing 'nigger' from popular culture? Do *you* know what animal's known as Nigger Man in Lovecraft's 'The Rats in the Walls'?"

"A rat?" guessed Rick.

"Not even close."

Damn, thought Scarlett.

He did hate being shown up.

With a pudgy pink face, bristles cropped short to hide baldness, and gold-rimmed glasses backed by an accountant's degree on the wall, Bill Tipple was the sort of overeducated paper-pusher who Rick feared would climb the ranks quickly by tromping on the fingers of hardworking street cops like him.

Kathy, however, saw Bill as a boon.

"How'd you make the link to Hardy?" she asked.

"Vancouver's now a go-to place to record hard-edged music. A black promoter named Steve Rackstraw, also known as the Fox, blew into town early this year with word of a new school of hip-hop music and rapping that was causing a buzz on the East Coast. He was talking up shares in a company he said was 'going to rake in bazillions once this sound catches on.' When those shares plummeted from ten dollars to one in the space of a few minutes, and it turned out the company had recently been stripped of all recording assets, Commercial Crime got called in by swindled local investors."

"The Fox still around?"

"Yep, and into something new," Tipple confirmed. "We put a tap on his phones to gather evidence. An unknown male called the Weasel showed up on the tapes. Days ago, I pegged him as Rackstraw's cousin John Lincoln Hardy. Then I saw your APB on him and put two and two together."

"Where's Hardy now?"

"Dunno. Only what's in the transcripts."

Spann picked up the papers her partner had dropped on Tipple's desk and flipped to an intercept logged in six days ago:

Weasel: I need time, man. To corral this filly in m' stable.

Fox: Uh-huh.

Weasel: Y'know? Get this filly broken so I don't need no rope to keep the bitch from splittin'.

Fox: Don't use yo' dick. Use Sister H.

Weasel: Can't hear ya. Hold a mo'. (Shouting: Turn that music down.)

(U/F: Come on, baby. Make me fe-e-el good.)

(Weasel: In a bit. Get yo' selfishness ready.)

Weasel: Ya still there, man?

Fox: Sounds like ya got yo' hands full. Take heed, cousin. Voodoo juju's comin'. Ya better be ready.

Weasel: I be ready.

Fox: When the Wolf calls, have yo' shit together.

Weasel: (Inaudible)…zombie walks.

Fox: By the by, where's H.G.? Bitch been split a week.

Weasel: I know. Cold. Real cold.

Fox: Better find her, man, 'fore the Wolf finds out. You'll be cold—stone dead cold—if there's a leak.

"H.G.'s gotta be Helen Grabowski," said Spann. "Sister H is heroin, so Hardy's using smack to break in a new hooker. Rackstraw doesn't know H.G.'s dead, and he doesn't want her screwing up whatever's in the works. Voodoo juju? Sounds like the Wolf's in charge. Know his name?"

"Not yet. Working on it."

"Are these taps the latest?"

"No," said Tipple. "We run a few days behind. Tape recorders catch what the targets say. It takes a while to listen and transcribe."

"If I told you that Hardy's the Headhunter and you're our best lead, would that motivate you to get those hard copies for us sooner?"

From the glint in his eyes, Kathy knew that the corporal saw sergeant's stripes. In his realm of tedious paperwork, the devil would be in the details, and the details would be mind-numbingly boring. Out of the blue, here was a chance for his bugging skills to bag the sickest of psychos.

"Give me a day and I'll have the wiretaps up to date."

"We've got thirsty ears, Bill."

"Okay, I'll have Rackstraw's phone monitored live."

"Got a face for him?"

Tipple fanned a sequence of telephoto shots across his desk. The snaps were of five black men exiting a brick warehouse in the heavy industrial area of Yaletown along False Creek. All were dressed in black fedora hats, black shirts, black leather jackets, and black jeans with red high-top sneakers, and each had a single chunky chain around his neck.

"The Fox," said Bill, tapping the center man.

"What about the Weasel?"

"Haven't got his mug. Just his voice on tape."

"I see where the stolen money went," Scarlett said, sneering. "The gold in Rackstraw's teeth and those fucking ain't-I-pretty chains."

Kathy frowned. With second-wave feminism at high tide, the genders had never been so polarized. Wouldn't you know bad luck had her partnered with not only a knuckle-dragging sexist but a racist as well?

She sensed there'd be trouble before this manhunt ended.

"'Zombie walks.' What does that mean?" she asked.

"Perhaps this." Bill handed her a flier for an upcoming concert. "That's Rackstraw's new project. Instead of stock fraud, he's putting together a band."

Spann perused the ad, which was for a gig the next night—November 1—at an underground heavy metal club in Gastown suitably called Hyde's.

The undead musicians were dressed like Baron Samedi. All four wore shabby funeral suits and top hats with tarot Death cards stuck in the bands. Black-ringed eyes in chalk-white faces were the sockets of fleshless skulls. Vertical lines on their lips made their mouths seem stitched together. The stage behind them depicted a steamy, moss-draped Louisiana bayou encircling the spark-spitting bonfire of an ominous African ritual. Bronzed by the flames and lost in the throes of demonic possession, nearly naked drummers and dancers writhed around a bare-breasted voodoo queen clutching a snake overhead.

The name of the band was written in bones.

Voodoo Juju.

As Robert DeClercq was pinning the autopsy report from Sister Angelica's postmortem to her segment of the Strategy Wall, he found that his hands were shaking from lack of sleep. It had been a grueling two-day stretch, and retirement had rusted him to the rigors of the first forty-eight hours in a murder investigation—let alone one inflamed by three odious killings that preceded it. His needs had now shrunk down to Scotch and a good night's rest, so he packed his briefcase and doused the office lights. That's when he realized the extent of the candlelight vigil outside.

So many tiny flames!

All afternoon, angry protesters dispersed by baton-wielding officers from the Take Back the Night rally downtown had regrouped on Heather Street, facing DeClercq's office. As the darkness of Halloween descended on the city, they began lighting candles, multiplying by the minute, to mourn their slaughtered sisters and pressure the Mounties to catch this monster.

While he took in the sea of lights, it happened again. Once more, Robert's mind slipped unwillingly into the Zone. Amid a windbreak of trees bordering the lawn that stretched to Heather Street, he saw that horrific cabin in the woods and, through its candlelit window, his daughter dead on the floor. With a jerk, he yanked the yo-yo to pull himself out of the hallucination, but the shutdown switch was on the fritz.

Jane lying dead...

Jane lying dead...

He couldn't snuff the vision...

The Headhunter's question yesterday...

Do you think you're up to this?

The Headhunter's answer today...

I guarantee you that it ain't your day.

Chop! Chop!

THE HIPPIE

On the Pastaza River, Ecuador, 1969

"Wanna do some acid?"

"Huh?"

"LSD. Wanna do some?"

"Oh...Uh, no...No, I don't think so."

Selena cocked her head and arched an eyebrow. "What's the matter, Sparky? Why the hesitation? You have done dope, right? You can't be *that* straight."

"I'm hip."

"Well, then." Selena shrugged her shoulders. "Acid ain't a turn-down. Grass, coke, bombers, speed—those you can let pass. But I'm talking acid, babe. The ul-ti-mate. Straight from God to Owsley to me to you. Don't tell me you haven't dropped acid?"

"No," said Sparky sheepishly. "I haven't done that."

"Fuck me, kiddo! Time for a trip! Think of the living you're missing. The fun you've never had. Try *everything* once, I say. Don't you agree?"

Hesitation...

"Yeah...I guess so."

"Good. It's settled. A-tripping we shall go."

She held out two tabs of White Lightning cooked up by Owsley, the legendary underground chemist who supplied Jimi Hendrix, the Grateful Dead, and the Beatles. Sucking a finger to wet it, Selena touched one of the hits and conveyed the hallucinogen to the tip of her protruding tongue. Once it had dissolved, she gulped.

"Your turn, Sparky."

She held out the remaining tab.

"The Magical Mystery Tour awaits. Down the hatch, pardner."

Following Selena's lead, Sparky dropped the acid and braced for its mind-tripping effect.

Nothing happened.

━━━

By chance, these Amazon trekkers had met in a steamy jungle town. Teaming up, they had whiled away yesterday's hot afternoon by paddling down the sluggish Pastaza River in a dugout canoe. As the sun beat down on the murky water, a shimmering haze floated up between the enormous trees that hemmed in both banks with the somber gloom of this equatorial forest. Beneath the leafy canopy, bright purple orchids clung to the bark, spiral creepers coiled like serpents from branch to branch, and poisonous fruits dropped into the underbrush to emit noisome odors in a landscape so alien that it could be at the bottom of the sea.

"*Cocodrilo*," Sparky said, nodding toward the bank.

With its glassy eyes half closed and its jaws half open, a gray-green crocodile slipped into the river and sank from sight, ready to gobble them up if the canoe tipped.

"Do crocs attack from down under?" Selena asked.

"I'm sure it's happened."

"Row faster."

"Aye, aye, Captain Hook."

With Sparky paddling at the stern, the hippie sat in the bow of the boat, facing backwards. Her long black hair was parted down the middle and she wore a narrow headband around her brow. Her tie-dyed shirt, knotted under her braless breasts, had been fashioned in a head shop in the Haight-Ashbury district of San Francisco, the epicenter of the counterculture earthquake back home. Her long legs emerged from a pair of khaki shorts, and the shoulder bag at her bare feet was stitched with cosmic designs.

"*Urubú*," said Sparky, gazing to the sky. "Nature's gravediggers."

Farther downstream, black-and-white vultures circled the air. As the canoeists drew closer, more flapped up from the bank into the trees, staring down in glum silence at having been interrupted midway through their meal. A musky stench made Selena wrinkle her nose—mired in the muck was a dead water buffalo with spears spiking out of its haunches. Both horns were smashed and splintered by too many blows from clubs, and the hide had been flayed to carve out meat. As the boat passed on, Selena watched the birds drop from the trees to continue their gobbling.

"I wonder who slaughtered that beast?"

"Them," said Sparky, jabbing the paddle at the jungle ahead.

Selena could barely make out a poorly constructed, thatched-roof hut with bamboo walls. In front, a filthy-haired woman whose face was painted with striped designs stirred a clay pot bubbling with stew over an open fire. Beside her, a child with spindly legs and a swollen stomach pulled the tail of a mangy, flea-bitten dog. Twenty feet away, a long blowpipe backed by a zigzag-patterned face extended toward them from a flowering bush.

"Jivaro," said Sparky, veering the canoe away from the bank.

"Headhunters?"

"Uh-huh. A generation ago."

"But no more?"

"That's what they say."

"Let's hope *they* got their facts right."

Late in the day, the trekkers branched off the main channel of the Pastaza River for a small side stream. Here, trunks dipped their leg-like roots in green water instead of the muddy flow scraping loam from the riverbed in its eastward journey to join the mighty Amazon. Overhead, a covey of vampire bats hung upside down in a hollow tree, their bellies bloated with blood. A mile in, the stream widened into a backwater lagoon. Beaching the boat on a mudflat, the two heaved their gear ashore to pitch camp for the night.

"Think it's safe to swim?"

"The Amazon's known for piranhas," said Sparky.

Selena winced. "Let's eat instead of being eaten."

They sat on the sun-dried mudflat, close to the water's edge, sharing simple fare and drinking *chicha*—a sweet and sour corn beer—from a glass jug. As the sun set and the moon rose, the jungle turned purple and the lagoon darkened from a sheet of hammered bronze to silver tinged with mauve. In the dying light, the hippie tossed a scrap of food into the calm water.

"Nope. Not a nibble. It's piranha-free."

Bullfrogs by the thousands croaked like drunks at a sing-along as fireflies flitted about the campers, now buzzed on *chicha*.

"So," said Sparky, "how'd you end up here?"

"A friend and I were at the Cow Palace in July, grooving to the Doors," Selena replied. "When Jim finished singing 'Break On Through,' we decided to break on through to South America. The following day, we stuck out our thumbs in San Fran to hitchhike south. My friend fell ill in Quito and flew home. I stayed behind and hopped a riverboat cruising into the jungle." She took another gulp of *chicha*. "How 'bout you?"

"My early years were spent in the bayous of New Orleans—"

"Hey, I was in the Big Easy last spring. Voodoo. Gris-gris. Marie Laveau. I love that juju stuff. That's where I scored a far-out talisman I got in my bag."

"My dad was dead. Then one day, my mom disappeared."

"Like, vanished?"

"Without a trace. I grew up in a foster home. Stayed there until I was of age to inherit Mom's estate. After that, I bummed around in search of adventure. In Caracas, I met a guy who was in the Peace Corps. I'm not a US citizen, so I couldn't join. But they gave me work as 'local labor.'" Sparky shrugged. "And here I am."

"What d'ya do?"

"Mostly paddle around by myself, taking water samples."

That morning, the hippie had opened her eyes to find herself alone at the campsite. It was only 6 a.m., but already the heat was stifling. After stretching her arms and rubbing the sleep from her eyes, she rolled over on her back and stared up at the sun-dappled canopy. The languorous smell of rotting fruit dulled her senses. Fluttering their wings, blue-and-yellow butterflies sipped dew from the ground plants. Higher up, a scarlet macaw, three feet from beak to tail, shrieked good morning.

"Zip-a-dee-doo-dah," Selena said, climbing to her feet. Swinging the shoulder bag that contained what the hippie called her tantra yoga kit—

the means to explore the upper chakras through sex—she traipsed from the forest shadows out to the sparkling lagoon. There, she found Sparky squatting at the water's edge, sealing the lid of a jar with tape sliced off a roll with a hunting knife.

"Morning," Selena said.

"You sleep well?"

"Like a log. Whatcha doin'?"

"Bottling a water sample for the Peace Corps."

"Why?"

"To test for tropical diseases."

"Outtasight!" Selena marveled, using her hand as a visor to keep the rising sun from flashing its blinding heat into her eyes. Not a wisp of cloud flecked the hard blue sky. "What a trip! This pool blows my mind. You finished work for today?"

"Yep," said Sparky, setting the bottle down on the bank and jabbing the Bowie knife with a nick in its blade in the baked mudflat.

"Good. The stars align."

"How so?"

Grinning, Selena reached into her shoulder bag and rummaged around, then she withdrew a small glass vial, popped its cap, and dumped its contents into her palm.

"What's that?" Sparky asked.

"Electric Kool-Aid. Wanna do some acid?"

———

"I don't feel good."

"It'll pass."

"No, really...I feel sick."

"Don't freak out on me, babe. Acid always starts in the gut."

"It's not my gut," Sparky moaned. "It's my *head*!"

"Shhh. Listen to the sounds."

Forty minutes had passed since they dropped the acid. While waiting for the rush to hit, they'd broken camp and moved their gear to the water's edge, ready to toss it into the canoe for a river trip. Now, they sat on the bank in the glare of the merciless sun, sweat streaming out of their pores as the acid overwhelmed them. Whatever Sparky had expected, it wasn't this. The river had somehow become a sound conductor, funneling every shriek of prey into the whispering gallery of this primordial jungle lagoon. Here, the pain of a lost world trapped in a green hell electrified into a tinny hum that rose in pitch to a nerve-shredding, brain-vibrating crescendo of metallic dread. Sounds bled into colors that took on geometric shapes, a phantasmagoric kaleidoscope that transformed reality into a Picasso painting. Sparky's heart lost its rhythm and throbbed to a chaotic beat. Sparky's lungs gasped in a struggle to suck oxygen out of this atmosphere of decay. Sparky's mouth was so dry that it *tasted* the color gray. The boundaries that divided body and self from the environment were disintegrating. The sweat seeping from Sparky's skin was evaporating quickly into the festering wound of this foul-smelling bog, a miasma that teetered on the cusp of extinction.

Evolution...

Devolution...

Going...going...gone...

Help!

What's happening?

My body is out of control...

"Fuck me!" Selena cried from light-years away. "What a trip. We're back in the Garden of Eden...Come on, Sparky. Let's shed these shameful clothes."

Reaching her arms skyward in worship of the sun, Selena uncoiled and rose from the bank like a serpent slithering up a tree. One by one, she unhooked the buttons of her sweat-stained, tie-dyed top, then shucked the garment like a snake shedding its skin. As her breasts burst forth, she tossed her head to shake down her black hair, and in a blink she was Medusa with toxic-fanged serpents hissing around her face.

Suzannah?

"Wanna try these forbidden apples?" Selena murmured seductively through Suzannah's lips. Cupping her breasts, she plumped them with a heft.

"Mommy?" Sparky whispered incredulously.

"Yes, child. I'm back."

"Mommy?" Selena giggled. "I've got your number, babe. You wanna suck these hunks o' heaven?" She gave her nipples a tweak.

Like a fishhook caught in the memory coils of Sparky's brain, the past was trying to tug the acid-tripper in by transforming Selena into Suzannah in her Medusa wig, but this time the hair was a nest of real snakes that squirmed and squirted venom from their curved fangs.

*Suzannah...Selena...Suzannah...Selena...*flickering back and forth.

Help!

What's happening?

My mind is out of control...

Selena was no longer human. She was perversion incarnate. Beneath her skin—half flesh-toned and half metallic blue—her muscles twitched a Morse code of erotic cues.

Sex...sex...dirty sex. Come and get it, Sparky...

Snaking among the milk ducts in her undulating breasts—first her left tit ballooned larger, then her right—veins and arteries pulsed with blood begging to spurt free from nipples as dry as a sunbaked riverbed. As Sparky gazed at the canyon between the snake-woman's tits, a small parasite called a *garrapata* latched on to one jiggly mound, then turned crimson as it sucked Selena's blood into its transparent body. Like a bolt of lightning flashing above Villa Diodati on the stormy night that Mary Shelley conceived *Frankenstein*, a horror zapped through the synapses of this hallucinator's mind. They say that as Lord Byron read verses from Samuel Taylor Coleridge's *Christabel* to the writers sequestered in that remote Italian retreat, the poet Percy Shelley—unhinged by advances on his wife by Dr. Polidori, the author of *The Vampyre*—fled screaming from that storytelling session in the throes of a vivid hallucination of a woman with eyes instead of nipples glaring from her breasts. And so it was with this voodoo hex from New Orleans. For leering at Sparky through Selena's nipples were Suzannah's hateful eyes.

"No! You're dead!"

"*Do I look dead? You can't kill me, Sparky.*"

"I buried you in the bayou!"

"*And guess what? This zombie has risen from her grave.*"

Selena's voice gurgled up from the depths of the lagoon. "Ground control to Sparky. You're zoning out, babe. Who you talking to?"

"I feel dizzy. I think I'm going to pass out."

"You need water, Sparky. A dip in the cool pool. Too much sweating has left you lightheaded. Here, let's get you out of those confining threads."

Sparky's head was spinning with paranoia and fear. As chemical psychosis snapped the anchor to reality, there went the last hope of reeling in. Sparky's clammy clothes seemed to dissolve onto the bank, fluttering down where the handle of the knife stuck up from the mud. A howler monkey hooted at them from the surrounding trees. *Zzzzzz*...A purple wasp with orange wings buzzed by. Having stripped her companion, Selena shimmied her own short shorts and underwear down to her feet, then kicked them into the air with naked abandon. A shiver ran down Sparky's spine at the sight of her bare pussy...

Tsantsa!

Then Selena turned and splashed into the dazzling lagoon. Like a series of afterimages strung in a row, Selena dissolved in a fountain of emerald water, then reconstituted herself in time to dissolve again. Waist-deep, she jackknifed her bum in the air and dove into the tropical pool, leaving behind a bull's-eye of sparkling ripples.

The heat flaming up from the sun-scorched bank was unbearable. Sparky was melting into a puddle on the mud and would soon be dead without a refreshing swim. The acidhead wobbled to the lagoon and waded into the tepid water. Just then, like a missile bursting from a submarine, Selena exploded from the depths in a whirlpool of rainbow drops with her body covered in...

Leeches!

Now Sparky was in full retreat, scrambling out of the water like a crab, hands and feet churning madly. Following closely behind, the Creature from the Green Lagoon evolved from the slime, lifting each scaly leg out of the ooze with a flatulent sucking sound, like a frogman coming ashore, eyes bulging and leeches licking like tongues.

"Fuck me!" the Creature gasped with Selena's voice. "It's positively primal! This pool is freakin' alive! Eat me, Mother Nature. Suck your daughter dry!"

"Eat me, Sparky. Eat me!"

No, Mommy! Please!

"Wanna gorge on forbidden fruit? I saw you drooling at my tits. We got our own little Woodstock here. If it feels good, do it!"

Looming over Sparky, who sprawled transfixed on the bank, Selena…
Suzannah…Selena splayed her dripping thighs, while all the black leeches
hooked onto her body began converging on the swampy black thatch of
her crotch, where…

Tsantsa!

…they wriggled together to form the tiny hair-snakes of a shrunken
Medusa head.

"*Eat me, Sparky,*" the labia lips commanded.

Ripped and freaked by LSD, Sparky cringed as Pandora's box yawned
wide to release the sexual monsters of this world and beyond. The shrunken
Medusa head…

Tsantsa!

…transformed into the squid face of Lovecraft's Cthulhu monster,
lashing its tentacles around its all-consuming mouth as the mesmerized
tripper gazed into the wormhole of creation.

That's when Selena—seeping sex from her sultry eyes, flaring nostrils,
and steamy mouth—bent down, tits swaying, to withdraw what looked
like a voodoo loa…

Damballa!

…from her shoulder bag on the bank, close to the handle of Sparky's
upright knife. The tongues of the snake god arced left and right from the
open mouths of miniature devilish faces that could be Janus, the Roman
god who looked to the past and to the future.

"Feel that, Sparky? I got the hots for you. The way you're leering at my
snatch, you got the hots for me. That's it, babe. Slip it inside…"

Sparky's fist closed on the knife.

"Now fuck me like there's no tomorrow!"

"*Sparky…*"

"Leave me alone!"

"*You're mine forever, worm-child.*"

"I hate you, Mother! Help me, Daddy!"

("*I'm here, Sparky. I am you.*")

Selena bucked as the blade slammed sideways through her neck. The
force of her pelvic thrust seemed to nail Sparky to the bank, then she went
into convulsions, thrashing about with her arms. Wham, wham, wham, her

body jackhammered her psychotic sex partner. The unearthly sound from where the knife pierced her windpipe was halfway between hissing and burping, as if Selena was slurping a milkshake dry. Then Sparky yanked the blade savagely across her throat and the hippie erupted into a volcano vomiting blood as her chin hinged back to reveal Satan's grin below.

Now, instead of pulling in sounds, the lagoon released a shriek of sexual ecstasy, scaring flocks of birds from the canopy of trees and working monkey colonies up to a fever pitch.

Sparky's *first* orgasm.

FISH SEE THE WORM, NOT THE HOOK

Vancouver, British Columbia, 1982
Sunday, October 31, 6:22 p.m.

As Robert DeClercq descended the driveway to his seaside home, the Headless Horseman from "The Legend of Sleepy Hollow" materialized in the wispy fog illuminated by the headlights of his car. The ghost was draped in a white shroud that ended at the neck, with crimson blood gushing down its chest. The apparition carried a pumpkin head under one arm, and the eyes and fangs of the jack-o'-lantern flickered with candlelight. Peering through eye slits cut in the shroud, the trick-or-treater drifted past DeClercq's car, lugging a bulging candy sack in its other hand. Flanked by Batman and an eyepatched pirate with a bushy black beard, the Headless Horseman galloped uphill to the next loot stop.

The Headless Horseman...

How fitting, the Mountie thought.

Before he could slip his key in the lock, the door to his house swung open on the Wicked Witch of the West. Genevieve had morphed into a green-skinned hag, with warts fouling her chin and her hair dyed as black as her pointed hat. Her body was sheathed in a long black dress under a flowing black cape, and as she held up a Scotch on the rocks in one hand, she loosened two buttons with the green nails of her other to give him a peek at her sinful red bra.

"Trick or treat?" she cackled.

"I'll take the trick—if that's the Scotch—and save the treat for later."

"*Much* later."

"Huh?"

"George Ruryk's here for dinner."

"Thought I saw his car at the top of the drive."

"Okay?"

"Of course." Though all he really wanted was a stiff drink and a deep sleep.

"George published a paper on trichophilia," she said.

"On what?"

"A shrink's fancy word for hair fetishism."

"Ah."

"Part of me's playing Watson. The other part's helping George. I hate thinking about him shuffling around that lonely high-rise. So I invited him here to enjoy the ghouls and goblins, and while I fill their sacks with candy, you can fill your brain with George's expertise."

"You're a wicked woman."

"Lucky you."

Behind him, footsteps rushed down the drive toward the door.

"I'll take that Scotch," Robert said, "while you button up. We can't have the neighbors suing you for inducing their sons' heart attacks."

As he crossed the threshold, the weary Mountie gulped a slug of whisky that burned all the way down. From the kitchen on his left came the mouth-watering smell of tourtière—Québec meat pie—his favorite comfort food. Another dram, then he set the glass down on the dining room table while he shucked his coat and swapped his shoes for slippers. Then he retrieved the Scotch and shuffled ahead to the living room, where he joined their dinner guest by the crackling fire.

What a jolt!

The Headless Horseman found himself facing Ichabod Crane.

Like the awkward, gangly schoolteacher of Sleepy Hollow, the head of the psychiatric program at UBC was a tall, skeletal man whose tweed jacket sagged loosely on his frame. In Ruryk's case, however, his bony look reflected a recent life-or-death struggle with flesh-eating disease contracted from a cut received by tripping over a stone on a summer stroll in Pacific Spirit Park. The race against necrosis had surgeons cutting chunks out of him, then grafting on skin to repair the resulting tissue damage.

"Hello, Robert."

"Hi, George. No, don't get up."

"Hope I'm not encroaching? I'm told you haven't slept for days. So pardon me for warming my bones and swilling your single malt."

"You're always welcome. *Mi casa es su casa.*"

"I have the feeling Genevieve plans to make me sing for my supper."

"Trichophilia?"

"Uh-huh."

"How goes your recovery?"

"Can't complain. I'm alive. I beat the cannibal bug. And your wife's a tonic for intimations of mortality. Halloween's got us psychoanalyzing kids based on their masks."

"Hope for the future?"

"No, same old shit. I envy you marrying Genevieve, one of my best students." He took a slug of his drink. "We've been discussing the Headhunter."

"If I refill your glass, will you give me your opinion?"

"Twist my arm."

As he carried George's empty glass to the sideboard by the Greenhouse door, he drained his own drink. The whisky relieved his tension like a clenched fist releasing a bird. While foghorns bellowed from the bay and the lighthouse swept its cyclops eye across misty whitecaps, he topped their glasses up with Scotch and ice, then returned to the armchairs by the fire.

"*Slàinte,*" the psychiatrist toasted his host.

"To your health too."

"Okay, let's get down to it. What do you want to know?"

"Genny says you published a treatise on hair fetishism. That's one of three theories I have for why the heads are taken. Is the killer collecting trophies? Is the killer a hair fetishist? Is the killer a cannibal eating his victims' brains? The hallmark in all four beheadings is that the women have jet-black hair—that is, if we include the nun's black cowl in the Polaroid we got today."

"Four defies coincidence," Ruryk agreed. "But there's no reason why your three theories must be exclusive. The Headhunter could be a fetishist collecting hair as trophies, and because he takes whole heads instead of just scalps, he could also be eating the brains."

"As an act of dominance over his victims?"

"Or to *become* them."

"Like Norman Bates in *Psycho*?"

"Yes. Ed Gein."

DeClercq knew the crimes of Ed Gein well. The Plainfield Ghoul was America's counterpart to Jack the Ripper. Gein's domineering mother was a religious fanatic who warned her son obsessively about the sinfulness of women. On her death, he turned his mother's room in their isolated Wisconsin farmhouse into a shrine. Then he set about robbing the graves of recently deceased local women to explore their anatomy. Eventually, he turned to murder to acquire better-smelling corpses, and that brought detectives to his door.

By 1957, Gein's farm had degenerated into a house of horrors. The stench of filth and decomposition was nauseating. In a shed, police found a female body strung upside down from the ceiling beams: decapitated, slit open, and gutted like a deer. Inside the farmhouse, skulls were stuck on Gein's bedposts, faces skinned from nine women were mounted on the walls, lips dangled from a string above the windowsill, noses sat in a cup on the table, and the victims' vulvas were stored away in a shoebox. Most telling, however, were the clothes he'd fashioned: a belt of stitched nipples, hands flayed into gloves, and a "mammary vest" tailored from a female torso so he could literally crawl into her skin and *become* his mother.

"Necrophilia, fetishism, transvestism, cannibalism—Gein displayed them all. And any of those paraphilias could be why the Headhunter takes heads."

"How do you see Gein's psychopathology?" asked the Mountie.

"He was full of love-hate feelings toward women resulting from his natural sexual attraction to them and the unnatural attitudes instilled in him by his overbearing mother. Those feelings developed into a full-blown psychosis. He'll spend the rest of his life in a mental hospital."

"Could that same psychopathology be going on here?"

"Yes."

"Some reports say deputies found a heart in a pan on Gein's stove. If the Headhunter's psychosis is similar to Gein's, might he engage in cannibalism for the female hormones?"

"To try to induce a sex change?"

"Whatever," said the Mountie. "I'm shooting in the dark."

"If sane women think eating their placenta will prevent postpartum depression and Asian males eat rhinoceros horn to boost their virility, imagine the fantasies that obsess psychotic minds, which, by definition, have suffered a break with reality."

Hamatsa? Voodoo? wondered DeClercq.

"What made you write a paper on hair fetishism?"

"While giving a lecture in Europe, I came across a fascinating German murder case. Do you understand how trichophilia evolves?"

"I think so, but enlighten me."

"A fetish is an object—or it could be a body part—on which the mind becomes so fixated that it's psychologically necessary for sexual gratification. Somehow, in childhood, sex becomes paired with the fetish, and that conditions the psyche as it develops. Hair isn't the most common fetish. It falls behind boots and underwear. But it's one of the kinkiest. Freud wrote a paper called 'Medusa's Head,' in which he equated decapitating that female monster with the castration complex aroused in a boy when he first sees female genitals without a penis."

"Might headhunting women give our psycho control over that Freudian fear?"

"Perhaps. Psychosis knows no bounds."

"What happened in Germany?"

"A girl came home from school and found her mother dead on the bathroom floor. Someone had bludgeoned the woman from behind with a hammer, before slashing her throat, severing her breasts, and placing them next to her head. Her pants were pulled down far enough to expose her pubic hair, but she hadn't been sexually assaulted. What puzzled police was a lock of *snipped* hair they found displayed in her right hand. It wasn't hers. The killer had brought it with him. He'd also tucked a clump of *her* hair in her other hand."

"What did the media tag him?"

"Der Haar-Killer," said the psychiatrist. "The Hair Killer."

"The Headhunter mutilates his victims' breasts too."

"Mother fixation."

"Was the Hair Killer caught?"

"Yes."

"How?"

"For weeks before the murder, a hair fetishist had preyed on local women going about their everyday lives. His MO was to sit behind them on a bus and snip a lock of hair without their knowledge. So strong was his compulsion that he constantly risked capture by collecting his trophies in public in broad daylight. The thrill of the chase revved him up for murder."

As he listened, DeClercq heard more maskers knock on the door...

"Trick or treat!"

...and the Wicked Witch giving them candy.

"Interpol linked the MO to an unsolved murder in Spain. A teenager had vanished while on her way to meet a young man for a date. Around the same time, a hair fetishist had been secretly snipping locks from women riding buses or sitting in theaters. In one case, a movie-goer felt her hair being tugged during a film, and she turned around to find a faceless figure masturbating in the dark. Only when she arrived home did she find a chunk missing from her hair."

"I take it they found the teenage girl?"

"Four years later, workmen repairing the roof of a church discovered a mummified body hidden behind a bricked-up wall in an unused part of the attic."

"Killed by the same ritual?"

"Her skull was caved in and her throat was slit. Her bra was cut between the cups just like the German woman's. Both breasts were severed and had been placed beside her head. The mummy's skirt was lowered to expose her pubic hair. The Spanish police found foreign hair in her right hand and a lock of her own hair beneath her left palm. The unknown hair was snipped and likely brought by the killer."

"So whodunit?"

"Who do you think?" asked Ruryk.

"The young guy the Spanish girl was on her way to meet."

"And ten years later, guess where he resided? In a rooming house across the street from the German woman."

"If head hair was his fetish, why expose both victims' pubic hair?" asked Robert.

"Good question."

"Reminds me of Reggie-No-Dick," said the Mountie, referring to John Reginald Christie, of 10 Rillington Place.

Robert was fading fast. All he desired was his bed. But his gut told him that this discussion was crucial to solving the Headhunter murders, so he forced himself into his second wind and raised the pubic hair connection to the Christie case.

There is no more infamous address in London than 10 Rillington Place. So much so that in 1954 the street was renamed Ruston Close.

In 1949, Timothy Evans—a mentally deficient lorry driver—walked into a Welsh police station and all but confessed to murdering his wife and fourteen-month-old daughter in his top-floor flat at 10 Rillington Place. Scotland Yard found the two strangled bodies in a backyard shed.

Evans stood trial for murder. John Reginald Christie, who lived in the flat below, was the Crown's star witness. Evans's defense? "Christie did it." The jury disagreed and found him guilty. So on March 9, 1950, Timothy Evans was hanged.

Three years later, Christie vacated his flat. When the upstairs tenant came down to clean up, he found three naked women dead in a hidden cupboard. Then Scotland Yard discovered Christie's wife buried under the floorboards and found two more women on digging up the backyard.

Christie, it turned out, was a necrophiliac. Abused by his father, coddled by his mother, and dominated by his sisters, he so associated sex with predatory aggression that he was rendered impotent unless in overpowering control. At school, his first go at intercourse was such a failure that it earned him the nicknames Can't-Do-It-Christie and Reggie-No-Dick. From 1943 to 1953, he cured that sexual dysfunction by luring women to his house, getting them drunk, and gassing them into unconsciousness, then strangling them and raping their corpses. On his arrest, police found a tobacco tin in which he kept tufts of female pubic hair.

In one of his statements, Christie confessed to killing Mrs. Evans. On July 15, 1953, the sexual psycho was hanged. What the hangman couldn't do was "unhang" Evans. So that led to an inquiry, and eventually to legislation that did away with the gallows in 1964.

"Pubephilia," Ruryk said. "That's what we call it. Sexual arousal fixated on pubic hair. But every sexual fetish has a flip side—a sexual phobia. Trichophobia is the morbid fear of head hair. Pubephobia is the fear of pubic hair. By caging his trophies in a tin, was Christie trying to overcome his fear?"

"Pandora's box *in reverse*?"

"Good analogy. In Greek myth, Pandora opened that box and released all the evils of the world. Did Christie hope to lock 'evil' *in* to master his sexual dysfunction? Was the German Hair Killer so fearful of women's sex organs that he transferred his pubephobia to less threatening female head hair, snipping it not out of arousal but out of fear?"

"Medusa's head?"

"Like I said, hair fetishism is one of the kinkiest paraphilias. The key to understanding the Headhunter's psyche will lie in what he *does* with his trophies."

"Enough of that," said Genevieve, joining the men by the fire. "The witch is finished using candy to lure Hansel and Gretel to her house in the woods. I've turned off the outside light. If you'll serve the tourtière, Robert, I'll wipe this gunk off my face so we can eat."

"Aye, aye, Captain."

"There's salad in the fridge."

The men gulped their Scotches and moved to the dining room. After Robert served the meal from the kitchen, he and George sat at the table.

"Dig in," said the Mountie. "The rule around here is that we don't eat cold food while we stand on formality. I'd also prefer if you talk while you eat. You're helping me unmask the Headhunter."

"You're looking for one of two 'psychos.' The killer is either an over-controlled aggressive psychopath or a deeply repressed psychotic."

"Break them down for me."

"An *under*-controlled aggressive psychopath is someone like Clifford Olson. He's sloppy, makes mistakes, and is likely known to police. An *over*-controlled aggressive psychopath is Ted Bundy. He's rigid and meticulous in his constraints, and thereby wears a mask of normalcy in his everyday life. He's more dangerous and elusive than the under-controlled type. At times of stress, however, he can't suppress the urges buried deep in his psyche, so he looks for an opportunity to lash out. Then the pressure is released and he returns to his 'normal' self."

"The mask of Jekyll hides the face of Hyde," said the cop.

"Exactly." George nodded his agreement. "The Chinese have a proverb: 'Fish see the worm, not the hook.' If the Headhunter's a psychopath, he knows who he is. The killer hasn't suffered a break with reality. He doesn't hear voices, he doesn't hallucinate, and he isn't in the grip of a delusion. Instead, he lacks all moral sense of right and wrong. He does whatever he wants for personal gratification, with no concern for the horrific effect on other people. His illness was most likely caused by past abuse from a female—odds are his mother—so he lures stand-in victims with his surface charm, then rips off his mask to reveal the sexual sadist he is."

"Why taunt us with the staged scenes and the Polaroid photos? To make *us* suffer?"

"Attention-seeking is common in psychopathy. The killer sees himself as superior to you. He doesn't make mistakes, and if he does, someone else is to blame. In effect, he's boasting: 'I can do no wrong. You haven't caught me in four chances. Puzzle over this.'"

"What do you make of the fact that we found no semen in the nun? The floater and the buried body were too degraded to test, but we did find sperm in the third victim, Joanna Portman."

"Perhaps he was interrupted?"

"That could be. There was a dog walker nearby."

"Or if sexual dysfunction fuels the Headhunter's rage, perhaps he can ejaculate only when the reality of his crime meshes perfectly with his fantasy of revenge. Maybe something about the nurse's death pulled his trigger."

The totem pole? thought DeClercq. *Hamatsa?*

"What if he's not a psychopath but a deeply repressed psychotic?"

"Then you're into the murky realms of split personality disorder, dissociation, psychosis, and a lot of mumbo-jumbo terminology that means little. The Headhunter murders are so 'crazy,' in the layman's sense of the word, that I think this killer has had some sort of break with reality. It's possible that Jekyll doesn't know Hyde exists. Sometime in the past, the Headhunter encountered a mental trauma so severe that his psyche splintered off a separate consciousness to deal with it. When you meet Jekyll, he appears normal, but—*unknown to him*—Hyde is possessed by a demon."

Voodoo?

Robert recalled what Al Flood had said when he wondered aloud what the Headhunter was trying to tell them.

"Or tell himself."

"Is mental illness inherited?"

"Yes," said Ruryk. "By nature and by nurture. Genes pass psychosis down from one generation to the next. And what parents do to their kids only makes things worse."

———

Robert knew he was in big trouble the moment Genny sat down at the table.

Once again, the Zone took over.

Her face was back to normal, but her auburn hair was still dyed black.

"It'll wash out," she said. Then, as if reading his concern, she added, "I'm a psychologist. I can't—and won't—live in fear. No monster out there is going to manipulate what I do with my own person. I'm flipping him my finger."

Pop! Pop! Pop! Pop!

Like flashbulbs going off, his overtired mind superimposed the severed head of each black-haired Headhunter victim on his wife's face.

THE ENFIELD

Monday, November 1, 3:50 a.m.

Horse hoofs thunder behind him as he runs for his life through a Kwakiutl village of longhouses and totem poles silvered by a full moon. Stacked up the totems are the heads of the Headhunter's victims, the severed neck of each woman bleeding black blood down on the hair below. Voodoo drums throb from the forest encircling the Native settlement, and eyeballs glare from the gloom between the trees.

Thrump…

Thrump…

Thrump…

Galloping hoofs narrow the gap between predator and prey.

He's afraid to look behind him for fear of what he'll see, so he sprints toward the bridge ahead while his heart hammers in his chest and sweat pours down his skin. This end of the bridge is flanked by several vertical poles topped with grinning silver skulls.

A horse whinnies behind him as he nears the safety of the far riverbank. Glancing over his shoulder, he sees the Headless Horseman rear up on his ghostly mount, with one glove gripping its reins and the other raising his pumpkin head in the air. The only colors in the black-and-silver dreamscape are the Horseman's scarlet tunic and the fiery orange face of the jack-o'-lantern.

"Daaaaddy!"

The scream of his terrified daughter chills him to his core as her face in the pumpkin hurls toward him from the Headless Horseman's hand. If ever there was a Hail Mary pass, this is it. He knows he has to catch her or his life won't be worth living.

"I'm coming, Jane!" he cries...

...and he stumbles toward the arcing head with lead weights on his feet, his heart bursting in his rib cage as his fingers close around her...

...but then he fumbles the catch and her pleading features slip out of his grasp...

...and the jack-o'-lantern tumbles down to smash to pieces against the planks of the rickety bridge...

...while the tubes in the Headless Horseman's neck stump whistle in triumph...

...and he...

Robert DeClercq awoke in a panic with his pulse pounding in his brain and his pajamas clammy with cold sweat, certain he was having a heart attack. Genny stirred beside him but didn't jerk from sleep, so he lay on his back in the darkness and willed himself to calm down.

Breathe...

Breathe...

Breathe...

Slowly, his heart stopped racing and his muscles relaxed. Once he was sure he wasn't in the iron crab of a coronary, the Mountie crawled out of bed, donned his dressing gown and slippers, and shuffled from the bedroom along the main hall to the kitchen by the front door. The savory smell of tourtière clung to the slumbering house.

While his wakeup coffee dripped through a filter, he descended the cellar stairs to the laundry room and put on whatever unironed clothes he could scrounge from the dryer. Then he retraced his steps to the main hall and angled into the library off the living room. The window wall faced English Bay alongside the Greenhouse, which bore a specific name because it was attached to, but not part of, the original bungalow. Side-by-side desks overlooked the outer harbor, but all he could see was gray mist swept by the lighthouse, and all he could hear were foghorns still groaning on the phantom anchored ships.

Oooo-wah...

Oooo-wah...

An ocean of moaning cows.

Robert switched on the overhead light to illuminate the floor-to-ceiling bookcases that lined the library walls. His books were on one side, Genny's on the other. Crossing to his half, he pulled a hinged shelf open to expose a secret wall safe, then entered the combination that popped the door. From inside, he withdrew a Victorian gunbox and conveyed it to his desk, where he lifted the lid to reveal the most legendary revolver in North-West Mounted Police history: Inspector Wilfred Blake's .476 Enfield.

Returning to the kitchen, he gulped a mug of coffee. The caffeine did nothing to clear the haze of last night's whisky and this morning's interrupted sleep. His mug refilled, he carried it and Blake's sidearm out to the Greenhouse and sat down at his auxiliary desk, still cluttered with research notes for his stalled book. It was a lot warmer out here than in the house. Turning on the desk lamp cast a pool of light, and the moment he saw the photos of Kate, Jane, and Genny, he knew what disabled him.

PTSD.

Post-traumatic stress disorder.

A mental condition recently categorized by psychiatrists.

Reliving past trauma.

His eyes locked on the photo of Kate performing Ibsen's *Rosmersholm* in Manhattan, and his memory took him back to that snowy evening in February when he had succumbed to the giddy joy of falling in love at first sight. Sergeant DeClercq was in the Big Apple on an extradition matter, trying to arrange the deportation to Canada of a fugitive hitman linked to the Montreal mob. Excluding Shakespeare, his favorite playwright was the "father of realism," Henrik Ibsen—*Peer Gynt, A Doll's House, Hedda Gabler, Ghosts,* and such—so the chance to see *Rosmersholm* couldn't be missed. Sitting in the front-row balcony and having rented opera glasses, he focused both lenses on the actress playing the lead of Rebecca West...and not once had they wandered from her during the entire performance. So smitten was the Mountie by Kate that he *had* to get backstage.

Romeo and Juliet.

Throw caution to the wind.

Star-crossed lovers.

Until a burly security guard stopped him at the stage door.

"You need a pass," he said.

It was one of those moments when life hangs in the balance. If he pressed on against all odds and won her heart, the sun would shine, birds would sing, and they'd live happily ever after. If he backed down at the first obstacle and allowed this magic moment to slip away, he'd end his days in the gutter, broken and alone, with stubble on his ruddy face and a bottle of hooch in his hand.

No fuckin' way, he thought.

And he wasn't a man who threw "fuck" around like Johnny Appleseed.

DeClercq flashed his regimental badge.

"Will this pass do?"

"No," said the brute, smirking at the bison head.

Which left the nuclear option.

Leaning in, the Horseman lowered his voice confidentially. "My friend, you don't want to call this wrong. You're forcing me to divulge privileged information. I'm in town looking for this guy." Robert fished the mug sheet out of his suit pocket. "He—I kid you not—is a psychopathic hitman for the mob. How'd you like to meet *him* in a dark alley?"

He let the guard read enough to absorb the bloodcurdling threat.

"I'm working with the NYPD on this."

He waved the card of the homicide officer who was his local contact.

"I have reason to believe this thug may—I repeat, *may*—have a fatal attraction toward the lead actress in this production. I don't want to alarm her. I'm here to find out—for safety's sake—if she's seen this guy hanging around. And while you're trying to keep me from protecting her, she could walk out the back door and *literally* meet this cold-blooded killer in *your* dark alley."

The guard winced. In poker, that's called a tell.

"See what I mean when I say you don't want to get this wrong?"

The guard let him pass.

Backstage was the usual hurly-burly after a performance—stagehands coming down from the flys, set decorators storing props, actors shedding costumes and complimenting each other. Robert wormed his way through the throng and down a warren of corridors to the dressing rooms.

Hers had a star on the door above her name card.

"Enter," she answered at his rap.

With his palms as sweaty as a teenage boy's on his first date, Robert opened the door and stepped into her realm.

"Ms. Burrows?"

"Yes?"

She turned from her mirror and looked him up and down.

"My name is Robert DeClercq. I...I have to confess that I took some liberties in my haste to make your acquaintance."

"Should I call Security?"

"I *am* Security," he said, stepping forward to hand her his RCMP badge.

Kate smiled and shook her head.

No doubt she'd been through this umpteen times with awestruck, besotted fans.

"What can I do for you, Mountie-man?"

"Allow me to buy you flowers—I believe that's stage protocol—and dinner at a restaurant or deli of your choice. We can talk Ibsen."

Now—years later—the Zone kicked in and superimposed on the *Rosmersholm* photo the horror of Kate's bullet-riddled body sprawled on the floor of their Montreal home. His bleary eyes took in every hole that was drilled through her flesh when the intruders ripped her with a machine pistol.

I am *Security*, he thought.

What a con.

The Headless Horseman nightmare was so fresh in his mind that he couldn't bear to look at the photo of Jane sitting in a pile of autumn leaves, with her head thrown back in laughter and sunlight caressing her curls. Was that another symptom of post-traumatic stress disorder? He tried to recall what he'd read about PTSD. Those plagued by the illness suffered intrusive flashbacks and night terrors. The onset was often delayed by years, until an increase in stress triggered the crippling symptoms: reliving the horror, day and night; struggling to fall asleep and stay asleep; grappling with strong feelings of guilt, shame, anxiety, and despair; trying to get intrusive thoughts out of your head while sights, sounds, smells keep setting you off.

Post-traumatic stress disorder.

DeClercq had its symptoms in spades.

His big mistake had been falling in love with his psychologist. After the deaths of Kate and Jane, he'd fled across the continent from Montreal to the West Coast, lugging his demons with him. Before long, the first symptoms of

PTSD had him tossing in his sleep, so he sought help from a psychiatrist rec-ommended by Vancouver Mounties. Dr. George Ruryk, however, was leaving for sabbatical in Europe, and he suggested that Robert undertake the talking cure with his best student, Genevieve Blouin. If only she hadn't been so be-witching, they might have dug down and pulled out the roots of his distress.

But she was…

So the heartbroken patient fell moonstruck…

And filtered what he discussed with her through a desire to paint his rate of progress in a glow that would win her approval, and that had ul-timately led him to invite her for a home-cooked meal to celebrate his success at therapy.

"What a house!" she had enthused, standing on the very spot where he stood now, while gazing out at the summer sunset over the Pacific. "Are you on the take?"

He laughed. "Like I told you, I was orphaned as a tyke. The aunt who raised me was well-off, and the money I inherited bought this place before property went through the roof."

"You'll make some gold digger a good catch."

"You're teasing me."

"Yes and no. You're too smart a man to fall for that trap. But you would be a *fine* partner."

"You think so? Why?"

"Don't forget, I've spent months inside your brain. They say you don't know what you've got until you lose it. So given a second chance at love, you'd cherish it, wouldn't you?"

"With the right woman."

"And who would that be?" she asked.

"If I were twenty years younger, she'd be someone like you."

"But not *me*?"

"I'm a realist, Genny."

"You sell yourself short," she chided.

His palms were as clammy as the night he'd talked himself backstage to meet Kate. During their sessions, Genevieve had been as professional as a headshrinker should be. But she was one of those second-wave feminists undermined by her irrepressible sex appeal. Her auburn hair was too wild, her green eyes sparkled with too much intelligence, her velvet lips were too sinful, and her figure left too little to the imagination.

"I see you have photos of Kate and Jane on your desk?"

"As you suggested."

"And now you comprehend what I mean by saying it *wasn't* your fault?"

"I hope so."

"It wasn't. It was simply the hand fate dealt you. If you hadn't been a Mountie, you wouldn't have got backstage. If you hadn't got backstage, you wouldn't have known Kate's love and the joy of Jane. It may have been too short a time, but it *was* worth it. And if you hadn't loved them—"

"I wouldn't have met you."

"Yes," she said matter-of-factly. "That's how fate works. Look at me. If I hadn't come of age in the Summer of Love, I'd not have had extensive experience with men. And what has that experience taught me? An awful lot of men my age are jerks. It's all about them, and my looks are all they want from me. What I see in you is a thinking man mature enough, and knocked around enough, to love me for *who* I am."

"That I would."

"Thanks to Kate and Jane."

"But there's a catch," he warned her.

"Oh? What's that?"

"I couldn't bear the guilt and heartbreak of losing another child."

"That too is fate."

"How so?" Robert asked.

"We all have crosses to bear, *chéri*. Mine is that I can't have kids."

"Is this ethical?"

"What? Us flirting?"

"Yes."

"Now you're teasing me."

"You *are* my therapist," he said.

"Not anymore. We're celebrating the cured you, aren't we?"

"May I kiss you?"

"I thought you'd never ask."

"And if I hadn't?"

"Then I'd have kissed you."

Now, in this gloomy hothouse, with Genny asleep down the hall, his eyes fixed on the third photo on his desk: the one of his suntanned second wife on their South Seas honeymoon, beachcombing in a white bikini while holding a conch shell to her ear.

Another con, he thought. *I was far from cured.*

Look at the mess I created.

Demons are crawling through the cracks in my mind.

Hubris has me crumbling.

And the stakes could not be higher.

If I buckle, Genny will know that our marriage is based on a lie.

And that she failed at her job.

Meanwhile, I'm teetering on the verge of failing at mine.

The Headhunter is calling the shots.

How'd it come to this?

The answer, of course, was obvious: his romantic con had never been put to the test. On the mornings he didn't have fencing, Robert was up before dawn to brew coffee and carry a steaming mug—if the weather was decent—through the Greenhouse and out its door to a knoll above the beach, where he would sit in a driftwood armchair and wait for a new day to brighten the horizon. Then he'd return to the house for breakfast with Genny, and after she departed for work at the psychology clinic, he would settle in here on the white wicker chair and write longhand at his own pace.

His had been the good life.

But then he got bored and yearned to return to the challenge of being a Horseman. That probably wouldn't have reawakened his PTSD had the Headhunter not immediately turned what should have been an arm's-length manhunt into a winner-take-all chess game that focused almost entirely on Robert's personal weaknesses.

Why? DeClercq wondered.

What am I to him?

Why does my gut tell me we have some kind of history?

What's the missing link that chains this killer to me?

Is it to me personally?

Or is it to what I stand for?

"Watch me shatter the myth that the Mounties always get their man."

Or is it something more?

An unfathomable prize to be awarded at the outcome of this bloody showdown?

Think, man. Think!

What could that coveted prize be?

Suddenly it was too hot in here and Robert couldn't breathe. Another symptom? Anxiety attack? Whatever the reason, he was in desperate need of fresh air. After a quick detour to bundle up and refill his mug, he took the coffee and the Enfield outside to slump in the driftwood chair flanked by an antique sundial on the fog-shrouded knoll by the sea. He was already exhausted, and the day had yet to begin. What fresh hell would dawn bring? A fifth victim? To his left, the Zone revealed images in the haze hiding North Vancouver: the headless bodies of the camper and the nun found near the harbor. Ahead, the Zone unveiled two more corpses across the fog-banked water: the nurse nailed to the totem and the floater in the river beyond. Could it be that the Headhunter had staged this taunt too?

Pull yourself together.

If not, you're going to break down.

He willed himself to concentrate on the talisman in his fist. The Horsemen were the last vestige of the British colonial army, the redcoats sent forth to conquer the world in Queen Victoria's name. When overwhelmed by hostiles and trapped in a last stand, the Horsemen were trained to hold the thin red line. That's what Robert had to do now if he hoped to be the last man standing.

"May the Force be with you."

Who said that?

He was a proud member of the most famous police force in history, and now that he was up against it, it was time to channel the power of the past to do what must be done.

He hefted the revolver.

They don't make 'em like this anymore.

Robert opened the .476 Enfield to check its load. Unlike modern-day revolvers, the six-shot cylinder didn't swing out to one side. Instead, the barrel dropped down on a hinge so the gunman could extract fired casings from among the live rounds. Designed and manufactured for the British Army by the Royal Small Arms Factory in Enfield, Middlesex, this gun was the sidearm of choice of the North-West Mounted Police from 1883 to 1911. Commissioner Lawrence Herchmer reported in 1886 that the Force was entirely armed with Enfields—1,079 in all—and his men were generally pleased with them, but concerned that the .476 round was too potent.

Too potent, thought DeClercq.

How often do you hear cops complain that they have too much stopping power?

He snapped the Enfield back together and hooked his little finger through the lanyard ring that once strung this handgun from the collar of Wilfred Blake.

A potent weapon indeed!

The gun had been found in the Rocky Mountains after the inspector vanished in 1897 while chasing a young Cree named Iron-child. Searchers sent to find Blake after the spring thaw had stumbled upon the Indian's remains, or what little the wolves had left behind. He was later identified from the beading on his tattered breechclout. Blake had left traces in a thicket near Medicine Lake, and on the far side of the water, close to Windigo Mountain, the trackers found Iron-child's shelter. Dogs then sniffed out Blake's Enfield in a pile of rubble at the bottom of a cliff face created by a recent earthquake.

The mountain above was inaccessible.

Ergo, the mystery of the lost patrol was never solved.

In researching his history of the Force, *Men Who Wore the Tunic,* Robert had found the inspector enigmatic too. Blake was a loner. He eschewed teamwork. Forged on the anvil of colonial battles around the globe, he had carved out a unique niche for himself in the Mounted Police: he was the Horseman dispatched to catch the ones who got away. The American press loved him; he was the source of the unofficial motto "The Mounties always get their man." The fact that so many came back dead only enhanced Blake's reputation—proof of derring-do struggles in the Great Lone Land.

The queen herself had given him the Victoria Cross for valor.

Several times, Blake had refused promotion. He preferred to stalk the wilds in a game of survival of the fittest. After he vanished, his Enfield was given to his illegitimate son, conceived with his young housekeeper at the

Regina barracks. Half a century later, when Blake's son was posted to the North, he left the revolver with Robert for safekeeping.

Like father, like son.

For Alfred had vanished too.

Now, as DeClercq sat on the knoll hefting the gun in his hand, the beam from the lighthouse morphed the fog into a snowstorm. The Enfield was channeling power from the past, and the Zone had Robert manhunting Iron-child as Inspector Wilfred Blake.

What would Blake do if the Headhunter tried to break him?

You know the answer.

He'd do whatever's necessary to ride this outlaw down.

Time to get to work.

As Robert gulped his coffee and stood up to climb the misty path to the Greenhouse, his eyes took in the warning etched around the antique sundial beside the driftwood chair:

The Time Is Later Than You Think.

BAXBAXWALANUKSIWE

8:42 a.m.

The streets of junktown before the overnight fog burned off resembled the set of a zombie film. Junk punches no time clock. Junk takes no coffee break. Junk is a never-ending cycle of shot need and shot nodding-off. The realm of a junkie gets reduced to spoonfuls of smack, horse, mud, tar, skunk, skag, H, dragon, hero, boy, and so on, spiked into scabby veins trying to shrink from the needle. Per capita, this town has the highest percentage of junkies in North America. So this morning, the zombies shambled out of their flophouses and lurched through the mist to find their pushers.

Shoot 'em in the brain.

That's how you kill zombies.

Shoot 'em in the vein.

That's how they kill themselves.

Peering out from the shotgun seat of the unmarked car, Katherine Spann took in the gaunt faces twitching like dead meat coming alive—the mainliner whose jaw hung as slack as that of a ventriloquist's dummy; the tranny in hooker's clothes who swished his hips as if to say, "You should see me in the nude"; the old woman with the toothless mouth, slumped against the wall of an alley with her arm flopping in the gutter as a drop of blood bubbled in her elbow crease.

"Gotcha!"

"Who?"

"Bax."

"Where?"

"There," said Spann, swinging open the passenger door before Scarlett hit the brakes. Then she was off and running as the Kwakiutl took flight.

Abandoning the prowl car where it was, her partner joined the chase.

Maple Tree Square in the center of Gastown was the birthplace of Vancouver. There was nothing here but logging camps until the day in 1867 when "Gassy" Jack Deighton rowed ashore with a barrel of whisky and asked the axemen to build a saloon so he could wet their whistles. The five roads that converged on that frontier pub were still in use, and the cops were cruising down one of them when Bax appeared in the haze. Around here, if you're a pusher and someone rushes at you, you turn tail and scram.

Bull or mugger, whoever's coming is not your friend.

Run, dude. *Run!*

This chase could have been taking place a century ago, for some of the buildings surrounding the cobblestoned square dated back to Victoria's reign. At one time, this hive of brick warehouses buzzed with boisterous hollers from three hundred taverns, but starting in the 1960s, the area was half reclaimed by trendy restaurants, hip boutiques, and the chambers of courtroom shysters. Pounding across the paving stones by Gassy Jack's statue—with the bronze figure standing atop a whisky keg, of course—the fugitive Indian dashed north on Carrall Street, then scrambled over a wire-mesh fence into the harbor rail yards.

From here, trains chugged thousands of miles east to Montreal.

Today, the CPR was shunting boxcars.

Bax hit the ground on the far side of the fence and took off again. If they lost him in the fog, the pusher would escape their clutches, so Spann scaled the eight-foot mesh and pounced beyond. When Scarlett vaulted over seconds later, the wire tore his pant leg ankle to groin, missing his scrotum by inches.

"Stop! Police!" Kathy yelled.

Bax gave her the finger.

The squeal of steel on steel and the slam of boxcars whamming each other were as grating on the nerves as fingernails scratching a blackboard. Oblong phantoms lurched across the fog like tanks in battle amid the smell of the salty sea and diesel fumes. It all reminded Spann of an ad she'd once seen for a record album. An engine and a rail car are about to be coupled together. A black slave bound in chains has had enough, and the old-time lithograph shows him hanging upside down to position his head into the gap between the closing plates. The caption reads: "Led Zeppelin"—or whatever rock group it was—"does things to your head."

Bang!

Squishhh!

Moral?

Track crossers beware!

Bax must not have seen the ad, for he suicidally threw himself under a boxcar the moment before it was shunted, lying on the tracks between the grinding wheels until the slowing cars gave him an opening to roll out the other side. Clawing earth to gain his feet, off he dashed.

Kathy was going to lose the chase if she didn't move fast, so the Mountie turned and jogged alongside the rolling stock until she could grab hold and scale the ladder up a tank car. Legging over the cylinder near its loading spout, she descended the rungs on the other side.

"See him?" Scarlett shouted from the top of the next boxcar in line, where a squawking seagull swooped down on the action.

"Quiet!" snapped Spann, listening intently.

Here, bordering the sea, the fog was thicker. Creeping off the water like a mariner's ghost, it shrouded the potholed access road along the harbor. Like the whale did Jonah, the mist had swallowed Bax. Her ears cocked, Kathy took in the lapping of waves on the shore, the incessant moan of foghorns from the inlet, the huff and hiss of the train behind her...and footfalls on the road to her left.

"He's heading for the SeaBus terminal, Rick."

"Get him," yelled her partner.

The pounding of her running feet drowned the Native's paces. As they neared the site being cleared for Expo 86—the world's fair was coming to Vancouver in four years—Kathy skidded to a halt and listened again. No more footsteps. Had Bax veered off the road? If so, where could he be? Back in the rail yard, playing chicken with the train? Or was he on the rickety pier jutting into the harbor?

No, not the pier, she thought. *I'd hear him on the planks.*

Unless…

You don't think?

Is Bax hiding under the pier?

In the beginning, the CPR's Waterfront Station was built on piles along the shore. As warehouses sprang up, so did marsh bridges and steamer docks. Now, those relics of the past were doomed to demolition. One of the condemned docks was beyond the four-foot gravel dyke that kept the sea from the road. Cresting the embankment, Spann peeked in under the pier. Sure enough, there was Bax, squirming his way through the piles and struts like a toddler on monkey bars.

What did the pusher believe?

That there'd be a canoe waiting at the end of the pier?

Dream on, fantasy dude.

Squeezing in under the ramp that slanted to the dock, Spann shinnied up supports crusted with barnacles and crawled along crossbeams treated with creosote. The sea below reeked of rotting fish and gray water flushed from ships in the harbor. As she closed on the Kwakiutl ahead, rats scampered past, blinking their red eyes in the clammy dimness.

The sound of Scarlett creaking on the boards above echoed into the crawlspace. Six…five…four feet between her and the Indian. Kathy almost had Bax by the leg when Rick dropped to his knees at the end of the dock and poked his head under the deck to grin at their boxed-in prey.

"Game over, pal," he said as Bax kicked Spann's hand away and rolled sideways off his perch into the foaming waves below.

"Damn!" cursed Kathy.

Filling her lungs with air, she tumbled in after the pusher.

From high on the dock, Rick watched both swimmers splash out from under the pier, then thrash around in the foggy sea, throwing punches at each other. Not only had his partner connected Grabowski to Hardy through Bax, but now she was single-handedly going to haul Bax in, thereby claiming the collar for herself. If Rick didn't get his ass in gear and wade into action, it would be *Corporal* Katherine Spann giving orders to *Constable* Rick Scarlett…well, ain't gonna happen!

"Damn!" cursed Rick.

This was no time to stay high and dry.

Sitting down on the pier, he pulled off his shoes and socks, stuck his gun barrel-first into one shoe to leave it on the dock, then stood up and dove into the choppy water to surface behind Bax. The moment his head was back in the air, Rick locked a chokehold around the Kwakiutl's neck and—having cut off his oxygen—snarled in his ear, "Give up or I'll drown you."

The Native surrendered by raising both arms.

Spann grabbed one wrist, Scarlett grabbed the other, and together they dragged their gasping captive onto the rocky shore to cuff and search him.

"J-J-Jesus, Blondie! I never made you for a narc."

"Tough luck, Bax," she said, tugging off his boots. One released a red balloon stuffed with gelatin caps into her palm.

"H?" she asked.

"No idea. You p-p-planted it on me."

A waterproof bundle fell out of his other boot. It was the junkie's outfit: hypodermic needle, plastic arm cinch, vial of water, blackened spoon, and cigarette lighter.

"Well, well, what have we here?" Scarlett mused, poking the image of the severed head in the V of the Indian's jean jacket. Bax was wearing the same dirty T-shirt he'd worn in the Moonlight Arms, the one with the nose-ringed Kwakiutl chief displaying four long-haired trophies.

Bax shivered.

"I n-n-need a fix," he groaned.

Junkies run on junk-time, and Bax's clock was winding down. His only retreat was another stab of the needle. His pupils weren't pinned, and that meant he hadn't fixed recently. Odds were he'd come out to peddle the caps supplied by his pusher—who, the cops suspected, was John Lincoln Hardy. That done, he'd scurry back to his lair and spike his own arm, then drift off to junk-land without a care in the world. Unfortunately, the intervening hot pursuit had exhausted his junk-ravaged body. Already, Bax showed signs of withdrawal. His nose was running and he was sweating, despite his cold dip in the harbor. The itch of water on their skin is vexing to addicts. That's why junkies don't take baths. Bax twitched in his wet clothes as if they were poison ivy. Soon, the entrails in his belly would cramp, and he'd double up, writhing.

"Have a heart, Blondie. I f-f-fixed you, remember?"

"I was *acting*, Bax."

"But I fixed you all the same."

"See the fix you're in now? I've got you for trafficking multiple times in the Moonlight Arms. The number of caps in this bundle will add another trafficking charge. On top of that, you're in withdrawal, and we both know what that means. Every tick of the clock moves you closer to going cold turkey on the cold floor of a jail cell, trying to keep your guts from squirming out of your mouth."

Rick jabbed the T-shirt harder.

"What's with this headhunter on your chest?" he asked. "I'll tell you what—you're a serial killer. You hate white men for what we did to your people. Stole your land, suppressed your culture, and locked your kids away to be sexually assaulted in residential schools. You take your revenge by raping and beheading our women according to the bloody ritual flaunted on your T-shirt. You stalked Helen Grabowski from the Moonlight Arms and Sister Angelica from the North Van Indian rez. The rest were random victims, chosen to confuse us and terrorize the city. The taunts are to rub the Mounted's noses in it. You're the Headhunter."

"Like hell. I'm j-j-just a junkie, man."

Bax shuddered, arms straining against the cuffs, as rattling took hold. He tried to spit on the beach in contempt, but his mouth was too dry.

"Hurts, huh?" Rick goaded. "What does Bax mean?"

No answer.

Wary.

"It's short for Baxbaxwalanuksiwe," said Kathy. "The cannibal god. Eh, Bax?"

"Jeez, Blondie. You hip?"

"The image on your T-shirt was shot by Edward S. Curtis, the foremost photographer of Native culture in the West. He also filmed *In the Land of the Headhunters* among your people. The guy on your chest is Qa'hila, a young Kwakiutl chief. The Lekwiltok—the Southern Kwakiutl—were headhunters feared as far down the West Coast as Seattle. Hok Hok, the cannibal bird, represents Baxbaxwalanuksiwe on your totem poles. And Baxbaxwalanuksiwe inspired Hamatsa, your cannibal cult."

"Cannibal cult?" said Rick. "That explains it. Even if you've got an alibi for some murders, other cultists could be out raping and hacking off heads."

"Where'd you learn that, Blondie?"

"Research, Bax. It helps to know who I'm busting."

"Why that T-shirt?" Rick asked.

"P-p-proud of my culture. Qa'hila's way cooler than some rock group."

"Let's take him in. We *got* the Headhunter."

"F-f-fuck you."

Withdrawal had Bax squirming like a can of bait worms.

"Easy, Rick. Let's hear what he has to say. No matter what, Bax is off to jail. Isolated till after the roundup. Can't let him ruin the undercover op."

Unbuttoning a cuff, Spann yanked the Indian's sleeve up past his elbow and pulled his arm out to examine its inner crease.

"Needle tracks that long mean you're hooked bad. If you don't fix *now*, you're heading for hell on earth. You have only one escape, so listen good. I know Hardy supplies you. I saw you meet in the alley behind the Moonlight Arms. This guy, remember?"

She fished the soggy NOPD photo from her pocket.

"Hardy's into voodoo. That fits the Headhunter's MO. As Helen Grabowski's pimp, he's tied to one of the victims. Tell us where to find him and I'll let you fix."

"I'm no rat."

"Yes, you are," said Rick. "Tell us where he is, or we let it leak you snitched on him. If that happens, you'll be one *dead* rat."

"Who knows?" Kathy said. "I could lose the paperwork on my undercover buys."

Bax's teeth chattered.

Goose bumps mottled his scabby skin.

Untying the knot in the red balloon, Kathy dumped its contents into her palm. After counting the caps, she stuffed twenty back in and pocketed the stash.

"Twenty caps are enough to charge you with possession for the purpose of trafficking. The five in my hand are for your fix. You choose, Bax. Hardy or hell on earth?"

Gripping one cap, she pulled it apart, releasing the white powder within to float off into the sea.

"Hardy?" said Spann.

She pulled another cap apart and set its heroin free.

"Two gone, three to go."

As Kathy gripped a third cap to scatter more than half of Bax's fix, the Kwakiutl cracked.

"Stop! I'll rat!"

"Uncuff him, Rick, and extend his arm."

Though they were in the open on the shore of the inner harbor, the fog allowed the cops and their quarry to hide in plain sight. As Rick cuffed Bax to him and grasped the junkie by his released wrist, Kathy cinched the plastic cord around his upper arm.

"How many caps do you fix?"

"I'm jonesing, Blondie. Load 'em all."

Spann emptied three caps into the spoon, added water from the vial, and flicked the lighter to cook the heroin. After drawing the junk into the hypodermic, she repeatedly tapped his inner elbow to raise one of the veins cowering near the bone.

"Look me in the eye, Bax, and don't try lying. The moment I smell bullshit, I'll squirt your fix into the sea. Have we got a deal?"

"Yeah. Hit me, Blondie."

"Answer first. Where's Hardy?"

"Honest Injun?" His smirk fell short. "I don't know."

"You're lying. A pusher always knows how to reach his supplier."

"You got it backwards, Blondie. Hardy's new to the skids. Him and his hooker blew in from New Orleans. That pimp's not into smack. Coke's his drug. All he wants Sister H for is to keep his whores hooked. Keep 'em in his stable."

"Backwards? How?"

"I don't know where Hardy is 'cause he don't push to me. *I'm* the source," said Bax. "*I* push to him."

———

Bax was gauching—nodding off—when the paddy wagon arrived. The Headhunter Squad had its own jail, the old BC Pen, a castle-like federal prison upriver in New Westminster. Opened in 1878, the Pen was decommissioned two years ago, after a series of riots and hostage takings. Slated for demolition but commandeered for this case, the Pen would play host to Bax until after tomorrow's roundup.

"I'm surprised you let him fix," Scarlett said as they hoofed up Water Street to their abandoned car.

"He's not the Headhunter. He's too smacked out for that."

"Still, you coulda let him stew."

"Why be cruel?"

"The guy's a hype."

"Not my style."

"Whatever." Scarlett shrugged. "We make a deadly team, eh? My good cop to your bad cop."

"Christ, I'm freezing."

"How 'bout a steam? If you're not hung up on modesty, I know a place near here. It's got private baths, and we can swap these wet rags for the plainclothes stored in our car."

"If the car hasn't been towed away, then I'm game."

Downtown Vancouver is warmed by a network of subterranean pipes that deliver high-pressure steam from a natural gas boiler near the Georgia Viaduct to office towers, the new football dome, and tourist landmarks like the Gastown steam clock. The pipe that powers that crowd-pleasing timepiece on the corner of Water and Cambie also heats the Gastown Steam Baths a few doors east, where the flying patrol cops paid for an hour of solitary sweating.

It was foggier in here than by the foggy harbor. Having stripped in the men's changing room and wrapped a towel around his taut waist, Rick was first to enter the small, white-tiled cubicle. Folding a towel on the slick bench, he slouched in one corner, listening to the steam hiss as he waited for Kathy.

Seeing the door open perked him up.

Hubba hubba!

Yowza! Rick thought.

Never had he seen a female in better shape. All the body beautifuls Rick eyed at the gym wouldn't stand a chance next to this Amazon. Kathy entered the steam bath naked but for two towels. One was tucked around her hips—*What an ass she has!*—and the other slung around her neck so both ends covered her breasts. With luck, sweat would adhere the fabric to her skin and pop her nipples.

What a pair of headlights! Rick marveled.

It took all the willpower he could muster not to reach out and whip the towel off her tits. What a fuck she'd be—more like a wrestling match. He imagined himself with his arms up her back, gripping her shoulders just to keep her on his cock when she came, screaming.

"Not bad, eh?"

"It's *hot* in here," she said.

He watched her fold a third towel onto the tiled bench.

Good. Don't want you scalding that sweet pussy.

When Kathy sat back against the wall tiles, she winced from the heat, and that jiggled her boobs enough to stir an erection beneath Rick's towel.

Oops! Can't let Omar the Tentmaker give me away.

To cool his jets, Rick closed his eyes and thought of the classic, time-tested Aesop fable one of his granddads had told him. An old bull and a young bull are coming down a hillside toward a field of cows. The frisky young bull bounces about and says to his elder: "Come on, Pops. Let's rush down and hump some of those cows!"

"Nope," sighs the old bull.

"How come?" the young bull asks.

"Because if we mosey on down as cool as can be, we'll get a whole lot more."

Wise words, Rick thought.

Bide your time.

Broads need to be tickled.

Bending forward to hide his erection, he opened his eyes while Kathy had hers closed and watched sweat trickle from the pores of her hot body.

Fuck me, Rick thought.

Do I want a piece of that!

EBONY

On his way into work at HH HQ, DeClercq stopped by his doctor's office to get a prescription for Benzedrine. When the doc gave him a quizzical frown, the Mountie explained: "I know what you're thinking, and you know from media reports what I'm up against. I know that speed burnt out the Beat Generation. But I also know that bomber pilots used 'wakey-wakey pills' to get them through the war, and that James Bond takes them in Fleming's novels when he has to stay alert. This case has me working around the clock in a desperate situation, and if there's another murder, there will be no option but to stay awake. I won't take them unless I have to, but if I must, I will. I need your help, Doctor. Desperate times call for desperate measures."

"I'm hesitant," said the doc.

"But you'll write the scrip? I've got four women's heads stuck on poles."

His doctor wrote the prescription, which Robert promptly filled at the pharmacy. Then, sitting in his car in the drugstore parking lot, he opened the vial and swallowed a benny with a gulp of bottled water.

By the time he reached the Heather Stables, DeClercq—though exhausted—was wide awake.

———

The scene on the foggy street in front of the Tudor building was surreal. Hundreds of female protesters carrying placards and chanting slogans milled in the murky mist. The sign that caught Robert's attention read, DECLERCQ IS A JERK! CAN HIM! Yesterday's attack on the Catholic nun, which was followed by the Take Back the Night riot in Robson Square, had lured CBS, ABC, NBC, and CNN—the newly founded cable news network—north across the border to cover the story. To protect the building in case of attack during another riot, the Mounted Police had deployed heavily armed ERT cops across the front lawn.

Besieged, thought DeClercq.

The Zone flashed an image through Robert's mind of the Bastille being stormed by irate Parisians during the French Revolution.

The guillotine.

Off with my head, he thought.

Inside, the main-floor squad room hummed with activity. Inspector Chan's Computer Command had whittled the skinner file down to a hit list of potential suspects based on their past sexual crimes. Tomorrow, the Headhunter Squad would fan out to check their alibis under the guise of "routine questions." Mug shots and printouts cluttered every desktop in the cramped bullpen, and knots of cops crowded around assignment schedules tacked to bulletin boards along one wall.

"Got a moment, boss?"

Mad Dog Rabidowski intercepted DeClercq at the foot of the stairs to his office. Rabid was in shirtsleeves and sported a shoulder holster, a rarity in the Mounted because it was more suggestive of American city cops than a cavalry regiment recruited from the British colonial army.

"What's on your mind, Constable?"

"There's trouble brewing with the Iron Skulls."

"Follow me."

They climbed the stairs, crossed the landing, and entered the corner office, where MacDougall and Rodale were already studying the Strategy Wall. With four murders to deal with, the collage had grown in complexity. The inspector and the sergeant looked more like generals maneuvering troops at the Battle of Waterloo.

"Sit down if you want," said DeClercq.

"I'll stand."

"So what's up with the bikers?"

"Special E has a snitch close to the motorcycle gangs, a mechanical whiz at constructing rigids that grip the street without wheel suspensions. The Iron

Skulls are meth heads into some sick shit. Yesterday, the Wimmin's Strike Force took bricks and razors to a pair of porn marketers: Artie Fripp at Get-A-Whiff Productions, and Kurt Schmidt, owner of the Kit Kat Klub and Theater. The snitch's tip is that those two scuzzbags want revenge, so they've hired the Iron Skulls to help 'em stage an S&M porn video called *Headhunter*. The rat says the Skulls are so methed out that they might make an actual snuff film."

"Course of action?"

"We hit the Skulls hard and fast. An ounce of prevention..."

"Okay. Do it."

Mad Dog was turning to leave when the superintendent stopped him.

"Is that a Ruger Security-Six strapped to your chest?"

Crap, thought Mad Dog. *He's heard too.*

"Yes, chief."

"What's the load?"

"Six rounds of .357 Magnum."

"Powerful gun."

"Yes, sir. Is this the James Bond moment?"

"How so?"

"In *Dr. No*, M orders 007 to swap his weapon of choice—a Beretta—for a Walther PPK. You want me to pack the Smith?"

DeClercq shook his head. Having used Bond himself to pry Benzedrine tabs out of his doctor this morning, he couldn't fault Mad Dog for playing the same card.

"When Wilfred Blake was on the hunt last century, he packed the potent Enfield .476 revolver and the Winchester Model 1876 rifle. If need be, he could requisition seven- and nine-pound cannons. And had he lived a year longer, a .303 Maxim machine gun. I don't believe in having my team underpowered for the task at hand. So if the Iron Skulls act out, I want you armed to blow their heads off."

———

"I haven't seen a shoulder rig like that for years," said MacDougall as the door shut behind Rabidowski. "Not since snub-nosed revolvers went the way of the dinosaurs."

"He's young," said DeClercq.

"He'll have an old man's back problems if he lugs a chunk that size around in a shoulder holster for a crippling stretch of time."

DeClercq smiled. "The price of looking macho."

"Ain't it the truth."

The Mounties refocused their attention on the grisly Strategy Wall.

"Update me," said the super.

"The sweep's ready to go, and the BC Pen's set up as an interrogation center. Expect to see your desk piled to the roof with harassment complaints."

Now was not the time for these Horsemen to be reined in by Canada's new Charter of Rights and Freedoms. For more than a century, the Force had policed under the British style of law, where the focus was on whether an accused had committed the crime. From here on, manhunts would veer toward the American model, where courts were obsessed with policing the police. Lawyers love nothing more than a newly minted law with every untried argument up for grabs, so they'd swoop down on the sweep and pick the bones of the Headhunter Squad like vultures in Death Valley.

Rodale, who liaised with the flying patrols, said, "Scarlett and Spann have shipped our first guest to the BC Pen."

"Who?"

"A skid row pusher named Bax. When she was undercover, Kathy saw him deal heroin with Grabowski's pimp." Rodale tapped John Lincoln Hardy's photo on the Strategy Wall. "They've also got Hardy on some Commercial Crime wiretaps talking voodoo and zombies."

"Where's Hardy?"

"On the loose. But they're closing in."

"See that Spann and Scarlett get all the support they need."

Rodale moved over to the shallow grave section of the wall and flicked the morning's pinup. "Now that she's been ID'd, Interpol wired this photo of Liese Greiner."

"Attractive woman."

"Macdonald and Lewis are tracking a creep who fits the Headhunter profile. A psycho named Matthew Paul Pitt. He lives in the bush and haunts strip bars. If Greiner ran out of cash while camping rough by the creek, maybe she found temp work as a stripper."

"Distribute her photo APB, including the flying patrols."

"Roger."

MacDougall gestured toward the totem pole quarter of the wall. "It appears Joanna Portman had a *secret* boyfriend. She wasn't as strong on Catholic religious beliefs as we were told. Her lover—married, with three kids—is a pathologist in St. Paul's morgue. We're checking him out."

"So the sperm found in Portman is likely from him."

"Which boosts our theory that the Headhunter's driven by sexual dysfunction."

"He can't come," concluded DeClercq.

"Or he hasn't perfected the fantasy that gets him off," MacDougall suggested.

"And the nun?"

The three Mounties moved to the final portion of the wall.

"Ghost Keeper canvassed the North Van reserve and turned up nothing. Sister Angelica was well liked by the Squamish Natives around her church."

"That was a long shot. They're not Kwakiutl."

"But Bax is," Rodale said. "When Spann and Scarlett nabbed him, he was wearing a T-shirt with a Baxbax-whatever-his-name-is *headhunter* on it."

"That fits the totem taunt. Grill him," said DeClercq.

———

For several hours, the cops fine-tuned the next day's dragnet of skinner file suspects. When Avacomovitch knocked on the door in the early afternoon, the three men broke for lunch. Jack and Jim headed for the canteen in the basement, leaving Robert and Joe behind.

"Good news, I hope," said DeClercq.

"Yes and no," said the Russian.

"Bad news first."

"*The Vancouver Times* just hit the streets."

Joe held up the front page.

BROKEN COP LEADS HUNT FOR PSYCHO, blared the headline.

HEADHUNTER MOCKS MOUNTIE, read the subhead.

The newspapers in this town were duking it out in a circulation battle. *The Province*—since 1898—and *The Vancouver Sun*—since 1912—had jointly ruled the kingdom. *The Vancouver Times*—a recent upstart—hoped to usurp the throne. At first, *The Sun* had scooped the market when its editor, Skip O'Rourke, received the *Buns and Boobs* ad and the two Polaroids from the Headhunter. But now *The Times* had fired back with some muckraking, and the target getting slimed with printers' ink was Superintendent DeClercq. The rag revived the vengeful aftermath of Quebec's October Crisis, illustrating its article with photos of Robert's home in Montreal as Kate's corpse was wheeled out to the meat wagon, and of the cabin in the woods where Jane's neck was broken. A telephoto shot of her devastated father being comforted by François Chartrand, the current commissioner of the Mounted Police, ran with a sidebar on the internal investigation into DeClercq's rampage, at which he was represented by the same François Chartrand. Is that why, *The Times* asked, this "broken cop" was brought back to lead the Headhunter Squad? Not because he was the best detective for the job, but because he was a charter member of the old boys' club?

"It's not what you know, it's who you know," the paper intimated.

DeClercq was *yesterday's* man.

And why, asked *The Times,* should this terrified city pay in blood?

Whoever had delved into his past had done a thorough job, unearthing the fact that he had been treated by—and later had married—Genevieve Blouin. Early this morning, a *Times* photographer had snapped a telephoto shot of Genny arriving at work, rushing it to the paper in time for the afternoon edition. Here, beside a story questioning just how much counseling had gone on between them, was a picture of his wife with her raven-black hair from Halloween.

Printed on the front page for all to see.

Including the Headhunter.

Joe was troubled by the change that came over his friend as Robert absorbed the implications of what he saw and read. It seemed as if the Mountie had suddenly sprung a leak, and all the energy Joe had seen when he entered the office quickly drained away. A tic twitched one corner of Robert's anxious eyes, and bags weighed down the flesh below as tension furrowed his face.

"When I was down and out," Joe said, "you were there for me. A defector burns all his bridges and leaves his life behind. You offered me work and welcomed me into your home. Now you're backed against the wall, and it's my turn to be there for you."

The Russian closed in on the Strategy Wall and examined the four Polaroid photos pinned there.

"The killer takes Polaroids because that film develops itself. He can't send his shots to a photo lab for negatives and prints. Nor, it seems, does he have a darkroom. What say we direct every seller of Polaroid film to ask purchasers for photo ID and then make a record of the names? If a customer balks at being identified, the seller should promptly phone in a description to the Headhunter Squad."

"I take it that's your good news?"

"No, this is."

From within his jacket, Joe withdrew a microscope slide containing a black splinter.

"While I was examining Liese Greiner's remains at the VGH morgue, I found this sliver lodged in a recent fracture at the lower front of her pelvic bone—just where I'd expect to find it if the Headhunter had kicked her in the crotch and transferred it from his shoe. It took a while to identify the wood as *Diospyros crassiflora*, a species used for elaborate carvings since ancient Egyptian times. It's jet black, hard, durable, and polishes to a high luster. People have used it for ritual masks, knife handles, gun grips, piano keys, and the black pieces in chess sets."

"Does it have a common name?"

"West African ebony."

———

"We got your message," Kathy said.

"About the taps," said Rick. As he looked across the desk at Bill Tipple, the manhunter thought the wiretapper had a "bum face." His pudgy cheeks were like the orbs of someone's ass, and his little mouth was pursed like a sphincter. Talking with him was like being mooned out a car window.

"Seen the APB that just came in from your boss?" asked Tipple.

"No," said Kathy. "We've been combing the skids."

Bill handed her the bulletin from the Headhunter Squad. It showed the Interpol photo of Liese Greiner and asked all units be on the lookout for West African ebony.

"Ebony?"

"Interesting, huh?"

"West Africa smacks of voodoo."

Like a smug poker player pushing his chips all in, Tipple shoved a pile of wiretap transcripts across his desk to the flying patrol.

"The taps are up to date, and Rackstraw's being monitored live. The only sign of Hardy is in the top three calls from two days ago."

Commercial Crime Section (Special "I": Electronic Surveillance)
Target: Steve Rackstraw (aka "The Fox").
Tape installed: October 30. 0900 hours. (Tipple.)
Tape removed: October 30. 1630 hours. (Tipple.)
U/M "The Weasel" now known as John Lincoln Hardy.
U/M known only as "The Wolf."

Outgoing local call: 1444 hours

Weasel: Hey.
Fox: Hey. Hey.
Weasel: What's happenin', nigga?
Fox: Waitin' on a call.
Weasel: I'm ready.
Fox: 'Bout that house youse knows?
Weasel: All moved in.
Fox: An' the filly?
Weasel: Hooked on Sister H. Now she hooks for me.
Fox: Biz good?
Weasel: Uh-uh. Stroll's too crowded. So many ladies out last night, they shoot at you. No need t' shoot at them. Pussy failed to drive them white boys wild.
Fox: H.G.?

Weasel: Nothin'. No worry, bro. Done an' dusted.

Fox: Play this right an' you'll move up.

Weasel: I ready.

Fox: Good. Be gettin' yo' juju soon.

(End of call.)

Incoming long distance call: 1557 hours

Fox: Hey. Hey.

Operator: I have a collect call from Mr. Wolf. Will you accept the charge?

Fox: I will.

(Pause.)

Wolf: It's cooking on the second. Pot boils over at midnight.

Fox: The cous'll be down to see ya.

Wolf: Better not fuck up.

Fox: He won't.

Wolf: *Au revoir.*

(End of call.)

Outgoing local call: 1601 hours

Weasel: Hey.

Fox: It's on. Time a nigga caught his ride an' was gone.

Weasel: Will do.

Fox: Enjoy the gumbo. Tell Momma hello from me.

(End of call.)

"'Cooking on the second' is likely tomorrow, November 2," said Spann. "Sounds like Hardy's on his way."

"Unless 'Be gettin' yo' juju soon' refers to the Voodoo Juju gig tonight," she suggested.

"At Hyde's," said Scarlett.

"Where's the Wolf calling from?"

"New Orleans," said Tipple.

VOODOO JUJU

10:15 p.m.

The towering wedge loomed out of the fog like a ship's prow. The fog-horns off the harbor added to the nautical daydream. In fact, the ship was a triangular flatiron building six stories high. The streets of Gastown aren't laid out in a grid because each follows what would have been the shortest route from the old lumber camps to Gassy Jack's saloon. Alexander Street formed one side of the wedge and Powell Street the other, so the tip of the prow jabbed into Maple Tree Square. The door in the tip was flanked by six Greek columns, and above the lintel, five bow windows stacked up to the roof. Residents on those upper floors would get no sleep tonight, for music boomed from downstairs at ear-bleed volume. The blood-red neon sign above the door glared HYDE'S.

"Voodoo Juju," Kathy said. "Hear the African drums?"

"Disco's dead," scoffed Rick.

"How'd Bill put it? Rackstraw blew into town with word of a new school of hip-hop music and rapping on the East Coast."

"Bass that loud'll jar your fillings loose."

"Swamp music."

"New Orleans."

"'Zombie walks,'" said Kathy.

Spann led the way down dingy stairs to a subterranean vault. Harsh light pulsed in time with the thundering bass, kinetic enough to bring on an epileptic fit. The sweet smell of marijuana mixed with cigarette smoke swirled up the stairs to meet the fog outside. *Boom-boom! Boom-boom! Boom-*

boom! The deeper they descended, the louder were the voodoo drums, amplified to a level that rattled their rib cages. A bone-crushing bouncer blocked the gate to hell, but their bison-head badges yanked his leash.

"Be good," he mouthed.

The *Boom-boom! Boom-boom! Boom-boom!* was too deafening for speech.

Back when this building was raised at the turn of the century, its underground beer hall extended beneath both sidewalks. The cavern the Mounties entered this day was larger than expected, and if the jackhammering bass cracked its foundations, they'd be crushed by rubble. The crowd was a mix of black and white, most of them wearing heavy metal leathers or retro punk. Those mobbing the stage thronged forward and back, pulsing like a human heart. Each one clenched a fist and leaned in with the beat of the drums. "People are strange, but people are nice," a freak from the acid-head sixties had written across the ceiling beam. Later, someone hardcore had scratched over that flower-power graffiti and replaced it with "Fuck you and your mother."

Boom-boom! Boom-boom! Boom-boom!

Voodoo Juju live was a riveting enactment of the concert poster the cops had seen back at Commercial Crime. On a screen at the back of the stage, alligators and water snakes snapped their jaws and bared their fangs while slithering through a dark bayou swamp overhung with mangrove trees dripping Spanish moss. Nudging Spann, Scarlett directed her attention to a trellis of skulls and voodoo masks that framed the musicians and dancers, all of them naked except for jockstraps and G-strings. Painted with luminous skeletons, the black bodies humped each other in time to the erotic beat like demon-possessed zombies writhing at a graveyard orgy. Hand-slapped voodoo drums and an electric bass drove the rhythm. Hendrix-style, the lead guitarist wailed a banshee squeal. The frontman wore a top hat crowned with a snake's skull and growled out a voodoo chant:

> *Papa Legba, ouvre baye pou mwen,*
> *Papa Legba, ouvre baye pou mwen,*
> *Ouvre baye pou mwen, Papa*
> *Pou mwen passé.*

Boom-boom! Boom-boom! Boom-boom!

As Rick stood mesmerized by the bouncing breasts, Kathy nudged him too. He followed her nod toward a door by the stage and discerned a silhouette lurking on the threshold. The strobe light flickered the man's features like faces in an old-time film. Steve Rackstraw—also known as the Fox—was clad in gangster garb similar to what he wore in Tipple's telephoto shots. His pencil-thin mustache dribbled down to his chinstrap, corralling lips smirking with self-satisfaction.

Flanking the stage, the flying patrol cops closed on the door. The scowl on his brow said Rackstraw smelled pork coming his way. Spann shone a penlight on her badge to confirm that suspicion. The music producer retreated backstage and shut the door after they followed. The wall between here and the stage was a support structure, so it dampened the noise enough for them to talk.

"Wha'?" asked the Fox.

He made no move to turn on the lights.

"We talk by yo' flash? Don' wan' no mofo bargin' in an' glare spoilin' da gig."

"You Steve Rackstraw?"

"Who you?"

"Constable Katherine Spann. And this is Constable Rick Scarlett."

"Wha'd I do?"

"Nothing."

"Den why da man botherin' me?"

"I'm not the man," said Spann.

"Yo' wan' shawty o' booty instead?"

"I like the band."

"Rock da house," said the Fox. "Dem niggas gonna be *big*." He shot Spann a warning look: I can say it, but you can't. So suck it up, honky.

"What's the chant mean?"

"Papa Legba, open da gate fo' me," he translated. "Open da gate fo' me, Papa / Fo' me to pass."

"Who's Papa Legba? Yo' grandpappy?" Scarlett goaded.

Kathy wondered why Rick felt the need to pick a fight with every suspect they questioned. The man carried a massive chip on his shoulder.

Recalling her premonition of trouble coming when they'd discussed Agatha Christie's *Ten Little Niggers* at Commercial Crime, she sensed it wouldn't be long until Rick pushed someone too far.

Spann wished she could dump him.

But she knew that if she tried, sexist blowback from the Force would take her down instead.

"Papa Legba guard da gate t' da spirit world. Papa Legba stan' between me an' da loa."

"Loa?"

"Voodoo spirits. Da Mystères. Da Invisibles."

"Speaking of *da* Invisibles, does Papa know the whereabouts of John Lincoln Hardy?" Rick asked.

Rackstraw drew back sharply.

"He is your cousin, isn't he?"

"Who say?"

"The New Orleans police. Forget about Papa. Do *you* know John Lincoln Hardy?"

"True dat. He da *white* sheep o' da family."

"White sheep. That's good."

"What'cha wan' 'm fo'?"

Rick wondered if the Fox was laying the chitlins accent on thick to play sly with him, making it hard to understand what the hell he was saying. The jive talk—or whatever they called this patois down in voodooland—seemed the same as what was in the wiretap transcripts, but until he heard the actual tapes, he wouldn't know for sure. If it did turn out that this juju man was pulling his chain—in what he was saying or how he was saying it—Rick would come back gangbusters and get a piece of him.

Piece of Spann.

Piece of Rackstraw.

Piece of mind, thought Rick.

"Last month," said Kathy, "Hardy arrived in town with Helen Grabowski. Grabowski was a hooker with a record in New Orleans. We know she was a junkie, and Hardy was her pimp. The pair lived together in a skid row hotel, and Grabowski worked the stroll in front of a local bar. On the night of October 17, two weeks ago, the drug squad picked up Grabowski for junk possession. After she got out of jail at dawn the next morning, she vanished until her corpse was fished out of the river."

Rackstraw shrugged.

"You hear about the Headhunter?"

The Fox nodded.

"Helen Grabowski's one of his four victims."

"No shit?"

"News to you?"

"Din know da ho. Din know 'er name. I bin slavin' in da lab on m' niggas' sure shot. Weasel try t' hussle me, but I blew 'm off."

"Weasel?"

"'Hood name. A'ways hittin' me up."

"Problem is, we can't find Hardy. He left the skids hotel. And until we question him, we can't cross him off our suspects list."

"Weasel no thug. Don' ha' da balls t' murk."

"He may have pimped Grabowski to a john who does. How do we get hold of him?"

"I da bro's keeper? No idea."

Liar, thought Spann.

Liar, thought Scarlett.

Tipple's wiretaps proved that Rackstraw knew where Hardy was, but they couldn't show their hand until they knew what was what with the Wolf in New Orleans.

Spann took out a card and passed it to the Fox.

"You hear from the Weasel, gimme a call."

"Fo' sho', honey drip."

Voodoo Juju stopped pounding, and the crowd beyond the door began whistling, hooting, and hollering.

Rackstraw gave his balls a heft.

Nostrils flaring, he sniffed as if to snort coke.

"Like I say. Sure-shot niggas."

The door flew wide, and for a moment, the Mounties were in the midst of a horror film. Skeletons still luminous from the stage lights swarmed the dark room. One by one, they streamed in like Baron Samedi's crew, raised from their graves at some Haitian crossroads. But then the overhead lights came on and the backstage vault lit up, and the blinking eyes of both Mounties took in piles of open packing crates. Most of the skulls and voodoo masks were mounted onstage, but those not being used in the act were stored back here in trunk-like wooden boxes, nestled in foam cradles to keep them from being damaged in transport.

"Han's off, whitey!" Rackstraw snapped as Scarlett reached for a mask.

Rick's eyes narrowed.

Kathy could smell the stink of hot testosterone in the air.

"Dats m' juju. Dem masks 'r' a hun'red years old. Keep yo' cotton-pickin' fingas off m' witchcraft. Dats da *blackest* wood der is. Wes' African ebony."

———

Rodale was at work on the Strategy Wall in DeClercq's office when the late-night call from Spann was patched through to him. As he listened to her recount the night's evidence, his eyes followed the connections in the Grabowski segment. From the photo of Hardy sent by the New Orleans police, she'd linked the hooker's pimp to Bax at the Moonlight Arms, and from that she'd learned Hardy was possibly trafficking cocaine. "That pimp's not into smack. Coke's his drug," Bax had told the flying patrol that morning. Next, she'd followed Hardy through Tipple's wiretaps, connecting him not only to voodoo and zombies in New Orleans, but also to West African ebony in the masks displayed by Voodoo Juju. And *that* linked Grabowski's murder to the ebony splinter Joe had found wedged in Liese Greiner's pelvic bone.

Victims one and two were joined.

"Lay it out, Kathy."

"Tipple says that Rackstraw blew into town early this year. So the Fox was here when Liese Greiner got raped and beheaded. If voodoo's his religion, and not just about selling music, it could be that Greiner's skull was mounted on the stage among the voodoo masks."

"Giving us a connection to the splinter in her groin."

"Right. The killer could have picked it up on his shoe *before* he kicked her."

"Keep going."

"What if the Headhunter's a cult, not a person? Somehow the psychology is tied to New Orleans. Rackstraw almost tore Rick's head off when he reached for one of the masks. 'That's my juju, my witchcraft,' he snarled. The guy is really into it. He's no dabbler."

"And Hardy?"

"The Wolf, the Fox, and the Weasel. That's how I'd rank them. Hardy's the low man on the totem pole, the fuck-up no one respects. But the man is family, so what can you do? The Wolf and the Fox have big plans for tomorrow—'The pot boils over at midnight'—and somehow Hardy's involved. It could be as a mule. Last month, he arrived in Vancouver with his meal ticket in tow. Was it a dry run to check the lay of the land? Grabowski's a junkie he puts to work on the stroll. Hardy hooks up with Bax to score her fixes. Maybe he wants to prove himself to his family and move up in the world? But when Grabowski gets busted for drugs, it endangers their plans. What if she snitches? So how better to erase a hooker than to make her a random victim of a serial killer?"

"Hmm. Who did her, then? Rackstraw?"

"Makes sense. He's got the most to lose. And he's accountable to the Wolf in New Orleans. If he killed Liese Greiner last summer for sex and photographed her severed head before harvesting her skull, why not add Helen Grabowski to his resume and send pix of both to *The Sun* to launch the Headhunter's reign of terror?"

"How do the nurse and the nun fit in?"

"Two more random victims to help bolster the serial killer story. And maybe it's about the voodoo as well. The two latest victims also lost their heads. For all we know, all four skulls could have been on that trellis tonight. We're talking about a blood cult that dates back to West African slavery, with roots that still thrive in Haiti and New Orleans. The key to what's going on up here is down in New Orleans, and my reading of Tipple's wiretaps tells me that's where Hardy is now."

"The boss says you get all the support you need. Tomorrow, you and Rick catch the first flight south. I'll call the FBI and NOPD to set things up."

DELILAH'S

As the name suggested, Delilah's was a strip bar for hair fetishists. Since pioneer times, the main industries of this province have been forestry, fishing, and mining. All those lonely, horny males lost in the woods, out at sea, or worming underground would hit the big city on their weeks off with cash in their pockets to blow on booze, strippers, and costly rolls in the hay. Obscenity laws had crumbled over the past decade, so now there was a strip joint aimed at every kink. It's unlikely the drunks in Delilah's had ever read the Bible or knew that Delilah was the femme fatale who learned the secret of Samson's strength and then betrayed him to his enemies. But having spent all day combing through the dives advertised in Matthew Paul Pitt's matchbook collection, Macdonald and Lewis were hip to the kink that lured Delilah's patrons.

"Ecdysiasts," Rusty said eruditely, nodding toward the stage.

"You're a quick learner."

"I *love* this job."

"Which peeler do you prefer?" Monica asked, her voice rising to a shout to be heard over the rock music and hooting pub din.

"The one on the right."

"Careful, sport, or *you'll* end up in Chan's skinner file."

The strippers working the side-by-side poles were identical twins. The one on the left had her head shaved bald and had shed her G-string to flaunt the blonde tuft between her legs. As the cops stood behind the raucous voyeurs in the smoky, dingy bar, the twin with the spiked punk hairdo whipped off her G-string to bare a pussy as pink and hairless as the day she was born. Their eyes darting to and from the scalps and crotches of the curvaceous twins, the fetishists could mix and match hair combinations to fit their quirks.

Some of the patrons were women, and they looked as tough as the men.

While AC/DC's "You Shook Me All Night Long" blared from the speakers and the twin on the left hung from the pole and spread her legs, a spotlight followed her slinking sister to the front of the stage, where she squatted above the nearest table and splayed her thighs for its gawkers. Reaching down, she plucked the glasses from the face of a wide-eyed sailor, wiped them across her vulva with her head thrown back in fake orgasm, then replaced the spectacles on his nose and sashayed to her pole.

The bar erupted in catcalls as dollar bills littered the stage.

A wobbly drunk bellowed, "I'll sniff your bicycle seat any day, lady!"

Monica elbowed her partner.

"You're blushing, Rusty," she teased.

"Am not."

"Are too. Is that why you're called Rusty?"

"Time to fish or cut bait."

They had perfected their trolling technique in the dozens of strip joints they'd visited before lunch. Rusty flanked the boozers and stood beside the stage, gazing out at the flushed faces amid a haze of blue smoke thicker than the fog outside. The pub stank of cigarettes and a hard day's sweat. As Monica zigzagged among the tables looking for Matthew Paul Pitt, Rusty checked the lustful leers trailing his bountiful partner around the room.

Meanwhile, the twins gyrated to Led Zeppelin's "Whole Lotta Love."

"I don't see Mr. Titstitstits," Monica yelled in Rusty's ear when the flying patrol reassembled.

"Me neither."

"Let's quiz the barkeep."

"I learned something as I watched these yobs ogle you."

"Yeah? What?"

"If you ever get tired of wearing red serge, there's a job for you onstage."

"Ha, ha."

The Englishman behind the bar had no time to waste on cops. He was a beefy lug with a ruddy scowl, cauliflower ears, and a bulbous, red-veined schnoz. But the bar was distant enough from the music to allow for conversation. The Brit grunted when Macdonald flashed her badge.

"Can't you see I'm busy?"

"This won't take long."

"Wot won't?"

"Routine questions."

"Coppers don't do nought that's just routine, lass."

"Seen this guy?"

She held up the mug shot of Pitt.

"Wot you want him for?"

"How do you Brits put it? 'Help with our inquiries'?"

"Oi, lookin' for Jack the Lad?"

"Speak English," she said, grinning.

"I lived in Leeds when the Old Bill were chasing the Yorkshire Ripper."

"Seen him?" she pressed.

"Has he got a name?"

"Matthew Paul Pitt."

"Maybe. Maybe not," said the lug. "Hard to suss, 'coz I'm at the bar, not the tables. The dirty raincoat brigade haunts this boozer. Most blokes just want the show. Bare an orifice up there and their eyes crawl into it. But some of the lads have the sneer to do what this Jack's done."

"So you know him?"

The barman shrugged. "Got a notion I tossed him out for bovvering one of the birds. But I bounce a lot of chancers from this pub."

"How 'bout her?"

The Mountie showed him the Interpol photo of Liese Greiner.

"Her I know. That's Liese. She stripped in here last summer."

"On the payroll?"

"Uh-uh. Amateur night. The punters got so stiff for her that the boss had her back. She peeled a couple of nights, then left us in the lurch. Didn't even collect her pay."

"Why?"

"Who knows? *Poof!* She was gone."

"Was that around the time you *might* have tossed Pitt out?"

"Could be."

"What do you know about Liese?"

"Nought except she was a looker with the bristols and a brill arse. Ask the boss."

"Where do we find him?"

"Behind the door at the end of the bar."

"Dexter Flesch, right?"

The lug smirked enigmatically.

"If *you* say, lass."

———

T. Rex was pounding out "Raw Ramp" as the Horsemen rapped on the door.

"Come in," replied a voice as soft as corn silk.

The cops entered the office.

If ever there was someone destined to run a joint like this, it was Dexter Flesch, Peeping Tom *extraordinaire*. He was in the skinner file as a probable threat to women because of his ingenuity at getting in their pants. At school, he was caught trying to drill a peephole into the girls' restroom. Then he hid a tiny camera in the toe of his shoe to snap surreptitious photos up their skirts. After he got expelled, the persistent perv showed up at a private girls' school wearing a white lab coat and announcing that he'd been sent by the College of Physicians and Surgeons to check the students for crabs. A clinic set up in the gym teacher's office would do, he said, and the girls should be brought to him individually for examination. But before he got to see his first patient, the police drove up, cuffed him, and hauled him off to jail.

He served a month, and thanks to his effeminacy, every day of it was hard time.

Bitch in the cellblock.

On his release, Flesch found work in the LA porn scene as a cameraman specializing in crotch shots. Now, years later, he was back in Vancouver, where—according to an anonymous tip to the liquor control board—he was running Delilah's through a false front to hide his criminal past. That tip was in the skinner file, so Macdonald and Lewis had seen it while they were planning their search through the pubs frequented by Pitt.

"Dexter Flesch?" asked Monica.

The office reeked of cloying perfume.

"*Delilah* Flesch," said the trans woman slitting envelopes open with a glittering dagger.

"Police," said Rusty, badge in hand.

"Yes?" The transsexual uncoiled from behind her compulsively well-ordered desk like a cobra rising from a wicker basket at the bidding of an Indian snake charmer. A plastic surgeon had sculpted her he-to-she looks. Cheek implants gave a feral slant to her blue-shadowed, mascaraed eyes. A nose job refined her feminized face. Her bee-stung lips had a permanent pout and were slicked vampire red. Her black hair was teased as wild as an hour's work could comb it. As you'd expect of someone with roots in the porn trade, her pumped-up breasts were *way* too big—the cleavage packed into her low-cut black dress made Marilyn Monroe seem flat-chested. Stiletto heels gave her extra height. All in all, Flesch looked like she should be hosting Shock Theater late on Friday night.

"Yes?" she repeated.

Macdonald met her halfway.

"We're with the Headhunter Squad."

The trans woman blinked.

"I don't understand," she said tensely. "What's that got to do with me?"

Delilah Flesch sniffed.

White powder caked her nostrils.

"We're told that a woman named Liese Greiner stripped here last summer."

"So?"

"So the Headhunter killed her and buried her in a shallow grave."

"What?!"

"The corpse in North Vancouver? Surely you've heard."

"You think that was *me*?"

The last word came out as a high-pitched squeal.

Flesch's face purpled with rage.

"You...you...you...*fucking pigs*! You're not going to stitch me up for *that* too!"

"Calm down."

"Screw you! Nobody calls *me* a rapist!"

Hysteria lit up her eyes.

Tears made her mascara streak.

Spittle spewed from the snarl that bared her teeth.

"Fucking pigs! Get the *fuck* out of here!"

Everyone has a flash point that will set off a powder keg of emotion. This visit from the flying patrol was the spark Flesch needed to ignite. It was the moment cops dread—when something innocuous provokes an explosive backlash from a suspect.

"Feast your eyes, fuckers!" Flesch screamed as she dropped one hand to the hem of her dress and yanked it up to expose her pantyless groin. Having had the nip and tuck of surgery, she flaunted genitalia as anatomically correct as any flashed by the strippers on Delilah's stage.

"I'm not a rapist!" she shrieked. "I'm a lesbian!"

"Look out! Knife!" Lewis yelled.

Flesch raised the letter opener as if re-enacting the shower scene in *Psycho*.

Straight from her shoulder, Macdonald jabbed a full-force punch at the livid, twisted face, connecting with the nose in a spray of blood from cracking bones.

The dagger clattered to the floor.

The cop kicked it away.

Flesch sank to her knees, wailing, "You ruined my face!"

Rusty grabbed the trans woman and cuffed her wrists behind her back.

Then he grinned at Monica.

"Who am I partnered with? Muhammad Ali?"

———

An hour later, Monica eased the car into the curb out front of Rusty's apartment block. They sat in their tomb surrounded by mummy wrappings of fog.

"You could have charged Flesch with attempted murder, Mon."

"Nah. The broken nose'll do. I can't send a transsexual back to jail for freaking out at the prospect."

"Your call."

"Pitt's our quarry."

"What a day."

"I'll say. Got a girlfriend waiting inside for you?"

"No. Who'd want me? I spent a year on the road with the Musical Ride. Now all I do is work and study in hopes I'll make Chan's team. You?"

"I've got no time for boyfriends. I'm building my career. Besides, female Horsemen seem to scare civilian guys away."

"Their loss."

"Must be tough on you, eh? Spending the day watching all those sexy strippers bump and grind, then climbing into bed with just your teddy bear?"

"My bear's female."

"Skinner file, here comes Rusty. By the way, thanks for laying none of that sexist shit on me."

"You got a job to do. Fair's fair."

"Got a sister?"

"Three."

"That explains it. Meanwhile, you and I are both constables, right?"

"Yeah," he said questioningly. "Same rank."

"So there's no question of sexual harassment by a superior officer. Fact is, I'm running on adrenaline and want to work it out. And you, I'll bet, have lover's nuts from eyeing those ecdysiasts. We're both consenting adults, and we're both single. We're also in our sexual prime, and neither of us is getting any younger. So—it seems to me—we have a decision to make: Do you go in alone while I drive away, or do we go in together, and tomorrow we pretend it was all a dream?"

"Mon, you owe me nothing. I only saved your life by shouting 'Look out! Knife!' to warn you."

"Tick-tock."

"Are you sure?"

"It's your call, sport."

TONTON MACOUTES

New Orleans, Louisiana
Tuesday, November 2, 3:45 p.m.

In this corner, wearing the red serge trunks, we have Constable Rick Scarlett of the Mounted Police, thought Katherine Spann as the four cops drove toward downtown New Orleans from the airport at Moisant Field.

And in this corner, wearing the stars-and-stripes trunks, we have Special Agent Luke Wentworth of the Federal Bureau of Investigation.

Gentlemen, let's have a clean fight.

Touch boxing gloves and come out swinging.

For reasons both historical and egotistical, the Mounted Police and the FBI don't get along. In the hierarchy of crime fighting by these "Children of a common mother"—as it says on the Peace Arch that straddles the border between their countries—each force sees itself as Batman and the other as Robin. Face to face, it's never long till there's sibling rivalry.

The legend behind the Riders of the Plains began with the Great March West to Fort Whoop-Up to squash American whisky traders and raise the Union Jack. Bub Walsh and Wilfred Blake intercepted Sitting Bull's Sioux and Cheyenne brethren as they fled across the border from Custer's Last Stand, wading into a clutch of warriors wearing bluecoat scalps to arrest a horse thief and enforce Canadian law. The Horsemen suppressed the Riel Rebellion and hanged the Métis leader on a gallows in their Regina barracks. They manhunted Almighty Voice around the Saskatchewan prairies, then blew him apart for killing three Mounties and a civilian. They policed the Klondike Gold Rush with a skeleton troop and a Maxim machine gun. They chased another cop killer, the Mad Trapper of Rat River, across the Arctic in the winter of 1932, the action reported live to the world by radio, before the final shoot-out on the Yukon's icebound Eagle River. They cracked through the Arctic icepack in the 1940s to make the *St. Roch* the first ship in history to navigate the Northwest Passage. By the time the FBI came to be, the Mounties were deep in a myth fueled by the American press, pulp fiction, and Hollywood films.

So eat my shorts, J. Edgar Hoover, Scarlett thought.

The legend behind the G-men began with Prohibition and the ensuing war on crime. Hoover's federal agents shot and killed gangster John Dillinger, Public Enemy No. 1, after the "woman in red" led him into a trap in front of Chicago's Biograph Theater. They gunned down Baby Face Nelson in a furious firefight that came to be known as the Battle of Barrington. They blasted matriarch Ma Barker, who cut loose with a tommy gun after the feds uncovered her hideout at Lake Weir in Florida. They almost shot Machine Gun Kelly, who kidnapped an oil tycoon but got caught without his signature weapon in Memphis, Tennessee, and had to give up while shouting, "Don't shoot, G-men!" Hoover himself arrested Canadian-born Alvin "Creepy" Karpis, the last Public Enemy No. 1, right here in New Orleans. After the boss yelled, "Put the cuffs on him!" Creepy had to be bound with an agent's necktie because none of the G-men had handcuffs. And then there was the so-called crime of the century, the 1932 kidnapping of the Lindbergh baby, which saw Bruno Hauptmann go to the electric chair. And the decades-long battle against the Ku Klux Klan. And all those innovative forensic techniques, like the crime lab, fingerprint scans, the most wanted list, coining the term "serial killer," and creating psychological profiling.

So fuck you and the horse you rode in on, Wentworth thought.

Boys will be boys.

"Quite the case you got up there," said the G-man.

"A doozy," said the Mountie.

"I hear your boss is cracking under the strain?"

"Who says?"

"American news."

"Well, that explains it," Rick said contemptuously. "We're down here, aren't we? On his okay."

"Yeah. *That* explains it," Luke said snidely.

"Whaddya mean?"

Wentworth, in a lightweight blue suit expensively tailored to his lean physique, glanced out the window at the Louisiana Superdome, hovering like a flying saucer come to earth. His sharp cheekbones narrowed to a thin chin and his dark hair was cut as conservatively as a banker's. Aviator sunglasses—a prop he could whip off to drill you with a withering glare—hid Luke's cunning eyes.

Image: Wall Street chic.

He looked more like a businessman than he did a cop.

"It means you're caught up in the crap peddled in Mountie comics. Sergeant Preston. Dudley Do-Right. All that shit. You've got a real-life psycho whacking off women's heads, and you're down here searching for voodoo queens and dug-up bayou zombies? If you step aside and let the big boys do the work, I'll send our Behavioral Science Unit up to solve it like that." Luke snapped his fingers.

Ow! Kathy winced. *G-man lands a blow below the belt.*

"When it comes to voodoo," Rick replied, "no one tops the Bureau. Reach into Hoover's 'twelve drawers full of political cancer' and wow us with your juju."

Ouch! Kathy flinched. *Horseman throws a sucker punch.*

Hoover clung to power for almost fifty years by hoarding an "Obscene File" full of sexual escapades and damaging dirt on eight presidents, eighteen attorneys general, several first ladies, countless celebrities, Martin Luther King, and anyone else he didn't like or thought might challenge him. His threats to leak what he had on the Kennedys kept them from kicking him out of the Bureau.

"Your telex mentioned zombies. Where'd you get that?" asked Luke.

"A wiretap. It said something about 'zombie walks.'"

"Who the hell believes in zombies these days?" the G-man said, jeering.

"I do," said Antoine Cheval from the driver's seat.

———

The way both Horsemen saw it, the G-man was just there to show the federal flag; Antoine "Tony" Cheval was the real deal. Rodale had asked the

NOPD for a black detective versed in New Orleans voodoo, so Cheval had met them at the airport to drive them into town. He was a heavyset Creole of Haitian ancestry whose lineage went back to the voodoo uprising that resulted in the first black republic. A snappy dresser who'd fit right in at a French Quarter jazz club, Cheval made Wentworth look like an undertaker.

"Want background?" he asked in a voice drained of accent.

"The basics," said Spann.

"In 1492, Christopher Columbus set foot on an island in the Caribbean that he called Hispaniola, meaning 'Little Spain.' In 1625, France established the colony of Saint-Domingue on the western half. As colonists carved out sugar, coffee, and indigo plantations, the slave trade brought them chained labor from West Africa. Along with that human cargo came an ancient religion based on blood sacrifice, possession by loa spirits, and fetishes hexing curses.

"The Africans called it voodoo, meaning 'spirit' or 'god.'

"When white masters forced their black slaves to convert to Roman Catholicism, *mambo* priestesses and *houngan* priests hid voodoo's loa among the church's saints. Syncretization equated St. Peter, who holds the keys to the kingdom of heaven, with Papa Legba, the loa gatekeeper to the spirit world. St. Patrick, who drove the snakes out of Ireland, represented Damballa, the mighty loa depicted as a snake whose twisting coils form the stars and planets, hills and valleys, and who fills the ocean by shedding his scaly skin.

"Saint-Domingue was a hellish place. Whipped by overseers, groaning slaves toiled from dawn till dusk. Those who stood up to their masters were tortured to terrify the rest: hung upside down, drowned in sacks, buried alive, spread-eagled over anthills, crucified in mosquito swamps, boiled in cauldrons of cane syrup, or stuffed in kegs spiked with nails and rolled downhill.

"Times like that," Tony said, "don't call for priests. They call for...?"

He waited.

"Sorcerers," said Kathy.

"Bokors serve the loa 'with both hands.' That means they conjure black magic as well as white. In voodoo, black magic is what raises zombies from the grave."

It was hot and muggy outside the car, but air-conditioning made the ride bearable for cops used to a more temperate climate.

"In 1791, the colony's slaves revolted," Tony explained. "The uprising began with a voodoo ritual at Bois Caïman—Alligator Woods—in the north. With voodoo drums pounding under a driving rainstorm, and one of the female dancers possessed by a loa, a bokor slit the throat of a pig and passed around its blood, inciting those who drank it to slaughter French slavers and torch their homes. That night, the northern plantations went up in flames, and voodoo cultists ran amok across the island. Whites by the thousands died in that rebellion, and when France abandoned its colony to be reborn as the Republic of Haiti in 1804, the survivors fled to New Orleans. Those who dragged their slaves with them also brought the loa, and soon voodoo drums throbbed in Congo Square.

"When I was a boy," Tony said, "the root doctor would sit on the porch and talk with Grandmammy. I'd be playing on the steps below, and eventually she'd lean over and spit on me. That meant they were discussing a topic I shouldn't hear. Likely Marie Laveau, our famous Voodoo Queen."

"What's a root doctor?" asked Spann.

"*Houngan*. The local voodoo man."

The car was passing a city of the dead. Because so much of New Orleans is below sea level, kept dry by levees and pumping stations that divert seepage into canals and Lake Pontchartrain, burial tombs are built above the ground. The early colonials had architects design their graves, and this boneyard was like a miniature city of narrow residences overlooked by ornate death statues.

Tony pointed.

"Marie Laveau is buried over there."

As the illegitimate daughter of a plantation owner and his mulatto mistress, Laveau was born "a free woman of color" in New Orleans at the time of the Haitian Revolution. Legend says she learned voodoo from a *houngan* named Dr. John. After 1830, she took charge of the voodoo rituals in Congo Square, rising to become New Orleans's undisputed Voodoo Queen. It's said she kept a snake called Le Grand Zombi, and danced with it to worship Damballa. People believed her juju was so potent that she didn't age, but in reality her look-alike daughter, Marie Laveau II, took over the rituals. By the mid-1870s, more than ten thousand spectators, black and white, would swarm to Lake Pontchartrain to see her perform. Today, Marie Laveau's tomb in St. Louis Cemetery No. 1 is chalked with red *X*'s drawn by cultists. They knock on the vault, turn three times in a circle, and shout wishes for the queen to grant.

"I did some digging into John Lincoln Hardy's family," said the NOPD cop. "Rumor is that N'Orleans has a *new* voodoo queen."

"Who?" Kathy asked.

"Hardy's mother. Jezila Dubois."

From 1915 to 1934, US Marines occupied Haiti. Soldiers came home with lurid tales of dead men raised from the grave by voodoo sorcerers. First, the witch doctors put hexes on their victims, who then fell ill and died within days. After the dead were buried, the bokors returned to dig the corpses from their coffins and zombify them. Revived by witchcraft, the undead were chained and hauled away to serve their black masters as shambling, bug-eyed slaves on farms and sugar plantations. Zombie tales started to appear in pulp magazines, and in 1931, *White Zombie* starring Bela Lugosi hit the screen.

"*I Walked with a Zombie*," said Kathy.

"Uh-huh. And all the films since."

It's easy to see why zombies are Haiti's nightmare. Death was the only escape for slaves on colonial plantations. Baron Samedi, the lord of the cemetery, is one of voodoo's darkest gods. He's depicted by modern-day Haitians as a chalk-skinned, skull-faced black man wearing a top hat, a black tuxedo, and dark glasses, with a skull-knobbed cane in his hand. Rude, crude, fond of tobacco and rum laced with hot peppers, the Baron revels in sex, porn, and debauchery. He's also the god you must please if you want to get to heaven, which Haitian slaves saw as a return to Africa—a leafy green place with no sugarcane to cut and no monstrous white master to serve. Only the Baron can usher you into the realm of the dead. When you die, he digs your grave and greets your soul after burial. If you offend him, or if a bokor casts a voodoo hex that turns you into a zombie, you'll be a slave forever, an eternal field hand.

"Zombies!" Wentworth scoffed.

The G-man took out a handkerchief and blew his nose.

"You laugh," said Cheval, "but that's naive. Voodoo necromancy is chemically based. Bokors concoct a zombie powder called *coupe poudre*—literally, 'strike powder.' They make it by mixing a poisonous neurotoxin found in puffer fish with dried and ground-up toads, lizards, spiders, and human remains. Inhaled, applied as a paste, or ingested in food, a dose of tetrodotoxin induces a paralytic, death-like state characterized by low body temperature, reduced rate of breathing, and a barely perceptible heartbeat. The catalepsy wears off after the undead are buried."

"Poe would freak," said Spann. "Premature burial was his ultimate fear."

"How do they breathe?" asked Scarlett.

"An oxygen tube sunk from the surface to the grave."

"Smoke and mirrors, eh?"

"When dragged from their coffins, the victims are groggy and traumatized. The bokors feed them a concoction made from a plant called datura, also known as jimson weed, devil's snare, and zombie cucumber. It's a mind-controlling deliriant that brings on psychosis. And just like that, you have the creatures of Haitian folklore—mindless automatons with gaunt features and gray skin who shamble about with fixed, staring expressions, mumbling slurred words in nasal tones," said Cheval. "Chemical zombies."

Voodoo is still the dominant religion in superstitious Haiti. So fearful are Haitians of bokors conjuring the undead that they hold protective vigils over the graves of beheaded corpses buried with gris-gris charms. Zombifying is a crime under Haiti's penal code, but that didn't stop Papa Doc Duvalier, the island's dictator from 1957 to 1971 (or his son, Baby Doc—its current president), from using dread of witch doctors and their juju creatures to quash resistance to his iron rule.

"Jezila Dubois and her sister, Zette, were born in Haiti. Their father was a bokor who taught them voodoo from an early age. In the 1950s, he married them off to Jeb Hardy and Vince Rackstraw here in N'Orleans, 'cause the men had a bayou network smuggling drugs from the Caribbean. John Lincoln Hardy, known as the Weasel, is the son of Jeb and Jezila. Tom and Steve Rackstraw, known as the Wolf and the Fox, are the sons of Vince and Zette. The sisters' father knew Papa Doc from his dabblings in voodoo before he became Haiti's dictator. When Duvalier needed henchmen to enforce his political will, he asked Dubois to conjure an image that would terrify his subjects. The bokor came up with the Tonton Macoutes, a name that plays off the Uncle Gunnysack bogeyman of Creole mythology."

Cheval glanced over at Spann, who shook her head no.

"Uncle Gunnysack kidnaps unruly children by snaring them in a gunny-sack—a *macoute*—and carrying them off to eat for breakfast," he explained. "Dubois suggested that Papa Doc dress like Baron Samedi, in a black fedora and business suit, with heavy or dark glasses. The Tonton Macoutes should sport straw hats, blue shirts, dark glasses, guns, and machetes. People believed the secret police were Papa Doc's zombies, summoned to rape and kill as they pleased. They burned Haitians alive and hung their charred corpses from trees as a warning to others not to cross them."

"Let me guess," said Kathy. "Dubois used his contacts in the Tonton Macoutes to funnel drugs through Haiti to his sons-in-law in your bayou?"

"Uh-huh. With a sideline in selling the cadavers and blood of murdered Haitians to universities and hospitals here in the States."

"You gotta be kidding!"

"Haiti's hardcore. That hellhole stews in fear. Papa Doc snuffed about thirty thousand people during his reign."

"So what became of Dubois?"

"Got too big for his britches. Tried to put a hex on Papa Doc, but it backfired. The Tonton Macoutes jumped him while Jeb and Vince were in Port-au-Prince arranging a drug shipment. Rumor is they hacked all three to pieces with machetes and fed the bloody chunks to sharks and swamp gators."

"D'ya have kids, Tony?"

"No."

"Ain't that a shame. You tell a spooky bedtime story." Spann crossed her index fingers to ward off the undead. "So what did Jezila and Zette do after the menfolk got chopped into luncheon meat?"

"The sisters ran a voodoo shop in N'Orleans."

"In the French Quarter?"

"No, in a run-down 'hood on the Mississippi River. They sold authentic gris-gris to practicing cultists, unlike the French Quarter phonies selling junk made in China to tourists."

"*Sold*? Past tense?"

"Sells, in the case of Jezila. She runs the store alone now. Until last year, Zette was the city's reigning voodoo queen. Jezila took her sister's place after a snake called Damballa strangled Zette during a voodoo ritual performed somewhere in the bayou on Haiti's Day of the Dead."

"When's that?"

"October 31 to November 2. The Day of the Dead coincides with the three-day Catholic festival of Allhallowtide: All Hallows' Eve, All Saints' Day, and All Souls' Day."

"Has this year's ritual been held?"

"Doubt it. This will be Jezila's first as voodoo queen. There's nothing on the grapevine about her yet, so I'll bet it's tonight."

"We've got a wiretap of the Wolf telling the Fox, 'It's cooking on the second. Pot boils over at midnight.' We've also got the Fox telling the Wolf, 'The cous'll be down to see ya.' And finally, we've got the Fox saying to the Weasel, 'Enjoy the gumbo. Tell Momma hello from me.'"

"Well, there you have it."

"Fill us in on what Tom, Steve, and John are doing," said Scarlett.

"Tom Rackstraw is trying to rebuild his pappy's bayou network. So the Wolf's been trafficking drugs in from the Caribbean. His brother, Steve, is trying to break into the music business, hoping to make it big with a new take on swamp boogie."

"Voodoo Juju." Scarlett nodded. "We saw them in concert last night."

"Any good?"

"Yeah," said Kathy.

"They wake the dead," said Rick.

"Muscling into the coke biz is dangerous in the South. You're sure to run afoul of the cartels. The Colombians, the Mexicans—they don't fool around. Easy to get your throat cut and your tongue yanked out through the slit. Who wants a Colombian necktie if there's a safer market? So if I had a brother in the Great White North, I'd be tempted to use him."

"Me too. What about Hardy?"

"Now that *his* momma's taken over as the voodoo queen, she's tied into whatever the Rackstraw boys are doing. Hardy's made his living by low-level pimping, but she hopes to move him into his cousins' get-rich-quick schemes. I'll bet that's why the Weasel flew north."

"Then came home for what's going down tonight."

"That's all I know."

"You've got damn good sources," said Spann.

"It helps to grow up in the neighborhood."

"I wonder what Hardy meant by 'zombie walks' in our taps?"

"You'll soon find out."

IRON SKULLS

Vancouver, British Columbia
3:50 p.m.

Vancouver is notorious for its outlaw biker gangs. That's why the Mounties have Special E: a squad tasked specifically with curtailing them. Special I is Tipple's mainstay, the listeners. Special O is the watchers, the cops who took down Olson. Special E is the gangbusters. And now there was talk of reconfiguring the Headhunter Squad into Special X—the psycho-hunters—once this case was solved.

Special X.

Mountie-speak for Special Extreme.

I like it, thought Mad Dog Rabidowski as he wheeled a Suburban with a cowcatcher welded to its grille through the Eastside streets, closing on the fortified clubhouse of the Iron Skulls. The squeal had come in from Special E's snitch that the possible snuff film was going down *now.* This afternoon, the Iron Skulls had grabbed one of the feminists who threw bricks at Artie Fripp of Get-A-Whiff Productions and razor-slashed Kurt Schmidt at the Kit Kat Klub and Theater. The porn merchants' backlash, according to the snitch, was to cast one of the attackers in a real-life snuff film and reap the profits.

Don't get mad. Get even.

Ka-ching!

Back in 1968, the Satan's Angels had shocked this town with two grisly crimes. In the first, that January, one of the bikers had bludgeoned a prospect to death with an iron bar in the gang's clubhouse just to see what it felt like to kill somebody. In the second, the next month, the bikers had abducted a hippie from Davie Street and driven him back to the same clubhouse to serve as their "butler." They stripped him, scoured his scrotum with a bristle brush, then had him scrub the floor, dance with a broom in the bucket, and masturbate. Twice they almost drowned him in an ice water bath, and if that wasn't enough, they placed a plastic fireman's hat on his head and ignited it so the bubbling goo dripped down his torso. Then they sodomized him with the broom handle and ran him around like a hobbyhorse.

Since then, rival gangs had warred to control this turf. The baddest of the bad these days were the Iron Skulls—a gang of neo-Nazis into cooking and peddling meth. So as the ramming van screeched around the corner and gunned it for the padlocked gate in their clubhouse fence, Mad Dog's heart pumped adrenaline into his blood.

"Hang on!" he yelled to his team.

Crammed into the back of the supercharged Suburban was a motley crew of heavily armed Horsemen. Last year, these men had trained with the SAS—the Special Air Services unit of the British Army—and if Mad Dog had his way, they'd soon be a ruthless team of paramilitary commandos in kick-ass uniforms. For now, however, the hardmen on this assault wore a mishmash of kits—a hodgepodge of toques, hoods, baseball caps, camouflage jackets, and overalls—and clutched a gamut of firearms, from assault rifles to pump shotguns to sniper scopes.

Bang!

Sparks streaked past the windows as they crashed through the fence, tearing the gate from its hinges. Gleaming motorcycles formed a chopper barricade in front of the reinforced door, but the van plowed through the line of hogs and caved in the brick wall. Shifting into reverse, Mad Dog burned rubber to extract the battering ram, then jumped out into the haze of dust belching from the breach.

"Raid!" a biker hollered as the ERT cops stormed in.

Pandemonium reigned inside the ruptured clubhouse. It was like a scene from the Second World War. Nazi banners hung on the far wall, flanking a huge human skull made of iron plates with a hog vomiting from its mouth. Motorcycle headlamps glared from the skull's eye sockets, both beams illuminating a terrified woman cuffed to the handlebars so the chopper's front wheel buzzsawed between her legs. Her clothes were ripped to expose her undergarments, and a ball gag filled her mouth.

The biker gripping her hair resembled a medieval headsman. His bare chest was mottled with a slew of tattoos—all Viking runes, Aryan symbols, and Nazi icons. His black leather pants and motorcycle boots glittered with silver chains caught by the headlamps. The mask hiding his face was a skull and crossbones, the knobs jutting from his neck like bolts from Frankenstein's monster. As the cops burst in, the muscled executioner was about to swing at his captive's throat with a headsman's axe.

"Freeze! Police!" Mad Dog barked to bring a halt to the scene being filmed by a cameraman with his back to the door.

The man behind the camera was Kurt Schmidt. As the porky porn purveyor craned his bowling ball–sized head around to face the intruders, Mad Dog took in the obsessive squint and moist, sneering lips of a pervert. A head case like him would go to sleep with an artificial vagina and a Suck-U-Lator on his bedside table, handy for if he woke up horny in the night. When his Alfred Hitchcock tummy rotated to follow his face, his belly bulged with bandages patching the slash across his bowels. He'd abandoned all hope of finishing his flick, and now his fingers worked frantically at trying to spring open the camera and expose the film to keep it from being used as evidence in court.

Fat chance, sucker, thought Rabid.

Like the Sioux responding to Custer's charge, the Iron Skulls scrambled for any weapons they could find: chains, pipes, tire irons, and baseball bats. Mad Dog's primary weapon was a Heckler & Koch MP5, but when he saw that these punks were bringing steel and wood to a gunfight, he slung the submachine gun over one shoulder and cross-drew the Smith and the Ruger from his waist and shoulder holsters. As both handguns cleared leather, the meth head in the skull-and-crossbones mask released the woman's hair and blitzkrieged toward him.

"Drop the axe!"

The Iron Skull ignored him, closing in for the kill.

"Stop or I'll shoot!"

And damn if the neo-Nazi didn't bellow a Valhalla cry.

Bam!

Horsemen are trained to shoot to kill, not to wing or maim. You don't fire your sidearm unless you're up against it. The clang of the slug striking the mask snapped back the biker's head, but it didn't stop the bullet from punching through his skull and his brain, spewing out blood and bone.

As all eyes jerked to watch the dead man bite the dust, another cop aimed his submachine gun at the ceiling and cut loose a burst that sent ejected casings twinkling through the headlamp beams and tinkling onto the floor. The blasts reverberating around the clubhouse seemed to clear the haze of meth clouding the bikers' minds, making them realize that the film being shot wasn't *Custer's Last Stand* but *The St. Valentine's Day Massacre*.

In their rush to arm themselves, the Iron Skulls had overturned Artie Fripp's wheelchair. The injured porn merchant crawled among the boots of greasy bikers with dirty hair that hung in matted hanks, some with ripped torsos from pumping iron in jail, others with flabby stomachs from swilling too much beer, but all with tattoos and scars revealed by sleeveless jackets patched with the gang's colors.

Iron Skulls.

MC.

Vancouver, BC.

Circling the skull and crossbones.

As the bikers were cuffed and led one by one out to the waiting paddy wagons, Mad Dog smiled down at the Ruger still wisping smoke from its barrel.

Nice piece, Spann, he thought.

LE GRAND ZOMBI

New Orleans, Louisiana
9:35 p.m.

LE GRAND ZOMBI, read the black-and-white sign above the voodoo shop door in this run-down neighborhood on the Mississippi River. The cops were parked in a vacant lot with the water at their backs, watching the goings-on in the shack through night-vision binoculars. Antoine Cheval was at the wheel with Katherine Spann beside him, while Rick Scarlett poked his head between them from the backseat. All three were pleased that Luke Wentworth wasn't along for this excursion. If he were, they'd have to put up with his snarky comments about whites wearing blackface. "Normally, I'd punch your lights out for racist minstrel shit like this," Tony had told them on handing the Horsemen black greasepaint to smear on their skin. "But I'll make an exception on this occasion, because where you're going, we can't have you shining like ghosts in the night."

"Rules?" Spann had asked as they were driving here.

"What can and can't we do?" clarified Scarlett.

"Are either of you packing?"

"No guns, Tony."

"Good. We can't have US citizens stopping Canadian lead. Also, there can be no arrests unless the NOPD spearheads the bust. You have no jurisdiction. Agreed?"

"Agreed," said Kathy.

"Agreed," said Rick.

"That gets the formalities out of the way. But I've got a gift that didn't come from me. Seems you bought it under the table in a seedy local bar."

From between his feet, Tony produced a paper bag and passed it to Kathy. Inside, she saw a Colt pistol fitted with a silencer.

"The gun's untraceable," said Cheval. "Where you're going is teeming with gators and snakes. Can't leave you unprotected in the bayous at night. The silencer's so you won't be heard by the voodoo cultists if you have to shoot some critter on the edge of the ritual ground. Under no circumstances do you shoot a human, living or undead. And if you do, you drop the gun in the bayou. Deal?"

"Deal," said Kathy.

"Deal," said Rick.

"That concludes a conversation we didn't have. I know nothing."

———

"Snack?" Tony asked his fellow stakeout cops.

"What'cha got?" asked Rick.

"Po'boy sandwiches. Shrimp, mayonnaise, and green tomato chow-chow on a baguette. Coffee and chicory to wash it down."

"Thanks," said Rick, unwrapping one.

"I'll pass for now," said Kathy. "Something's going on in the shop."

The vacant lot was more a junkyard than an empty space: clumps of foliage, rusting cars, old tires, and such. Their prowl car was a clunker in the shadow of a tree, with three black faces lost in the dark interior. The shanties across the riverside road were derelict. Some had mud walls and corrugated iron roofs, others broken-hinged doors and peeling shutters. Even this late at night, the Mounties sweated profusely in the mobile oven while they took in foreign sounds and smells: the throb of swamp boogie from a distant bar, the crack of a nut bursting as it fell to earth, the creak of a chair rocking on a veranda, musky odors from the river in the muggy air, the scent of tobacco flowers.

Le Grand Zombi was the real thing. Against this backdrop of decay could it be anything else? The denizens haunting this green realm—as seen through Spann's binoculars—undoubtedly traced their bloodlines back to West African slaves who conjured voodoo spirits under the crack of plantation whips. Candlelight burned inside the door to Damballa's lair, where Spann could see a cluttered altar against the far wall. The altar was made of ebony carved to resemble a human skull, with the jaws yawning wide so the lower teeth formed a counter and the upper teeth a canopy. Gone were all slave-era trappings of the Roman Catholic Church. No Christian statue flanked by oleographs of St. Peter and St. Patrick. Instead, a glass vivarium in the base of the altar caged a slithering boa constrictor that looked to be around eight feet long, judging from its coils.

Back to basics, thought Spann.

"Doesn't look like a place to buy Love Potion No. 9."

"For that, you go to the tourist shops in the Quarter," said Tony. "Jezila Dubois specializes in black magic—gris-gris and fetishes that do harm."

"Voodoo dolls?"

"Yes, but not like Hollywood peddles. Most African fetishes are shaped like dolls. But the doll isn't fashioned after the person hexed, and pins aren't jabbed in to cause pain. The doll is a conduit to the spirits. The hex is channeled from the spirits through the fetish to the one you want harmed."

"Now I know," said the Mountie.

"But gris-gris is more effective."

"Why?"

"It's tailor-made. 'Putting a gris-gris' on your enemy brings bad luck. It's what slaves used to throw on the doorsteps of their plantation masters. How many blacks in N'Orleans do you think hate whites? You want to lay a hex on whitey, come to Le Grand Zombi. See the boxes on the shelves to the left and right of the altar? They contain animal bones, graveyard dust, sharks' teeth, bats' wings, cats' eyes, roosters' hearts, and doves' blood mixed with sap, fossils, stones, poisonous roots, hair, nails, horns, salt, pepper, gunpowder, the little finger of a suicide, and the shroud of a rotting man."

"No shit?"

"Uh-huh. Hexes are prepared at the altar, in the skull's mouth. The altar contains the four elements: salt for earth, incense for air, candle flames for fire, and of course water. The white porcelain pots on the floor house the loa and the spirits of the dead. Jezila stuffs a small bag made of red flannel or leather with whatever's required for your particular hex. The pouch always contains an odd number between three and thirteen. A drawstring shuts the bag, and you're ready to sow misfortune."

"Mumbo jumbo," said Rick.

"Better hope so, because you two are out to mess with a hardcore voodoo queen. And she'll throw her blackest of juju at you."

"At the window? Is that Jezila?" asked Spann.

Cheval raised his binoculars.

"That's her," he said.

The Haitian who stood at the window staring out into the darkness wore a white tignon—knotted scarves wrapped around her head like a turban—above the blackest of skin stretched tight over jutting cheekbones. Her gaunt features looked predatory. As near as Kathy could tell through the distorting green lenses, she was around fifty, with arched eyebrows and full red lips. Hooped earrings dangled from her lobes, and a necklace looped down her chest like a snake.

"Eye the door," said Tony.

The Mountie swung her binoculars to focus on a huge man filling the doorframe. She watched him crouch and wiggle the vivarium out of the altar.

John Lincoln Hardy, thought Spann.

———

The stakeout team watched Hardy drive a gangster-era black hearse around from the back of the shop to the front door. Fenders and running boards adorned the outside, and curtains covered the compartment that normally received the casket. Hardy returned to the shop and opened the vivarium. From it, he lifted the boa constrictor, transferring it to a big burlap sack. Slinging the sack over his shoulder, he accompanied his mother to the hearse, and while she climbed into the front passenger's seat, he lugged the snake—which was squirming in the bag like the kidnapped kids of Haitian folklore—to the rear door and swung it in.

"Tonton Macoute," said Kathy. "Uncle Gunnysack."

"Love the hearse," said Rick.

"It's rebuilt," said Tony. "Lots of relics get recycled for Mardi Gras."

"You can tell that from here?"

"No, I saw the chassis when I installed a bumper bug."

Reaching under the dashboard, Tony flicked a switch. "Open the glove box, Kathy." Inside was an electronic screen pulsing a dull red. A blip from the homing device attached to the hearse moved across a map of the bayou swamps when Hardy drove away.

"They're heading for Houma," said Tony, as he cranked the ignition and wheeled the clunker off the vacant lot to shadow the body buggy.

"Question is, will this jalopy make it?" said Rick.

"Looks decrepit on the outside to blend in. But it too's been rebuilt."

"Hot Rod Tony?"

"*Thunder Road*, Canuck."

By moonlight, they followed the hearse deep into Terrebonne Parish, more than two thousand square miles of marshland with only one city. In the 1750s, the French-speaking settlers of Acadia, in eastern Canada, were forced to flee from their homes when the British took control. Relocating here, they called the area *terre bonne*—meaning "good earth"—and the Acadians became Cajuns.

In Terrebonne, the line between liquid and earth is vague and always changing. Lazy bayous carve pathways out of soggy soil, curving and twisting and curling back on ill-defined channels until fresh and salt streams merge into bitter brackish water. Lose your way in this terrain and you could be gone forever, buried alive in a grave of mud—if the alligators and water moccasins don't get you first. In the antebellum period, Terrebonne had over a hundred plantations worked by slaves. As the cops left Houma and pressed on into the dark, they skirted a slaveowner's mansion topped with a widow's walk. There, according to legend, the man's wife paced mournfully for years, watching the haunted bayou for his ghost to return.

Southern Gothic.

There was no need for the ghost car to ride the bumper of the hearse. The tracking bug informed them when Hardy turned off the main road, and the numbers displayed down the side of the screen calculated the distance between the Weasel and the cops. Nor was it necessary to use headlamps—moonbeams silvering the stagnant streams made it bright enough for Tony to navigate. At first, the roadside was lined with shanties and the night stank of fish, excrement, and garbage. But the deeper south they snaked, the more the dirt track degenerated into potholes filled with water. Soon there were no hovels, and Terrebonne became no man's land. In fact, it was doubtful that this mist-covered bog qualified as terra firma.

The blip stopped moving.

"End of the line," said Tony. "These are pirate swamps. Back when buccaneers marauded ships in the Caribbean, they rowed up these bayous from the Gulf of Mexico and supposedly hid their treasure somewhere here, never to be found. If you stumble across any booty, I want my share."

"Where now?" asked Rick, eyeing the motionless blip.

"Follow the drums. Hear them?"

Kathy cocked an ear.

"I hear 'em. Beyond the crickets and frogs. What's that noise?"

"An alligator."

"I'll carry the gun," said Rick. "You bait him, Kath."

"Where will you be, Tony?"

"Parked in that thicket, ready to vamoose. The mosquitoes are voracious. Don't get eaten alive. And be careful, or I'll be waving goodbye to zombie Mounties at the airport."

———

On foot, they walked the soggy road to where it sank into smelly water. Strange that the black hearse was the only vehicle parked there. They angled left along the spongy bank and weaved through gnarled cypress trees draped with Spanish moss. There were no footprints to follow. The swamp quickly sucked in any holes. Without moonlight, it was dark and foreboding in the trees. Nooses of moss tried to strangle them, while roots tripped them up and gigantic spiders lurked in webs strung ten feet across. Through tendrils of fog, they could see flames dancing in the distance, and with every step, the throbbing of drums grew louder.

Boom-boom! Boom-boom! Boom-boom!

Not the amplified pounding of Voodoo Juju back home, but the hand-slapped thudding once heard in the jungles of West Africa, Saint-Domingue, and New Orleans's Congo Square.

Now there was chanting…

With no one here to translate…
But that didn't matter…
They got the idea…

Ki mele mwen, Danbala, Ki mele mwen,
  Ki mele mwen, Danbala, Ki mele mwen,
  M pagen Mama, M pagen Papa,
  Danbala, ki mele mwen!

DAMBALLA

Midnight

They hid in the shadows of the trees and watched the ritual. A spit of land connected the bank of the bayou to an island that humped out of the water where it spread into an algae-covered lagoon. A bonfire blazed on the island, spewing sparks into the night while serving as a beacon that lured in boats from all directions. Some were motorboats up from the Caribbean. Others were Cajun pirogues carved out of tree trunks. Not all the cultists were black. A few were white or Hispanic. For as far back as the slavery years, New Orleans's voodoo has attracted all races.

One by one, the flat-bottomed boats motored, paddled, or poled to shore. A big iron cauldron bubbled on a cooking fire apart from the central blaze. "The pot boils over at midnight" was evidently more than a figure of speech. A caged animal was hauled off each boat. The drums were pounding to invoke the African loa from the spirit world, but there had to be energy for the gods to communicate with mortals. By sacrificing animals, cultists combine the life force of their beasts with the life force of the loa. So now the night quivered with the shrieks of terrified goats and chickens as worshipers chopped off their heads or hung them from a gibbet to slit their bellies.

Hackles rose on the Mounties' skin as they witnessed the bloodletting. The ground around the mossy gallows was littered with animal bones. Obviously, the ritual island had seen many slaughters. The bones crunched under the feet of the butchers wielding cleavers and knives. A shadow against the orange-red bonfire, one man held up a goat's head and drank blood from its throat. Is that what created the Headhunter? A blood fetish spawned in this swamp that warped into sexual vampirism?

A bayou bloodsucker?

Is there a Creole name for that?

Another cultist pulled the guts out of a still-twitching goat. His arms red to the elbows, he carried the glistening viscera to the boiling cauldron and dumped them in. Others followed, and meat from every sacrifice went into the pot. The Mounties recalled what the Fox had said to the Weasel: "Enjoy the gumbo. Tell Momma hello from me." But this gumbo wasn't for nourishment. At least, not for humans.

Spann wondered if the island was a bayou graveyard for runaway slaves. No mossy headstones jutted from the hump like rotting teeth, but there was a squat stone mausoleum shining eerily under the light of the moon. Jezila Dubois—the new voodoo queen—sat cross-legged on top, flanked by Tom Rackstraw, made up as Baron Samedi, and her son, John Lincoln Hardy. Her head was still wrapped in the tignon, and the sleeveless dress she wore was as white as the stone.

The drummers thrashed animal hides stretched over hollow logs.

Boom-boom! Boom-boom! Boom-boom!

The cops watched intently as several cultists put on ebony masks carved with the demonic scowls of West African voodoo gods. If they had this right, the masks were full of cocaine, and this was the New Orleans smuggling route that Tom Rackstraw—the Wolf—hoped to revive from its heyday, when the Tonton Macoutes had killed his dad and his uncle, Jezila Dubois's husband. From here, the coke would be shipped to Steve Rackstraw—the Fox—in Vancouver.

Was Hardy—the Weasel—its mule?

Odds were.

Boom-boom! Boom-boom! Boom-boom!

This wasn't the Baron Samedi of Voodoo Juju or Mardi Gras, dandified in a top hat and funeral tuxedo, his face artfully made up to resemble a skull, holding a death's head cane in his hand. That was a Baron for the masses, for the consumer crowd, for folks willing to pay money for voodoo fantasy. No, this was a lord of the cemetery in real life—*this* cemetery in the bowels of the bayou. Naked except for tattered black pirate pants, this Baron Samedi had painted his skin with some sort of goo and covered it with graveyard dust, wiping it off to give the impression of a skull. The "cane" he held was a human leg bone, and as the cultists—some masked, others barefaced—danced between the bonfire and the mausoleum, he pounded the crown of a human skull in time to the drummers' beat.

Boom-boom! Boom-boom! Boom-boom!

Switching the bones for a bottle of rum, the Baron left the mausoleum and joined the wanton dancers. He whirled in a circle and pitched forward as if to hit the ground, but recovered at the last moment and gyrated again. A woman who sashayed toward him swung her wide hips provocatively and flounced her heavy breasts. Then a look of bewilderment consumed her seductive face, and as the loa of sex and debauchery seized her, she clenched her teeth, slapped her forehead, and clawed at the nape of her neck. She was mounted, however, and the spirit rider perched on its horse whispered in her ear.

Boom-boom!

The Baron took a swig of rum and spewed the mouthful at her. Crying, choking, grinding her jaws and shaking her head, the woman sank into convulsions and crumpled to the damp earth. A drummer dashed over and beat his drumskin so hard it burst, and as the mounted wretch shrieked—

Boom-boom!

A grasping hand shot up out of the ground.

The zombie's clutching fingers got entangled in her hair. They yanked her head from side to side as a hole yawned in the earth. Clods of dirt erupted as the buried man struggled to break free from his subterranean prison. Then his head popped up, smeared with mud, his bulging eyeballs blank and empty. The Baron digs your grave and greets your soul after burial, and he'll turn you into a zombie if he pleases. Now he ordered the undead man to rise from his interment, so he tossed the convulsing woman aside, rose rigidly with both hands at his thighs, and stood staring at the moon while he moaned deep in his throat.

For the Horsemen lurking in the shadows, the garbled words "zombie walks" from Tipple's wiretaps took on new meaning.

"Damballa!" the cultists cried as all heads turned to face the crypt.

Boom-boom!

Uncoiling herself like a serpent, Jezila Dubois rose from the roof of the mausoleum. With a sweep of her arm, the white dress fluttered away from her skinny body and floated like a ghost in the humid air. Unwrapping her tignon like a mummy exposing itself to prying eyes, she bared a nest of dreadlocks tipped with water moccasin skulls. As she began to undulate, her limbs as fluid as seaweed at the mouth of the bayou, John Lincoln Hardy untied Uncle Gunnysack's bag and handed Le Grand Zombi up to his mother.

"Damballa!" the cultists chanted.

The Voodoo Queen held the boa constrictor high above her head so moonlight rippled across the scales heaved by its powerful muscles. Slowly, the snake slithered down her body and burrowed its snout into her vagina. As Damballa flowed from the spirit world through Le Grand Zombi to take possession of the Voodoo Queen, Jezila Dubois splayed her legs wide on the roof of the crypt and lowered herself like a limbo dancer until her shoulders almost touched the stone. As she pumped her hips in time to the pounding of the drums, the cultists shed their own garments to get ready for the oncoming orgy.

Jezila's wail as she climaxed would wake the undead.

"Holy fuck," Rick muttered.

"No matter what you hear, size matters," whispered Kathy.

Baron Samedi prodded the zombie toward the mausoleum. As the reptile pulled out of the Voodoo Queen and slid up her torso between her breasts to glare into her eyes, Jezila rose inch by inch from her limbo crouch and again stood with the snake held above her head. Damballa's possession was evident from how she flicked her tongue and conversed with Le Grand Zombi through hissing.

"L'Appé vini, le Grand Zombi. L'Appé vini, pou fe gris-gris," chanted the cultists.

Boom-boom!

From the roof of the mausoleum, the Voodoo Queen dropped the boa constrictor onto the zonked-out zombie. She hissed to the serpent as it wrapped its coils around the resurrected corpse, squeezing tighter and tighter to strangle the undead man into silence. Abruptly, the drums stopped beating so all could hear the bones crack. As reanimation was crushed out of him, the zombie fell to his knees and toppled.

John Lincoln Hardy uncoiled the snake and stuffed it back into the sack. Then he set a line of red gris-gris bags along the edge of the crypt at his mother's feet. Baron Samedi pried open the zombie's mouth and wrenched out its teeth with a pair of pliers. Four men dragged the tooth-less body to the shore and hurled it into the bayou. A rustling in the swamp told the cops that gators were coming, and soon there was thrashing that turned the algae red. Meanwhile, at the eerie tomb, an exchange occurred. As each cultist removed the ebony mask from his or her face and handed it to the Voodoo Queen, she dropped a bloody tooth into the smuggler's bag as thanks.

With a zombie tooth in every pouch, Jezila's gris-gris was *wanga.*

"Bad luck" indeed!

As the ritual devolved into an orgy of sexual frenzy—the drums thumping in time to a sea of humping hips, the bodies dripping sweat as they were mounted by loa and mounted each other, twisting, contorting, convulsing, and shaking until eventually they'd all collapse from exhaustion—the Horsemen slipped away.

"What do we tell Cheval?" asked Kathy.

"Nothing for now. Not until Hardy's in our hands back home."

"That was murder."

"No, that was a voodoo cult running afoul of a snake. Exactly the same thing that happened last year, when Zette got strangled. And there's no body. Gators saw to that."

After they climbed into the car and Tony headed off into the night, Rick returned the silencer-equipped Colt to the New Orleans detective.

"Didn't need it," he said.

"Good," said Tony. "Get what you want?"

"Yes. And then some."

WATCHERS

Vancouver, British Columbia
11:20 p.m.

Kuntz was the name of the strip bar on the inland side of the Dollarton Highway, which ran along the harbor from North Vancouver to Deep Cove on Indian Arm. The neon sign above the door flashed two alternating strippers: one standing with her clothes on and the other squatting with her clothes off and her thighs spread wide. Local politicians outraged by the sign had fought a battle to have it changed, but the owner, whose birth name was Sidney Kuntz, accused his opponents of having dirty minds.

"Kuntz? Wasn't he the heavy in Conrad's *Heart of Darkness*?" asked Rusty.

"I believe that was Kurtz," replied Monica as she pulled to a stop in front of yet another sleazy joint from Pitt's matchbook collection.

"Mad Dog told me a funny story about this dive."

"Do tell."

"You sure? It comes with a content warning."

"Nothing shocks me."

Last night's fog had failed to return and bright stars pinpricked the fathomless sky. They could just make out the North Shore Mountains jutting from behind the raucous pub. Posters flanking the door announced that the Ice Queen was back by popular demand. Inside, the woman onstage bumped and jiggled to "Ain't That a Shame" by Cheap Trick.

"One of the regulars at Kuntz has a religious wife who drags him to Catholic mass on Sundays. At a church social, he confessed his evil passion to the priest, an affable guy known for his sense of humor. Intrigued, the priest said he wanted to tag along one night, but there was a stipulation: 'You don't call me Father, and I won't wear my collar.' So off they went to chug beer and see the star performer—"

"The Ice Queen?" said Monica.

"Yep," Rusty confirmed. "And guess what? They scored a table on gynecology row."

Monica groaned, rolling her eyes. "I suppose gynecology row is the line of tables hugging the front of the stage?"

"You got it," Rusty said, laughing. "And it seems the Ice Queen earned her moniker from a unique sexual talent. She can stuff an ice cube you know where and shoot it out into the crowd for one of her admirers to catch in his drink."

"Scotch on the rocks?" said Monica.

Rusty grinned.

"Anyway, on the night in question, guess who was the fortunate gawker to have lady luck's ice cube splash into his drink?"

"Father Incognito?"

"The sinful Vatican priest. Come next morning, the pious wife dragged her reprobate husband off to mass, where he took his place in line to receive the body and blood of Christ. The priest, nursing a hangover, placed the host onto the man's tongue. Then, instead of having him sip from the communion cup, the wayward father substituted a glass of red wine in which—"

Monica guffawed.

"There was a floating ice cube."

In light of the sex scandals besmirching the Catholic Church, Macdonald had little doubt that Mad Dog's tale was true. If her job had taught her anything, it was this: repressed sexuality will always warp. It's called a sex drive because it advances survival of the species. Monica's time investigating sex crimes had given her a key to the cellar where people hide their orgasmic secrets. *There isn't a person who isn't fucked up sexually,* she thought. *It's all a question of how you hide it.*

For as long as she could remember, she'd yearned to be a Mountie. "Girls can't be Mounties. Only boys," her father told her. Young Monica devoured every Nancy Drew mystery, then moved up to cozy soft-boiled puzzles by Agatha Christie, and finally reached the hard-boiled stuff...

or so she thought. All those tough guys writing about the sexual under-ground, where sloe-eyed, enameled hussies flashing cleavage and leg ranked as femmes fatales. But then, in 1974, the Force recruited its first troop of female Horsemen, and Monica learned what the sexual under-belly was *really* like. Judging from what they put down on the page, most hard-boiled crime writers plotted in the missionary position.

Kuntz, she thought. *The cesspool of bottom-feeders.*

Tell it like it is.

Don't wimp out and sanitize it for fuddy-duddy readers.

Like John Lennon said, "Gimme some truth."

From the door of the club came the voice of Roger Daltrey singing about Mama having a squeeze-box and Daddy never sleeping at night.

"That's our cue," said Rusty.

"Into the heart of darkness," Monica replied.

As the cops stepped out of their car, Macdonald patted her hip to con-firm that her gun was holstered there if needed. Was it a premonition? The hackles on her skin warned something was about to happen.

Across the lot and through the door, they entered the strip bar in time to see that the Ice Queen was a talented gal indeed. Her hair exploded from her head in a burst of silver spikes. Her eyes were smudged with black, and her lips were slicked ruby red. She must have asked the plastic surgeon for the largest pair he had, for no woman in her right mind would want a boob job that balloony unless there was a reason. The reason, it seemed, was that the mob in this pit of sexual degradation was into female cartoons as phony as the women on the club's blinking neon sign. To the haze of smoke produced by the puffing drunks, the Ice Queen was adding a cloud of her own. Squatting knees-wide on the stage above gynecology row, the stripped-down ecdysiast was smoking a cigarette with her vagina.

The cops split up and wormed their way around the edges of the crowd. As she scanned the faces hypnotized by the smoke-ringed Ice Queen, Monica thought she knew the source of her premonition. She imagined these troglodytes mindlessly prowling the streets of Vancouver later tonight in search of emancipated women to fuck to—

She froze to the floor…

Her skin went from tingle to crawl…

For there, leering up at the Ice Queen from gynecology row, was the unmistakable twisted face of Matthew Paul Pitt.

Inspector Jack MacDougall was the watch commander at HH HQ when Monica's call for assistance came in at a quarter to midnight.

"We found him, sir. Matthew Paul Pitt. Got him under observation at a North Shore pub."

"Crime committed?"

"No."

"Evidence for arrest?"

"None that I can see. But I'm thinking that if he's sleeping rough, we may find the missing heads at his bush camp."

"Good work. Hang on while I call Special O."

The nondescript building next to the Trans-Canada Highway, on the north bank of the Fraser River, was home to Cascade Consulting. The company's business was unclear, but whatever it was, consultants had to come and go all night. Thanks to its roadside location, they had their choice of routes.

Quick response.

Only the RCMP brass knew what Cascade Consulting did. For reasons that no one can now recall, "Oscar" was the code name for Special O—the "O" as in "observation" trackers of the Mounted Police. Oscar's "watchers" were Mounties versed in state-of-the-art surveillance techniques created by British, American, and Israeli spies. It wasn't uncommon for Special O to have as many as a hundred disguised cops tailing a single suspect, backed by satellites, homing devices, infrared cameras, and gyroscopic binoculars. Monica—Nancy Drew reader that she once was—would have been tickled to know that the watchers even used a surveillance system diagrammed on page 246 of *The Hardy Boys' Detective Handbook*.

If it ain't broke, don't fix it.

Tonight, the ghost cars that left Cascade Consulting for the bridge across the inner harbor to the North Shore were tasked with tailing Matthew Paul Pitt from Kuntz to his lair.

THIN RED LINE

Wednesday, November 3, 3:45 a.m.

"Daddyyyy!"

A shrill scream shatters the moonlit night as he struggles to close the distance between himself and the open door of the cabin in Quebec's Laurentian woods. The harrowing shriek is Janie's, and it chills him to his marrow. The crossbow in his quivering hands is cocked, loaded, and ready to let vengeance fly, if only he could run faster than he's moving now. Why, when every second counts, do his legs plod as if they're made of lead? When he glances down to see what's impeding his sprint, he's surprised to see that his feet are sinking roots into the ground, transforming him from a father desperate to reach his child into some sort of plant-man from science fiction.

"Daddyyyy!"

All the fear in the world is bottled up in her cry.

"Help me! I'm scared!"

Panic grips him as he drops the bow and grabs hold of one leg, tugging his thigh as hard as he can to wrench his rooted foot free. When that limb refuses to budge, his hands switch to his other leg and yank, yank, yank until his foot begins to rise. Half the forest floor seems to cling to his roots as chunks of dirt tear loose from the moist soil. His heart strains in his chest and pain shoots down his arm when he hauls his land-locked leg with him. But suddenly it releases, and then he's lumbering toward the cabin while trees crash down around him.

"I'm coming, Jane! Hold on!" he shouts to her disembodied voice.

The forest turns silver as moonlight gleams in through the clear-cut swaths. The steps to the cabin door are flanked by four severed heads mounted on poles:

Helen Grabowski, Liese Greiner, Joanna Portman, and Sister Angelica. How many warnings like this did he see in the adventure films of his youth? Turn back, explorer. Headhunters and cannibals await you.

Up the steps and across the porch, he stumbles into the cabin, still trailing torn roots in his wake. At first, he's blinded by darkness. Then he sees the face of his daughter in the far corner, where a moonbeam slants in through a broken window.

"No!" he howls, for Jane has no body. She's nothing but a head stuck on a stake like the Headhunter's trophies by the door.

"I knew you'd come, Daddy," she cries through tears of blood.

———

He jerked awake to find he'd fallen asleep at his desk. Moonlight spilled in through the seaside window and sheened wet drops on the polished desktop. His palm dampened as he ran a hand down his face, telling him that he'd been crying in his sleep. His head ached from the drugs, his back was stiff, and a charley horse cramped his leg. Massaging the muscle eased that pain.

The panic attack had him too wound up to go to bed. The side effects of the Benzedrine were kicking in: overstimulation, restlessness, insomnia, anxiety, paranoia, depression, and tremors. High blood pressure made his heart pound in his chest, flushing his face. Elevated body temperature had him shivering. He was paying a steep price for mental alertness, and if he OD'd on bennies, amphetamine psychosis was next.

That would compound his PTSD.

And lock him in the Zone, which was already out of control.

If only he could hold out long enough for something to break in the case.

A day or two.

Hopefully.

I've got to keep going, he thought.

As he had for the past two mornings, Robert crossed to the wall safe hidden behind his books and unlocked it to fetch the .476 Enfield that had once armed Wilfred Blake. He carried the gun along the hall to look in on his sleeping wife, and found Genny bathed in moonglow with her black hair a spider's web on the pillow. As he watched her breasts rise and fall with each slumbering breath, the clothes tree by the window cast its shadow across her like a secret lover in their marital bed.

"I adore you," he murmured, before he went to the kitchen to brew strong coffee.

After bundling up against the cold and filling a mug with steaming caffeine to jump-start his weary body, Robert trudged to the Greenhouse and jinked through the rose bushes, several of which were showing signs of neglect and scattering wilted petals on the tile floor. Exiting by the water-front door and climbing the knoll, he slumped down in the driftwood chair beside the moonlit sundial. With his coffee in one hand and the Enfield in the other, the modern redcoat journeyed back in time.

When you find yourself going down for the count—like Robert did now—British military history is full of stirring icons to help you soldier on.

The Battle of Balaclava is known for the Charge of the Light Brigade. On October 25, 1854, while British soldiers fought the Russians in the Crimean War, a miscommunication in the chain of command sent the British light cavalry charging in a frontal assault against a Russian artillery battery with excellent fields of fire, instead of one that was in retreat.

Lord Tennyson captured the action in "The Charge of the Light Brigade":

> *Half a league, half a league,*
> *Half a league onward,*
> *All in the valley of Death*
> *Rode the six hundred.*
> *"Forward, the Light Brigade!*
> *"Charge for the guns!" he said:*
> *Into the valley of Death*
> *Rode the six hundred.*
>
> *Cannon to right of them,*
> *Cannon to left of them,*
> *Cannon in front of them*
> *Volley'd and thunder'd;*
> *Storm'd at with shot and shell,*
> *Boldly they rode and well,*

Into the jaws of Death,
Into the mouth of Hell
Rode the six hundred.

That's how Robert felt this morning: shell-shocked on all sides. Plagued by nightmares that wrenched him out of sleep, leaving him too exhausted to face another stressful day, he'd fallen into a vicious cycle of popping bennies to keep alert, then downing Scotch or Ativan to knock himself out.

How did Wilfred Blake maintain his sanity?
Think of the horror and stress he faced in all those far-flung battles.
What mettle drove him on?

The Battle of Balaclava is also known for another iconic image. Early that morning, a Russian cavalry force of twenty-five hundred men was on the road to the disorganized, vulnerable British camp. All that stood in their way were the vastly outnumbered 93rd Scottish Highlanders on foot. Sir Colin Campbell is said to have told them, "There is no retreat from here, men. You must die where you stand."

Military convention held that a firing line should be four men deep. Campbell had his troops form a line just two deep. As the Russian cavalry charged, the Highlanders fired three volleys. Confronted by a thin line of infantry, the Russian commander concluded that the Scotsmen were merely a diversion masking a much stronger British force, and he ordered his cavalry to withdraw.

The war correspondent for *The Times* wrote that he could see nothing between the Russian charge and the British camp but the Highlanders' "thin red streak tipped with a line of steel." In the popular imagination, this became "the thin red line," a symbol of British stalwartness in battle, and a metaphor for any thinly spread military unit holding firm against attack.

Rudyard Kipling immortalized the phrase in "Tommy":

Yes, makin' mock o' uniforms that guard you while you sleep
Is cheaper than them uniforms, an' they're starvation cheap;
An' hustlin' drunken soldiers when they're goin' large a bit
Is five times better business than paradin' in full kit.

Then it's Tommy this, an' Tommy that, an' "Tommy, 'ow's yer soul?"
But it's "Thin red line of 'eroes" when the drums begin to roll,
The drums begin to roll, my boys, the drums begin to roll,
O it's "Thin red line of 'eroes" when the drums begin to roll.

In time, the police changed that to "the thin blue line." The Mounties, however, are the last remnant of the British colonial army, and with their red serge tunics, they still reflect the original phrase.

DeClercq channeled Blake's mettle through the Enfield revolver.

A day or two.

With luck.

I've got to hold out.

Time to form a one-man thin red line.

——

Clutching her dressing gown against the predawn chill in the house, Genevieve stood at the library desk and gazed out at her beleaguered husband slouched above the sea. For days, she'd watched him disintegrate, both mentally and physically, under the crushing pressure of this rampage. Now, he'd absentmindedly left the drawer of his desk unlocked and ajar, baring the bottle of Benzedrine pills. In his psychological quandary, Robert was playing with nitroglycerin.

Genny had to buttress him.

But what could she meaningfully do?

If she went to the Mounted Police, she knew they'd wrench the case from him, which would only add to the public thrashing he was undergoing in the media. She wondered if he subconsciously blamed her for failing him as a therapist. He'd come to her as a patient, and she fell in love with him. After too many romantic trysts with males of the Me Generation, she found it refreshing to meet a man who was attracted to her for *her*, and not for what she could do to gratify *him*.

But she had merely patched over his psychological cracks.

And now he was tumbling into fissures that had been chiseled wide by the Headhunter.

Then it struck her.

Yes, she thought. *That's what I'll do.*

After Robert drove off to work another grueling shift, she canceled all her appointments and sat down at his walnut desk. The files he'd brought home were an overview of all pertinent leads in the ongoing manhunt, so she settled in to read them cover to cover, and by late afternoon she had a detailed understanding of what he was up against.

Then she phoned the man she knew was smitten with her.

The guilt she felt over manipulating him was trumped by the guilt she felt over failing her husband in her capacity as a psychologist. All her life, Genny had found it easy to make men fall for her. Anglo males in particular go gaga for a French temptress. It's the nature of testosterone. If you can pout like Brigitte Bardot in *And God Created Woman,* Englishmen will crumple at your feet. This man was like that: head over heels for her. Perhaps thirty years from now, attraction between the sexes would be more evolved. But Genevieve wouldn't hold her breath. Human beings were primates clad in a thin veneer of civilization.

She wouldn't hurt him.

Just play on his Franco fantasies.

"*Bonjour.* It's Genny."

"What a pleasant surprise."

"I need your help."

"Anything."

"Have lunch with me tomorrow?"

HEX

New Orleans, Louisiana
8:35 a.m.

Threatening clouds rumbled north from the Gulf of Mexico. When the tropical storm cracked open, blinding light silhouetted the horizon in stark relief. A boom of thunder hit the car like a cannon volley as the cops drove toward Moisant Field. Each subsequent flash of lightning was more searing than the last, and each blast of thunder pounded at a shorter interval. As they neared the airport, the *son et lumière* show exploded above their heads, and rain rattled down in a drum roll.

"I checked the airlines," Antoine Cheval said, his voice louder than the clatter outside. "John Lincoln Hardy and Tom Rackstraw have seats on the flight after yours."

"Where to?" Spann asked.

"Seattle. There, they connect with a small commuter plane to Vancouver."

"Any luggage?"

"Yep. A cargo shipment is flying with them. The bill of lading says the package contains antique voodoo masks."

"Perfect," said Kathy. "We'll stop them at Vancouver Airport and search the cargo for drugs. What better way to import coke than in a shipment of stage props for Voodoo Juju, a band currently recording and performing in Vancouver? Cocaine smuggling has a minimum sentence of seven years, so arresting Hardy for that will give us a chance to squeeze him for information about Helen Grabowski and his whereabouts when each of the Headhunter's victims met her fate."

Special Agent Luke Wentworth was once more along for the ride, still wearing his signature shades despite the torrential downpour.

"Too bad you're not here longer," he said as the car pulled up at the airport. "You could have seen the tourist sights, like Chalmette Monument. That's where General Andy Jackson chased the Redcoats out of town at the Battle of New Orleans in 1814."

Jerk, thought Kathy.

Asshole, thought Rick.

Sibling rivalry.

And one-upmanship.

Vancouver, British Columbia
7:45 a.m.

A maelstrom of trouble awaited DeClercq as he pulled into the parking lot between the Heather Stables and the forensic lab. The protesters milling about the street had grown in number and turned nastier overnight. As the Horseman climbed out of his Citroën, one of the women rushed up to his car and spat in his face. "Pig!" she snarled, her eyes bloodshot with rage. Then she ran away.

Wiping the spittle off his cheek, he crossed to the Tudor building. Bright morning sunshine danced along the thicket isolating the lot from the building's front lawn. As soon as he pushed open the front door, he was embroiled in organized confusion. Bulletin boards were papered with graphs charting the victims' heights, weights, ages, and even the outside temperature when each was last seen alive. As tech workers installed more phones to keep up with the volume of tips, the stacks of paper on the rows of desks grew visibly by the minute. An ant line of filing clerks weaved along the aisles, bringing this and taking that away. At one desk, a police artist sketched a face "seen" by a psychic.

His day began putting out the brush fires that had been sparked by yesterday's lightning strikes. Robert sat in the U of his horseshoe-shaped desk, flipping through telephone messages from irate politicians and lawyers. The dragnet of sexual deviates in Chan's skinner file had yet to produce a feasible suspect, but as predicted, the legal sharks sniffed blood in the water and were circling to be the first to chomp the Mounties using the Charter of Rights.

The raid on the Iron Skulls clubhouse and the narrowly averted snuff film had the AG and the mayor passing the buck to him.

News organizations across the country had latched on to *The Vancouver Times* story of the "broken cop" and were probing for his reaction to every development.

Rodale popped in at noon to update him on the flying patrols. Special O had shadowed Matthew Paul Pitt to his bush camp, but a search of his lair this morning after he'd wandered off to forage breakfast had turned up no trophies or incriminating evidence. Scarlett and Spann were on their way back from New Orleans, having witnessed a bloody voodoo ritual that gave credence to the idea that the Headhunter belonged to a cult.

Late in the afternoon, the meth building up in DeClercq's body caused another panic attack. Standing alone at the Strategy Wall, he intuited from the accelerating pace of the killings that the Headhunter was going to strike again that night.

In a blink, the Zone expanded the Strategy Wall from four sections to five.

The fifth head on the board was Jane's.

"Daddyyyy!" she screamed.

The silhouette behind her seemed to be cast by Jane's head, but then he realized that the faceless black-haired shadow was the Headhunter's next victim.

Ottawa, Ontario
5:30 p.m.
Politics, he thought.

The Mounties are administered by the federal solicitor general, which meant that Commissioner François Chartrand had political masters to please. To complicate matters, the past few years had seen control of Parliament switch back and forth between the major political parties. Another election seemed always on the horizon. And so Chartrand had been summoned to this hardwood office in one of the Victorian blocks flanking the House of Commons for a tongue-lashing about his decision to appoint Robert DeClercq to lead the manhunt.

"Have you seen the papers?" the solicitor general asked. His ruddy gin-and-tonic face attested to his longtime membership in Ottawa's leading old boys' club, the smoky backroom social hub from which the country had been run for over a century.

"I've read them," said Chartrand.

"Including *The Vancouver Times* piece on DeClercq, his wife, and his kid?"

"I didn't need to read that one. I *lived* that tragedy."

"No playing tiddlywinks, François. The situation's explosive. The Opposition is grilling me in question period. They want to know what's being done to ensure there's not another killing. DeClercq is damaged goods. He's yesterday's man. Did you see him on the news last night? He looks burned out. If he's not good media, what use is he to us? We're selling confidence, plain and simple."

"I'm not selling anything. I'm trying to catch a killer. DeClercq's the best psycho-hunter we've got. His record speaks for itself."

"Bullshit!" The solicitor general slammed his desk. "It looks like you took him out of mothballs because he's your buddy, and now that he's stumbling, you're stonewalling."

Chartrand bit his tongue.

Like so many politicians, this guy was a blustering dolt.

"The PM wants him yanked. Is that clear enough? Replace DeClercq with a team of the best cops from across the country. Put an assistant commissioner in charge so it looks like we're being proactive. We can't afford to have another dead nun, for Christ's sake."

Again, he slapped his desk for emphasis.

"If DeClercq goes down in flames, *you* go down with him."

———

The wind off the Ottawa River buffeted Chartrand as he came out of the stone building into rush hour traffic. Civil servants queued for buses on Wellington Street as government ministers craving a drink hurried by trailing their retinues of eager-faced clerks and hangers-on. The commissioner found an empty bench facing Parliament and the Peace Tower. From his pocket, he withdrew the cigarette case Robert had sent on his promotion and took out his last Gauloises for the day.

François tamped the tobacco on the motto etched into the silver: *Maintiens le Droit.*

Lighting the smoke, he sucked nicotine deep into his lungs.

Every man has his breaking point, and Robert was in the eye of a hurricane battering him from all sides. The Mounties had never stalked a foe as cunning as this one. With public hysteria rising, how long would it be until the nightmare of Robert's past consumed him?

This was no time to command from the rear.

Tomorrow, Chartrand would fly to Vancouver to reinforce his friend.

Time to help Robert hold the thin red line.

Vancouver, British Columbia
4:30 p.m.

"We've been hexed. Those masks are cursed," said Spann.

"What a screwup!" Scarlett snarled.

After they'd arrived from New Orleans, they'd hung around the airport terminal, waiting for Hardy and Tom Rackstraw to land from Seattle. They'd arranged to have customs agents pull them aside, search the shipment, drill the masks, and let the cops squeeze them. But when the passengers disembarked, the Weasel and the Wolf were nowhere to be seen. A call to Seattle informed them that both men had missed the flight. Apparently, they were smuggling the voodoo masks by a secret route.

"We should have bugged the cargo," said Spann.

"We should have tailed them instead of thinking they'd come to us."

"I smell the Fox."

"Me too."

"Wanna bet he warned them after we crashed the Voodoo Juju gig?"

"What now?" asked Scarlett.

"We brief Tipple. And wait till they surface again."

11:30 p.m.

"Sparky."

"Shut up! Go away! Leave me alone!"

"Sparky, really! Is that how you talk to your mother?"

"You're dead and buried! You're not here!"

"Oh, but I am, child. Come downstairs and stroke my hair."

"You're bald, Mommy."

"Not that hair, silly. The black hair below."

"I won't do it."

"Yes, you will. Eat me, Sparky."

"No!"

"Do what I command. I fixed it so that you'll be mine forever. You'll have no lover but me."

"No!"

"Do it or I'll tell on you. Do you want the police to know you killed your father?"

"You killed him, not me!"

"We killed him together. Remember how he died in that wasteland of white? How his face contorted as the poison took effect? How the yellow spittle froze to his mustache? How the terror took hold when he grasped what you and I were doing to him?"

"I was a toddler! Don't blame me!"

"Who else can be blamed, Sparky? They can't jail me. I'm dead and buried, as you point out. You're the only one who knows I live on in your head."

"You make me do bad things."

"Discipline, Sparky. Spare the rod and spoil the child. What's a mama for if not to teach you self-control?"

"Why do you torment me?"

"I loathe your father, and I don't have him. Look in the mirror. Are you not your father's child? When you don't have the one you hate, you hate the one you have."

"I'm done."

"No, you're not. And you never will be. Come down and stroke my hair. Come see how black it is. Black. Black. Black. As black as your evil heart."

"No."

"Yes."

"No! AUUGGHHHH!"

"Say you love me."

"No."

"Yes."

"No! AUUGGHHHH!"

"Say you love me."

"Please, Mommy! No more. My head will explode."

"Say you love me."

"I hate you! AUUGGHHHH!"

"Say you love me."

"I hate you! AUUGGHHHH!"

"Say you love me."

"I…"

"Say it."

"I…"

"Say it, worm-child!"

"I love you, Mommy. You fucking cunt!"

MEDUSA'S HEAD

Thursday, November 4, 7:00 a.m.

Does life get better than this?

At twenty-seven, Natasha Wilkes had one of the best jobs in town: pop culture reporter at *The Vancouver Times*. She got free tickets to all major events—rock concerts, festivals, movies, hit plays, dance performances, book tours—along with passes to interview celebrities. Her latest assignment was this pre-season spread on cross-country skiing in the North Shore Mountains. So here she stood, on the snow-covered deck of a rustic ski chalet high on the south-facing slopes of Hollyburn Mountain. The chalet had been comped to her for a week so she could glide as free as an eagle along miles of virgin backwoods trails lined with ice-boughed evergreens and report her bucolic adventures to commuters currently snarled in bumper-to-bumper traffic.

Nice work if you can get it.

And I've got it, Natasha thought.

Another perk of this assignment was designer skiwear. Last weekend, *The Times* had run a promo piece on her upcoming columns, and there she stood, long black hair ruffled by the breeze, with her figure enhanced by an electric blue snowsuit. This morning, as dawn poured molten gold on Grouse and Seymour Mountains to the east, she was flaunting a scarlet jacket and black ski pants for today's photo shoot.

Eat your hearts out, poor lowland stiffs.

I'm queen of this eagle's nest.

The snowbound chalet clung to the peak uphill from the access road. She was to hook up with the photographer at the parking area. A ski trail led across the mountainside from the chalet to the lot, so Natasha zipped up her jacket, tugged on her toque and gloves, and lugged her skis down the slick steps from the deck to the crest of the trail. Snapping the boards onto her boots, she pushed away with her bamboo poles, unaware that Sparky—who was stalking her—lay in ambush just ahead.

———

So weary was DeClercq from yet another restless night that he slept through the alarm. Genny had left for work by the time the bedside phone woke him.

"G'morning."

"Bad news," said Jack MacDougall. "Another headless body."

"Where?"

"On the mountainside above your home."

"Who?"

"Brace yourself. It's Natasha Wilkes. Pop culture reporter at *The Vancouver Times*."

I'm done for, Robert thought.

———

The best way to the murder scene was on cross-country skis. The access road was clogged with police cars and forensic vans. Black Lux, a German shepherd with the K9 unit, had helped Ident sweep the path of contamination. When the cop guarding the end of the trail gave DeClercq the all-clear, he clamped on his skis and laboriously poled up the slippery incline to a slash of red snow across the narrow run. No wonder sleep deprivation was used to make captured spies talk. Days ago, he had been in tip-top shape. This morning, he was exhausted by the time he reached the crime scene.

"Robert." Avacomovitch emerged from some nearby trees.

"Joe. Where's the body?"

"In here," said the Russian, gesturing to the firs that lined the uphill side of the path across the mountain's face. As he spoke, the cold alpine air turned his breath into mist. It made Robert shiver.

"Who found her?"

"A *Times* photographer. When she failed to meet him at the parking lot as planned, he skied toward the chalet and spotted this blood line across the trail."

"Christ, will we see the body in today's paper?"

"No way," said Joe.

"That bad, huh?"

"About as bad as it gets."

"Got a theory?"

"Based on marks left in the snow, the Headhunter hid in these evergreens on the edge of the trail. He could have poled in from anywhere. See the holes in that drift where he stuck his skis as he switched to snowshoes? Natasha Wilkes skied down the path from the chalet, and when she passed the Headhunter, he coldcocked her from behind. Then he picked her up, both skis still on her feet, and carried her into the trees."

"Weapon?"

"A broken branch."

"Swung like a baseball bat?"

Joe nodded. "Then tossed away." He handed Robert a pair of snowshoes. "There's no room for skis in there. Lean on me and strap these on."

Balancing on one leg and then the other, DeClercq switched footwear.

Shoving through the branches, the Russian led the Mountie in from the path. The woman lay spread-eagled in a drift of blood-soaked snow. Her scarlet jacket and black ski pants had been slashed apart from her neck to her crotch, baring her breasts and her genitals. Her arms, stretched wide in a crucifixion pose, had ski poles rammed through both palms. The killer had staked her feet to the ground by sinking the backs of her skis into the snow. The icy blood matting her pubic hair indicated that she'd been the victim of a sadistic rape. The knife gash across her breasts exposed two ribs. Her head had been hacked off at the neck, and in its place an iconic face stared up at Robert from a crimson halo and turned him to stone.

Like it did in the classic Greek myth.

The depravity of this crime scene made him physically sick. It was all he could do to keep the bile from bubbling into his mouth.

"Nicked blade scratched the vertebra," said Joe, squatting by the stump of neck.

"Voodoo mask?"

"Could be. Rodale says Spann and Scarlett saw snake worshipers in New Orleans."

The whup-whup of a helicopter passing overhead loosed snow from the trees. The chopper was scanning the mountainside with infrared, searching for any signs of body heat that would smoke out the fugitive killer.

Careful not to smear any prints with his surgical gloves, Avacomovitch eased the mask out of its deep-red bed of snow. Carved from West African ebony, Medusa's face and head of snakes shone jet black. According to myth, any man who stared into the Gorgon's eyes turned to stone. To slay her, Perseus followed her reflection in a polished shield and cut off her head.

"Ebony?" said Robert.

"Like the splinter I found in Liese Greiner's pelvis."

"And the masks at the Voodoo Juju concert."

Straightening up, the doctor met the Mountie's eyes. "Could be coincidence," he suggested.

"Let's hope not."

Lowering his gaze to the bloody pubic hair, DeClercq recalled his conversation with George Ruryk about Freud's paper "Medusa's Head." The good doctor had explained that Freud saw the decapitation of Medusa as a representation of the castration complex. It was possible, he said, that the killer took his victims' heads as a way of regaining control over that most primal fear.

The squawk of a walkie-talkie behind him drew DeClercq's attention. MacDougall was pushing in through the firs along the ski run.

"I radioed Special O," he said. "The watchers have had Matthew Paul Pitt under round-the-clock surveillance since the night before last."

"Well, that strikes *him* off the list."

"We're doing a house-to-house of every cabin on the mountain, and Ident techs are combing the access road for tire marks. We've asked West

Van police for a list of all traffic stops and tickets issued over the past twenty-four hours. And we're about to reinterview every suspect on Chan's skinner list to map where each has been since Natasha Wilkes was last seen alive."

"Call the AG and have him increase the reward."

"Will do."

Just then, a voice came over Jack's radio. It was the K9 master. "Inspector, can you meet me at the blood trail? Lux has found something."

The psycho-hunters retraced their steps to the path. The bennies had Robert spiraling into a funk of depression that warned him something worse was coming.

A German shepherd's sense of smell is a hundred times stronger than ours, and a police dog is trained to sniff into the wind and pick up foreign scents. Black Lux and his master waited at the downhill edge of the trail, where the slash of blood across the path disappeared into the woods. A police dog works for the praise of its master, so Lux was being treated to a reward.

"What'd you find?" MacDougall asked.

"Is this your scenario, sir? The vic skied down this path from her chalet. The perp waylaid her on the *summit* edge of the run, then hauled her *uphill* into the bush and cut off her head. Leaving the body behind, he carried his dripping trophy back *downhill* and across the path so the blood streak would attract attention from whoever skied up from the road."

"Joe?"

"That's how I see it."

The dog handler looked pleased.

"From here, the blood and snowshoe tracks descend to a ski run that crosses the face of the mountain to the parking lot. There, he bagged his trophy, swapped his snowshoes for cross-country skis, and made his escape."

"Is that what the dog says?" asked DeClercq.

"Tell him, Lux."

Trained to respond to certain words, the German shepherd barked.

They followed the dog handler and his charge into the trees, stopping by a tangle of bramble canes flanking the trail of blood.

"Lux found these."

Fetching a pair of tweezers from his Murder Bag, Joe plucked three threads from one of the thorns.

Two of the threads were black. The other was scarlet.

"Puzzling," said DeClercq.

The forensic scientist nodded. "If the Headhunter murdered the girl in the *upper* woods, how did these threads from her clothes end up on this thorn?"

SCAPEGOAT

1:05 p.m.

Five hundred tape recorders filled the room in which officers from the Commercial Crime division gathered wiretap evidence on Steve Rackstraw and other suspects in Tipple's crosshairs. Each pair of machines had a master and a slave. The master recorded the evidence that would be heard in court; the slave made a working copy for the investigation. At the moment, some recorders sat dormant, some had their reels turning, and some started up or shut down according to changes in voltage on the bugged lines. When a suspect made or received a call, the act of lifting the phone's handset altered its electric current, and that kicked in the recorders.

"Action," said Tipple.

The reels bugging Rackstraw's phone began to spin.

The corporal flicked a toggle switch to route the call to a loudspeaker so Spann and Scarlett could hear the intercept.

"What's happenin'? Been waitin' on ya, nigga."

Rackstraw was tense.

"Dey tailed us, Fox. A'mos' nailed ma ass."

Hardy was scared.

"Who?"

"Feds. Pigs. Heat. F-B-fuckin'-I."

"How?"

"Wolf don' like da vibe when we flew into Seattle. Yanked da shit from da plane an' missed da flight north. Scored some wheels an' 'scaped east t' cross in da boonies. Found a border post wit' a lonely guard. Jus' dis side, da feds moved in t' bust us. I grabs a mask an' runs like hell into da trees. Cross da border, I wired a car an' drove t' Vancouver. Arrived las' night an' hid t' see if I's hot 'fo' callin' you."

"Where's Wolf?"

"Don' know. Feds could have 'm."

"Bad juju, nigga."

"Got da C, man. Wha' do I do?"

"Don' muck me."

"I's hidin' in da bush an' snuck out t' phone."

"I mean it, nigga. Don' come near me. Da mountain shack's safe. Go t' ground, lay low, an' I'll come to ya in a coupla days."

The line went dead.

The tape recorders shut down.

"Fuck!" said Rick, pounding his palm with his fist. "Wentworth screwed us and kept us out of the loop. No wonder we got stonewalled when we called the Yanks and asked 'em to look into *our* missing suspects. Wentworth's out to steal our bust. That asshole must have tailed the Wolf and the Weasel from New Orleans. When they veered off course and didn't catch the second plane north, he made his move. Followed them east way out hell and gone, then went in gangbusters to nab them in the States. He'll lord it over us. He'll get credit for taking the Headhunter down, and we'll have to beg him to gather evidence."

Kathy nodded. "That about sums it up."

"The prick would probably ask the Force for *my* corporal's hooks."

Kathy turned to Bill.

"Where's the Fox now?"

"At his Yaletown studio. Voodoo Juju spent the night laying down tracks. Stakeout saw them leave, but not Rackstraw. He likely hung back to wait for Hardy's call."

"How come he talks so freely?"

"Because he thinks he's smart. Rackstraw knows his phones at home and work are probably tapped. Doubly so since you two crashed his gig. But he thinks no one knows his studio shares a basement with the building next door. From the outside, it looks like an empty warehouse boarded up against squatters. The Fox rents that shell through a crooked lawyer."

"How'd you pick up on that?"

"Not only are we tapping his phones but we've got bugs in the walls, including the cellar. Crooks seem to think it's safer to talk underground. Eventually, we picked up the sound of a squeaky hinge. It sounded like a door being opened and closed. Special I crept in one night and checked it out. They found a secret passage behind a wall of shelves, and that led to the cellar next door. The room is empty, except for a phone on the floor. We tapped that line too, and now we can hear the calls that will make our case."

"But how do they hook up? The Fox can't be sitting in that empty basement all day, waiting for calls to come in."

"The Wolf or the Weasel dials the number next door. Whoever's calling lets it ring twice, then hangs up. The call blinks a warning light on the studio's mixing board. That tells the Fox to slip downstairs and use the secret passage. Five minutes later, the caller phones back."

"Sneaky."

"Uh-huh. But not sneaky enough."

"How do the room bugs transmit?" asked Rick.

"Radio links."

"Can you shut them down?"

"Sure. Flick of a switch."

"Have you got a skeleton key for the cellar next door?"

"Yep. The key opens a door off the alley out back."

"Okay. Rackstraw screwed us—he didn't have Hardy contact us like we asked. Hardy screwed us—he didn't catch the flight from Seattle to Vancouver. Wentworth screwed us—he tried to grab Hardy and the Wolf on his turf. I'm tired of being screwed. If Hardy's the Headhunter, we can't let him hack off another head. Rackstraw knows where Hardy is, and he's going to talk. Here's the plan: I need the key to the cellar next door. I'll radio when I'm in position to have you switch off the bugs. Can't have Big Brother listening to me interrogate the Fox. Once the bugs are dead, you call the cellar phone, and that will light up Rackstraw's mixing board."

"Deal," said Tipple. "As long as I'm in for the kill."

Rick turned to Kathy.

"Well, Dickless Tracy? You with me or not?"

1:10 p.m.

Nat Bailey was born in Minnesota in 1902. He came to Vancouver as a kid, and learned to hustle by hawking peanuts and hot dogs at baseball games. Then he turned his 1918 Model T truck into a mobile lunch counter to serve tourists parked at Lookout Point. The lazier automobilers were slow to get out of their cars, so Nat invented the carhop tray: a plank of wood that stretched across the seats from window to window. In 1928, he launched his first White Spot drive-in restaurant, and by the 1950s, Nat was serving ten thousand cars a day at his string of restaurants strategically dotted around town.

To this day, the Spot is a local legend.

Joe's stomach was rumbling as he drove down Hollyburn Mountain from the crime scene, on his way to the lab to test the snagged threads, so he turned into the White Spot at this end of Lions Gate Bridge and parked his rented car to get himself a Legendary Burger Triple "O."

When in Rome, as they say.

While passing the front window, he peered in to see if there were available seats, and that's when he spotted Genevieve DeClercq having lunch with a man much younger than her husband. He recognized her at once from her recent photo in the paper. A woman as striking as her, you don't forget. What was troubling was that Joe could tell at a glance that she was flirting with the man: she had one too many buttons popped, and occasionally, to make a point, she touched his arm.

More worrying, however, was the look in her lunchmate's eyes.

Poor Robert, Joe thought.

It's a bad time for this.

His wife's fooling around on him with a guy who's madly in love with her.

1:35 p.m.

Robert entered his office to find Commissioner François Chartrand sitting at his desk, clenching the phone tight enough to crush it.

"Yes, Prime Minister," he said with distaste. "I hear you loud and clear. You'll have my resignation as soon as I return to Ottawa."

The Bullet hung up the phone.

"Time's run out on us, my friend," he said matter-of-factly. "The thin red line just collapsed. The Opposition has been giving the government hell over the Headhunter case. No arrest is bad politics. I flew out here in a last-ditch effort to lend you support. The manhunt you've put together"—he swept his arm to take in the Strategy Wall—"is as comprehensive as I'd hoped. Unfortunately, this morning's murder has the PM seeing red, and to cover his political ass, he's making us his scapegoats. I've been ordered to clear the way for a new task force that arrives tomorrow. 'Dream team' is the term he used. Fresh-faced hotshots led by an assistant commissioner. Tomorrow there'll be a press conference to announce you've been sacked. Once I'm back in Ottawa, I'll get the chop."

"I'm sorry, François."

"For what?"

"Taking you down with me."

"It's not your fault that we're up against a conniving monster. After *The Vancouver Times* turned on you, the Headhunter stalked Natasha Wilkes to squeeze the most ink from his crimes. This afternoon's edition just hit the streets."

Chartrand gestured at the newspaper on DeClercq's desk.

The big, bold, black headlines read:

BLOOD ON HIS HANDS.

BROKEN COP SACRIFICES TIMES REPORTER.

SACK HIM!

"Is that why the PM called?"

"He's ducking for cover. Vancouver MPs are screaming, and he needs to be seen doing something. That's why *our* heads are on the chopping block."

"No reprieve?"

"None that I can see. Go home, Robert. I've been ordered."

He slouched in disgrace to the parking lot, where he found his Citroën in no shape to drive. All four tires had been slashed, flattening his car to its rims, and someone had scratched the word "pig" multiple times into its paint.

"Pig" as in cop?

Or "pig" as in chauvinist?

Abandoning the Citroën, he walked to Cambie Street and caught a cab home.

3:05 p.m.

Detective Al Flood had returned to the Vancouver Police Department's Major Crime bullpen to reinterview the drug squad cops who busted Helen Grabowski on the night she disappeared. He hoped they might recall something that was overlooked at the start of the Headhunter investigation. He was still questioning them when Inspector Fleetwood, gingerly clutching an envelope in both gloved hands, clomped up the stairs from the entrance hall and growled, "Flood. My office. *Now!*"

"Uh-oh," said the tougher of the two drug bulls.

"Got shit on your shoe?" smirked his partner.

Puzzled, Al crossed to the inspector's cramped office, stepped in, and shut the door.

"What's up, chief?"

"This," said his gruff boss, holding up the envelope. "It was shoved into the book return slot at the public library."

"Another barb from the Headhunter?"

"Yeah."

"With a Polaroid of Natasha Wilkes's head stuck on a stake?"

"Close, but no cigar."

To avoid contamination, the inspector covered his desk with sheets of fresh paper, then dumped the contents of the envelope onto the white surface.

Not a Polaroid, but a roll of film.

And with it a note, jigsawed together from newspaper clippings.

Never give a sucker an even break.

Had enough, Robert?

If you want more, develop this.

RUSSIAN ROULETTE

3:07 p.m.

Steve Rackstraw sat hunched at the mixing board in his Yaletown studio, taking a break from working on tracks for what would hopefully become Voodoo Juju's hit record to snort more lines of coke off a handheld mirror, when the red light blinked on. He'd told Hardy not to call him on the secure phone unless it was urgent, so now—fueled by paranoia from too much blow—his overwrought mind conjured up nightmare scenarios of oncoming doom.

Had the feds nabbed the Wolf south of the border?

Were the Horsemen closing in on the Weasel's hideout up Grouse Mountain?

Or—worst of all—was this call to warn him that *he* was about to be taken down?

Sniff, sniff...

Shiiiit, he thought. *Big C, I'm amped.*

Shoving back from the array of mixing board dials and sound level meters, the Fox slinked like his namesake down the stairs to the studio's basement, where he pulled open the squeaky-hinged shelves that led to the secret passage into the cellar next door. As he flicked the switch that illuminated a bare bulb dangling from a cord overhead, he felt the muzzle of a gun pressed to the nape of his neck.

"Freeze or I'll blow your head off."

Rackstraw froze.

"Cross your wrists at the small of your back."

He did as ordered.

Whoever held the gun to his skull snapped a pair of handcuffs on his wrists. The coke had fried his brain so completely that the Fox now imagined himself peeping out through a cyclopean eye drilled through his head by a bullet. Baron Samedi waited for him to play this wrong.

"What you want?"

"Hardy. You were supposed to find him, remember?"

"You dat cop?"

"Turn around, black boy, and look me in the eye."

Rackstraw felt the barrel pull back from the base of his skull. When he turned around, he was surprised to see *two* cops flanking the secret passage. They were the same Horsemen who'd crashed the Voodoo Juju gig earlier in the week—the ho with the rack who could blow him any day, and the northern cracker with the KKK in his eyes and a phantom lynch rope in his fist.

"Step back, nigga, and stand under the light."

"Why we down here?"

"So the shot won't be heard if you fuck up."

The cokehead's eyes were like glass and the stink coming off him said he'd feared a confrontation like this all his life. As the white boy aimed the muzzle at his sweating forehead, Rackstraw retreated into the cone of light. Five minutes were up. Would Hardy call again?

The Horseman flipped open the revolver's cylinder and emptied the six cartridges into his palm. Then he dropped all but one bullet into his pocket. The remaining shell was slotted randomly into one of the six chambers, and Scarlett then spun the cylinder like a gambler turning the roulette wheel. When it stopped, he flicked his wrist to snap the cylinder back into the frame.

With the gun locked and loaded, the cracker said, "Round and round it goes, and where it stops, nobody knows...except *you*, Rackstraw."

The crazy cop aimed the .38 at the bridge of the Fox's nose, about a foot from his eyes so he could see the slug among the holes.

"I took this off a pusher who OD'd on a speedball. It's a clean piece that can't be traced to me. It must've fallen into the hands of the gangster who claimed the dead pusher's turf. A gangster none too pleased with you trying to muscle in on his action. Is that why he broke into this cellar, hauled you down from your studio next door, and blew your brains out of your skull?"

The Redcoat cocked the hammer.

The cylinder revolved, inching the bullet closer to the firing chamber.

"Where's Hardy?"

"Don' know."

"Yes, you do. Play him the wiretap, Kath."

The blonde ho pressed a button on a small tape recorder and the Fox heard himself talking to the Weasel just a couple of hours ago.

"I mean it, nigga. Don' come near me. Da mountain shack's safe. Go t' ground, lay low, an' I'll come to ya in a coupla days."

"We know the coke comes in through the New Orleans bayou. When the pot boiled over at midnight, we were there. We saw your aunt—the Voodoo Queen—dance with Damballa the Snake. We watched the Wolf and the Weasel collect the coke-filled voodoo masks. Minutes ago, the FBI scooped up your brother in Washington State. Everything you've said on the phone—including the phone in this room—has been recorded. The call that brought you down the stairs was from us, not Hardy. No matter how you look at it, you're going down. The only remaining question is this: Who's the Headhunter? Is it Hardy alone? Or Hardy and you together?"

"No fuckin' way!"

"Spill it."

"I ain't killed no one."

The Horseman whacked the bare bulb to start it swinging. The wobbly light turned the cellar into a black-and-white horror film as the hand-cuffed man's drug-addled mind transformed the shadows on the walls into grotesque monsters.

Sniff, sniff…

Voodoo juju messed with his head.

The cracker's face was so pale that he could have been a zombie.

"The reporter the Headhunter killed this morning was *my fiancée*. I could let it leak that you squealed on the bayou smugglers. Let them and the Wolf take care of you. But I want blood for what's been done to *my heart*. Either you give up Hardy or…"

The Redcoat pulled the trigger.

Click!

"You're dead."

The lone bullet moved next to the firing chamber.

"Where's Hardy?"

The Redcoat pulled the trigger.

Click!

This was it!

The lone bullet moved *into* the firing chamber.

"No!" yelled the Fox.

"Where's Hardy?"

"Don't shoot! He's up Grouse Mountain!"

The cracker pressed the .38 to Rackstraw's temple as the ho held out a map, and just like that the Fox gave up the Weasel.

After the hideout had been fingered, the Redcoat pulled the trigger.

Click!

"Damn," said the pig. "It's a dummy bullet."

The Horseman released the cylinder, popped out the dummy shell, and reloaded the S&W with six live rounds.

"We're going to put you on ice while we check out the shack. If it turns out you jacked me around, I'll be back to teach you the meaning of law and order up here. You Yanks let your West go wild and tried to tame it later. We marched the Mounties west before the settlers arrived. *Big* difference. Step out of line and you get cracked like a walnut. If Hardy's not at the mountain shack, I'll return with a full load and *crack* you."

Rackstraw believed him.

━━━

"That was harsh," Spann said as the wagon took the Fox away. "Black boy? Nigga?"

"Ends and means, Kath. He coughed, didn't he?"

"The fiancée was a nice touch."

"Punks always think you've got a personal motive for going berserk."

"At least you warned me the bullet was a dud."

"Want your corporal's hooks?" he asked.

"Yeah."

"So let's go get Hardy."

THE TIME IS LATER THAN YOU THINK

3:10 p.m.

Robert DeClercq came home to an empty house. No sooner had he closed the door than he headed to the sideboard in the living room and poured himself a stiff Scotch. He snapped back an ounce to dull the weight of failure that was dragging him down, then topped up the glass and carried it through the Greenhouse and out the waterfront door to the knoll above the angry sea. Squawking gulls were flying in, signaling a storm, and thunder rumbled among the dark clouds boiling in from the Pacific. Robert collapsed in the driftwood chair and gulped several more drams, then his bleary eyes fell on the ominous prophecy etched into the weathered sundial: *The Time Is Later Than You Think.*

It certainly is, thought the Mountie.

The rain clouds storming in toward his house cast a black shadow across the waves, and as the darkness engulfed him, the jaws of depression consumed his indebted mind. He'd agreed to a pact with the devil in the form of Benzedrine, knowing that he'd pay the price of hellish side effects later on. Now the devil had come for his due, so Robert gave in and got sucked into a sinkhole of gray, gray, gray...

He couldn't surface.

The downward pull was too strong.

When his glass was empty and dull rain began to fall, he trudged back to the Greenhouse and locked the door. His favorite piece of music was Beethoven's Piano Concerto No. 5—the *Emperor* Concerto—with all its grandeur, bold melodies, and heroic spirit. For years, he'd thought that's what he'd like played at his funeral—something uplifting for his mourners to see him off. A yearning to hear it one more time beat back despair and dejection, so Robert fetched the photo of Jane from his desk and carried it and his empty glass into the living room. He splashed another slug of Scotch and spindled the record on the turntable, then lit a fire and sat by the hearth to listen and reflect.

Hold on, Janie. I'm coming.

Hollow words.

In addition to failing his daughter, he'd failed the five raped and beheaded women. He thought of Arthur Miller, another playwright who, like Ibsen, spoke to his soul. Miller's play *All My Sons*, which Robert had seen in New York with Kate, was based on true events. A father's son dies in a plane crash during the Second World War. It's revealed that the father sold cracked cylinder heads for aircraft engines to the air force, causing twenty-one other pilots to crash and die. At the end of the play, the father gasps, "They were all my sons."

Like him, DeClercq had covered up cracks, and because of that five women were dead.

Maintiens le Droit.

He'd failed in his duty.

Natasha Wilkes, Sister Angelica, Joanna Portman, Helen Grabowski, and Liese Greiner.

"All my daughters," he muttered.

In rushing off to the crime scene, he had skipped both breakfast and lunch, so now the whisky hit him as hard as a sucker punch. Rising unsteadily to his feet, Robert paused the record and weaved toward the kitchen to scrounge a bite to eat. Unexpectedly, the front door swung open and Genny stepped into the dark hall.

"You gave me a fright," she gasped. "Your car's not parked outside."

"Mechanical trouble," he fibbed. "I took a cab."

"Are you ill?"

"Just overtired. I haven't been sleeping."

When he flicked on the light, he got a jolt of his own. His wife was not a woman to flaunt her sexuality, but here she was in more makeup than she ever wore to work, with her top unbuttoned enough to display her cleavage and wearing jeans that hugged her hips like a coat of paint.

She's got a lover, he thought.

"What brings you home?" she asked, leaning forward to kiss him on the cheek.

"The commissioner flew in from Ottawa with reinforcements," he lied. "I let François use my office to get up to speed on the Strategy Wall. He suggested I go home and catch up on some sleep."

"Nightcap?" she asked. "I smell Scotch."

"Hopefully it will knock me out and I'll saw logs till dawn."

"Good. You look beat."

"And you look ravishing, Genny."

"*Mea culpa.* I've done what I shouldn't do. I've manipulated a board of chauvinistic men into financing a recovery house for battered women."

You're lying, he thought. *Just like me.*

Was it surprising that this day had come? He'd married a vivacious French beauty who turned countless male heads. Was it not inevitable that she'd be attracted to younger men as the age difference between them grew more pronounced over time? And he had conned her about his mental state, which she had surely realized by now, and that would diminish her professional self-worth. Put that together and the outcome was obvious: a younger man had made his move when she was receptive.

All's fair in love and war…and he had lost at both.

"What brings *you* home?"

"Changing for dinner," she said. "Tonight's the night my students are having potluck for me."

"I forgot."

"Should I cancel and stay home with you?"

"You can't do that after all their work. You're a super teacher and deserve their praise. Besides, I'm about to crash for the night."

"You sure?"

"Definitely."

Moving slowly to hide how tipsy he was, Robert went to the liquor cabinet next to the sideboard and fetched a bottle of vintage port.

"Here. Take this."

"I thought you were saving that for a special occasion?"

"Better that many enjoy it in celebration of you than I selfishly hoard it for myself."

She kissed him on the lips.

"That's *why* I love you," she said.

4:48 p.m.

As Robert fell restlessly into a pit of PTSD and meth nightmares—sweating, trembling, and tossing in bed—Genevieve locked the front door and eased herself into her sports car. Wedging the bottle of port between the bucket seats, she cranked the engine, shifted into gear, and drove up the leaf-strewn incline onto Marine Drive.

A car was parked fifty feet back along the road. As Genny drove away, the car started up and followed her.

Sparky was at the wheel.

RED SERGE

7:07 p.m.

Sparky had followed Genevieve DeClercq to a cozy log house nestled in the trees of North Vancouver, close to the creek that rushed down Lynn Canyon from the mountains. The night was full of water sounds: pounding rain, gurgling gutters, and the turbulent stream. The only light flickered from the cheery windows of the rustic gabled cabin. Inside, the killer could see shadow puppets moving across the bronze hearth.

Had DeClercq's wife not stopped to pick up a passenger, she'd be dead by now.

Tick-tock…

Time was tight.

If only she'd venture outside.

The cutlass in Sparky's hand was two feet long. It was the kind of machete used for cutting cane in the Caribbean islands—with a difference. A round ridge ran along the spine of the razor-sharp blade from the wooden handle to the blunt tip. Close to the handle and loosely held around this ridge was a sliding six-ounce weight. One swing of the cutlass would shoot the weight down the blade to its tip, adding force to the blow. No need to strike twice or saw back and forth with a weapon like this. A single slice at Genevieve's neck would take her head clean off.

"*Sparky.*"

"Shut up! Leave me alone!"

"*Sparky, really! Is that how you talk to your mother?*"

7:15 p.m.

For hours, Joseph Avacomovitch had toiled away in the RCMP's forensic lab, subjecting the black and red threads found at the Hollyburn Mountain crime site to a battery of tests with high-tech equipment. "Every contact leaves a trace," according to Locard's exchange principle. In other words, every killer will leave a clue at and take a clue away from the murder scene. Trace evidence is what's found in minute samples of hair, fibers, soils, paint chips, glass fragments, and such. Fibers fall into three categories: *natural* fibers from plants, animals, or minerals, such as wool, silk, cotton, jute, and asbestos; *manufactured* fibers like rayon and acetate, made by dissolving raw cotton or wood pulp and extracting cellulose to regenerate into threads; and *synthetic* fibers created from polymers, like nylon and polyester. To categorize the fibers left behind by the Headhunter at this morning's murder scene, the Russian used microspectrophotometry, gas chromatography, and refractive indexes. First, Joe bombarded the fibers with wavelengths of light, some of which were absorbed and some of which passed through. By assessing the absorbed wavelengths, he was able to determine not only the nature but also the exact color of each thread. For the chemical composition, he used gas chromatography to decompose the fibers and analyze their separate components. Having completed those tests, Joe reached several conclusions.

The two black fibers caught by the thorn were a synthetic nylon from a modern-day water-repellant garment, likely a raincoat or a jacket. That didn't help much.

The red thread, however, came from a natural twilled worsted fabric with diagonal ridges on both sides in a two-up, two-down weave. It was the type of serge used to make British-style military uniforms, and the color was an exact match for the Mounties' iconic tunic. But Joe's laser tests had revealed something else. Molecular changes occur as a fiber ages. If two men don identical red serge tunics cut from the same fabric, everyday wear and tear will soon make them different—body oils, perspiration, bleaching by sunlight, laundering in hot or cold water. Eventually, the passage of time *dates* the uniform.

Hmm, thought Joe, creasing his brow.

If this thread is from a red serge tunic, the uniform is more than fifty years old.

7:31 p.m.

Genevieve's car was parked ten feet away from the foliage where Sparky skulked. The rain was hammering so hard that it dropped a murky curtain between here and the dark front door, and because of that, when the door swung open and hearth light spilled out onto the welcome mat, the Headhunter had to squint to make out what was going on.

Tick-tock...

Yes!

Sparky's watch said there was still enough time to pull this off.

If only...

A blurred figure emerged from the rain-swept cabin down by the creek and gradually took shape as it—no, *she*—ascended the gushing slope toward the sports car. Was it the driver or the passenger she had picked up? Sparky gripped the machete hard in anticipation.

Yes!

Hunched and hooded against the downpour, the woman approached the driver's door. As she inserted the key in the lock, Sparky crept toward her from the evergreens. As the woman opened the door and bent in to retrieve a bottle of booze from between the bucket seats, the Headhunter broke cover, slid the weight back to the handle, and positioned the cutlass high to one side.

Shhhhhhew...

Perhaps she heard the weapon swish as the weight shot forward and the machete whipped sideways like a scythe, but then—

God, no! Am I having a stroke?

Defying the force of gravity, her world flipped upside down. The woman's awareness spun round and round like a discus tossed at the Olympics. The spinning wrenched the hood off her hair, and black strands slapped around her face like Medusa's snakes. The ground came up to meet her and slammed into one cheek, then her dizziness stopped abruptly as what should be horizontal turned perpendicular.

That's my body!

This can't be! she freaked.

I've lost my head!

I've lost my head!

I—I—I—

She tried to scream, but her vocal cords were cut. A severed human head can survive for up to a minute on the oxygen in the brain's blood. She watched as, yards away, her headless corpse twitched on the driveway, alive with cadaveric spasms. The blood spurting from her neck's arteries waned as her heart slowed and then finally stopped.

I—I—I— she thought as boots splashed toward her head in the rainy puddle where it lay. Crouching with the bloodstained cutlass in one hand, the Headhunter reached down and clutched the dying trophy by its long black hair.

I—I—I—

The head got stuffed in a bag.

I—i—i…

The brain ran out of oxygen as Sparky fled into the night.

FIREFIGHT

Ghost cars converged from all directions on a parking lot behind a bankrupt pizzeria at the foot of Grouse Mountain. In the hours that followed his encounter with Steve Rackstraw, Rick Scarlett had recruited a handpicked team to arrest John Lincoln Hardy and search his hideout on the North Shore peak. The Horsemen who gathered around the map in the pizzeria's loading zone were Scarlett, Spann, Tipple, Lewis, Macdonald, and Rabidowski.

"Sure you don't want the ERT squad?" Mad Dog asked.

"No way. As big busts go, this one'll join the Mad Trapper of Rat River. *We* found Hardy. It's *our* show," said Rick.

"Just checking."

Rabidowski was dressed in black and armed to the teeth. His face was smeared with greasepaint.

"Are you not muscle enough?"

"That I am," said Mad Dog.

"Who's got the search warrant?" Rusty asked.

"I do," said Kathy.

The downpour made it hard to hear. Clad in dark rain gear for this nighttime mission, the Mounties were wired up with earplugs and mouthpieces. There'd be next to no light where they were going, so they all had night-vision devices too.

"What's the plan?" asked Monica.

"Lean in," said Rick. He beamed his flashlight on the map of the North Shore slopes. "Like I told y'all earlier, here's the Grouse Mountain shack." He ran his index finger up Capilano Canyon, tracking the river to Cleveland Dam and the lake that supplies Vancouver's drinking water. Higher up, his finger traced a rutty road leading to ski huts that had been there even before the first chairlift soared to the snowcapped summit overlooking the Pacific Northwest.

"The shack's as rustic as they come. No electricity. An out-of-the-way hidey-hole fit for a fugitive. The kind of refuge you'd expect of smugglers who go to ground in Louisiana bayous. One of our choppers flew by the shack this afternoon and checked for signs of life. No body heat. No glint of light from the windows."

"Where's Hardy now?" asked Rusty.

"Don't know," said Rick. "If he snuck in after the flyby, he's inside. If not, we know he's coming. Rackstraw said that's where he'd meet him. And the shack'll be more comfortable in this deluge than hiding in the bush."

"Okay," said Tipple. "Who does what?"

"We drive two vehicles up the mountain past the dam. Rusty, you and Monica park here"—Rick indicated a spot on the map—"where the old road branches off to the shack. Alert us if you see a black guy in the bush. We'll press on up the forest road to beyond the shack. There, Bill and Mad Dog will wait in the car while Kath and I double back to scope Hardy's hideout. If he's inside, we'll call you and all close in together. If he's not there, we'll search the shack and wait for the Weasel to show."

"Got it," said Rusty.

"Questions?" asked Rick.

There were none.

"Good. Let's rock 'n' roll."

The night-vision devices strapped to their eyes turned the mountain woods green. The pathway to the shack was in worse shape than the pioneer road. The rain hammering down had turned the dirt to mud and erased their footsteps behind them. The evergreens around them shuddered from the downpour. The night-vision goggles picked up ambient light, so Rick and Kathy could see there was no glow escaping from the shack. That meant either Hardy wasn't inside or he was asleep.

Kathy took in the structure before her. The steep-angled roof of the A-frame was built to shed snow. The moss patching the walls had accumulated for decades. The rickety chimney told her that the only source of heat was a wood-burning stove. The pile of wood near the door had been chopped recently. All in all, it could be a hermit's shack or a hideaway from the chain gang.

"No smoke," radioed Rick. "The place looks deserted."

"Copy that," said Mad Dog in his earplug.

"B&E time," Kathy transmitted.

They circled the ramshackle hut, casing the joint. Through a grubby window, they could see a single room with one door. An outhouse served as plumbing. On completing the circuit, they approached the door and cranked its handle. Rusty hinges creaked open.

"Lock's been jimmied," said Rick.

"Likely Hardy. The Fox wouldn't meet him, so Hardy had no key."

"If he's been and gone, I wonder where he went?"

"Scrounging food?"

They stepped inside, shut the door, removed their night-vision goggles, and switched on their flashlights. The pools of light illuminated the hovel—a potbelly stove for cooking and heat, sticks of furniture that no respectable burglar would steal, a library of ancient paperbacks going moldy. Dust and dirt grimed everywhere, and cobwebs tattered the rafters. A fairy tale witch would be at home.

"Is that blood?" Scarlett asked.

His torch illuminated several red drops dotting the plank floor. As the Mounties squatted on the heels of their rubber boots, they heard Monica's voice in their earplugs.

"Heads up, rockers! Black man driving a black Jeep just turned off into the bush. He's coming your way. Rusty and I will follow with no headlights."

"Bill? Mad Dog? Get that?" Rick asked.

"Roger."

"Loud and clear."

"Bill, stay with the car to cut off Hardy's retreat. He'll likely park at the mouth of the path that leads to the shack. Mad Dog, hoof it down and reconnoiter his arrival. No gangbusters until Hardy enters the hut. We'll be waiting for him inside. When I say go, Rusty and Monica will block the road below, while Bill wheels down to hem in the Jeep where it's parked. If Hardy attempts a dash from the shack back to his Jeep, Mad Dog will take him down on the path."

"I'm outta the car," said Rabid, "and off to recce."

The cops in the hut focused their attention on the blood spots. One of the drops formed a half-moon at the edge of a plank in the floor. The other half-moon should have stained the adjacent board, with the crack between the planks bisecting the circle.

Spann touched the blood with her finger.

"It's fresh," she said.

"See the string tucked in the crack?" said Scarlett. "Want to bet it pulls up a trapdoor? The trap was open when the blood dripped. The missing half fell into the hole."

Spann yanked on the string, and just as Scarlett predicted, a square in the floor opened up. The shack was built on stone blocks to let the mountain runoff through. Reaching into the black pit, Rick brushed his hand against a soggy sack hanging on a hook screwed into the underside of the floor. On lifting it out, he untied the drawstring cinching the bag, pulled open the top, and shone his flashlight in.

"We've got 'm, Kath! Severed head and all!"

"Prints," she cautioned.

Sheathed in latex gloves, Rick rummaged in the sack and withdrew a head, grasping it by its black hair as if he'd plucked it from the basket under a guillotine.

"Natasha Wilkes?"

"Could be. Or the head of the woman attacked tonight," said Spann.

"That was nearby along the highway. Easy enough for Hardy to drive up and hide the trophy before heading off again."

"What else you got, Santa Claus?"

Scarlett swapped the bloody head for two weapons in the sack. One of them was a Bowie knife with a nicked blade. That nick would leave scratches on a victim's vertebrae if the killer sawed the knife back and forth. No sawing was necessary with the other weapon, a two-foot-long machete with a sliding weight to augment the centrifugal force of its swing.

"Hardy's here," Mad Dog reported through the earplugs.

"ETA?"

"As long as it takes to walk the path. He's parking the Jeep. He's getting out. He's carrying two bags. One has groceries. The other's bigger."

Rick and Kathy doused their torches and stood in the dark, waiting for their quarry to swing open the door. The night-vision goggles gave them the element of surprise. They would see Hardy before he'd see them. The Mounties drew their .38s and checked the loads. Rick held the two weapons by their blades in his free hand. Kathy retrieved the severed head from the sack and held it up like Perseus had Medusa's snake-haired face, ready to turn the Weasel to stone.

"Radio silence," Rick broadcast. "When I say 'Go,' go."

The rain drummed the roof like a garage band. The hut was cold and damp at this altitude. The smell of death came off the severed head. Something scraped the door, but it didn't open. The Horsemen held their breath.

They waited.

They waited.

What was Hardy doing?

Abruptly, the door crashed open and a glare flashed in their eyes, blinding both cops. The cutlass and the Bowie knife clattered to the floor so Rick could tear off the goggles without dropping his gun. The severed head thumped to the planks so Kathy could shuck her own glasses. All the pandemonium was caused by Hardy lighting a kerosene lamp, but it turned the element of surprise back on the Mounties and gave the Weasel an opening to launch a counterattack.

"Police!" yelled Rick.

That had the same effect as waving a red flag at a charging bull.

The enraged giant filled the doorway from jamb to jamb. Light from the flickering lamp sheened his scarred face, which was twisted into a mask of hate. Whitey was gonna get his! To ready himself for action, Hardy had dropped the voodoo mask in his other hand. The West African ebony split open and plumed coke powder into the air. With a snap of his wrist, Hardy hurled the oil lamp at Scarlett. Spewing kerosene, it splashed Rick's arm before it smashed on the wall behind him. In trying to avoid the fireball, the Mountie jerked back and cracked his head against the wood. Normally, kerosene isn't flammable at room temperature, but this low-grade oil was cut with something to make it burn more brightly.

Whoosh!

Rick's arm ignited as he tumbled to the floor.

"I'm on fire!" he shouted as the kerosene-spattered wall also burst into flames. As Scarlett rolled onto his stomach to smother his burning arm under his body, Hardy scooped the Bowie knife and the cutlass off the floor. Looming over the prostrate Mountie, the pimp was in mid-swing when Katherine Spann fired.

Bam!

The first bullet drilled his cheek and blew out the other side. The blast boomed like artillery in the tight confines of the room.

Bam!

The next bullet caught him in the temple, shattering his head into a shower of blood, brain, and bone. The hut shook on its stone blocks when Hardy hit the floor.

The shack seemed on the verge of exploding too. Hot summers had dried the wood in here for decades. Despite the rain, the flames were spreading fast. Hardy had dropped both beheading tools, so Spann tossed them out the door, along with the severed head. While fire licked around her, she grabbed Scarlett by his good arm and hauled him behind her, desperate to vacate the hut before hungry flames consumed it. None too soon, for the shack collapsed minutes later.

The smell in the air reminded her of a summer barbecue.

BREAKDOWN

9:01 p.m.

He stands in front of the Strategy Wall, facing the Polaroid heads. The severed heads aren't frozen in the grimace of death. Instead, the faces writhe and contort on their stakes, like the victims of Vlad the Impaler—the inspiration for Dracula— spiked by the thousands on sharp poles so the Romanian sadist could listen to their screams while he ate. To hear the silent screams from the Strategy Wall, Robert has to read lips, and the word shrieked by all his daughters is "Daddyyyy!"

Now the heads melt down their stakes like guttering candles, and blood from the Wall pools around his feet.

———

He jerked awake in the pitch-black room and reached for Genevieve, seeking affirmation from her warm body. But what he felt was cold flesh destined for the grave, and when he switched on the bedside lamp to confront the horror, his daughter lay sprawled beside him in the same broken-necked pose that had torn the heart out of him years ago at that cabin in the woods.

"Enough!" he said, shielding his eyes and shaking his head.

Another look and the ghost was gone.

Before going to bed, Robert had unplugged the phones to keep the world at bay and draped the windows with blackout curtains to shut out the light. Throwing back the covers, he sat up drenched in sweat and shuddered as the chill of night goose-bumped his skin. He padded to the bathroom and took a cold shower to steel himself for what he knew he had to do.

In *For Whom the Bell Tolls*, Hemingway wrote that a man who commits suicide is a coward. But even Papa shot himself in the end. The Germans have a word for it: *Selbstmord*—"self-murder." It's an act of free will that offers escape from a fate worse than death. Only those who spend their lives telling others what they can and cannot do call euthanasia and suicide sins. A free thinker has the right to choose the moment of his death, and the right to die a good death instead of a bad one. Hemingway said, "The real reason for not committing suicide is because you always know how swell life gets again after the hell is over." But in the end, he didn't believe it, and neither did Robert. In reality, the cavalry never rides to your rescue in the nick of time.

The question was: Should he wear the uniform?

He'd devoted his life to the Mounted Police and done the best job he could. In his heart, he knew he'd earned the right to die with honor, so he stood in front of the mirror and donned the full dress uniform of the Royal Canadian Mounted Police. The red serge tunic strapped under the Sam Browne belt, displaying his medals, decorations, sword, whistle, and lanyard. Brown gauntlets tucked into the belt. Blue serge riding breeches with a yellow side-stripe. And last, long boots with jack spurs.

I'll die with my boots on, he thought.

How else should a Mountie go out? At a Horseman's funeral, a riderless horse offers a "last ride" with the dead cop's boots reversed in the stirrups.

Robert carried the iconic Stetson along the hall from the bedroom to the library, setting it down on his desk overlooking the harbor. From the safe behind the bookcase, he fetched two guns: Inspector Wilfred Blake's Enfield and his own Smith & Wesson. He wrote a note on what to do with Blake's historic revolver, then tagged the weapon with the note and returned it to the safe.

Next, he wrote a farewell letter to his wife:

Genny,

I have left this world and gone to find my beloved Jane. Don't open the door to the Greenhouse. Call François Chartrand. He'll clean up the mess I left behind.

Never doubt this: I love you and am thankful for the time we had together.

But I'm a haunted man, and this is the only way I can escape from my demons.

I've left you everything.

Find someone worthy of you and have a better life.

Please forgive me.

Robert

He carried the Stetson, the gun, and the letter to the living room and set them down on the sideboard. He placed a bottle of Scotch next to them to fortify his nerves, then taped the letter to the Greenhouse door. Because it was his sanctuary, there was no window between the outbuilding and the living room. There was no danger that Genny would peer in and see his corpse.

"Robert!"

For the second time that day, his wife came home unexpectedly. Hat on his head and gun and bottle in his hand, he had one foot in the Greenhouse when she burst through the front door.

"The phone's dead. I couldn't reach you. It was awful! A student went out to my car to fetch the bottle of port and she was—"

"Goodbye, Genny," he said.

Entering the Greenhouse, he closed and locked the door.

It took no more than a second for her to grasp what was happening. From her psychology sessions with would-be suicides—and especially cops—she recognized the signs. The uniform, the gun, and the locked door were all giveaways. For an hour, she'd been embroiled in the aftermath of the Headhunter's sixth murder, and all the while, Robert was preparing to top himself. When she'd finally cabbed it home—because her sports car was part of the murder scene—she'd found this!

Genny panicked.

There wasn't time to stop him.

No way could she smash through that solid wall of wood. And by the time she'd exited the front door, circled around the bungalow, and gained access to the Greenhouse from outside, Robert would have shoved the gun into his mouth, pulled the trigger, and blown his head apart. Even if she made it, what could she yell that would yank him back from the brink?

Still, she had to try.

Grabbing the knob, she gave it twist and wrenched open the front door, only to find the threshold blocked by the bulk of Joseph Avacomovitch.

"Where's Robert?"

"In the Greenhouse! He's going to shoot himself!"

A sweep of the Russian's arm sidelined Genevieve. He too had been trying to contact Robert, and while he was driving over to discuss the red thread with his beleaguered friend, he'd heard news of the firefight on Grouse Mountain.

What happens when an unstoppable force meets an immovable object? At six foot four and 285 pounds, the forensic scientist was a hulk to be reckoned with. Like a human battering ram, he thundered down the hall and through the living room, hunching his head to his barrel chest and leading with his shoulder, until he hit the hothouse door full force.

It didn't stand a chance.

With cracks of protest, the lock ripped free and the hinges tore from the jamb. Amid a spray of splinters, the door crashed into the Greenhouse. Joe rode it like a surfboard across the tile floor, trailing potted plants and clumps of dirt in his wake.

Robert sat in the wicker chair with the gun barrel in his mouth. The muzzle was aimed at his brain. As he snapped back the hammer and his finger closed on the trigger, he glanced down at his friend's white pompadour and wire-rim spectacles craning up to face him.

"Don't do it!" Joe yelled. "A flying patrol brought him down!"

COP A FEEL

Friday, November 5, 4:45 p.m.

"To *Corporal* Katherine Spann."

Rick raised his Manhattan in a toast to her promotion.

"To *Corporal* Rick Scarlett."

Kathy raised her champagne flute to him in return.

The flying patrol clinked glasses.

"The Queen Mum drinks champagne, Kath. I'da thought soaring the ranks calls for hard bar."

Rick knocked back his cocktail—two parts whisky to one part vermouth—then popped the cherry into his mouth.

"Bubbly's the drink of celebration."

"Whatever." His fist punched the air. "Fucking A, eh?"

"Yep. Fucking A."

The revolving bar atop the harborside hotel was filling fast with the after-work crowd as the downtown office towers emptied for the weekend. Another day of rain had turned the sky gray, and that was darkening fast as evening settled in. The cops were seated side by side on padded barstools, watching the mixologist pluck colorful bottles from the shelves to concoct his potions.

Rick signaled for another double Manhattan, and when it arrived, he raised his glass again.

"Here's to the Bullet. The man's got balls. Rumor is he and DeClercq were about to get the chop when—let's be frank—*we* saved their bacon. That's why the hotshots from back east had arranged a media scrum for this morning. To give 'em the bum's rush. Trust the Bullet to make an entrance in full red serge and stride to the podium to break the news: *DeClercq took the Headhunter down.* All the brass could do was applaud as reporters ran to file their stories."

"What a show," Spann agreed. "The media loves us."

"You more than me, it seems." Scarlett tapped the newspapers fanned out on the bar as he gulped his drink and ordered a third.

"Easy does it, Rick, or I'll be rolling you home."

"Tits, eh? You got 'em. I don't."

The front pages showed the Amazon Mountie—as one headline put it—in the aftermath of the firefight up Grouse Mountain. According to the stories, she not only gunned down the psycho terrorizing Vancouver, but also saved her partner from being killed *twice*: first from the knife that the Headhunter used to cut off his trophies, then by the flames engulfing his hideout.

"*I* found Hardy, not you," Rick said bitterly. "But my mug's not in the limelight."

"You were in the ambulance having your burns treated when the photogs swarmed in. I was out in the open, so I drew the cameras. That's all."

"Horseshit."

"What does that mean?"

"You stole the spotlight because you're a woman. Must really turn your crank, huh? Being one of the first female recruits to make corporal?"

"How's me being female relevant? You got promoted too. We're the same age and have served for the same length of time. *That's* why I made corporal."

"Mark my words," Rick said, slurring the words to be marked, "you'll make inspector on sex alone, and I'll still be down to corporal."

"Gender."

"Huh?"

"It's gender, not sex. And I'll climb the ranks on merit. Not fuck my way to the top."

"Women trumping men. That's the future."

"No, that's destiny. Centuries of inequality need leveling out."

"At *my* expense?"

The bar was turning blue with cigarette smoke. She drained the last of her champagne and waved to the bartender for the check.

"I'll get it," Rick said, fumbling his wallet onto the counter.

"Not my style. We'll split it."

She tossed some bills down beside the papers.

"I can't even buy you a drink?"

"I pay my own way."

"Whatever."

"Why are you so angry, Rick? Too many things rile you."

"It used to be a man's world."

"Not anymore. Get used to it."

The Manhattan is a drink that can hold its own with the martini. Straight alcohol. Rick had slammed his three back so fast on an empty stomach that he was having trouble holding his booze. His steps were unsteady as they walked to the elevator that would take them back down to the street, and his face was flushed the color of vermouth.

"You're drunk," said Kathy.

"No, I'm not."

The elevator was empty except for them. As the door closed, he leaned across her to punch floor 12 and managed to trip on his own foot. As Kathy pulled Rick toward her to break his stumble, he grabbed one of her breasts and gave it a hard squeeze.

"Now that's copping a feel," he said, chuckling at his pun.

She shoved his hand away.

"What gives?" she snarled, clenching her teeth.

"I got us a room."

"No way. Back off, Romeo."

Rejection jabbed him like a picador.

Rick saw red.

"You've been asking for it since you stripped down for that steam."

"You've got to be kidding! I was cold and wet, just like you."

"You don't like cock?"

Veins snaked at his temples and whisky fumes belched in her face.

"I don't fuck cops. Get that through your head. It's nothing personal. The job's the job, and bed-hopping's not part of it."

"Aren't you the frigid one?"

"I'm warning you, Rick. Pull back while you can."

The elevator stopped at the twelfth floor and the door slid open on an empty hall.

"What's a stud gotta do to get somewhere with you? Know what? You hold your cunt too tight!"

His body pinned her to the wall as his uninjured arm scooped down and his hand grabbed her pussy. Spann reacted by lifting one leg and kneeing him in the groin. Scarlett yelped and dropped both hands to his balls. The force of the blow crumpled him to the floor. Stepping out of the elevator, Spann wedged the standup ashtray from the hall against the door so the lift wouldn't move until Scarlett recovered. No good would come from having it descend to the lobby, igniting a scandal while their names were still in the news.

Kathy then pulled open the fire door and ran down twelve flights of stairs.

Shit, she thought.

Now I've got to watch Rick.

Part Two

WHAT'S UP, DOC?

ONE MIND'S I

I saw Dr. Ruryk today, and this is what he told me: "The compulsion you're feeling about the severed heads is probably tied to the recent death of your mother, which has revived unresolved anxieties over the death of your father when you were young.

"The mind has ways to protect itself from traumatic horrors—*unconscious* psychological coping techniques that dispel anxiety. We call these defense mechanisms. Freud, as you'd expect, is the man who came up with the concept. The first mechanism he discovered was repression. Repression means forcing a painful thought or feeling out of conscious awareness. Think of it as locking a criminal away in a dungeon. Repression is the jailer holding the key. The forgotten thought or feeling is still alive and yearns to escape, but it has to trick the jailer into letting it go. And to do that, the 'criminal' disguises itself as neuroses like phobias, compulsions, and obsessions, or in extreme cases, as psychoses like hallucinations and delusions."

"I get the picture," I said.

"Freud would not be pleased with me painting it that way."

"How would he put it?"

"'Life is not easy!'" Dr. Ruryk shook his head with a sad smile. "Freud said our mind consists of the ego, the superego, and the id. The id represents our biology, our instinctual demands, our drive to fulfill our wants, needs, and impulses. The superego represents control, the rational and moral reins that stop us from doing what the id wants. Caught in the middle is the ego—our 'I'—the part of our mind that tries to mediate between the id and the superego. If conflicting demands on the ego can't be resolved, we suffer anxiety. Anxiety is an upsetting inner state that our mind seeks to avoid. When we feel threatened, overwhelmed, or about to collapse under the weight of it all, anxiety serves as a distress signal, alerting the ego that its survival—and with it, the survival of the whole organism—is in jeopardy. To protect us, the ego brings an *unconscious* defense mechanism into play to manipulate, deny, or distort whatever thoughts or feelings are distressing us."

"So I've repressed something from my conscious mind?"

"Probably."

"To do with the death of my dad?"

"Are severed heads not linked to what happened to him?"

"Yes. But what would I be repressing?"

"Guilt, perhaps. Repressed thoughts are often tied to feelings of guilt from the superego."

"You said I've *probably* repressed something from my conscious mind. Why 'probably'?"

"Repression's only one of many defense mechanisms. There's also regression, projection, dissociation, displacement, reaction formation, sublimation, and so on."

"Weird that I suddenly feel compelled to blow up these heads."

"Whatever's locked in your dungeon is once again tricking the jailer to try to escape. You have no memory of what was repressed, but it still festers in your unconscious."

"Is there a cure?"

"Psychoanalysis. Our aim is to bring your repressed thoughts, fears, and memories back to the level of *conscious* awareness. We delve into your childhood for the cause of the repression, and then use realization to show you why your defense mechanism is no longer needed."

"How do I start?"

"With a journal. Sit down and record everything you recall about your father's death and your consequent obsession with severed human heads."

"Then what?"

"I'm referring you to a clinical psychologist I trained—and by the way, she's the best student I ever had. She'll delve into your childhood."

"What's her name?" I asked Dr. Ruryk.

"Genevieve DeClercq."

Why do humans so fear a severed head? Stick them on poles in the jungle or on hooks at the Tower of London and we recoil in terror that shakes us to our core. Is it because we know a severed head can live on after the heart stops beating? Back in 1793, at the height of the Reign of Terror in the French Revolution, as many as fifty people a day went to the guillotine. Executioners would watch for any still-conscious heads—those that didn't succumb to shock from the whack of "the national razor"—and hold them aloft so they could see their headless bodies. A French scientist condemned to death on the guillotine told his student to count the number of times his severed head blinked to learn how long it lived on. The eyes blinked twenty times.

When I was a boy in the fifties, there were still haunted forests to play in. They're all gone now. Everything's been developed. In those days, the word "pedophile" rarely popped into parents' heads, and kids were free to run until hunger drew them home. The thicket of bush between me and my grade school had two tracks through the jungle-like underbrush: the Witchy Path and the Ghosty Path. The Witchy Path ran through a clearing encircled by several crude totem poles. The clearing was spooky on a misty fall day but could be sparkling in the snow. The Ghosty Path was bisected by a spring-fed marsh, and if the Huck Finn raft was waiting on your side, you could pole across. If not, you had to retrace your steps and use the Witchy Path instead.

One day, I was on my way to school when something strange happened. The Thunderbird, the Cannibal Bird, and the Big Mouth Monster—the three figures on top of the totem poles—began flapping their wings, snapping their beaks, and gnashing their teeth. I ran for my life, got to class, and immediately threw up on the floor. During my walk up the Witchy Path, I'd become so feverish from the flu that I hallucinated.

The school sent me home. As I wobbled along in delirium, my dad drove by in his patrol car. He picked me up to take me home, with a stop along the way at the drugstore for medication. And because I'd be sick in bed for days, Dad gave me a dollar to buy ten comic books.

The comic racks were at the back of the store. To reach them, I had to pass long shelves of adult magazines—everything from *Life*, *Playboy*, and *Ellery Queen's Mystery Magazine* to the armpit slicks. The "armpit slicks"—also known as "men's sweat mags," or simply "the sweats"— were lurid pulp magazines produced to appeal to the adventure fantasies of vets who'd fought in the Second World War and Korea. Their covers boasted bodice-ripped pinup girls and bare-chested heroes struggling to survive in exotic locales against attacks by wild animals, piranhas, and headhunters.

The headhunters grabbed me halfway along the shelves.

By then, my temperature was over a hundred. I wasn't just frozen in my tracks by the cover of *Real Man's Adventures*—I was sucked off my feet into the brutal world it depicted. There I sat, in a dugout canoe in the steamy Amazon rainforest, facing a man's man in safari khakis with a rifle gripped in one hand. Three canoes manned by Jivaro headhunters boxed us in. The Indians had black hair to their shoulders with bangs circled by red headbands. Warpaint streaked their faces and torsos. They were armed with blowpipes, barbed spears, and beheading knives. The knives had been used to hack the heads off enemy warriors, and those trophies were stuck on bamboo poles at the prows of their canoes, warning the soldier of fortune and me about what was in store for us.

To this day, I recall every detail in that grisly ring of heads.

The eyes were rolled back in their sockets and slivers of pupil peeked out from under the lids. Blood trickled down the cheeks like red tears. The mouths hung slackly open, baring tongues and teeth. The ears were pierced with white pegs and shiny gold rings. It was as if the heads had been torn from the bodies. Instead of clean cuts from razor-sharp machetes, the skin at the necks dangled in tatters.

When a hand clamped my shoulder, I almost died of fright.

"Does that cover scare you?"

The voice was my dad's.

He was standing behind me at the magazine shelves.

"Yes," I said.

"It's frightening to *me*, and I spent several years fighting a war. You're ill, son. You've got a fever. That cover is playing tricks on your mind. You'll run into lots of scary sights in life, so let me show you how to deal with them."

He reached over my shoulder and turned the cover facedown.

"Out of sight, out of mind," he said.

On the back of *Real Man's Adventures* was an ad for Charles Atlas, "The 97-Pound Weakling who became 'The World's Most Perfectly Developed Man.'" "Hey Skinny, yer ribs are showing," sneers a beach bully to a light-weight stick in front of his bikini-clad girl. Then the bully kicks sand in their faces. Feel humiliated? Do something about it. Charles Atlas is your pal. "What's My Job?—I Manufacture Weaklings into MEN! Let Me Make YOU a New Man—In Just 15 Minutes a Day!"

My dad came home from the Second World War with a chest full of medals and a reputation as the go-to-guy if you're in trouble.

He became a Mountie, and I idolized him.

A neighbor several doors away wasn't so lucky. He returned from com-bat with a mental disorder and a Luger pistol he'd taken off a German soldier he killed. The man had a hair-trigger temper that would explode in rage, and he told his young son on threat of a beating *never* to touch the gun.

Back then, Cowboys and Indians was the favorite neighborhood game. One day, while his dad was at work, the boy found the Luger—which was loaded—and blew off his own finger. My dad answered a phone call from the injured boy's desperate mom, who screamed that her husband was on his way home to skin his son alive for disobeying his order. I remember my dad rushing out the door and sprinting away.

On arriving home, the berserk vet burst in with his belt in his hand, the buckle hanging down to make good on his threat. His terrified son was hiding behind my dad, who told the man that he was to blame for keeping a loaded gun in the house, and that to get at the boy, the father would have to go through *him*.

Not long after that, my world fell apart.

My dad was investigating a gang of heroin traffickers. A tip came in to the Heather Stables that he was on the take, and the caller said that if the Mounties checked under the seat of his patrol car, they'd find a wad of cash. Another tip alerted the press to a corrupt Horseman, and my dad was suspended from duty. I recall schoolkids telling me my dad was crooked.

A week later, the plane he was in vanished.

The Cascade Mountains east of Vancouver are known to pilots as "the graveyard of the air." Clouds storming in from the Pacific buffet them, and air currents change in the blink of an eye. Downdrafts can cause pilots to lose lift under their wings.

While climbing over the Cascades, my dad's flight to RCMP headquarters in Ottawa ran into a deadly winter storm. The ice on the wings grew so heavy that one of the DC-4's propeller engines burst into flames. Unable to maintain altitude, the plane had to return to Vancouver, and while it was flying blind over the jutting peaks, its radar blip went dead.

Search planes were scrambled, but the turbulence got so violent that rescuers wearing safety belts were torn from their cockpit seats. With visibility nil, the search was suspended. Then it snowed every day for a month.

My dad was still missing when my mom sent me to the store for a quart of milk. Because the new *Batman* would be in, I headed straight for the comic racks. The headhunter cover of *Real Man's Adventures* must have sold well, for the magazine had hired the artist to do another one. This time, the jungle explorer stood his ground in front of a grass hut, the Amazon village in flames around him as he pointed his rifle at two retreating Jivaro Indians. The natives were shown only from their chests down. Both wore loincloths around their waists. One carried a machete smeared with blood. The other held a spear. They both gripped cords that looped through the mouths of heads dangling beside their knees. Once again, the gruesome trophies had been hacked off enemy warriors. This head's eyes were closed. That head's eyes rolled back. Blood dripped from one mouth. The ragged necks were gory.

I was sweating from every pore as if scorched by tropical heat.

This time I wasn't hallucinating from the flu. But my first encounter with *Real Man's Adventures* must have conditioned me, for like Pavlov's dog, I was being tugged into the cover against my will.

I was hypnotized…

Mesmerized…

And then it happened.

The front head's eyes flicked open, and I was staring *at my dad's face.* He wasn't there to turn over the cover. And I realized in that moment that he'd never again be there to protect me. I was on my own to brave life's horrors.

"Dad's dead!" I gasped as I turned and ran from the store. In my haste to escape from whatever was wrong with my mind, I struck the door so hard that I shattered its glass.

It took ten stitches to stop my hand from bleeding.

I still have the scar.

Days later, I knew that something was seriously wrong.

My mom sent me to the drugstore to buy fresh bandages for my hand, but when I tried to enter, I couldn't get through the door. It was as if it were blocked by an invisible force field from a science fiction film. I couldn't cross the threshold.

Kids in the 1950s knew that if you went nuts, you were "sent to Essondale." Men in white coats arrived from that nuthouse above the Fraser River to lock you in a straitjacket and haul you off to a padded cell with a barred window. There, they pumped you full of drugs that made you drool, fried your brain with electroshocks, and cut out the rotten part with a scalpel.

You scream, but no one hears.

It wasn't long before my friends knew I was crazy. There are only so many times you can go to the store and ask your pals to buy you comics while you wait outside. Eventually, I told Gord—my eight-year-old best buddy—that I was off to the nuthouse.

"We can't let 'em put your brain in a jar," he said.

It was Gord who hatched a plan to "break the spell." He'd go into a drugstore and scout the magazine shelves. Then he'd come out and tell me where not to look. Two more friends would grab my arms and drag me in through the door. When I was compelled to glance where I shouldn't, Gord would throw his coat over my head to blind me while the other boys hauled me out to safety.

And guess what?

It worked.

In hindsight, I see the defense mechanism. If I couldn't get into a store that stocked magazines, I wouldn't run the risk of seeing a headhunter cover and having to confront the horror that my dad was dead. I was the 97-pound weakling with sand kicked in my face.

Come spring, the snow in the Cascades thawed and search teams finally spotted the wrecked plane. My dad was dead—no escaping from that—and it helped that I never saw another magazine cover by that same artist. My mom was devastated. She never got over the trauma. Whether my dad was really a crook stayed unresolved. But until she died last week, Mom resolutely maintained that he'd been framed by the drug gang.

As soon as I was old enough, I applied to join the RCMP. The Bible says that the sins of the father will be visited on the son, so that's what happened to me. I could see it in the recruiter's eyes as he reviewed my family history. And as predicted, I failed to get in.

Gord went on to become a promising surgeon. But less than a year into practice, my childhood friend succumbed to brain cancer.

I gave the eulogy at his funeral.

———

So *this* is what they mean by love at first sight!

Well, I'm smitten.

I don't know what I expected when Dr. George Ruryk said he was referring me to his best student, a clinical psychologist named Genevieve DeClercq.

It certainly wasn't this heavenly creature.

I've never had luck with women. I don't know why that is. I look at myself in the mirror and think, *Surely I'm not that bad to look at? I'm relatively intelligent. I treat women with respect. But I guess I just don't have that magic we call sex appeal.*

Freud asked, "What do women want?" Or something like that.

I have an answer.

What they *don't* want is me.

Now I also know why I don't have sex appeal.

Genevieve got it all!

If I were a woman, I would never—repeat, *never*—stand next to her.

We sat in her office at the university. I told her about my compulsion to blow up the Polaroid photos of the Headhunter's victims' heads, all the while wondering if she thought I was some kind of freak. Polaroids of four women were currently pinned up on her husband's Strategy Wall: Liese Greiner, Helen Grabowski, Joanna Portman, and Sister Angelica. The blow-ups on my wall at home were ten times as large.

"How do you do it?" she asked.

"Enlarge them?"

"Yes."

"I have a darkroom in my apartment. I take a photo of each Polaroid and then enlarge it."

"Why the darkroom?"

"I have a powerful telescope with a camera attached. Astronomy is my hobby. No, it's my passion. On clear nights, I take my telescope into Stanley Park and snap pictures. Then I blow the shots up at home to study at leisure."

"Sounds fascinating. What do you see?"

"Canals on Mars. Clouds on Jupiter. Saturn's rings. Nebulae. Every night is different. I'm never bored if I'm lost in space."

"When did you blow up the first severed head photo?"

"The night my mom died."

"Not before?"

"No. I thought I was cured in childhood."

"Cured of what?"

"My obsession with headhunters."

"Tell me how it began."

So I told her. And as she was scribbling notes about my internal landscape, I was falling head over heels in love.

What a woman!

How the light glistened on her jet-black hair. How her green eyes shone with intelligence. How alluring she was without even trying. She smiled and I tingled. She spoke and I tingled. I couldn't get enough of her French accent. Still, I knew she was way out of my league.

"What's the last thing you said to your dad before he took that flight?"

"I can't recall."

"What's the last thing you said to your mom before she died?"

"'I'm sorry, Mom.'"

"Sorry for what?" Genevieve asked, putting down her pen.

"Everything, I guess. She lived an unhappy life. My dad's death gutted her."

"How was that your fault?"

"I don't know."

"What's the last thing your mom said to you before she died?"

"She was high on morphine. She was babbling."

"What did she say?"

"I don't recall."

"I think you do. And it will help if you tell me."

Suddenly, I felt anxious. My palms got clammy. Sweat trickled down my ribs from my armpits. My heart hammered in my chest.

"She said, 'He wasn't a crook.'"

"Your dad?"

"Yes."

"Did you think he was?"

"No."

"Then why did she say that?"

"Oh, God!"

"What?"

"I know what I said to him before he took that flight."

"You remember?"

"Yeah. I asked him, 'Are you a crook?'"

"Why did you ask him that?"

"Because the kids at school were telling me he was."

"Did he answer?"

"Yes."

"What did he say?"

"He said, 'No, son. I'm not a crook. And I'll prove it.'"

"His last words to you?"

"Yes. Before I went to bed. And when I got up the next morning, he'd left."

"Where did your mom say he'd gone?"

"She said he was flying to Ottawa because he loved me. My dad was off to see the RCMP brass to prove he wasn't a crook *to me*."

"When did you hear he was missing?"

"Later that day."

"So for years, you have repressed the idea that *he died because of you*. And consequently, you think you ruined your mom's life too."

"But what does all that have to do with severed heads?"

"What better way to 'trick the jailer'—as Dr. Ruryk likes to say? You feared those pulp magazine headhunters as a boy, but your dad saved you. Are severed heads not the ideal way to punish yourself for what you think you did?"

"Not think. *Did!*"

"You're not to blame. Your dad didn't have enough time to put that trip together after what you said. He must have already had it booked. I'll bet he was summoned by the brass. Your mom said he was going to build himself back up in your eyes. Then fate—*not you*—dealt the ace of spades."

"That's the death card?"

"Yes. And you've blamed yourself ever since."

I could literally feel the weight lifting off my shoulders. I wondered if this was what Dr. Ruryk had meant when he talked about using realization to show me why my defense mechanism was no longer needed?

"What about now?"

"With enlarging the Polaroids?" She shrugged. "Wrong place, wrong time. The severed heads mesh with your buried neurosis. Then your mom died, and her last words revived the guilt you thought was laid to rest long ago. Blowing up the photographs is an attempt to trick the jailer again."

"Where do I go from here?"

"Let the realization that you're not to blame sink in."

"How will I know if I'm cured?"

"It will be clear if the Headhunter sends another taunt. If you don't feel compelled to blow it up, you'll know."

———

Out of the blue, she called me.

"*Bonjour.* It's Genny."

"What a pleasant surprise."

"I need your help."

"Anything."

"Have lunch with me tomorrow?"

We met at the White Spot in West Vancouver. The moment I saw her, I knew she was playing to my French fantasy. One too many buttons undone, but that was okay with me. I could moon over her from now until the twelfth of never.

"How are you doing?" she asked.

"We'll find out soon. The Headhunter attacked a reporter this morning. Natasha Wilkes. It won't be long until we receive another Polaroid."

"Do you feel anxious?"

"Not like before."

"That's a promising sign that psychoanalysis is working. We've brought your repressed fears and memories up to conscious awareness."

"You helped me, so how can I help you?"

"It's my husband."

"Go on."

"I don't know where to turn."

"Is he in trouble?"

"Yes. The same kind of trouble as you."

"Because of his past?"

Genny nodded. "The deaths of his daughter and his first wife."

"I know the story. We all do."

"His cracks go even deeper than yours, and I'm afraid the Headhunter's out to break him."

"My lips are sealed. I promise."

"I fear he's cracking up, and I'm the one to blame. He came to me for psychological help, and instead I got romantically involved."

The confident and professional Genevieve of three days ago was gone, and now she was a haunted woman. For her to be confiding marital secrets right off the bat meant she was at her wit's end. If she went to the Horsemen, they'd pull her husband from the saddle, and that would be as humiliating as it comes. I've known cops to eat their guns for less.

Her only hope was an outsider with a stake in *her*. That's why she was playing to my fantasy. Turning herself into a sex siren to save her husband. For the briefest of shameful seconds, I considered letting Robert DeClercq crash and burn. That would open up the field for me to make a play for her. But every morning when I shave, I must face myself in the mirror. A man who cannot face himself is no man at all.

She touched my arm.

Reaching out.

"I'll do what I can," I said. "You can count on me."

One of the flying patrols was searching for John Lincoln Hardy. His photo was up on DeClercq's Strategy Wall. He might not be the Headhunter, but he was surely Grabowski's pimp. Rodale had shown me a transcript from a wiretap indicating that Hardy—aka the Weasel—had got another girl addicted to junk to make her hook for him after Grabowski vanished.

Fox: That Ms. Billie Holiday I hear behind you, man?

Weasel: Yeah, pussy purrs for her. She da cat's meow. I need time, man. To corral this filly in m' stable.

Fox: Uh-huh.

Weasel: Y'know? Get this filly broken so I don't need no rope to keep the bitch from splittin'.

Fox: Don't use yo' dick. Use Sister H.

Weasel: Can't hear ya. Hold a mo'. (Shouting: Turn that music down.)

(U/F: Come on, baby. Make me fe-e-el good.)

(Weasel: In a bit. Get yo' selfishness ready.)

Weasel: Ya still there, man?
Fox: Sounds like ya got yo' hands full…

After lunch with Genevieve, I detoured to the VPD bullpen to talk to the narcs who'd busted Helen Grabowski on the night she disappeared.

"Any sign of Hardy?"

"Not a peep," said Detective Bernie Zebroff.

"Don't suppose you recall anything more about Grabowski?"

"Just what's in the report."

"After she vanished, did Hardy pimp a new hooker?"

"Yeah. Charlotte Clarke."

"Know where she hangs out, Bernie?"

"Corner of Jervis and Barclay."

"Got a mug shot?"

I heard footsteps clomping up the stairs from the entrance hall.

"Flood. My office. *Now!*" growled my boss.

"Uh-oh," said Zebroff.

"Got shit on your shoe?" said his partner.

Puzzled, I crossed to Inspector Fleetwood's office, stepped in, and shut the door.

"What's up, chief?"

"This," said Homicide's top cop, holding up an envelope labeled FOR THE POLICE. "It was shoved into the book return slot at the public library."

"Another barb from the Headhunter?"

"Yeah."

"With a Polaroid of Natasha Wilkes's head stuck on a stake?"

"Close, but no cigar."

To avoid contamination, the inspector covered his desk with sheets of fresh paper, then dumped the contents of the envelope onto the white surface.

Not a Polaroid, but a roll of film.

And with it a note, jigsawed together from newspaper clippings.

Never give a sucker an even break.

Had enough, Robert?

If you want more, develop this.

Genevieve's burden just got worse. This would destroy her husband. *The Vancouver Times*—Natasha Wilkes's tabloid—was already crying for his blood.

A roll of film, I thought.

Imagine the detail this *will reveal if I blow it up on my enlarger.*

———

There's been another murder! A student beheaded in North Vancouver's Lynn Canyon as she left a party to fetch a bottle of booze from a car.

This will surely be the final nail in DeClercq's coffin.

Poor Genevieve!

The news came through as I cruised the streets of the West End, looking for Charlotte Clarke. In the beginning, there was Gassy Jack and his keg of whisky. As Gastown sprawled west to become the city of Vancouver, settlers built their homes near Stanley Park. In the 1960s, a construction boom bulldozed those houses to raise a jungle of phallic towers, and now streetwalkers had strolled in to comfort all those apartment dwellers. The lights weren't red, but the advertising campaign was the same. Hookers stood under the streetlamps on every West End corner, flaunting their wares for johns in curb-crawling cars.

I found her right where Zebroff had suggested: on the corner of Jervis and Barclay.

Here's what I was thinking.

I was brought into the case by the murder of Joanna Portman, the nurse nailed to the totem pole. Portman was the only victim found with semen in her vagina. Sperm hangs around for up to thirty-six hours after intercourse. If the Headhunter had ejaculated in Portman, why did he come in just one victim? The more logical conclusion was that Portman had a secret boyfriend, and he had deposited the sperm *before* she was attacked. Later, the Headhunter Squad had tracked her lover: a married pathologist who worked in St. Paul's morgue. That brought Portman back into line with the other victims. The Headhunter likely suffers from male orgasmic disorder. Events in his past have warped him psychologically. Unable to climax via conventional intercourse, he blows a load in his head when he rapes and stabs the symbolic stand-ins for the woman who caused his sexual dysfunction.

To help Genevieve, I had to start somewhere.

The Headhunter manhunt began when Detective Bernie Zebroff and his drug squad partner arrested Helen Grabowski out front of the Moonlight Arms. John Lincoln Hardy, Grabowski's pimp, had yet to be interviewed, and he couldn't be crossed off the list of suspects. Charlotte Clarke—Grabowski's replacement—could be the source of two leads. One, did she have any idea where her pimp was? And two, did Hardy have a sexual dysfunction that fit the psycho's profile?

The downpour was torrential as I pulled in at the curb. Charlotte Clarke stood in the glare of the streetlight, holding a clear plastic umbrella overhead so the light could shine through on what she was selling without getting her skintight minidress wet.

I leaned over and rolled down the passenger window.

The hooker approached my car.

"Want a date?" she asked, her jet-black mane framed by the window.

"Hop in," I said.

She ducked into the car before she furled her umbrella.

"What'll it be, handsome? Blow job? Straight lay? Around the world?" she asked.

"Information," I said, flashing my badge.

"Shit! Not a bust?"

"I'll give you the price of a cap if you answer two questions."

"You'll lemme go?"

"I promise."

"Bet I can guess. You want to know where Big John is?"

"That's question one."

"Let's see the moola. I don't fuck, or fuck people over, without getting paid upfront. Hookers and criminal lawyers work by the same rules."

I held up seventy dollars between my index and middle fingers.

She plucked it.

"I don't know where Johnny is. We met in a club and banged all night, then he turned me on to junk. He said his filly had left him, so his stable was empty. If I turned tricks for him, he'd protect me, keep me in H, and drown me in champagne if his gig worked out."

"What gig?"

"Dunno. He dumped me and scrammed."

"Where'd you live?"

"A cheap hotel. He checked out while I was peddling ass here." She was getting twitchy and itching to fix. "That it?"

"Question two. Was Hardy able to come?"

"Come?"

"Get his rocks off."

"I know what it means. But that's a fucked-up question. *Everyone* comes for me."

"Did he?"

"You're *serious*? Of course Johnny came. When you screw for money, johns don't ring your chimes. Big John, however, was hung like a stud." She winked. "Johnny's wad blew me across the room."

I mulled over the wiretap transcript Rodale had shown me.

(U/F: *Come on, baby. Make me fe-e-el good.*)
(Weasel: *In a bit. Get yo' selfishness ready.*)
Weasel: *Ya still there, man?*
Fox: *Sounds like ya got yo' hands full…*

If the Headhunter was driven by male orgasmic disorder, Hardy wasn't the killer.

———

On my way back to HH HQ, I stopped at the forensic lab to pick up a duplicate negative from the roll of film I'd dropped off earlier. My plan was to work until midnight, then take the film home and see if I was still compelled to enlarge it. I was typing a report in the squad room when Inspector Jack MacDougall entered and blew a whistle.

"We got him!" he told the room. "A flying patrol gunned down the Headhunter on Grouse Mountain. Caught red-handed with a trophy and his beheading tools."

Cheers erupted.

MacDougall waved a bottle of Scotch and called for paper cups.

"Dead or alive?" someone shouted.

"Dead," said the inspector.

"Who?"

"John Lincoln Hardy. Helen Grabowski's pimp."

Fuck me, I thought.

———

I woke up with a raging hangover. The Headhunter Squad had celebrated well into the night, and my first thought—after groaning with pain—was that Genevieve would be happy.

Lucky Robert DeClercq.

Waking up with Genny beside him.

Imagine reaching out and having her fall into your arms.

It took three cups of coffee to cut through the sludge bogging down my brain. I have no idea how much I drank in the cop bar last night. As I turned on the TV to see how Hardy's takedown was being spun, I felt no compulsion to go to my darkroom and obsess over the latest images. What a weird labyrinth is the human mind. All my life I had suffered from repressed guilt over my father's death, until Genny's talking cure had slain the Minotaur in my maze.

Lucky me, I thought.

The remaining question was: Should I develop the negative anyway to search for clues?

Answer: Yes. That's my job.

To prove that a brand-new me was now in the driver's seat, I went out for breakfast. Scrambled eggs with sausages beat back my hangover. I circled Lost Lagoon, the artificial pond between my West End apartment and Stanley Park, and still felt no compulsion. Once back in my suite on the top floor of the four-story building, I entered my darkroom and enlarged a single print off the negative. As I worked, I wondered why the Headhunter had switched from Polaroid photos. Was he worried we were checking up on buyers of that film?

Whoa! I thought.

What's that?

A print off a negative is a whole lot sharper than a Polaroid. The head-shot hanging from two clips on a drying line in the red gloom of my darkroom measured a foot across by three feet high. Anxiety no longer squirmed in my gut as I stared at the severed head. Like the others, it had been mounted on a stake with its pointed tip jutting up from the top of the skull. I took in the bloodshot eyes. I took in the nose gushing blood. I took in the tongue with its bite marks. I took in the strands of jet-black hair adhering to the spike. Then my gaze ran down the pole to the spot where all the Polaroids had been cropped. But here, the stake continued on into a bucket full of sand.

A Polaroid lets you see the shot you've taken *before* you show it to people. But a negative keeps its contents secret until you develop a print.

The Headhunter probably had no intention of including this bucket of sand on the roll of film he sent us, but the camera had captured it.

What's that mixed in with the sand? I thought, moving in close to the print. *Maple leaves?*

———

Kerrisdale is an affluent, fuddy-duddy part of the city. The neighborhood took its name from Kerry's Dale, an estate in Scotland where a socialite friend of the bigwig who headed the British Columbia Electric Railway grew up. Kerry's Dale meant "little seat of the fairies," and it was easy to imagine fairies living in this yard—as English a garden as ever there was in *British Columbia*, now put to bed for the winter under a quilt of autumn leaves. As I rapped on the door of this maple-embowered bungalow on a street lined with chestnut trees, I heard scurrying noises inside. So the queen of the fairies was at home.

The door cracked an inch on its burglar chain.

An eye peered out at my waist level.

"Yes?" she asked.

"Good morning, ma'am," I said. "Are you Elvira Franklen?"

"Who are you?"

"Detective Flood of the Vancouver Police."

"Got a badge?"

I flashed the tin and my VPD ID.

"Eh, what's up, Doc?" she asked in a nasal voice while pretending to chew a carrot.

I frowned.

"The card says your name is Almore Flood."

"So?"

"Bugs Bunny. You *do* know who Bugs Bunny is, right?"

I nodded.

"Almore Flood? Elmer Fudd? Bugs Bunny's archenemy?"

"I get it."

"Shhh. Be vewy, vewy quiet. I'm hunting wabbits," she whispered, mimicking Elmer Fudd's catchphrase.

"I prefer *Al*," I said.

"I prefer *El*," she teased, mimicking *my* voice. "Tsk-tsk, Detective. You should be proud of your name. If I can live with Elvira, you can stomach Almore."

"Point taken."

"Have you come about the library book? I told them I'd return it. It's not *that* long overdue."

"Are you pulling my leg?"

"A little."

"Actually, I've come for help in solving a murder."

"Good grief! Really?"

"Really."

"Then *do* come in, Detective! *Do* come in," she gushed, sliding off the chain and swinging the door wide. "Pardon my bunker mentality. Last week, we had a home invasion no more than a block away. You're lucky I didn't blast you with a blunderbuss."

The woman was an octogenarian. She was less than five feet tall—about the size of a dwarf—and she had white hair combed down in a Caesar-like bowl and bulgy blue eyes twinkling with mischief. She wore a frumpy wool suit fastened with a brooch.

She reminded me of Yoda in the Star Wars films.

With smaller ears.

As I stepped into the book-lined hall, something furry brushed my leg.

"Scat, Maigret! Shoo, Poirot! Leave our guest alone."

"I like cats," I said.

"Good. I have eight. The scruffy one at the end of the hall is Mike Hammer."

The bedraggled feline looked like he'd been on a bender.

"You have a lot of books," I said as she ushered me down a long hall lined floor to ceiling with hardcover novels.

"A Toronto paper pays me to review crime fiction. They send me dozens of books each week. Most are shelved upstairs. One day the floor will collapse."

We turned into a room that looked like Queen Victoria's parlor crossed with Sherlock Holmes's study. Relics of the empire and death on paper. Among the knickknacks that cluttered every surface was a collection of coronation mugs, including one for Edward VIII, who was never crowned. What drew my attention, however, was the rogues' gallery covering one wall: dozens of autographed photos of famous crime writers.

"Impressive," I said.

"Conan Doyle signed his a year before his death in 1930. Agatha Christie autographed hers for me when I had tea at Greenway, her estate in Devon."

"How did that happen?"

"I was on a Christie bus tour that stopped for lunch in Torquay. Eccles cakes are a weakness of mine, so I bought one in a shop to munch at the beach. A wasp lured by the sugar landed on my finger and stung me when I tried to swat it away. I didn't know I was allergic. My finger had ballooned to twice its size by the time a stranger on the street rushed me to a chemist's. She was friends with Dame Agatha, and after I missed the departing tour bus, she took me with her for tea at Christie's home."

Elvira clapped her hands.

"Spade, Marlowe, jump down and give the detective your seat."

I didn't know cats could be wrangled.

Both pounced down from an overstuffed armchair facing a tea table set with a Brown Betty pot in a crocheted cozy.

"Speaking of tea, will you join me?"

"Gladly," I said.

The tea table had four bone china cups, a cream-and-sugar set, spoons, knives, and a lazy Susan stocked with Eccles cakes and scones with clotted cream.

"I was about to gorge myself when you knocked."

"Good timing," I said.

She poured me a cup of tea.

"The queen drinks Poonakandy, and so shall we. Cream? Sugar?"

"Both. One lump."

"Eccles cake?" she asked.

Selecting a plump one, I bit into the scrumptious round of flaky pastry filled with currants and glazed with demerara sugar.

"Some people call them squashed fly cakes, but I prefer flies' graveyards," she said. "Now, enough suspense, young man. Let's talk about *murder*."

I set down the cup and cake and opened my briefcase. From it, I withdrew a large cropped photo of the sand and leaves in the bucket supporting the pole that held Natasha Wilkes's head. Just the sand and leaves, with nothing else to give the case away.

"A body was dumped in Vancouver wrapped in a tarp," I lied. "It may be a gangland hit. We found this mix of sand and leaves inside the cover. If we can identify the leaves—"

"That might tell you *where* he was killed," said the mystery maven, rubbing her hands together with the thrill of the chase.

"No flies on you," I said.

The chair in which she sat was obviously her reading spot. The side table was piled high with books and also held her reading glasses and a magnifier like Sherlock Holmes uses. When she put on the glasses, she resembled a wise owl. She took the photo from me and focused the magnifier on it.

"*Acer macrophyllum.* The bigleaf maple," she said, after enlarging and examining some of the leaves. "A large deciduous tree native to southwestern British Columbia. See how deeply incised the palmate lobes are? The bigleaf maple—as you'll deduce from the name—has the largest leaves of all maple trees."

"How many are there in BC?"

"Millions, I would think. But these leaves mixed in with the bigleaf maple leaves are different," she said, moving the magnifier across the photograph. "They're *Acer pseudoplatanus*. The sycamore maple. See how the leaves are smaller? About half to three-quarters the size? They're not as deeply lobed. And they're not native to BC. The sycamore maple grows in Eurasia, from France to the Ukraine."

"And how many of these are there in BC?"

"None," she said.

"None?"

"Not unless one"—she waved the photo—"has been transplanted."

"You already knew that, didn't you?"

"Yes," I confessed. "I spoke with some botanists at UBC and VanDusen Botanical Garden. They said if I could find someplace where *both* maples grow, that would likely be where the body was wrapped in the tarp. And if I hoped to identify such a place, I should start with the go-to expert on maples, Mrs. Elvira Franklen."

"*Miss* Franklen," she corrected.

"They said you've been a member and president of various horticultural societies since the 1930s."

"The 1920s. I joined when I was eighteen."

"So can you help me?"

"Finish your cake. Drink your tea. And follow me."

When I had done as I was told, we crossed the book-lined hall to an open door. From within came the smell of air freshener struggling to mask the odor of kitty litter.

"Carella and Nancy Drew," she said as two cats exited the room.

"And the eighth cat?"

"Dr. Fell. He's off in a locked room."

I laughed.

"You get it?"

"*The Three Coffins*," I said.

And I thought *I* was obsessed! The room we entered looked like a public library: rows of pamphlets, mimeographed sheets, newsletters, magazines, and yellowed newspaper clippings with aisles in between. Each stack was labeled with a tag listing its contents: *The Arborist: June 1931 to September 1952*; *The Horticulturalist's Digest: 1923 to Now*; *"Comedy" and "Tragedy" Tree Plantings in Stanley Park's Shakespeare Garden: 1921*; and so on. There were piles of flowers and leaves pressed in wax paper.

"I'm a bit of a hoarder," she said.

"It's a needle in a haystack. This could take *years*."

"Then I'd better get started."

"You're going to hunt through all this to find the location of two maple trees?"

"I've spent my life reading detective stories and you think I don't have the time to work on a *real* murder case?"

Miss Marple lives, I thought.

———

A week later, I was back at my desk in Major Crime. The Horsemen were holding a regimental dinner that night to celebrate cracking the Headhunter case, and as VPD liaison, I was invited. Yesterday, I'd been fitted for a rented tux, and as I stood in front of the mirror thinking, "*The name's Flood...Al Flood,*" the tailor said, "I don't know where you're going, sir, but I guarantee you'll be the best-dressed man there." More like a penguin in a sea of red serge.

The phone rang.

"Major Crime. Detective Flood."

"Elvira Franklen here. I found your maple trees."

"I'll be right over."

Mike Hammer met me at the door as Elvira swung it wide. He looked in worse shape than the last time. His owner waved a mimeographed newsletter in the air and used it to lure me down the hall and into the parlor, where tea was waiting.

"I found this article in the July 1955 issue of *Pacific Planter*."

Intrigued, I read:

Ready for War, But Hoping for Peace

Maple trees flourish above Mr. Albert Stone's atomic bomb shelter. Mr. Stone acquired his property on the Slough at a public auction of land confiscated from the Japanese during the Second World War. "It was a fish shack before the Japs attacked Pearl Harbor," he told this columnist.

Mr. Stone is a character.

Today, we stood in his Freedom Garden alongside the South Arm of the muddy Fraser River. This writer asked him why he'd planted maple trees—a bigleaf and a sycamore—above his nuclear fallout shelter. "Is that not a strange juxtaposition?"

"No," said Mr. Stone. "When the Commies send their nukes and the Big Hot One is on, I'll be ready for them. Till then, me and the missus will sit in our Freedom Garden."

And that, dear reader, is what brought this columnist here today. For beside his sapling of Acer macrophyllum *stands the only* Acer pseudoplatanus *in Western Canada. It's a hardy little sycamore maple, and certainly worth the drive on a Sunday afternoon.*

"My wife is from Eastern Europe," Mr. Stone explained. "She brought that seedling from the garden of her family home. It was her Freedom Tree..."

I skimmed the rest until I found Mr. Albert Stone's address.

Then I leaned over and kissed Elvira on the cheek.

"You rival Sherlock," I said.

———

The Steveston hardware store had a sign in the window: SMALL BOAT FOR RENT. ENQUIRE WITHIN. This store on the South Arm of the Fraser River was cluttered with nautical gear like ships' barometers, blocks and tackles, yacht braid, anchors, corks of every size, and Greek fisherman's caps. The old salt behind the counter was mending a fishing net. A sign on the wall above him read: FOLKS WHO BELIEVE THE DEAD NEVER COME BACK TO LIFE SHOULD BE HERE AT QUITTING TIME.

"Help you, matey?"

"I want to rent your boat."

Britain had ruled this part of the world since Captain Cook sailed into Nootka Sound in 1778. British imperialists, as they did everywhere, settled the best land. Immigrants who came to work for them—like the Chinese who built the railroad—and downtrodden refugees fleeing despotic realms were left to scrounge the badlands. The sloughs along the Fraser were nothing more than swamps, fingers of water thick with marsh plants that thrive in muck and alluvial sediments, with names that capture the feel of the place: skunk cabbage, bog orchid, and cuckoo flower. Cuckoos, it seemed to me, like Mr. Albert Stone.

Hard to imagine a *worse* place to build a 1950s Cold War atomic bomb shelter.

A nutcase.

It takes one to know one.

Early on in the Headhunter case, I had been a headhunter neurotic stalking a headhunter psychotic. But thanks to Genevieve, I had shifted my focus and now I was a detective out to tie up a loose end that bothered him.

Question: What became of the Headhunter's missing trophies?

The only severed head found in John Lincoln Hardy's Grouse Mountain cabin belonged to the student beheaded that same night.

So what happened to the others?

My cop's nose told me the answer could be found with those maple leaves that fell in the garden next to Mr. Albert Stone's bomb shelter, and that's why I was in this motorboat put-putting up the Fraser River toward what I hoped was the aptly named Gravesend Reach.

November afternoons don't come darker than this. The clouds overhead were soot black and loomed low. The choppy water heaved the boat up and down, making me queasy. The sounds and smells of the river and the wetlands besieged me. How fitting that as I cut the motor and paddled toward the slough, I was circled by birds of prey: a bald eagle and a hawk.

The slough stank of dead fish.

In the 1890s, Lulu Island had not been cleared. The delta was dense with trees, and the Fraser River was rich with salmon runs. Steveston, the local village at the mouth of the South Arm, was just a clutch of canneries. Dozens of them. It took a day to trek here from booming Vancouver, so struggling immigrants clustered in shantytowns on the sloughs to make a living off harvesting the fish. At low tide, the backwater channels were streams. At high tide, they were inundated with fresh water from the river and salt water from the sea. The squatters' shacks were raised on pilings or floated on scows. Nets were dried on racks and stored in rickety sheds. Outhouses emptied into the sloughs. The land behind was cleared for crops, and the fishing out front was done by muscle work. Hand-built boats came and went with the tide.

All that changed, however, when the Hell's Gate rockslide of 1913 blocked the Fraser Canyon and nearly destroyed the river's sockeye salmon run. Fishing gave way to logging that polluted the water, and then came the Depression. By the 1950s, this slough was good for nothing but the doomsday hideout of a crackpot survivalist like Mr. Albert Stone.

Now even he was gone, and the slough was a ghost town.

The perfect lair for a madman.

In the waning stretch of day, this was a gray shadowland. A derelict houseboat half submerged in the water clogged the mouth of the slough. Paddling around it, I glided deeper into the throat of darkness. The abandoned shanties along both mucky banks were rotting and falling apart. Most were made of shiplap and crumbling shingles. Because this intertidal mire lay outside the dyke, floods had battered the docks, pilings, railings, and fences. Abandoned boats were everywhere, but none were seaworthy.

Whatever plank road or boardwalk had once carried those *Pacific Planter* readers scampering across Lulu Island's marshlands to see Mr. Stone's sycamore maple, it was long gone. Anyone who tried to traverse that boggy stretch would go down in quickmud. Those who made it to the slough would have no way to reach the isolated bomb shelter and its overgrown garden, for the shaky wooden bridge that spanned the backwater to the Fraser River silt bar had collapsed. The only route in was by boat.

Seen from the slough, the bomb shelter was a concrete oblong wedged into the island. The bottom half was lined with sandbags to insulate the bunker from floods. Some bags had burst, spilling sand onto the bank, where it mixed with autumn leaves falling from the maples. Squatting on top of the concrete oblong was a military surplus Quonset hut from the

Second World War. The semicylindrical shed was plugged at both ends by half-moon walls. Rain had rusted the metal, streaking it like a bloody head wound.

I moored the boat to the creaking dock and climbed a wobbly staircase to the hut. The steel door was locked, and the front wall had no windows. The hut was smaller than the bunker, so a narrow ledge gave me passage to the rear. The shed's back wall also lacked doors and windows, but I spotted a three-foot-square plate bolted to the concrete, between the ledge and the rising ground. At one time, this was probably how Mr. Stone fed supplies into the bomb shelter. But judging from the corroded bolts, the plate hadn't been moved for decades.

I, however, had burglary tools in a Nike carryall I'd brought along in case. The crowbar made short work of the plate and it snapped right off.

Instantly, I jerked back.

The bomb shelter reeked of cooked human flesh.

Cannibalism?

At times like this, I longed for a two-way wrist radio like the one Dick Tracy wears in the funny papers. Think how easy it would be to get a judge to grant a search warrant on a mobile phone, instead of having to motor back to Steveston for a phone booth.

But that's science fiction.

Still, "exigent circumstances" allow a cop to search without a warrant if there's imminent danger of the loss, removal, destruction, or disappearance of evidence…and surely I could shoehorn this warrantless break-in into that law.

Shining my VPD flashlight into the square hole, I saw a chute full of cobwebs and rat shit. Nothing does like doing, so I let the Nike bag slide down the grubby tunnel to clear the way, then—gripping the butt of the flashlight in my teeth like a miner's headlamp—followed it in headfirst.

Pulling with my fingers at the tip of my outstretched arms and pushing with my toes at the end of my straightened legs, I was inching, inching, inching down…until I got stuck.

Claustrophobia!

In a fearful flash, I could see myself stuck here forever, screaming down into this concrete straitjacket until finally—after how many days?—I starved to death. If neurosis had crippled my mind before, would this make me snap?

Calm down.

Think.

Panic won't help.

Exhale and relax your muscles.

Make yourself shrink.

Wriggle from side to side to smear the Wet Coast slime and moist rat shit.

That's it.

Slick the path.

Claw with your fingers.

Breathe out.

Shove with your toes.

You're moving.

Keep going.

And all at once, I tumbled to the floor.

Hundreds of tiny rat bones were illuminated by the pool of light in front of my face. Gaining my knees and then my feet, I picked up the torch and shone it around. There were no signs of the survival supplies Mr. Albert Stone had stockpiled to weather a nuclear winter. Instead, this foul pit was the dungeon of a psychotic's unconscious mind come to life. Mardi Gras and voodoo masks by the dozens glared from the green-slimed walls. One was gone—I could see its outline—and I wondered if it was the Medusa mask left behind at Natasha Wilkes's beheading?

Probably.

I swept my flashlight around the room, revealing a stage as macabre as the one at the Grand Guignol. In front was a wooden table set with butcher and taxidermy tools. A chair faced the table. Whatever work went on there, it was ghoulish. A cooking pot worthy of the witches in *Macbeth* sat on a propane burner beside the bloodstained surface. The closer I stepped, the stronger grew the smell of cooked human flesh. Then my flashlight caught the source of that flesh mounted atop five sharpened stakes rammed into buckets of sand and maple leaves.

Five female skulls.

Originally, these skulls had been five severed heads, back when the lifeless faces of Liese Greiner, Helen Grabowski, Joanna Portman, Sister Angelica, and Natasha Wilkes had stared blankly into the cold lens of the Headhunter's camera. Later, the flesh of each victim was evidently peeled off and cooked in the pot, leaving the five mounted skulls that confronted me now. Or perhaps the heads themselves were boiled in the pot to free them of flesh so the skulls wouldn't rot.

Welcome to my nightmare.

Beyond the table, there was a weird dressing area. The mounted skulls formed a semicircle around a standing mirror and a tailor's dummy. The mannequin displayed a Mountie's red serge tunic. The insignia told me it had once belonged to an RCMP corporal, but I could see from its wear and tear that this garment was about half a century old. It was the Headhunter's killing uniform.

No doubt this was the source of the red thread found on the thorns at the Hollyburn Mountain murder scene.

Was this red serge relic its Jekyll owner's attempt to dissociate his Hyde persona?

You bet, I thought.

It gave the phrase "dressed to kill" new meaning.

My mind's eye saw the faceless killer dressing in front of this mirror, admiring himself as he transformed into the Headhunter to escape the bonds of his unconscious mind, before creeping out of this hellhole to rape and behead.

Question: Whodunit?

Was the answer in the wooden box on the table?

As I lifted the lid to peek inside, my flashlight caught red eyes at the periphery of its beam. When a river rat sank its teeth into my ankle, I stumbled back in revulsion and dropped my torch.

Shattering, it rolled away and left me in the dark.

But not before my eyes had glimpsed the contents of the box.

I'd found the Headhunter's trophies.

Eight shrunken heads.

Plus something even more chilling.

Part Three

SPARKY

As I was going up the stair
I met a man who wasn't there.
He wasn't there again today.
I wish, I wish he'd stay away.
—Hughes Mearns, *The Psychoed*

TSANTSAS

Friday, November 12, 5:15 p.m.

"They're gone!"

"*How?*"

"I don't know. They were in the box on the table."

"*And Damballa?*"

"It's gone too!"

"*What about your father's rag?*"

"That's still on the dummy."

"*How'd the thief get in? Jimmy the door to the hut?*"

"No. It's secure. And the door at the foot of the stairs is locked."

"*The supply chute?*"

"I don't think so. I can't see any light coming from the top."

"*There wouldn't be if the intruder put the outside plate back on.*"

"Someone knows!"

"*And you're to blame. Those tsantsas will be your downfall. Did you really think controlling them would give you control over me?*"

"Help me, Daddy!"

"*He can't help. We poisoned him, remember? You saw him puke his guts out in the Arctic snow. You saw me cut a hole in the ice and shove him in. They never found his body. I hope a polar bear ate him. Just another lost patrol in the myth of the Mounted Police. He was a weakling trying to live up to his legendary dad. 'Thin red line' and 'Always get their man.' His dad thought so little of him that he didn't even pass on his name. Is your name Blake? No. That's because your father*" *was a bastard in every sense of the word. I never should have married him. But my dad raped me, and I was in need of a savior. It turned out that your father was an abuser too. He made me have you. I didn't want a kid. So you're here, worm-child, to pay for what he did."*

"I hate you, Mommy!"

"Who cares? I'll torture you forever."

"Daddy loves me. He kills *you!*"

"Let's see Daddy save you now. The Mounties can't get me, but you'll rot in jail for life because you created and kept those tsantsas. Fate, Sparky. Fate."

Crunch!

"What was that?"

"You stepped on some rat bones."

"Uh-uh. Something's smashed on the floor."

"What?"

"Glass. But I don't see what it's from."

"Sweep your torch."

"Found it. Under the mirror. It's the intruder's flashlight."

"Pick it up."

"There's a label. In case it gets lost."

"Read it."

"'Vancouver Police. Detective Al Flood.'"

6:25 p.m.

Genevieve closed Flood's journal and looked him in the eye. They were sitting in the front room of his apartment above the glittering Lost Lagoon. An hour ago, he'd phoned her at home and asked if they could meet as soon as possible. When she'd asked why he was skipping the Mounties' regimental dinner, he cryptically told her he'd be going after they discussed developments in the Headhunter case.

"What developments?" DeClercq's wife had asked.

"You'll see when you get here."

While she was fighting rush-hour traffic through Stanley Park, Al had showered and changed, but not into a tuxedo. The tux was still in a plastic bag hanging by the door, for there'd be no celebrating at the regimental dinner after he lobbed his bomb. When she arrived, Genny was dressed in casual clothes for a laid-back evening at home. Only Horsemen and police associates attend the annual dinner.

"Well?" asked Al.

"I don't know which is worse. If what you wrote is fantasy, I fear for your mental well-being. And if it's the truth, I fear for the Mounted Police."

"You asked me to help save your husband from ruin. I promised you that my lips would be sealed, that I'd investigate as best I could, and that you could count on me. Once the hook was through my cheek, I had to follow the line to its source. Tonight, I'm keeping my promise."

She waved Flood's journal in the air.

"The story's incomplete."

"You arrived before I finished recording today's events. When I broke the flashlight, I plunged the bomb shelter into darkness. I had no matches. If there was another way out, I hadn't spotted it. That meant I could only go back the way I came in, pushing the Nike bag in front of me up the chute. I dumped the contents of the box into the bag, added two knives I grabbed off the table for fingerprints, then stuffed in my jacket to make myself smaller."

"What's that smell?"

"Rat shit."

"Smeared on the bag?"

"It was grueling. To get back up, I had to claw at the sides and push with my toes. After returning the boat, I drove home, phoned you, cleaned up, and wrote until you arrived."

"So John Lincoln Hardy was framed?"

"Yes."

"The head and the weapons found in the mountain shack were *planted* there?"

"Right."

"By a Mountie?"

"It could only be. That person snuck in and set up the frame while the takedown was being planned, then drove to the staging point to join the assault team."

"What's in the Nike bag?"

Al unzipped the top and yanked it open.

Genny peered in.

"Are those what I think they are?"

"Tsantsas," said Flood.

———

Each of the shrunken heads—except for the nun's—had long black hair, its length accentuated by the size of its small face. Each tsantsa was no larger than a navel orange. Each trophy had pasty skin, shriveled and creased. The eyes of each head were sewn shut, as was the mouth. But unlike the shrunken head in the Vancouver Museum—which both Al and Genny had seen—the lips of the heads in the Nike bag weren't stitched shut like those of the tsantsas made by Jivaro Indians in the Ecuadorian jungle. Instead, these pursed lips were pierced by six small gold rings, and those rings were laced together like a shoe with a long black thong.

"How many heads are there?"

"Eight," said Al.

"Do we know who they belonged to?"

"Each head has a tag tied to one of the rings. There's no head for your student—that was the one used to set up the frame—but the five other Headhunter victims are here."

"And the remaining three?"

"Apparently, they're prior victims."

Al pulled on a pair of disposable gloves and held up a shriveled face.

"This one's labeled SELENA, ECUADOR, 1969."

"I wonder who Selena was?"

"Judging by the date, she was the first victim."

"And Ecuador is where the killer learned to shrink heads?"

Flood nodded. "From the Jivaro."

"And the other two heads are from…?"

"New Orleans."

"So there *is* a Hardy connection?"

"I think that's a coincidence. Liese Greiner was killed long before Hardy came to Vancouver. By chance, Grabowski had ties to New Orleans. My gut says that the Headhunter has a *separate* connection to that city. The fact that Hardy was from Louisiana had no bearing on the case, but it made us *believe* there was some link to voodoo."

"If you were the Headhunter," Genny asked, "how would you shrink my head?"

"Hmm. Well, I'd start by mounting your head on a stake and snapping a photo of it to taunt the police. Next, I'd slit the back of your scalp from the top of your skull down to your neck, peeling your skin off the bone toward your face. I'd make cuts at your ears, eyes, and nose, leaving your skull bare except for your eyeballs and lipless teeth. Then I'd fill a pot with water and bring it to a boil, submerging your flesh by its hair for half an hour. When I fished it out, your face would be half its current size."

"That would explain the smell of cannibal meat in the bunker."

"Don't remind me."

"Bad, eh?"

"It made me retch."

"Okay, so what next?"

"I'd hang your rubbery head from a hook to dehydrate it. I'd want your skin to be pliable, but not squishy. Later, to draw out remaining moisture and accelerate the dehydration process, I'd take a bunch of stones of various sizes and heat them on a propane burner. While I was waiting for them to get hot, I'd scrape the tissue from the inside of your head with a knife, pull down your upper lashes to close your eyeholes, then stitch your lids tight with black cord. I'd use two-inch splinters to keep your lips shut, and cotton to plug your nose and earholes. Lastly, I'd sew up the slit in the back of your head."

Genny shivered at the thought.

"That would leave me with an empty glove into which I'd drop the hot stones, starting with the largest. I'd roll them around like a gambler tumbling dice, being careful not to scorch your skin. As the stones decrease in size, so will your head. Next, I'd heat sand in a frying pan and pour it through the open neck to reach the crevices the pebbles can't. That would shrink your head to the size of my fist, and then I'd mold your boneless features to keep your likeness."

"And *voilà*," said Genny, eyeing Selena's miniature head.

"But there's one thing I don't get."

"What's that?"

"The rings through the lips. The Jivaro shrink heads to trap an enemy's vengeful spirit inside. That's why the headshrinker's final act is sealing the mouth. He pulls out the skewers and stitches the lips together with a black thong ornamented with beads or frayed into tassels."

"So why does the Headhunter pierce the lips with rings and lace them together?"

"Got a theory?"

Genny pondered for a moment, then said, "Let's assume the Headhunter's a sexual psychotic, and these shrunken heads are fetishes. Displacement is a defense mechanism. Sexually abuse a child, and the child's unconscious mind may redirect its aggression onto a powerless symbolic substitute that becomes a sexual fetish. In this case, the sexual fetish traps the symbolic abuser inside."

"But why the lip rings?"

"A female has *two* pairs of lips—her mouth and her labia. A dominatrix will pierce her genitals and lace her labia shut to flaunt her superiority over her submissive sex slaves. If you crave getting even with a woman like that for whatever she did to you, is there any better displacement than these fetishes?"

"I think you nailed it," said Flood.

"So who's the Headhunter?"

The detective reached into the Nike bag and withdrew something more chilling.

Genny's eyes widened.

And a light went on in her mind.

AMBUSH

The foreboding clouds of the afternoon began to spill rain as Sparky parked a block away from Detective Al Flood's Lost Lagoon apartment. Obtaining the VPD cop's home address had been easy. All members of the Headhunter Squad had to supply off-duty emergency call-out information: home address, phone number, and vehicle license plate. Beneath the rain slicker, Sparky was dressed in the red serge uniform of the Royal Canadian Mounted Police for tonight's celebratory regimental dinner. The event was being staged at the Stanley Park Pavilion, a short drive away. If luck was with the Headhunter, Flood would be dead and what he had stolen destroyed within a few minutes, and Sparky would be at the venue in time to savor a predinner Scotch with the rest of the squad.

The cocaine was an afterthought.

A week had passed since the Headhunter case reached its fiery climax at Hardy's shack on Grouse Mountain. In the hour before that alpine assault, Sparky had driven up to plant the head of Genevieve's student and the two decapitation tools to frame Grabowski's pimp. While searching the shack for a suitable hiding place, the psycho had discovered not only the cubbyhole beneath the floor but also a bag of cocaine dangling from one of the hooks there. In this city, coke will finance an escape to Timbuktu if necessary, so Sparky had stolen the stash and kept it in the bomb shelter for a rainy day.

A rainy day like *today*.

Late this afternoon, Sparky had boated downriver to the bomb shelter to dispose of the fetishes that could unmask the Headhunter: the eight tsantsas, Damballa, the bloody red serge tunic, and the mounted skulls. Flood's meddling, however, had forced tonight's showdown.

What would I do if I were you, Sparky had wondered, weighing the implications of seeing Flood's name on the broken flashlight.

First, I'd take my findings home and clean up. I'd be smelly and grubby from my crawl down and back up the chute. Then I'd drive the short distance to the Stanley Park Pavilion, knowing that both DeClercq and the Headhunter would be there at seven. I'd take the chief super aside and show him what I found, and together we would make the arrest that would skyrocket my career.

So, pondered Sparky, *what's my countermove?*

Easy.

Like the Horsemen in every western, I cut Flood off at the pass.

Pocketing the bag of coke from Hardy's shack, the Mountie stepped out of the car and crept down the alley behind Flood's apartment building. The rain was drumming on the trash cans. Across the lane from the entrance to Flood's underground garage, smoke billowed out of an alcove. Glancing in, Sparky saw the red glow of a burning barrel. It was illegal to burn trash, but thank God for scofflaws. Toss in the shrunken heads and they'd instantly burst into flames.

Now if only…

Yes! thought Sparky, heading down the ramp to the underground lot and spying a car with the cop's license plate in slot 404, Flood's apartment number.

Damn.

What have we here?

Now that's a complication.

For parked in the visitor's slot beside the detective's aging Volvo was a low-slung Triumph TR7 with the same plate number as the car the killer had followed from DeClercq's home in West Vancouver to the Lynn Valley house where the student mistakenly lost her head.

DeClercq's wife knows my secret?

Then she dies too.

No matter how this played out, the coke was essential. Originally, Sparky had planned to make Flood's death look like a gangland hit. People would think that like his father, the VPD bull was a dirty cop. He'd run afoul of drug dealers by confiscating their coke for his own profit, so they whacked him. To make it work, Sparky had brought along a piece taken off a junkie who'd OD'd on smack.

You could never have too many guns.

To activate the frame, Sparky headed to the passenger side of Flood's Volvo. Crouching down, the psycho used a screwdriver to pry the hubcap off the front wheel. Wearing gloves so not to leave fingerprints, Sparky packed the coke around the axle and snapped the cap back on, then turned toward the lot's exit ramp. The plan was to scale the fire escape to apartment 404, where a window might provide a clear shot at the meddling detective and DeClercq's wife. Then the Headhunter would climb in to retrieve the stolen tsantsas.

The rain was clattering so hard that any gunshots would be muffled.

Uh-oh...

What's that? Sparky thought.

The elevator was rumbling down to the parking lot.

The killer slipped away to hide behind a concrete pillar.

Clang!

Off fell the hubcap, exposing the bag of coke.

"One car? I'll drive?" said Al.

Having repacked the Nike carryall, he'd tucked his journal in on top and zipped up the bag. He gripped it tightly as they rode the elevator down.

"I'll brief Robert," Genny said. "Then you can join us."

"How will he react?"

"He'll do what must be done."

The elevator bumped to a halt and the door slid open. The parking lot was dimly lit by low-watt light bulbs in wire mesh fixtures. Support pillars cast shadowy bars across the floor. Flood's Volvo was parked nose in against the right-hand wall. The passenger's side faced them as they approached from the lift, with the driver's door closer to the ramp up to the alley. Genny's car was this side of Al's, so the cop didn't notice the pried-off hubcap until he rounded the TR7's trunk and unlocked her door.

Vandals? he wondered as he pocketed his keys.

"Freeze!" a voice behind him barked.

The detective whirled. The moment he saw the gun barrel poking around the pillar in the center of the parking lot, his hand went for the snub-nosed revolver clipped to his belt. His jacket was open, so the gun cleared leather and Flood pulled off a shot as a bullet ripped through his chest. Trapped like this between the cars, he was a sitting duck in a shooting gallery.

"Duck!" he yelled at Genny as he dropped the Nike bag and motioned her down by slapping his freed-up palm on the roof of her car.

She was crumpling to the floor when the shooter fired again. The muzzle flared yellow, then there was a thunderclap. The explosion echoed around the underground lot. The slug hit the bumper of Flood's car and ricocheted in Genny's direction. It caught her in the eye and lodged in her brain. Al had no doubt that she was dead before she hit the ground.

He'd be dead too if he didn't react this second.

Flattening himself behind the ineffective barrier of the Nike bag, Al wriggled like a crab beneath his car. The pain in his chest was excruciating, and he struggled to breathe. The shot had collapsed his left lung, and his head felt woozy. He knew if he stayed pinned under the car, the Mountie would spray gunfire across the floor and hit him. And so, fighting against the pain, he kept inching sideways until he emerged on the far side of the Volvo. Grabbing the door handle, he pulled himself to his knees.

Run, he thought.

No. Plan your move first.

Al's only hope of survival was to escape from the lot. He was bleeding profusely and felt sick to his stomach. The Headhunter probably knew that he was severely wounded, and that holding back for a moment would weaken him for the kill. The alternative was to close in while Flood was still an active shooter, and all it would take was a lucky shot by the VPD detective to turn the tables on the Horseman's winning hand.

Well, that moment was almost up and the countdown clock was ticking.

Al had begun this shootout with six bullets.

He had five left.

"That's all, folks!"

Porky Pig...

Jesus, I'm slipping...

No backup rounds to reload.

He hadn't come prepared for a life-or-death gunfight.

Dumb me.

His car was parked twenty feet from the exit ramp. From here to the dark alley was a straight-line dash with no obstacles. A single bulb overhead was the only light. Was it worth one of his five precious bullets to knock it out? His clothes would be black against the dark mouth to the lane, and he'd stand a better chance of making it alive.

Bam!

The bulb exploded.

Now Flood was on the move, staggering and stumbling toward the sanctuary outside. Something warned him that he was about to get shot, so he swung his gun hand back toward the pillar where the Mountie was hiding and triggered two more rounds.

In return, a bullet zipped by his head. He heard the whine as it passed his ear. The Horseman must have jerked for cover, for the next shot veered wild and pinged off one edge of the garage opening in a spray of concrete dust. Both shooters were down to two slugs, and Flood was beginning to think he'd make it out alive. Then the Headhunter's fifth round slammed him in the back, blowing a chunk from his shoulder and knocking him to the ground. The injured man, however, had landed in the alley, and with a Herculean effort, he dodged to the left, which put the wall of the underground lot between him and the Mountie's gun.

Trailing blood, Al half crawled, half lurched away.

First things first.

The plan was changing by the minute.

The unexpected arrival of Flood and DeClercq's wife had nixed the idea of the gangland hit. There'd be no time for Sparky to check the detective's apartment for any evidence he may have left behind. It was probably all in the Nike bag anyway, which meant he couldn't be allowed to leave the parking lot alive. Using the underworld gun was no longer feasible. The rain wouldn't muffle the booms of gunfire in the confined lot. If patrol cars responding to 911 calls closed in on the Mountie at the scene, it would be damn hard to explain having used an illegal firearm to shoot it out with Flood. No, the firefight had to be with Sparky's own gun.

And to make it look like self-defense, Flood had to fire too.

That's why Sparky had yelled, "Freeze!"

Flood was forced to draw and shoot.

Now the trick was to make it look like the shootout had erupted when the dirty cop refused to be taken alive during a drug bust.

From the concrete pillar, Sparky sprinted to Flood's car. DeClercq's wife was dead, so that took care of her. Any footprints the Mountie left in the blood would be dismissed as checking Genny's vital signs and searching under the car for the dirty cop. After fetching the bag of coke and slamming the hubcap back on, Sparky swung open the passenger door that Flood had unlocked. The Headhunter leaned under the passenger seat and stashed the drugs, the junkie's untraceable gun, and the screwdriver that had left toolmarks on the hubcap, then set the automatic lock and closed the door. The keys were in Flood's pocket, so anything found in the Volvo had to be his.

The frame was now complete.

Next, the shrunken heads.

Already, sirens wailed in the distance. Sparky grabbed the Nike bag off the floor, checked that it had left no outline in the blood, and ran up the ramp to survey the alley. Flood was crawling on his hands and knees a short distance to the left, and as Sparky dashed across to the burning barrel, the wounded cop took refuge in the adjacent alcove.

The sirens drew nearer.

Unzipping the Nike bag, Sparky watched the eight tsantsas and the cop's journal tumble into the red-hot embers. At once, the shrunken heads burst into flames, and the stench of burning hair sizzled up from the barrel. In a flash, all that remained was a handful of gold rings, and then the journal that gave them meaning disappeared too. Fearful that the bag itself might smother the inferno, Sparky wiped it free of fingerprints and stuffed it in a trash can.

Fuck you, Mother!

Burn, witch! Burn!

Now the journal was ashes.

And the cover-up seemed complete.

Flipping open the .38 and emptying it of casings, Sparky used the glow from the burning barrel to reload with six live rounds.

Okay, Mr. City Bull.

Now it's you and me.

SHOOTOUT

"Every man's life ends the same way," according to Hemingway. "It is only the details of how he lived and how he died that distinguish one man from another."

That says it all, thought Al.

The difference between a good death and a bad one?

You die for a reason.

Slumped in a garbage can alcove in a dark alley on a rainy night wasn't Al Flood's idea of a good death. While sitting vigil beside his mom's deathbed, watching her breathing get shallower by the minute, he'd taken her gnarled hand in his and whispered in her ear, "Mom, it's Al. I hope you can hear me. I promise I'll see you reunited with dad up on the mountain."

Well, her ashes were in his apartment, waiting for spring to come. Because of the early snowfall, no chopper could land safely at that altitude, so he hadn't been able to scatter her remains on the cairn marking his dad's grave. And if this psycho killed him, he'd break his vow to his mom.

Not without a fight.

Die for a reason, he thought.

Genevieve had asked Al for his help. Look where she was now: sprawled dead in a pool of blood because he'd called her tonight.

I have a score to settle.

Die for a reason, he thought.

Al wasn't going to die like a mutt in a spray of bullets when the Headhunter crooked an arm into the alcove and fired without breaking cover.

Die for a reason.

Make these two shots count.

For his last stand, Al squirmed as far back as he could in the stinking alley nook. He'd planned to build a barricade out of the garbage cans, but then the muzzle of his gun clinked against glass. Feeling behind him, he found a window in the brick wall funneling light into a cellar. The sirens were so close that if he could buy time before the shooting began, the cavalry might arrive. With the butt of his .38, he shattered the glass, then stretched himself flat and rolled into the hole.

The window was high in the cellar, so Al tumbled to the floor.

Peeking into the alcove to aim and finish off the cop, Sparky saw Flood vanish into a rectangular mouth in the far wall. With seconds to spare before a patrol car reached the alley, the Headhunter ran across to the window and peered into a pitch-black cellar.

There was no alternative.

If the killer didn't crawl in after him, Flood was home free.

Had Al gone down the rabbit hole, like *Alice in Wonderland*?

It was that surreal.

The red-and-blue wigwag lights of a patrol car in the lane beyond the window lit up this phantasmagoric storage vault for stage and movie costumes. In the blackness, Al had wormed away to the right from where he hit the floor. Now he lay crumpled on his side between rows of clothing racks. He was running on adrenaline, and his head spun like a whirling ride on a carnival midway as he took in creatures pulsing under the strobe lights. He saw Mickey Mouse and Daffy Duck and the Last of the Mohicans. He saw Henry VIII and Marie Antoinette and the Count of Monte Cristo. He saw Lady Macbeth and Punch and Judy and the Man in the Iron Mask. Across the far end of the aisle were military uniforms: British Redcoats flanked by

Scottish Highlanders at the Battle of Culloden and American Patriots in the War of Independence.

Die for a reason.

At this end, Al was surrounded by classic celluloid monsters. When he was a boy, the magazine *Famous Monsters of Filmland* was in its heyday. Each month, he'd cut out photos and tape them around the walls of his bedroom until there was no more space. Once, his mother had asked him how he could sleep in such a room. He told her, "They protect me."

Here those monsters were again, some hanging from wall hooks, some on mannequins: Dracula, Frankenstein's monster, the Wolf Man, the Mummy, the Creature from the Black Lagoon, the Phantom of the Opera, Mr. Hyde, the Hunchback of Notre Dame, King Kong, and Godzilla.

The cellar went dark.

The light from the window was blocked.

A thud hit the floor.

Flood was no longer alone.

If ever he needed the protection of the monsters on the wall, it was now.

———

Sparky hit the floor, rolled, and crouched below the window. The blood smear on the tiles said that Flood had crawled off to the right, so the psycho branched left. If he was still conscious, he'd be waiting for the Headhunter to follow his trail.

Instead...

Yes, there he is!

Wheezing from his punctured lung.

Behind the racks in the next aisle, at the other end from the Redcoats.

Redcoats?

I ask you: Does cover come better than that?

Sparky shucked the rain slicker to bare the red serge uniform beneath, then crept along the side wall in behind the Redcoats. As the Headhunter inched forward between two mannequins, aiming the .38 down the aisle at Flood's last stand, the thin red line grew by one. On the far wall, facing the Headhunter, was Boris Karloff's costume from the 1932 horror film *The*

Mummy. Except for its cracked, withered face—modeled on the Egyptian pharaoh Ramses III—the monster was wrapped in tattered, rotting bandages with both arms crossed on its chest.

A memory from 1957 clawed at Sparky's brain: Mardi Gras in New Orleans on an oppressive night when the Axeman went berserk in Suzannah's House of Discipline.

"Mummy!" Sparky gasped.

———

Through the peephole in the door of the four-foot-square cage buried in this dungeon, the traumatized child eyes Mother at work.

The mummy hangs suspended from a meat hook in the ceiling. At least, it looks like a mummy: this beseeching monster encased in a concrete overcoat of bandages soaked in plaster of Paris, its arms outstretched as if crucified. The full-body straitjacket has five holes: four in the blank face for eyes, nose, and mouth, and one lower down for the man's cock and balls.

"What's that for?" Crystal had asked earlier, when she first entered the well and saw the potter's wheel.

"We're going to make a mummy. A Freudian mommy, in fact."

"I don't get it."

"You will, baby. Tonight's guest has special needs that pay *very* well."

To the left of the door stands a yawning iron maiden painted like the sarcophagus unearthed in King Tut's tomb. Inside is a naked wax figure pierced with holes made by spikes aimed at the mannequin's groin. On the floor in front of the waxwork sits a potter's wheel with a foot pedal to spin it. Earlier, the Axeman had stood naked on the slowly revolving circle as Suzannah encased him in bandages dipped in a bucket of plaster of Paris mixed with water. After the casing had hardened, she'd winched her client up to the meat hook.

"*No!*" gibbers the mouth hole now. "Not *more* needles!"

"Momma's boy," Suzannah sneers as she struts around the drain in the center of the floor, her stiletto heels clicking on the stones.

"*Don't!*"

"A boy who fails his momma has to suffer."

The mummy swings to and fro on its chain as the man inside writhes. The dominatrix closes in to jab a needle through his genitals. The head of his penis is already a pincushion of spikes.

"One more."

"No! Please—"

"A boy should love his momma."

Suzannah shoves the last needle through her client's scrotum. As a primal scream of sexual ecstasy and unbridled pain bounces around the circular pit, the Axeman ejaculates from the hole in the plaster. Thrashing around on the hook and jerking within the white casing, the mummy begins to crack free from the straitjacket. Chunks of plaster break off the monster's body as the man inside falls from the hook and grabs the hatchet slung on spikes in the iron maiden.

"Bitch!" he snarls as he vanishes from the peephole.

Sparky hears the chain snap taut as Crystal shrieks and tries to retreat from the Axeman. The girl is tethered to the wall close to but not within sight of Sparky's cage. As she screams, the Doberman pinscher slams repeatedly against the bars that seal the tunnel from the Mississippi. The torches flaming around the pit cast Crystal's outline across the floor.

"You killed Momma!" the Axeman yells.

In the shadow play, his silhouette strikes the cringing girl with the hatchet.

"Bitch!"

Clang!

"Bitch!"

Clang!

Sparks and bits of flagstone fly with each whack of the axe, then the girl's arm plops down near the drain and quivers as the fingers close into a fist. Now the shadow man falls to his knees and chops in a frenzy as bones crack and the ravenous hound growls for meat. The gush of blood circles the drain while the Axeman's silhouette devours hunks of the hacked-up girl.

Sparky's eye, however, is locked on Mommy. Having earned lots of money off this year's Mardi Gras, Suzannah has one more act of revenge against her hated husband. As she slinks toward the peephole, she drops her Medusa wig. With each strut, bits of her costume disappear. The shaved scalp with its blue veins. The knee-high boots. The studded collar and the fishnet stockings. The corset and the scarlet garters. Only when the peeper sees nothing but Mommy's jet-black pubic hair glinting with six gold rings laced shut with a black thong does the creaking leather and rasping nylon cease.

"Help me, Daddy!"

Gloves with cut-off fingertips unlace the thong cinching Mommy's lips together, and as the door to the cage unlocks, the dominatrix orders, "Eat me, Sparky."

"Daddy! Where are you, Daddy? Help me, Daddy! Please!"

(*"I'm here, Sparky. I am you."*)

———

He wasn't going to make it. He was about to pass out. He could do nothing more than curl up in a fetal position, fighting off waves of blackness. As visions flashed before his eyes—of that lonely grave on a snowy precipice, and his mother's ashes never to be reunited with his dad, and his dream lover lying dead in a pool of blood—Flood struggled to focus on what he could see in the pulsing light, and what he could hear through the din of the police siren wailing beyond the window.

Then the siren fell silent, and Al caught a word gasped at the end of the aisle.

"Mommy!"

There, among the Redcoat costumes, two shoes stood firmly planted on the floor. The Mountie wore the red serge tunic and was aiming a .38 at the wounded city bull's heart.

Die for a reason.

"For her," Al choked.

He pulled the trigger of his own .38.

Two shots rang out.

RICOCHET

Sunday, November 14, 8:20 p.m.

Six floors below, the traffic along Burrard Street was rainy white noise. Behind him, in the ICU of St. Paul's Hospital—the hospital in which Joanna Portman had worked—the nurses talked in whispers and wore noiseless shoes, and the crash carts hummed along the floor on rubber wheels. In here, where newly appointed Chief Superintendent DeClercq sat beside the wounded officer's bed, the sound of life-support machines offered hope. The beep, beep, beep of the heart monitor. And the phew, phew, phew of the ventilator.

"You're going to make it," Robert said. "You're out of the woods."

The patient slept on.

There was no sign of awareness.

"I knew your father. He was my CO in Montreal before he went missing. Not only would he be proud of you, but your bravery's the talk of the Heather Stables. Putting yourself in danger like that was beyond the call of duty. You'll be getting a medal."

Beep...beep...

Phew...

"Your marksman badges are well earned. You killed Flood with a single shot to the head, even though he'd shot you in the chest first. We're slowly piecing together what happened in the parking lot. We found an unregistered firearm and a bag of cocaine locked in his car. Ballistics matched the gun to several underworld hits. Flood's father got embroiled in similar behavior and was never cleared of being a dirty cop. Flood himself had mental problems

| 409

so severe that he sought help from Dr. Ruryk and my wife, Genevieve. I have no idea what she was doing with him on Friday night, but it doesn't look good. Joseph Avacomovitch once saw them having lunch, and apparently they looked a little too comfortable with each other. I don't want to believe it, but her fingerprints were found on a glass in Flood's apartment, even though she told me she was staying at home while I was off celebrating our triumph in the Headhunter case at the regimental dinner."

Beep…beep…

Phew…

"I don't blame you for her death. I blame Flood. The shot that killed her wasn't direct. Ballistics say it was a ricochet off the bumper of Flood's car. The lab matched metal traces on the slug. What made you suspect Flood of drug trafficking, or worse? Did you get a tip from a snitch? The fact that you detoured to check it out while decked out for the red serge dinner is what makes you a *real* Mountie.

"*Maintiens le Droit.* You're a credit to the Force."

Outside the room, people erupted into action. An alarm summoned nurses to the patient next door. A crash cart followed, metal jiggling on metal. Gasping, choking, calls for drugs against cardiac arrest, and the whir of defibrillator paddles led to repeated cautions to "Stand clear." An unmistakable death rattle shut down the commotion, and soon the lifeless body left for the morgue. Meanwhile, in the street below, the Doppler effect of a wailing siren signaled more grief as an ambulance approached the emergency room.

Beep…beep…

Phew…

"I was surprised to see your name on the list of Mounties selected for the Headhunter Squad. I met your mother only once, on the day you learned to crawl. Your dad had invited me home for dinner a week before you three departed for his new posting up north. Suzannah was a statuesque and striking woman. While she was in the kitchen, you made your first move. On hands and knees, you crawled toward your dad. 'Bet you've never seen eyes sparkle like that, Robert. My kid's going somewhere, mark my words. Come to Daddy, Sparky. Daddy's proud of you.' After he vanished on Arctic patrol, I lost touch with your mom."

Beep…beep…

Phew…

"I brought you something special that your father left with me. He didn't want to chance losing it up north, and he knew my interest in the history of the Force. For years, I've held it in trust for you. I was going to present it to you at the regimental dinner."

DeClercq withdrew the .476 Enfield revolver from its box.

"This sidearm belonged to your grandfather, Inspector Wilfred Blake. He almost single-handedly forged our unofficial motto, 'The Mounties always get their man.' Now it's yours, to carry on the tradition. It must be something in your DNA. Something in your genes. First you take down the Headhunter. Then you take down Flood. Keep it up and you might rival the myth of Wilfred Blake."

There was a flinch on the bed.

The eyes fluttered open.

"Welcome back," said the chief superintendent.

Faintly, around the breathing tube, Katherine Spann smiled.

FRANKENSTEIN

Monday, November 15, 10:45 a.m.

The man who drove the garbage truck was called the Perfesser. No doubt he had another name, but Jeff had yet to hear it. The Perfesser was in his fifties, a short, squat fellow with a ruddy drinker's complexion. Each day he began this garbage run with a hip flask full of whisky, and each day he drained it while Slim took the wheel to drive the truck back to the city's sanitation yard. Before becoming a garbageman, the Perfesser had sailed the world in the merchant marine, an experience that made him—in the words of the inbred banjo-picker who swamped at the hopper with Jeff—"the world's foremost authority on women, liquor, and life."

Slim was a tall, skinny string bean in his forties. His overalls hung on his bony body like a potato sack. In Jeff's mind, he was Laurel to the Perfesser's Hardy. Slim favored a floppy farmer's hat that made him look like a hillbilly. When he cracked a shit-eating grin, his mouth flashed an orange-toothed smile stained by chain-smoking. Slim rolled his own.

Jeff was dubbed "the Kid" by the older men. As you'd expect, he did most of the heavy lifting. Jeff was taking a year off from university and drudging as a swamper to earn needed cash. Now, as the garbage truck turned into the alley behind Lagoon Drive, he jumped down from the hopper to empty the nearest trash cans into its trough while Slim puffed a ciggie and watched him work.

"Coffee break," the Perfesser yelled from the cab of the truck.

Jeff pulled the hydraulic lever to compact the rubbish in the hopper, then took off his gloves and went forward to escape the smell.

Slim stepped on his ciggie and followed.

The Perfesser filled three Styrofoam cups from a thermos and passed them around, then topped his own with a splash of booze. Leaning against the truck, the three men slurped their hot java. The heavy rain of the past few days had stopped overnight, but the alley was still wet.

"How 'bout we play Peepin' Tom?" Slim suggested.

"Kid? It's your turn."

"Okay by me," said Jeff.

Peeping Tom was the game they played to defeat boredom. The older men had initiated Jeff into it his first day on the job, when they learned he was studying archeology.

"Ah," the Perfesser had said then. "You want to be one of those guys who digs in the ground, looking for the garbage left by ancient people to figure out how they lived?"

"Sort of."

"If you wanna be an academic garbage collector, there's no better job than this to practice your future work. We're a gold mine, Kid."

Fishing a pack of rolling papers out of his overalls, Slim had tapped some loose tobacco onto a thin sheet, rolled it one-handed into a cigarette, then licked the gum, sealed it, and stuck it in his mouth. Striking a match on the zipper of his fly, he'd lit up and sucked it.

The hillbilly was Boswell to the Perfesser's Johnson.

"Perfesser says a man ain't worth shit if he thinks he's above cleanin' up the garbage left by others. A man's garbage is the face behind his mask. Tell him, Perfesser."

The ciggie jiggled on Slim's lower lip as he spoke.

"Once a week, I walk this garbage route on the *front* of the street. Since the wife left me, I got lots of time. I peek in our clients' windows. I watch 'em do their chores. I listen to 'em chatting with their neighbors. I take in the masks they put on to fool the masks they meet. After I've got a handle on who they pretend to be, Slim and I go through their garbage to tear off the masks."

"The Sherlock Holmes and Watson of the alleyway?" Jeff had joked.

"Wanna play, Kid?"

So here they stood, six months later, in the alley behind Al Flood's apartment three days after he died, draining their cups for another round of Peeping Tom.

"Choose a can," said the Perfesser.

"That one," Jeff replied, indicating a plastic trash container flanked by metal bins.

"Good choice. I've snooped those folks before."

A slug for the Perfesser and a puff for Slim, then the voyeurs approached the can and removed the lid. Opening a Swiss Army knife, the Perfesser slit the garbage bag on top and tore it open.

"What do you see, Jeff?"

"An empty box of condoms. Tissues smeared with lipstick. A *Hustler* skin mag. A week of TV dinners. A pair of airline folders for Reverend and Mrs. Bleeker. Travel pamphlets for Hawaii. And Sunday school papers for what appears to be a Bible-thumping church."

"Got the picture?"

"Sort of."

"Except you're missing a piece. *Three* people live in the apartment that belongs to this garbage can: the reverend of a goody-goody church; his sinless wife, who wears no makeup; and their pious fifteen-year-old son, who's currently home alone while his parents travel."

"That horny little monster," Jeff said, laughing.

"We're all horny little monsters, Kid. Question is whether we hide it."

"One more?"

The Perfesser swept his arm out grandly. "Choose a can."

"Let's try the next alcove."

They sauntered up the alley to a garbage nook across the lane from an underground parking lot drooping yellow crime scene tape. Here, the cans were stored with a barrel full of sodden ashes and sooty metal rings. Lifting one of the lids, Jeff removed a Nike athletic bag. Spreading both handles, he pulled the zipper apart to look inside.

"Empty," he said.

"The side pocket's bulgin'," Slim pointed out.

Opening it, Jeff withdrew a puzzling black object sitting on top of two knives. Carved from ebony, it resembled the steer horns he'd seen strapped to the grilles of cars from Texas. The miniature faces carved in the middle reminded him of the Roman god Janus in his archeology books. One face looked to the future, the other to the past. These two heads, however, depicted voodoo gods. Each miniature face had an open mouth, and from each mouth protruded an eight-inch rounded tongue carved to look like a snake. Damballa was the voodoo snake god, if Jeff recalled correctly.

"Well?" said the Perfesser.

"I think it's some kind of fetish."

"The woman in that apartment lives by herself."

"So?"

"She has several girlfriends."

"So?" Jeff repeated.

"When I was sailing the world, we often docked in the Caribbean. Back then, Barbados had a dive bar called Larry's Nitery. If you greased his palm, Larry would lock the doors for a girl-on-girl sex show. I watched two women use one of those to make Shakespeare's beast with two backs. That's from *Othello*, Kid. Theirs was fancy, like the one in your hand. But plastic double dildos are sold in every sex shop in this city."

Slim slapped his thigh.

"Musta been a hard thrust to chip the nose like that."

One of the faces had cracked and splintered. A sliver of ebony wood was missing from the nose of that voodoo god.

"A dyke's prong turns a woman into a man," chortled Slim.

"Same as Frankenstein's monster," said the Perfesser, taking a swig from his flask. "The creature was stitched together with pieces from *different* people."

The swampers waited for the Perfesser to fetch the truck. Jeff dropped the double dildo into the Nike bag, then tossed it into the trough. He emptied the rest of the cans on top and pulled the lever to compact the trash. Gears meshed in the hopper, and the fetish was gone.

"Didn't I tell ya?" Slim said. "World's foremost authority on women, liquor, and life."

"That you did."

"Perfesser taught me the garbageman's lesson of life—and I'll pass it on."

"Do tell," said Jeff.

"Perfesser says, 'In this city—in *any* city—the *real* garbage ain't what we dump outta the cans. It's some of the folks who fill 'em.'"

AUTHOR'S NOTE

This is a work of fiction. The plot and characters are a product of the author's imagination. Where real persons, places, or institutions have been incorporated to create the illusion of authenticity, they are used fictitiously. My thanks to the many helpful officers in the Royal Canadian Mounted Police, the Vancouver Police Department, and the New Orleans Police Department who answered my research questions. Inspiration was drawn from the following non-fiction sources:

Burroughs, William S. *Junkie: Confessions of an Unredeemed Drug Addict*. New York: Ace Books, 1953.

Butler, William Francis. *The Great Lone Land: A Narrative of Travel and Adventure in the North-West of America*. London: Sampson Low, Marston, Low & Searle, 1872.

———. *The Wild North Land: Being the Story of a Winter Journey, with Dogs, Across Northern North America*. London: Sampson Low, Marston, Low & Searle, 1873.

Gray, Marcus. *Route 19 Revisited: The Clash and London Calling*. London: Jonathan Cape, 2009.

Horrall, S.W. *The Pictorial History of the Royal Canadian Mounted Police*. Toronto: McGraw-Hill Ryerson, 1973.

Larson, Frances. *Severed: A History of Heads Lost and Heads Found*. London: Granta, 2014.

Parfrey, Adam. *It's a Man's World: Men's Adventure Magazines, the Postwar Pulps*. Port Townsend, WA: Feral House, 2003.

Rossmo, D. Kim. *Criminal Investigative Failures*. Boca Raton, FL: CRC Press, 2009.

———

Michael Slade is the alter ego of various collaborators.

Hyde to their Jekylls.

The original version of *Headhunter* was conceived by a firm of criminal lawyers.

Here's one voice.

———

In 1883, my great-grandfather, George "Scotty" Murdoch, crossed the Canadian Prairies through Cree and Blackfoot territory in a wagon drawn by an ox and a mule to set up trade as a harness maker at the North-West Mounted Police stronghold of Fort Calgary. There, he settled among the Natives outside the fort and learned their language.

The Blackfoot called him Leather Man.

In 1884, Scotty Murdoch collected enough signatures and money to have two hundred local settlers incorporated as the town of Calgary. He was elected Calgary's first mayor and served as its first judge. All the while, he kept a journal that's now in Canada's national archives. In it, he describes a court case this way: "A strange sight, civilians, military, and Indians in paint looking in at the windows."

I was born in 1947 in Lethbridge, Alberta—the site of Fort Whoop-Up, the whisky trading post that was the reason the Mounties were formed—when Scotty's children were still alive. So I grew up on *real-life* stories of the Wild West and the red serge Riders of the Plains.

Ergo, Wilfred Blake.

My mother, Vivian Murdoch, grew up in a small Alberta town with a population of one hundred. On graduating from nursing school in Edmonton, she hopped a train through the Rocky Mountains for adventure in Vancouver, taking a job at a hospital in a small Kwakiutl village up the West Coast, the Land of the Headhunters. The chief's son had arthritis, which my mom helped alleviate with a hot wax treatment, and as thanks the chief carved her a totem pole. That's how I became aware of the mythic reality of Baxbaxwalanuksiwe, Hok Hok, the Hamatsa cult, and the Lekwiltok headhunters.

For as long as I can remember, I have been enthralled by Native culture.

And none more than the culture of the Kwakiutl, now known as the Kwakwaka'wakw.

Ergo, Bax's T-shirt.

When I was a preschool boy, my family got a dog. My dad was an airline pilot, so we named the puppy Jet, after the new planes then coming into service. One day when I was riding my tricycle, I was attacked from out of nowhere by a mad dog. Jet heard me scream and came running to the rescue. As I stood on the bike seat, the dogs fought around me, and every chance the rabid beast got, it jumped up and bit my leg. Finally, the neighbors responded with weapons, and the police put down the monster. The doctor told my mom that if not for Jet and my winter layers of long johns, jeans, and a snowsuit, I would have lost my leg, and maybe worse.

The name of the beast that savaged me?

You guessed it.

Sparky.

My father, Flight Lieutenant (later Captain) Jack "Johnny" Clarke, was an unlikely warrior. At the height of the Battle of Britain—when he was working as a professional artist for Associated Screen News in Montreal— he volunteered to fly with the Royal Air Force. Against great odds, my dad survived forty-seven combat missions in the Second World War, only to die in a freak winter storm in the Cascade Mountains—"the graveyard of the air"—when I was nine. My father was larger than life, and his death hit me hard. My overwrought mind threw up a weird force field that kept me out of magazine shops. My best friend, also nine, saved me from myself. Gord Thorson later became a trauma surgeon, until brain cancer felled him. I gave the eulogy at his funeral.

Ergo, Al Flood.

In 1967, after my final second-year university exam, I caught a flight to Zurich in search of adventure. Rich folks were doing *Europe on 5 Dollars a Day*, but I was a pauper traveling on a buck and a quarter—hitchhiking, youth hostels, and student meals. I was determined to go behind the Iron Curtain, even though, with the Cold War raging (the invasion of Czechoslovakia was the following year), it had taken me nine months to get the necessary visas. There were no flights to the Soviet Union from the West, so in Vienna I climbed aboard a train stamped with the hammer and sickle, and trundled east for days, heading for Moscow.

What a trip!

My undergrad studies were in modern history, and I was going where the action was. Naysayers had warned my mom, "If something goes wrong, you'll never get him out." And—my favorite—"You know how Americans feel about Reds. They'll think he's a Commie and bar him from the States." My mom shut them all down. "When his father was his age, he was locked in combat over Nazi Germany," she said. "I won't discourage him."

Oh, there were adventures.

And yes, I almost got arrested by the KGB.

In Leningrad (now Saint Petersburg), I went to the Hermitage Museum, founded in 1764 by Catherine the Great. As I backpacked around the rest of Europe over the next three months, I added the Munch Museum in Oslo; the Rijksmuseum in Amsterdam; the Louvre, the Musée du Jeu de Paume (the Impressionists), and the Musée Rodin in Paris; the British Museum, the National Gallery, and the Tate in London; and a whole lot more.

But isn't life ironic?

Have you read Somerset Maugham's "The Verger," a classic short story about twists of fate?

All that high-minded culture is lodged in my brain, but thanks to a bout of the flu, the artwork that changed my life, turned me into a novelist, and put this dark thriller in your hands was a lurid painting of headhunters on the cover of a so-called armpit slick.

Fate.

I was called to the bar in 1972 and set up practice on Maple Tree Square in Gastown, the heart of skid row. What a dynamic era in which to practice criminal law! Vietnam War draft dodgers flooded the city, the counterculture was duking it out with the establishment, the Gastown Riot took place out front of my office, junkies shot up in my restroom as heroin poured in from the East, and Canada had a new prostitution law.

Can you guess who got the first soliciting case from legal aid?

Bingo!

Lawyers love nothing more than a new law. All arguments are open, with no one there before you, and it took less than a minute to get the case thrown out of court. What I was about to learn, though, was that hookers have a network to protect themselves against "bad dates," and as William Burroughs wrote in *Junkie*: "Criminal law is one of the few professions where the client buys someone else's luck."

The more luck a lawyer has, the more he has to sell.

Almost overnight, I was "the hookers' lawyer." My waiting room was full of sex workers: scores of women, men, transvestites, transsexuals, and—wait for it—dominatrices. I'd long known that one day I would try my hand at writing, so I made it a habit to ask each new client two questions:

"Who was your kinkiest john?"

"What was your most dangerous date?"

Research.

———

Here's another voice.

I was born in 1947 in Regina, Saskatchewan—the site of Depot Division, where all Mounties are trained, and the headquarters of the Force from the Wild West era to 1920.

In 1959, my future law partners and I attended the same high school, but after grade seven, they switched to a new school that had opened closer to their homes. I remained at the old school. With the war in Vietnam, flower power blossomed, and Vancouver's 8th Avenue became known as Chemical Row. Drugs devastated not only my working-class neighborhood but also my family.

When I was at law school in the early 1970s, my younger brother disappeared. His body was never found, but there was a murder trial, and the accused was acquitted.

I watched firsthand the impact that murder has on families on both sides of a case, the local community, and society in general. In seeking resolution to that crime that was never resolved, I switched from studying corporate finance to the realm of criminal law.

That's how I ended up practicing in the firm on Maple Tree Square, in the heart of Vancouver's skid row.

The result?

The city awash with drugs depicted in *Headhunter*.

Which Vancouver was then—and still is today.

———

Back to Scotty's great-grandson.

My first murder trial was an ugly one. My client was found standing on his head in a urinal in the restroom of an upcountry bus station, screaming, "I'm Jesus Christ!" He'd driven there in a stolen car and got three months in jail. Each morning behind bars, he'd shit in his hand and smear himself and his cell. One day while hosing him down, the jailors found a torn-up "death warrant" aimed at his wife. They ignored it. He was released. And in a full-blown psychotic fit, he pulverized her with a baseball bat in front of their kids.

That's when I entered the case.

Even the Crown psychiatrists had to admit that my client was psychotic, and it wasn't hard to win a verdict of not guilty by reason of insanity. He was sent to Riverside, Vancouver's forensic psychiatric hospital, where I visited him one day after picking up some business cards from the printer. While I was off speaking with his psychiatrists, my client "borrowed" a few. And when I got back to the office, the phone began ringing.

I was about to learn that psychos network too. Those sent to Riverside for treatment after trial mingled in a hospital setting with those being evaluated before trial. My client was handing out my business cards while talking up the "hotshot mouthpiece who got me off."

Burroughs: lawyer's luck.

Over the next decade, I defended a slew of accused murderers, and I argued the last death penalty appeal before the Supreme Court. Many of my cases involved insanity, and as one judge injudiciously put it, "Counsel, it seems you've cornered the crazy market."

Accused don't open up to cops trying to put them in jail. Accused don't open up to headshrinkers trying to plumb their minds. Accused, however, do open up to lawyers, who they know are bound by client privilege and can't repeat what's said.

Research.

In the 1970s, police went overboard with their wiretaps. The upshot was that I got copies of every word uttered by a gang of pimps who'd crossed the border to work the northern strolls.

The result?

New Orleans and voodoo.

When I was called to the bar, there were no female Mounties. The first troop graduated from Depot Division two years later. The courts were bursting at the seams, and police, criminals, lawyers, and witnesses milled together in cramped spaces. One day, my thirsty ears overheard a male Mountie sneer to another, "Who wants a cunt watching his back in a firefight? But she can blow me in the car on a boring stakeout."

A plot light went on in my mind.

Ergo, Rick Scarlett.

In one of my longest cases, I helped defend thirty-three corner-store owners who'd been charged with selling "dirty books." To bankrupt the porn distributor paying for the retailers' defense, the Crown proceeded by indictment to jack up the bill. Two can play that game, so we elected trial by jury in all thirty-three cases, which would clog the criminal courts for years if the Crown didn't blink.

Hey, the law's a chessboard.

And the mind behind this novel's plot also moved its chess pieces.

So there I stood at the evidence table, waiting for "the dirty assize" to start, when my eyes skimmed over the piles of porn and fell upon an object euphemistically called a "marital aid."

Another plot light went on in my mind.

The result?

This novel's twist.

The Slade-of-hand.

One of my toughest trials was the Surrey Baby Kidnapping Case. Two women from San Francisco sought work at a Vancouver hospital. One became obsessed with a baby in the nursery, and later—under the ruse of a postnatal-care visit—pulled a knife on the mother in her home, tied her up, and fled with the newborn stuffed in a bag.

The Mounties swung into the saddle and called in the FBI, who arrested both women in California and retrieved the baby. The extradition case had me shuttling to and from San Francisco, and when the trial began, the redcoats and the suits got into a pissing contest over who reigned supreme. That's how one of them let slip the absence of a document that set my client free. The other woman got life imprisonment.

The result?

Rick Scarlett versus Luke Wentworth.

In the early 1980s, a recession hit. Interest rates skyrocketed, and to save cash, the government cut funding for legal aid. The downturn in business gave me an opening to write my first novel, which I hammered out at a white-hot pace on a miniature typewriter that my mom had bought me in grade eight. The dogs of debt were nipping at my heels from the cost of building a new office, buying a home, and providing for a three-year-old who repeatedly knocked on the door of my hideaway to find out what Daddy was doing.

A single take—straight from my brain with no time for rewrites—went into print.

Headhunter, published in 1984.

Well, more than thirty years have passed since then. The Mounties, I am pleased to say, embraced *Headhunter*. Not only was I invited to their Red Serge Ball, but I've been a guest speaker at their regimental dinners. Because the novel was based on what I had experienced while practicing criminal law, subsequent events have buttressed its themes. By 2015, almost four hundred female Mounties had launched a lawsuit alleging years of sexual harassment, bullying, and abuse. The RCMP commissioner recently took a stance against racists in the Force. Canada's despicable crimes against its Native people have been exposed in public forums, and indigenous women by the hundreds are missing or have been murdered. In the years after *Headhunter* was published, in what's known as the Pig Farm Case, Robert "Willie" Pickton confessed to the murders of forty-nine women he'd lured off the streets of skid row. In searching Pickton's squalid farm, the Mounties found skulls cut in half and stuffed with hands and feet, the remains of a victim crammed in a garbage bag, and a handgun with a dildo attached to the barrel as a makeshift silencer. Forensic teams recovered the DNA of thirty-one women. Pickton fed body parts to his pigs, and after the animals were slaughtered, he gave the pig meat away to friends.

One of the women butchered was a long-time client of mine.

Headhunter, of course, is fiction, but the stories that inspired it worked their black magic on me, from the horrors of my traumatic boyhood to the years spent practicing criminal law in the sexual underground of Vancouver. Because this thriller was created before writers used computers, a paper book had to be scanned into a digital file to convert it to an e-book, and that process spurred me to completely reimagine the story with 20/20 hindsight from all that's happened since.

"Give me some truth," said John Lennon.

And that's what I hope—through dark fiction—I've done.

Slade
Vancouver, BC
July 1, 2017

www.ingramcontent.com/pod-product-compliance
Lightning Source LLC
Chambersburg PA
CBHW021123260626
47169CB00005B/1424